Magpie   New Writing

introduced by **Andrew Motion**

A CCPA paperback
Magpie

First published in Great Britain 2000

All rights reserved

No part of this publication may be reproduced, stored in a retrieval system or transmitted in any form or by any means without the prior permission in writing of the appropriate, individual author, nor be otherwise circulated in any form of binding or cover other than that in which it is published and without a similar condition including this condition being imposed on the subsequent purchaser.

The publishers would like to thank Faber and Faber Ltd., for permission to use the quote from Seamus Heaney's poem 'Whatever You Say, Say Nothing' from the collection *North* on p.203.
The excerpt from Gaston Bachelard's *The Poetics of Space* on p.179, is © 1958 by Presses Universitaires de France. Translation © 1964 by Orion Press Inc. Used with permission from Viking Penguin, a division of Penguin Putnam Inc. The quote on p.109 is from 'Handsome Is as Handsome Does' by V.S. Pritchett reprinted by permission of PDF on behalf of the Estate of V.S. Pritchett.

International copyright © retained by individual authors

ISBN 0 9536072 1 6

Typeset in Plantin Light

Printed and bound in Great Britain by Biddles Ltd., Guildford, Surrey

Acknowledgments

Magpie is grateful to the following for their support, advice and enthusiasm throughout its production:

Jon Cook, Andrew Motion, Max Sebald, Paul Magrs, Denise Riley, Esther Morgan, Val Striker, Aileen Davies, Alita Thorpe, Colleen Clayton, Annie Ogden, Julia Bell, Bill Bigge, Julian p. Jackson, Johnny Rich and Rupert Hopkins.

Many thanks also to Andy Vargo, Phoebe Phillips, Vicky Winteringham, Mike Oakes, Anastacia Tohill and Vanessa Vargo at the Norwich School of Art and Design.

The Magpie Team

Alison Boulton, Becky Deans, Julia Lee, Jane Monson, Andrew Proctor, Anne F. Stairs, Jo Wood.

Cover design by Michelle Lawrence.

Contents

Andrew Motion Introduction   7

Clare Allan Extract from Lipstick and Melleril   9

Alison Boulton In Search of Peter   19

Helen Cleary Extract from A Narrow Track   33

Martin Corrick Sunshine House Extract from The   45
                    Navigation Log

Douglas Cowie Back and Forth   59

Fflur Dafydd The Heroics of Hair   69

Deborah Davis Court Pastoral   81

Rebecca Deans The World of Insurance is Looking Up   87

Sarah A. Fairhurst Hakataramea   93

L. B. Fisher Dress You Up   101

Adam Foulds Eight Poems   109

Sophie Frank Extract from Disappearance   121

Clare George Extract from The Cloud Chamber   133

Leonie Gombrich	Extract from The Assumptionists, Part III	143
N. Johnson	Extract from Buddy Meansville	147
Panos Karnezis	Deus Ex Machina	167
Simone Knightley	Extract from Sightlines	179
Julia Lee	Diapason	193
D. W. Lewis	At the Post Office (after Chekhov)	203
Kenneth Macleod	Swimming	207
Paula Main	not in gods or angels	219
James Mckenzie	dogfight	229
Jane Monson	Shouts from the Skin	239
Sandra Newman	Extract from The Church of the Unexpected	255
Kate North	No Particular Method	265
Jeff Nosbaum	Five Poems	275
Andrew Proctor	One Step Ahead of The Spider	281
Dina Rabinovitch	Extract from The Spice of Life	293
Ben Rice	Jamaican Bananas	295

Rhian Saadat Leave of Absence	307
Sharon Sage The Change	319
J. Shaw Extract from Pusher	329
Clare Sims Extract from Dusk	335
Jessica Smerin Extract from Killing God	345
Cherry Smyth Playing Celine	357
Anne F. Stairs Comfort Food	363
Lorna Thorpe Extract from The Ashram	371
Kate Weinberg Reflex	381
David Whatley Extract from The Eye of a Little God	389
Katharine Whitfield Extract from Unreturning Track	401
Clara Wigfall Slow Billows the Smoke	411
Joanna Wood The Fire Mountains	421
Biographies	428

ANDREW MOTION
Introduction

Magpie is the latest in a distinguished series of anthologies containing work by students on the Creative Writing MA course at the University of East Anglia. The students also edit, design and publish the anthology.

The Creative Writing MA, founded thirty years ago by Angus Wilson and Malcolm Bradbury, has long had a reputation for excellence – thanks greatly to its association with Ian McEwan and Kazuo Ishiguro, both of whom were students on the course. But these, and other high profile authors, have benefited from their time at UEA because it allowed them to concentrate on writing. The course provides a dedicated opportunity for experiment, imaginative adventure, self-discovery and self-analysis.

Magpie gives vivid proof of the benefits, both in the prose and in the poetry that it contains. (A poetry 'option' has been available since I took over the course from Malcolm Bradbury five years ago.) It is an anthology which delights in diversity, which celebrates risk, and which shows its contributors being as watchful in the wide world as they are shrewd in their apprehension of interior states. It is an eclectic book, as its title indicates, but one made up entirely of things that shine in the writers' eyes.

There is a special pleasure in reading gifted writers at the beginning of their writing lives: the sense of promise, combined with the excitement of discovering that many skills and qualities are already well-developed, is a potent mixture. Like its predecessors, *Magpie* is at once expert and explorative: a gleaming witness to the health of new writing within the university and at large.

CLARE ALLAN

Extract from **Lipstick and Melleril**

ONE

There's no way I'm to blame for what happened. All I was trying to do was help her out. And anyway, it was her that asked me, it's not like I offered or anything, and I've done the same for loads of people and it's never happened before.

The thing is, she was in the wrong place anyway, or that's what we all reckoned. And I can't see how I was supposed to know any different either, with so much lying and deceiving as you'd never believe it, and me about the truthfullest person there, and that's saying something.

Even now, I still haven't got it quite straight in my head. Sometimes I think she had to do it, because there was nothing the matter with her, and she was that desperate to prove that there was. But then I start thinking how if Poppy was willing to kill herself, just so as they'd believe she was a dribbler, then I reckon she must actually have been one. So what did she have to pretend for in the first place? You see what I mean, it doesn't make sense.

One thing's for sure, and that's that they fucked up big time. It's not that I'm overly bothered or anything, but it doesn't half piss me off, when I'm sat there taking all the rap, and them lot's getting away scot-free. I'm way too trusting, that's my problem. I believe what people tell me. Or I used to. I've learned my lesson now. You're best not paying attention what anybody says, 'cause most of it's just shit, and the rest stinks even worse.

It might seem weird that she asked me to help, but it wasn't really. The thing is, I had a bit of a reputation for filling in the forms. I don't know why, but I was just really good at it. I got that many people high rate you wouldn't believe it. And, strictly hush-hush, I could probably name at least a dozen sniffs, who shouldn't have got anything at all and are set up for life now, and all because of me.

I was practically born in the system, put down at birth for a place in the bin. My mum was a dribbler, and her mum as well, except she never saw her hardly, because in those days they just locked you up and threw away the key. When I came along, they didn't even bother to check. They just marked it down along with my weight and blood group, or whatever. Schizophrenic. I got a social worker for my fourteenth birthday, and by seventeen I was doing my first six month section.

When my mum was around, they didn't have Disability Living Allowance. If you were mad, you were pretty much broke as well. Now it's quite lucrative. I mean, not compared with doing a proper job or anything, but compared with being on the dole or even just on the sick, it's not bad at all. Then you've got your bus pass and your council flat, and your added extras here and there, and all in all, it's quite a good time to be a dribbler. As long as you know how to fill in the forms.

TWO

I realise I'm getting all ahead of myself, but if you just bear with me, I'll try and double back. I'm really bad like that. I kind of assume that if I know something, then everybody else must know it too, and I forget that I've still got all the explaining to do. Like if I'm walking along with someone, and I'm supposed to be showing them the way, and then I suddenly realise that I've just been following them all the time, and we're miles away from where we're meant to be.

So first of all, I should probably say that when it all happened, we were going to the Dorothy Fish. Sometimes I find it hard to believe there can be anyone alive, or dead for that matter, who hasn't at one time or another wound up at the Dorothy Fish Psychiatric Day Hospital. Practically everyone I know has been a patient there at some point. And the weird thing is, that out of all those hundreds, if not thousands, of people, I've never met one who can honestly claim that it helped them. Not a single one. That's the only thing I can guarantee if you go to the Dorothy Fish. You'll come out worse than you went in.

Anyway, in case you've never been, or in case you don't recognize it, because, obviously, I can't go giving you the real name, or they'll sue me for libel or slander or whichever it is, and I'll bet you they'd never let me off for being a dribbler either. Do you know what I'm saying? I'm mad as a mushroom when it suits them to stick me on the ward and drug me till the eyes are popping right out of my head, but if they want to sue me for saying how crap they are, which is only what everyone knows anyway, then all of a sudden I'm as sane as the number nine bus, if you get what I mean.

So the Dorothy Fish is this psychiatric day hospital, and it's set on the first floor of the Abaddon Unit, which is a huge red tower of a building, built out of brimstone or whatever, where all the dribblers in the borough go to be locked up and lobotomised by Dr Belial and his team of Satanic Nurses.

The Dorothy Fish is a day hospital, which means, in case you're a complete virgin dribbler, that you go there every day, and then, every evening, when it closes, they kick you back out into the caring community so you can sit out another sleepless night in your 'Category A' priority council flat.

Upstairs at the Abaddon, stacked one on top of the other, above the Dorothy Fish, are the in-patient wards. These are pretty much like the day hospital, except that you get a bed, and you don't get to go home or anything. And sometimes the day patients envy the ward ones, like when its cold or raining or whatever, and they can't be arsed to walk back down the hill, and sometimes the ward patients envy the day ones, like when they fancy a good old booze up and a night or two on the town.

The general idea at the Abaddon is that the worse you get, the further up you go. Compared to the dribblers on the second floor, the day patients seem quite normal, a bit weird maybe, but not seriously round the bend. Compared to a fourth floor inmate, a day patient comes over as pure, unblemished sanity. And so on. After the fifth floor, the wards are kept locked. Nobody goes in or out. Even the staff don't mix with the outside world. Between the lower floors, the patients move up and down quite freely, but after the fifth, you must cross some sort of Rubicon or whatever, because the sixth is known as the floor of no return. Even with all the boasting and bragging and blatant exaggeration that goes on amongst your average group of dribblers, I've never met anyone who claimed to have got higher than the fifth. And if they did then I wouldn't believe them.

I don't know how many floors there are. The lifts stop at five, but if you go out and stand across the street, you can see there's a lot more than that. The truth is, the tower's so tall that you can't even see the top of it. It seems like it just goes up and up and up and up forever. It goes up so high that you can't make out the windows any more, and then it goes up still further until all you can trace is this faint red line disappearing into the sky. I reckon if you got hold of a special telescope or something, really powerful, so you could count up all the floors, then you'd run out of numbers to count them with before you got near the top. Which just goes to show you how mad they must be up there.

The Abaddon Unit is set at the top of this enormous hill and, from our common room, you can see right across London. You can see the white dome of St Paul's, and the blinking tower of Canary Wharf and the Old Bailey, and Centrepoint, and everything else as well. When it's clear, you can see all the way to the other side, where the hills start up again, which is about a hundred miles away. It's a totally amazing view, and that's just from the first floor. The higher up you go, the further you can see. It's easily the best view in London. And I'd be surprised if it wasn't the best view in the world.

What I can't understand is why nobody's snapped the place up and turned it into a Japanese hotel or something. I mean, the building's complete shite and everything inside, but if they did it up, it could make an absolute fortune. The only reason I can think of why it's still full of dribblers milking the state, instead of Japanese businessmen bringing in truckloads of money, is that nobody's ever thought of it. They will though. One of these days some entrepreneur's going to wind up in there, with depression or something, and he'll look out the window and that'll be it. Instant cure. I bet they'd sell it, as well. Just like that. And stick all the dribblers in Wembley Stadium or the Millennium Dome or wherever. The thing is, though, when entrepreneurs crack up, which they do, quite often, they always go private and check themselves into the Priory or the Charter Chelsea or somewhere, with mahogany loo seats and potted palms and salmon en croute for dinner. No one important ever goes near the Abaddon, which is probably how the place has survived so long.

I used to spend a lot of time staring out at that view. I used to think how, just in the space of our window, there were all these millions and millions of sniffs, all living their sane little lives in their sane little flats, and going out to work every day, and eating their sandwiches at lunchtime, and always being balanced and normal, and then there was us, screwed up like litter and dropped by the world outside, then stuffed into bin bags and tidied away in our tower. We didn't know them, and they didn't know us, and the weird thing was that that was how I liked it. I know it sounds strange, because the Abaddon was really just a human rubbish dump, and a mouldy one at that, piled with such battered old crap as you'd not even look at for salvage, but still, my biggest fear all the time I was there, was that they'd suddenly decide I was normal, and send me back down the hill.

THREE

I told you about how the Abaddon was really grimy and everything, well that's putting it pretty mildly, to be honest. The smartest bit was Security downstairs, and that wasn't overly smart, either, but it was massively cleaner and newer and fresher than anywhere else in the building. Everyone had to go through

Security to get in or out. Doctors, nurses, patients, visitors, even VIPs, if any of them ever came near the place, which I doubt. There was a fake leather sofa, and loo roll in the toilet, and a long traily pot plant on a stand. The security guard was this huge Nigerian body builder called Sharon. He was well over eight foot tall, weighing a good forty stone, and all of it gleaming muscle. He sat there all day, in a cage by the entrance, flicking through fitness magazines and watching the door. If you weren't either patient or staff, you had to fill in a visitor's sticker and wear it all the time you were in the building, just to prove who you were, and make sure you didn't get taken for a dribbler and dragged off and injected or whatever. Once Sharon had you labelled, or ticked off in his register, then he'd punch this round black button on the counter in front of him, and the sliding jaws would open, and above them, written in sulphurous flames, and at least a dozen languages (this was an inner-city area) was the one rule you couldn't break, even if you wanted to:

ABADDON ALL HOP, YOU WHO ENTER HEAR.

Dorothy Fish was on the first floor. There was a sign pointing you up the stairs, but the smoke funnelling down from the common room created a sort of tunnel around you, so it was pretty much impossible to wander off course anyway.

The common room itself was large, square and horribly overheated. It smelled of a mixture of stale cigarette smoke and curried fatty lamb. The kitchens were through a door on the far side, and every so often this would swing open and give us a blast of frying oil. Two walls of the room were all windows and a couple of these were always boarded up because someone had taken a chair to them. Through the bits that weren't boarded up, you could see, on one side, the view I already told you about. On the other side, you looked onto the car park, which was where all the doctors left their four-wheel-drives while they were busy torturing patients. I always thought it was just as well they had four-wheel-drives, in case some dribbler lost it half way up Mount Everest or something.

We day patients sat against the back wall in two rows of plastic covered chairs, set facing each other, and smoked. The ward patients sat in two rows under the windows and smoked. We put our feet up on the coffee tables, and flicked our ash in the brown metal bins. They put their feet up on the tables and flicked their ash on the carpet. That was because they didn't give a shit. Generally speaking, the ward patients gave even less of a shit than the day patients.

The carpet was the filthiest carpet you've ever seen. I don't even know what colour it was, it was so filthy. The walls were a pale shitty brown from all the smoke, and above our heads there was this line of dirty yellow rectangles, where they used to have pictures, except they had to take them down because people kept throwing cups at them and breaking the glass. You could still see the splashes where the coffee had run down the walls. In one of the rectangles, someone had got a blue biro and scratched out a cock and two balls, carving their artwork deep into the plaster.

Outside the common room, there were loos with no loo roll in them, and they flooded every week, because people used newspaper instead, which blocked up the pipes and everything, and it must have cost them a fortune to keep unblocking them, but they still never worked it out that it would be cheaper just to give us some toilet paper. Then there was this corridor with the staff room and some other rooms as well. And the staff sat in the staff room all day, drinking real coffee, like we never got, and doing wordsearches and reading those true story magazines and waiting for something to happen. The other rooms were meant for holding therapy groups and meetings and things like that, but half the time the staff couldn't be arsed to run them, and the rest of the time we couldn't be arsed to go, so it worked out that we never really saw each other.

All round the common room, there were these panic alarms, that looked like red mushrooms or something, sprouting out of the walls. You were supposed to press them if someone lost it, so the staff could come and sort them out. But sometimes we used to press them anyway, just to see them all come racing in.

FOUR

At the Dorothy Fish we all fitted into the system. We knew who we were. There was Tina, who was always saying sorry, like everything was her fault or something, and she was very thin and middle aged, with her hair in a bob that turned under, just right, and she wore her best clothes, all clean and ironed, like she was going to church. And you couldn't see it, because of her sleeves and everything, but Tina used to slash her arms to pieces, really badly as well, and she was the one who always fetched the tea.

Then there was Sarah, who was fat and blonde and smelt of toilet freshener, and she used to bring in cut-price tobacco that she bought from this man in the launderette on Saturday mornings, and sell it to us for a mark up. Only she claimed she didn't make any money out of it, but we all knew she did, except no one ever challenged her, because then she'd have sulked forever. And besides, none of the rest of us could be arsed to get out of bed on a Saturday morning and go and find out.

Dawn had had a course of ECT that went wrong, and now she couldn't remember anything. I mean, like if you had a conversation with her, she'd ask you the same thing about a thousand times, and each time it was like she really wanted to know. What happened was that when they were giving her the shock, they had all these students standing round the bed, who were supposed to be learning how to do ECT so that then they could become doctors or whatever. Or maybe they were doctors already, I'm not sure, and they just needed to learn about working the machine. I think they were students though. Anyway, there were loads of them in there, all squashed round the bed, and this one student, who wasn't paying attention properly, leant on the button by mistake, and they hadn't set the dial or anything, so Dawn got this monumental electric shock. It was so enormous that it blew every fuse in the Abaddon, and all the lights went out and all the TVs went off and all the patients started rioting, and it blew all the memory out of Dawn's brain as well.

But what Dawn was really brilliant at was making tables. We had this wood workshop place, and none of us ever went in except for Dawn, and she used to go in there pretty much all the time. She made so many coffee tables that we didn't know what to do with them, and she never got bored of it, because she couldn't remember that she'd ever made one before. We all took at least three home, and we gave one to every single dribbler in the borough, and all the day centres and crisis centres and drop-in centres were so full of tables you couldn't get in them any more, and there were still about a hundred left over for the common room.

Cath was 42, and she had a 28-year-old daughter, Mandy, and Mandy had a sixteen-year-old son. At different times I'd been on a ward with all three of them. And they all of them suffered from depression and they all self-harmed and they all tried to top themselves on a regular basis. There was a time when if you went down to A & E on any night of the week, chances were you'd find one of them in there, having their stomach pumped. Once I went for a drink with Cath, and she ended up getting totally off her head, and she told me that she reckoned all three of them had got the same father. The thing is, Cath was abused as a little kid, sexually, I mean, by her dad, and that's how she got pregnant with her daughter. And what she reckoned was that he did the same to Mandy, even though Cath really tried to protect her and everything. She asked her once, and Mandy went totally mental and wouldn't answer, which is a bit suspicious anyway, if you think about it. If it *is* true, and I'm not saying it definitely is or anything, 'cause I can't be sure, then that means that Cath's grandson, Jason, was also her half-brother. Put like that it sounds really bad, so I'm not surprised she had to get pissed to come out with it.

Cath was the most amazing scrabble player. She was so good that nobody would play her any more, because she always won. She knew all these totally weird words that nobody had ever even heard of, and she had this book that proved they were allowed and everything. It got really annoying in the end, and everyone got so pissed off that she started playing on her own. She had one of those fancy professional sets, with a turntable thing underneath, and she set it up every morning, and just sat there playing all day, and when she made a really good word, like EQUINOX or something, she'd swing it round and show us. It worked much better like that.

Then there was Brian, who used to be a butcher, and he couldn't stop washing his hands, so he used to spend all day in the toilets bent over the sink, and his hands were so dried up and cracked and wrinkled that they looked like they belonged on a really old man, and not Brian, who can't have been much over 30. Every two hours, he'd come out and take a five minute break, and he emptied the bins and tidied the tables and took all our cups back to the kitchen.

And there were lots of other people too. About twenty of us regulars, and twenty more part time, but I won't go on, because I'm sure you get the picture by now. And this is supposed to be about Poppy anyway, and how I helped her with filling out the forms. Because that's where I fitted in. I was the one who was brilliant at forms.

FIVE

Her name was Poppy Shakespeare, and for all I know, and for all she knew either, she might have been related to the really famous one, like he could have been her great-great-great-great-great-great-grandad or something. I don't think so though, not unless he was black, which he certainly wasn't meant to be, at least not from the picture I've seen. It would really crack me up though if he was. I mean, after all this time of them pretending he was white and everything, if he'd really been black all along. That'd be pretty hysterical. And then if it turned out he was Poppy's grandad or whatever, as well. Just think of the money in that! All that copyright from all those plays! Because I read about it somewhere, that you have to pay the writer every time you do one of their plays, even if they're already dead and everything. And they're always doing Shakespeare. I notice it now in the paper. I never used to pay much attention, but now that I'm looking, I see him all the time. And then there's the films as well, because they make millions, and she'd have to get her cut. Maybe that's why they never told her. I'm only joking, though. I don't really think he was her grandad. I mean, it's pretty unlikely anyway. It would have been good though. Because then she wouldn't have needed DLA.

Poppy wasn't actually black. Not properly, but then she wasn't white either. And the black part can't have come from her mother, because, although I never saw her till the funeral, when I did she was definitely white.

Sarah can be quite insensitive really. She doesn't mean it badly, but she can still be quite insensitive. I mean, there's no way I'd have said anything, but Sarah just came out with it, and asked Poppy if she was half-caste. What was really funny was that Sarah thought she was being so mature and everything, like if someone gets turned down for DLA, or they show up with their throat in stitches, or something like that, and instead of avoiding the subject, you bring it up deliberately so there's no awkwardness or whatever. Well, that's what Sarah was trying to do, and she was smiling and nodding before Poppy had even answered, just to show how accepting she was and that it didn't make no difference to her.

For a second I thought Poppy was going to go mental, and I was all geared up for it and waiting to see how she'd be. I mean, to call a half-caste person half-caste is about as insulting as you can get. They didn't used to mind so much, not when I was a kid, but then they decided they'd rather be called mixed race. After that, if you forgot and called them half-caste, they'd think you were saying it just to piss them off. I reckon it's up to them really, to decide what they want to be called, so mostly I just go along with it. And if they change their minds again, and want to go back to being half-caste, then I'll go along with that as well. It doesn't worry me. But it was just like Sarah not to pay attention and stick her great clumsy hoof in it, and her being so sensitive and sulky as well, about anything to do with her.

Well, Poppy just sat there, flicking her ash in the bin and making out like she hadn't even heard. So then, of course, being Sarah, she has to go and repeat the question. And this time Poppy looks up at her, but like totally uninterested, like she can't even be arsed to think up a reply.

"You talking to me?"

And Sarah's all nodding and smiling, and starting to look a bit nervous, on account of her biting off more than she'd intended. "I was just wondering if you were half-caste," she goes. "I mean, you've got such a lovely warm complexion. Do you have any African blood?" That made me laugh, that did, especially the bit about the 'lovely, warm complexion'.

"Half-caste?" says Poppy, frowning like she's really having to think about it. "You know, I'm not sure. But at least I'm not half-cholesterol. Jesus, just look at you! I'm surprised they don't roll you out and use you to make mince pies."

Well, there was no need for that. It was bang out of order, by anybody's standards. But I couldn't help finding it pretty amusing, as well. And it shut Sarah up for the rest of the day, which was a bonus. So after that, nobody ever tried asking Poppy again and I still don't know how much of her was black, exactly. I reckon it was less than a half though, so maybe a quarter. I would say something like a third, except I can't see how that would work out.

ALISON BOULTON
In Search of Peter

Cal and I spent all of the first day in his elderly, family-sized Volvo. We left his children sitting at a table in a Paris street drinking coke from bottles with straws, mopping up fried egg with fat chips. They accepted kisses. They waved. Two fair sturdy boys fidgeting either side of the Australian girl, anxious to leave the dusty street with its sharp smell of unfamiliar food. Already, in their imaginations, on the train to EuroDisney.

My children are in Amsterdam with their father. I regret their absence; that they aren't here in Paris, squirming and arguing on the plastic chairs beneath the parasol. That the goodbye took place before they were quite awake, still in pyjamas.

Cal and I travelled south from the French capital, into the afternoon heat. Crossing mile after mile of empty French countryside; the *Autoroute du Soleil*. We planned this trip on Christmas cards, cumulatively, each year more insistent:

Cal, Kate, Chris and Jamie,
Happy Christmas
Love from Emma, Tom, Will, Rosie and May
PS: Shall we do it this year? I might be able to get away for a couple of days during half term.

Emma, Tom, Will, Rosie and May
Seasons Greetings
Love Cal, Kate, Chris and Jamie
PS: Sorry. In the middle of a job move which will probably mean a house move as well. Difficult to plan anything. But we must do it. Let you know when things have settled down.

During those years Cal and I were busy playing Happy Families, constructing lives as we had been taught they should be. We stayed up at nights nursing the children we had screamed at during the day. There was never enough time. The things that we should have done got postponed. The people that we should have been were neglected, buried under piles of dirty nappies, pushed into cupboards with sacks full of bright plastic toys. We lived in bubbles and spoke only to people like us.

Then Cal's wife died. Her name on the Christmas card became a space as if Cal was unable to close the gap: *Love Cal,   Chris and Jamie.* The children added in a rush after a pause, after an absence. For the first time we could see that we did not have forever and the structures we had built around us were not safe. The trip, that had been half dream, became imperative. We had to look for Peter, of whom we had neither seen nor heard for more than a decade.

A postcard:

How about Spring Bank Holiday? Phone me.

A phone call:

"Cal? I can meet you at the Gare du Nord around lunchtime. Man in scruffy T-shirt? I'm sure I'll recognise you. Nope, forget the pink carnation."

Of course I recognised him, although his hair was darker. It was as if her death had taken some of the light out of him.

Until this journey I had not seen Cal for five years. And then, for hour after hour, there was only him to look at: Cal and the long, curved road. The man I remembered is now fused with this one, the same and different. Underneath both the boy remains, for Cal and I were at school together. It was always Peter, Cal and me.

"Will he be there, do you think?" It must be the fifth or sixth time we have asked each other this question. We ask each other the other question too: why do we want to find him? We cannot answer either of them.

In the car we talk. A car can be a confessional. The formality between us, erected by the years we have been apart, is slowly dissolved by the small space. We pick up fragmented pieces of history and hold them out to each other for inspection.

"Do you remember that flat I shared with Peter? The one above the sweetshop?" Cal asks.

I do. Three first floor rooms with greasy curtains in the main street of our small town.

"It belonged to Steve Draper's dad. Wasn't really fit to live in."

"They demolished it soon after you left."

"I don't think that was our fault."

"Probably not." The flat assembles itself in my head, then crumbles. "I watched them do it." I was standing across the street in the doorway of Woolworths as the windows caved in at a blow from some huge iron ball suspended from a crane. The curtains were still hanging as the wall fell.

"I've got a picture of you both there, actually. Eating sausages and baked beans. Pete's wearing a woolly jumper with the sleeves rolled up. You can hardly see his face because of his hair."

"Hair and eyebrows and bright blue eyes. And the way he sort of lolloped around. He even lolloped when he was sitting down. How did he do that?"

"Don't know. More relaxed than us. He was reading a book about Chairman Mao."

"And sleeping with that druggie from Bristol. That turned into a bit of a mess."

"Maybe that's why he went off grape picking. Do you think he was really more relaxed?" I've often wondered this.

"Hard to tell."

"He didn't seem to care."

Cal shakes his head and overtakes on the inside. A small blue Citroën hoots loudly.

"What did he do that for?"

"You overtook in the wrong lane."

"Ah." He grins. "Fuck."

"He sent me six brandy glasses for a wedding present, you know. Funny thing to send through the post. Five arrived intact."

"Brandy glasses, eh? Very French. But that was a good wedding, Emma."

Yes, I think. The wedding was good. A boiling hot day in midsummer and a cricket match on the green.

"Do you remember? There was even a hot air balloon."

Cal is getting tired.

"Shall we pull over, get something to eat? I'll drive if you like."

"You don't have to drive. That's OK."

We stop anyway. I unpeel the sticky fabric of my dress from my back, reach for a band to curl the hair off my neck.

"Never needed air-conditioning before. I suppose Kate and I always flew when we went on holiday."

"Drives like this are horrible with children. Always asking how far it is, when can we stop? They want to eat or drink or pee or throw up."

We park at a service station next to a lorry with a British number plate. I am still fiddling with my hair.

"Your hair is exactly the same as it was when you were eleven. Did you know that?"

I recall a photo of us on a youth hostelling trip to Wales. He is absolutely right.

"Have you ever had it any different? In between times I mean?"

"No. Why?" I frown. He gives me the shifting, sideways glance that was always part of him.

"You've got quite a sweet face. I thought you might have had it shorter."

"Should I have done?" To show off my quite sweet face, presumably.

"Not necessarily. I just thought... well, it was a long time ago."

"Twenty-five years. Your hair has gone dark."

"I don't know when it did that."

We buy orange juice, sticks of bread with brie and coffee to keep us awake.

"How much longer do you think?"

"Maybe three or four hours."

"Good." It seems like we are almost there.

"Do you want to sit down?"

"No."

"Pete didn't go on that youth hostel trip, did he?"

"Nope. I don't think they let him. Or maybe he didn't want to. But I remember he came to Boulogne. I was curled in a heap on the ferry feeling terrible and he made me go out on deck, get some fresh air. Then someone up wind was sick all over Draper."

"Poor old Draper. Do you know what happened to him."

"No idea."

"Those were the days." There is a moment of silence. We ignore it, scanning the half empty tables, the counter with its exquisitely wrapped sweets, the fridges full of baguettes and soft cheese.

"More coffee?"

"Please."

Cal slips francs into the machine and returns with strong French coffee. I can't be bothered to ask for milk.

"Do you remember my mother?"

"Yes." I remember the polished house, the big woman with starched grey curls and the small man in the corner, keen to chat, full of nervous energy. I remember Cal in the kitchen stirring drinks with a spoon, rarely looking at anyone directly, always those quick, flicking glances.

"After Kate died, on the day of the funeral, my mother arrived. I hadn't seen her for months. Do you know what the first thing she said to me was?"

I shake my head.

"She said, 'Aren't you going to shave?'"

We stare at each other. This look lasts longer.

"I couldn't say anything. Kate would have done. She wouldn't have stood for that." Pause. "Ready?"

"Yep." We throw the styrofoam cups into the bin.

Outside a team of ants crawl drunkenly over a lolly melting on the pavement. They chase its sweet, red juice into the road.

"Would you like to live somewhere warm?"

I glance at Cal. The sun is too much for me. It makes my skin prickle. "I'm not sure."

The English lorry driver is finishing his coke.

"Where are you two off to?"

"Mirmande," says Cal. At least we have a place in mind.

The trucker wants to talk.

"Mirmande? Lovely part of the country. Just been down that way myself."

"Really?" Cal has decided to humour him. "What's the road like?"

"You want to get off this autoroute, see some real scenery. It won't take that much longer."

"You reckon?"

"Take the N86 at the next junction. I go that way all the time."

"All right, then. Cheers."

"Have a good trip." The lorry driver waves as he pulls out. Cal and I examine the map. The way he has suggested winds with the river. It will put hours on to the journey.

"Shall we do as he says?" Cal asks.

"Maybe another time."

Back in the car it is much, much hotter. I fish in my bag for sunglasses.

"Do you want some music on?"

"What shall we have?"

"Manic Street Preachers. It's the last one Kate bought before she died."

"That's fine."

I think: Kate has come with us in a way that she would not have done if she were still alive. But I am unable to resent her presence.

Mirmande lies deep in the Rhône Valley. It's late in the evening when we reach it and already dark. The village of rambling stone cottages slopes up the mountain side and is crowned by a small, ancient church, softly lit as if by candles.

"My God," Cal gasps. "Just look at that." It is as if we have arrived at a place of pilgrimage, far more beautiful than either of us have dared to imagine. We park the car and stretch our legs, wandering at random through the narrow streets and staring out across the dark plain dotted with lights.

"He must be here."

"Why?" I ask reasonably.

Cal shakes his head in wonder. "Because if you ended up

here for whatever reason, you wouldn't ever want to leave it."

"You're just being romantic. Too much sunshine." But he's right.

We are looking for a bar, Peter's last address. The only possible place is a restaurant with a terrace full of English and Dutch voices.

"Pete wouldn't hang out there." Cal is disappointed. "But we could get some food."

"It's probably expensive."

He laughs. "I work for a merchant bank, remember. I'll treat you."

I had forgotten. The unshaven man in the grubby T-shirt does not remind me of merchant banks. We find a table and order fish, salad and wine.

"So what do we do next?"

"Find a hotel? Look in the morning?" I say this reluctantly. The night seems too good to give up on.

"Or we could ask the waiter?"

"Go on then. You speak French."

"I wonder if I do." I compose the sentence in my head, discarding the Dutch that has insinuated itself to the front of my brain, digging further back for the verbs I conjugated at school.

"Nous cherchons un ami. Il s'appelle Peter."

The French waiter smiles enigmatically causing Cal and me to giggle.

"Peter Reeve?" He rolls the initial R making the name sound suddenly unfamiliar. "I know 'im. You want to telephone?" We nod, grinning. If only we'd known it would be so easy. The waiter disappears inside to find the number. Cal and I look at each other and at the same time shout: "Yeees!"

The Dutch and the English smile benevolently from their respective tables.

Quite soon Peter is there, lolloping up the hill with his peculiar, distinctive gait. He slips easily onto the backdrop of uneven streets. He shakes our hands. The floppy hair has been cut off and his English has become gutteral, uncertain, from years of speaking French.

"What are you doing here, then?" He pulls a chair up to our table and orders Calvados for us all.

"We came to see you." It seems a bit silly, put like that. How can we tell him we planned for four years and drove for nine hours?

"We wondered where you were."

"Here. I've been here for years. Since I came back from Hong Kong. I nearly got stuck there. Had to sleep with some American woman, pay my way."

"On a boat?"

"Yeah." He turns to me. "Got your Christmas cards."
I had sent them all here, to this restaurant that was once a bar.
"Hey, Jean-Luc, this is the one who sent the Christmas cards."
The waiter smiles.
"Well, you can send the next one to my proper address."
"I might not send you anymore."
Peter raises his eyebrows.
"Well, you didn't write back."
"Nope. They nearly got me into trouble, actually. Sophie, that's my wife, thought you must be an old lover."
We look at each other. This was always impossible. Peter and I have the same birthday. We always felt like twins.
"I've brought a photo of my children with me. I'll show it to her."
"Good. I've got a kid, too. Girl. She's called Hélène."
Cal finishes the Calvados and orders three more. I shake my head and pour mine into the glasses of the others.
"So what are you doing, Pete? Still grape picking?" Cal asks.
"Nope. Cherries. But I'm supervisor now." He laughs. "That means I organise the orchards. Make sure the trees are pruned and stuff. Don't do much picking anymore. It's a nice life. How about you?"
"I work for a merchant bank."
"A merchant bank! Christ, Cal."
Cal shrugs. "I knew you'd say that. It pays well."
"That's alright then. You can buy the drinks."
"I was going to," Cal says quietly.
We are silent for a moment, then Peter says:
"You know, the thing I remember about school, how I ended up here and you ended up in a merchant bank – and fuck knows where you've ended up, Emma."
"Nowhere much."
"What I remember is when old Barnes said, 'Anyone who wants to go to university go through that door.' Remember that?"
Cal and I nod.
"And I just sat there. I thought, 'I'm not going through any door.' No doors in my house."
It is getting late. The Dutch and the English have drifted away. There is only us, left sitting on the terrace.
"Cal and I need to find a hotel."
"You can stay with us," Pete offers. "We've got other people staying, friends of Sophie's, but we can squeeze you in."
I have spent the whole day folded into the car. The whole day talking to Cal. What I want, more than anything, is silence.

"Not tonight, thanks. Maybe tomorrow when Sophie's had time to get used to the idea."

"Did that seem like Peter?" Cal asks, as we walk up the hill to the hotel with the three crowns on the wall.

"I think it did." But it's not enough, not yet. We haven't got what we came for. We were together too long in the car without him. He isn't with us as he used to be. He has kept separate. But there is still tomorrow.

"We have to decide now," I say, "how many rooms we're going to ask for."

"I don't mind," he replies. "I don't mind sleeping with you. We can if you like. We can still be friends."

I need a better offer than that to give up the thought of a cool bed in an empty room; to break my wedding vows.

I smile. "Two, then. One each. I need some space tonight." I can't tell if he's relieved or not.

We have telephoned from the restaurant. We ring the bell. A large woman with waved grey hair appears in a silken dressing gown.

"*Deux chambres, s'il vous plaît.*"

She waves her hands delightedly. The situation seems to please her. She reaches for keys.

"*Vous êtes copains.*"

"What did she say?"

I translate for Cal. "She said we're just friends."

Cal laughs.

Peter's wife is pale as a moon with heavy breasts that have leaked milk on to her blouse. Their small, dark child stumbles after her, clutching her skirt. The house is dark, whitewashed, made of lumps of thick stone like a cave. Sophie's paintings hang on the walls, intense and full of bright colours.

"It used to be a pig sty," Peter says with a gesture that encompasses the whole building. He pulls down a photo album which we examine politely. The transformation of his house. "I renovated all this with my own hands."

"His own hands and a roll of sellotape," Cal jokes when Peter has gone to fetch coffee.

I examine Peter's hands. They are large, broad, disproportionate to his body.

Now I am inside I see that Pete has told the truth. He has built a house without internal doors. Even the bathroom only has a curtain. It makes me feel uncomfortable.

"I need doors to shut other people out," I tell him.

He shrugs. "Why?"

"Because," I say slowly, "I'm not as contained as you."

The friends are still there, an artistic couple from Lyon with a fat-cheeked baby whom Cal instantly adores. We tell each other that we miss our children. In fact we want to show them off as these other people are presenting their child to be admired and remarked upon.

The babies fill up the day. They are sick, need feeding. The washing up never seems to get done. I fidget and do it. I wipe the surfaces and rinse out the dishcloth. The housewife in me refuses to leave be. Sophie seems not to notice. Certainly not to care. Peter and Cal talk about property prices and drink beer from bottles on the grass outside. The couple from Lyon decide to go shopping and their departure drags as they search for the baby's comforter. In the afternoon Peter takes us to the orchard where he works and we are allowed to pick fruit. The cherries are heavy and sweet. There has been too much rain, he explains. Cal and I pick bag after bag of cherries to take home. Hélène has cherry juice dripping like blood from her mouth. She clings to her father and stares mistrustfully at us. We cram the cherries into our mouths and see how far we can spit the stones.

In the house a meal has been prepared, chicken with bread and red wine. I am not clear if this is lunch or dinner. Time seems to have shifted.

"You can stay here tonight," Sophie says, in French. "I have prepared the beds." She is preoccupied, mostly, with the child, who won't eat. Occasionally she glances at Peter. She talks to the other couple who are fiery and animated, arguing with each other about the brochure for an exhibition they are planning. But I need to walk, not to sit.

Cal and Pete agree to come with me. We set off up the hillside as the afternoon sun dips.

"I'll take you to a medieval village. It's not far. People are beginning to move into it again and do up the houses."

"It's wonderful," says Cal, as we pause, gazing down the mountain at the flat, blue river, winding through the valley. Peter nods. I pick stems of wild rosemary and chew on its bitterness.

The village is half buried amongst trees. A goat stands with full udders, tethered to a stump. It looks up with interest as we approach.

"We'll go and see Marieke," Peter says. "She's Dutch. She'll give us tea."

Marieke is standing in her doorway. Perhaps she has heard our voices.

"*Bonjour.*"

"*Bonjour.*" They kiss. Three kisses.

"Three in Holland," says Marieke.

"Four here," Pete insists.

Marieke is older than us, tall and Anglo-Saxon looking with wide hips under a shapeless skirt.

"These are my friends from England." Pete spreads his arm to include Cal and me.

"Come in." Marieke has switched languages as the Dutch always do.

We enter a large rectangular room. The light is grainy because the windows are narrow. It has a lingering smell of damp stone. In the centre, beneath an overhead light draped in a spangled shawl, is a square table of scrubbed wood. At the table sits a man with wild dark hair, a wide moustache and eyes the colour of ploughed earth. He stands and offers his hand.

"Pierre," he says.

Peter is nosing round. "You've done up the kitchen since I was last here." Through an opening I can see an old calor gas cooker and a twin tub. A kettle is heating on the stove. I think of my kitchen with its dishwasher and fitted cupboards. I catch Cal's eye and guess that he is thinking the same.

Cal sits down at the table next to Pierre.

"English, eh?"

Cal nods.

"You know Peter?" The man speaks our language with difficulty.

"He's an old school friend," I say in French. Was he? Here it seems this cannot possibly be true. Pierre nods as if pondering this deeply. He is interested in Cal, despite the language barrier.

"And you have come to visit?"

"That's right."

"Why did you come?" I can't see what sort of answer this man is expecting. He is looking directly at Cal. Cal seems nonplussed.

"My wife died," he replies, suddenly.

"Ah." Pierre's English appears to fail him completely. His eyes do not leave Cal's face. "Thank you," he says at last, as if this has explained everything.

Cal looks at me. I cannot rescue him. Marieke and Peter emerge from the kitchen with a tray of tea.

"Who was that?" Cal asks as we stand once more in the dying sunlight beside the goat. He shakes his head as if to free himself from the intensity of the room.

"That's Pierre. He's usually stoned."

"Can we walk a bit further?" I don't want to go back to the house yet. I want to stay out here on the mountain.

"OK. I don't come up here much. But I think if we take this path we can walk in a circle."

We set off once more up the hill. We all walk quickly. We are chatting, remembering bits and pieces, asking about people we used to know.

"Do you remember that *Alice in Wonderland* play we did when I was the Red Queen and you were the king? You were short then, Pete. You only came up to my shoulder."

"I was a late developer."

"What were you in that, Cal?"

"I was a tree."

"I don't remember a tree in *Alice in Wonderland*."

"I think Miss Jackson wrote the part especially for me."

"Sophie's worried about Hélène. She's losing weight and won't eat anything. You two know about children. What do you think?"

"She might be allergic to something. Kate had allergic reactions to all kinds of things."

Pete and I look at each other and at Cal, who is looking at the ground.

"It might be worth getting her tested," I say.

We have come to a fork in the path.

"I suppose we'd better go down or the others will wonder where we've got to." We turn and through the trees see the Rhône again, now a flash of gold. The light on the path is becoming opaque. The stones stand out on the brown dirt turned to pearls by the dusk. We begin our descent of the mountain. The track twists unexpectedly to the right.

"Are you sure you know where we're going, Pete?"

"No. I told you, I've never been up here before. Why would I want to come up here?"

We walk on. The western sky is streaked with crimson. The night is quenching the heat of the day. Cal says: "I think we're going in completely the wrong direction."

This seems to be true. We don't feel inclined to double back. Probably we are not even sure that we can double back. We have to keep going.

"At least you're getting your walk, Emma."

"That's alright. I want to be tired."

"I reckon, if we go that way we'll end up back at the village." We take the track Pete indicates. Cal stops to pee behind a tree.

It is very nearly dark now and the trees have lost their colour. They have become dense patches against the murky sky. The river, when it comes into view, has lights dotted here and there along its bank. The distant lanterns of people chasing out the night.

"I think I recognise this bit."

"Is it the village?"

"Yep. Look, there's the goat." It stands, mournful now, still tethered to its stump.

"The rest should be easy. Come on."

Filled with new energy we follow Peter. A slice of moon, huge and yellow, has appeared on the eastern horizon, but the path is dark amidst the trees. We walk and walk, but the track melts into grass. We have arrived at a small, wooden shack and a grove of pear trees.

"Well. That was the wrong way."

"Don't you know the way back from the village?"

"It's a long time since I've been there. I haven't got any sense of direction."

"Neither have I," say Cal and I together. We giggle.

"Back to the goat then."

The goat regards us through bored eyes. She has taken our measure.

"We'll try this way. I think I remember that tree," says Cal. We try his way. It winds steeply through the wood until the ground becomes boggy.

"Well," he laughs nervously. "That wasn't it."

We head back up the hill to the goat.

"That's where we need to get to. Look, you can see the house."

"Let's just head for it," mutters Cal, and he is off before we can stop him, across a meadow of knee high grass, past disused beehives. He scrambles over a barbed wire fence and is soon thirty yards in front. His form flickers uneasily in and out of shadows. Pete follows shaking his head, then pauses to help me.

"Come on, Emma." There is an urgency in his voice. I have to keep up. We have to keep with Cal.

"Er, Cal," Pete shouts. "I'm not sure this is a very good idea."

The moon has risen now, full and powerful. It spotlights Cal as he charges on through the undergrowth. I follow with Pete whose lollop has quickened. It's almost a jog. I'm only just managing to stay with him.

"Shit," Cal yells. He has stopped abruptly. The white of his shirt trembles like a flag in the gentle wind. "It's a fucking ravine."

He is standing on its very edge. We rush up to him and all three of us gaze down to where we have not fallen. A sheer drop of hundreds of feet into the valley below. Pete puts a hand on Cal's shoulder. The moon has a smoky blue ring.

"I think we'd better look for the road."

It is nearly midnight when we arrive back at the house that Peter built. The three French friends are sitting around the table smoking and drinking beer. It is only the English who walk up mountains under a full moon. They look up and greet us but no comment is made on the length of our absence. They seem neither surprised nor concerned.

Cal and I take our seats at one end of the table. Peter brings in more beer. I light one of Sophie's cigarettes and take a long drag. The smoke wraps itself around the lamp. The children are asleep upstairs, in Paris and in Amsterdam. We sit, six of us, in the house without doors and talk.

For Steve and Pete

HELEN CLEARY

Extract from **A Narrow Track**

This is an extract from a novel that chronicles the last three years of a family's life. The setting is Singapore; the decade, the 1970s. From the point of view of a child we learn about understanding; from the point of view of that child's adult we learn about knowing.

Eleanor could not understand why they had to spend so many hours on the jumbo jet. As her brothers slept, she fiddled with their shoelaces, tying them together. And she attempted conversation.
– Is it far to Singapore now?
– Not too far.
– How far is it, Dad?
– I don't know in miles.
– But how far is it, Dad? How much time?
– About ten more hours.
With a cocktail stick he fished a green olive from the martini that had been delivered in a plastic glass to his flip-out table. He popped the olive into his mouth and sucked the stick.
– How many hours is ten hours?
– Ten, Elly. I've just told you. Don't be daft.
– Then how many minutes is ten hours?
– Six hundred.
– Six hundred. How long is a minute, Dad?
– You know how long a minute is, Elly.
– Show me.
He knew this game. They had a routine.
– Pleeease.
– Oh, OK.
Eleanor sat up on her knees so that she was at his eye-level. She breathed into her father's ear; he batted her away as if she were a mosquito. He undid the button on his shirt cuff and rolled back his sleeve. There was his gold and silver watch. A whole minute was up when the thin hand, a spider's leg, had travelled all the way round the watch face. Eleanor's dad always

removed his watch when he shaved. Clunk onto the porcelain sink top. He covered his face in foam, his pink lips looking even pinker, then scrabbled for his razor in the bathroom cabinet. With his fingertips rubbing back and forth he wiped steam from the mirror to make the squeaking sound of bickering turkeys. Occasionally he had to change the blade, gingerly removing the paper-thin, silver oblong from its waxy packet. Eleanor could see through a line down the middle, like looking through a keyhole or a door that was ajar. Razor blades gathered a chalky film of dried soap and toothpaste if they were left, discarded among other bathroom detritus. He was careful, the blades were sharp and Eleanor was not allowed to touch them. Her dad had to shave, he said:

– Otherwise your Mother wouldn't kiss me.

They didn't kiss much anyway.

Sometimes, before he shaved, Eleanor's father chased her around the house. When he caught her he nuzzled his bristle against her belly, jutting out his lower lip and moving his jaw from side to side. She writhed and screamed and afterwards looked at her stomach. Nothing.

To look at his watch, Eleanor held her father's wrist. She felt the hairs on his arms. Using the flat of her hand she brushed them the wrong way. They stood upright, then slowly relaxed back towards the skin. She did this when he let her sit next to him in front of the TV, but he didn't watch much TV, he was always at work. He tried to come home before her bedtime so that they could have a chat. That's what he said.

Eleanor always asked what he did at work and he always said the same thing:

– We saw some elephants eat bananas and they got stuck in their trunks.

And Eleanor always asked:

– What did you do, Dad?

– Everyone had to put both hands on their trunks and squeeze – one after the other.

– Show me how, Dad.

Her dad would put one hand over the other and clench his fists as if he was squeezing something with both his hands, tubes of toothpaste Eleanor always thought. Then Eleanor would put one hand over his and her other hand over the first. And they would both clench their fists. Then her dad would put one of his hands on top of Eleanor's and she had to be quick and put her hand on top of his hand. They both did this alternately, getting higher and higher until Eleanor could no longer reach. Even on tippytoes. Then he grabbed her under the armpits and swung her under his own armpit before taking her up to bed. That's how she held her bear, Muggins, too, under her arm as if he were a wrapped parcel. Eleanor had decided that she was her father's bear.

Eventually the crates from England arrived on the back of a lorry and their suitcases came in a taxi. The crates had numbers and words stamped on them in black ink which seeped through the wood's grain spreading tendrils. But the suitcases came too late: they had already bought new clothes. The whole family had caught the bus into the island-city centre. Eleanor couldn't believe the noise, especially as they walked through China Town where everyone rode Raleigh bicycles and rang their bells. Lots of people called out to passers-by, the words were strange to Eleanor. Some of the bicycles backed onto little seats sheltered by green concertinaed awnings.
 – They're called rickshaws, you sit in the back and they taxi you round.
 – Can we have a go, Mum? On the ricksaw.
 – Rickshaw. Maybe next time.
 – You wan' ride? One dollah.
Men pedalled rickshaws to make a living. They came up close and said:
 – Ride? One dollah.
 – No.
Eleanor's father sounded stern. He didn't pedal a rickshaw for a living. Maybe he didn't think he could. Eleanor thought it looked like fun, something her mum would like – her mum often had a bad back and had to go to bed.
 The colours red and gold were everywhere. Chinese characters like small mazes or a pile of sticks were scrawled everywhere too.
 – What do they mean?
 She asked her brother Sean because he was the oldest.
 – I dunno stupid. It's in Chinese.
 Nick pointed to a sign.
 – They're in English too. She only wants you to read them out to her.
 People stood on the side of the street frying food. Squashed chickens were hooked to rails that lined shop windows.
 – Look, Squinter! Must've been run over by a steam roller.

Just after they got a new car the Amah moved in. She lived next to the kitchen. The car was silver. The Amah was called Hasnah.
 Hasnah wasn't very tall and she was thin, thin like a cat. Her

face was round and soft, she had large brown eyes and when she smiled she showed a rotten tooth. She parted her long hair in the middle and pinned it into a crisp, tight bun. To comb it she would put her head on one side and hold out the hair with one hand, as if it were a piece of rope, while she brushed downwards with the other hand. Occasionally the comb would stick, catching on a knot, and Hasnah trickled her fingers through her hair to ease the comb from the tangle. Sometimes Hasnah pulled thick black clumps from her comb and put them in the bin where they crouched like ugly animals in captivity.

Hasnah's room smelt different to the rest of the house; not the scent of perfume or the aroma of food but the two mingled together. Sometimes Hasnah offered Eleanor food, when they sat together in her room – tiny fish that flashed silver and crackled against each other. They were crunchy, lacked eyes and were very salty to taste.

When Eleanor went to school Hasnah patted her head and put her school bag over her shoulder.
– Nice.
Hasnah smiled. Brown tooth. Eleanor wanted to paint it white.
Her new school was different to nursery. Grown up: she had to wear a uniform in white and yellow check. The colour of the chicks she had seen in the National Science Museum of Singapore. Her mum and dad had taken her there in her dad's car. They listened to *Bat out of Hell* by Meatloaf. 'Two out of three ain't bad' – Eleanor's favourite song, she knew the chorus. But she didn't dare sing in front of her father.
The chicks were in an incubator, huddled together. Eleanor had lots of questions to ask.
– Are they chicks when they're in the egg?
– No, they turn into chicks whilst they're in the egg. Then they hatch out and become chicks.
– So why do they need a mother?
– The mother hen makes the egg inside her then lays the egg.
– Then what happens?
– Then the hen has to sit on the eggs and keep them warm so they can grow. The incubator does the same.
– Oh. So is a hen a mannal?
– A what?
– A mannal. Like a lady.
– Oh, you mean mammal?
– Yes.
– MaMMal, Elly.
– Yes. Mannal.

– No, M. a. M. M. a. l. With two 'M's for Mum.
– Mammal?
– That's it.
– Well, is it?
– What?
– Is a hen a mammal?
– No, no, birds aren't mammals. They lay eggs.
– Oh. OK. So can you put babies in an incubator?
– Yes.
– Really?
– Yes.
– Did I go in one?
– No, Elly.
– Oh. When a chicken grows an egg inside her how does she lay it?
– She sits down and it comes out of her.
– Really, does it come out of her bottom like poo?
– Yes, sort of.
– Really?! Mum, that's disgusting. How come we can eat eggs if they're chicks that have come out of a hen's bottom?
– Well… um. Oh Elly, it's too hard to explain.
– Dad.
– Yes?
– I'm never eating an egg again.

Eleanor got annoyed when her mum and dad laughed and she moved closer to the incubator. She put her hand against the glass and was surprised to find that it was warm to her touch. As she pressed her chin and nose to the glass for warmth an egg cracked and a pink-brown beak poked through shell, first splitting a milky film that surrounded it.

– Mum! Look!
– Yes, it's hatching, Eleanor.

Hasnah was part of our lives – she lived with us – she had a small room at the back of the house. She was my friend. She must have seen so much. Heard so much. Two and a half years she spent with the family; three and a half, if you include the time after Mum, Nick and I left. Of course the others often forgot – or chose to ignore – her presence. Well, hiding the truth from the Amah would have been a further worry. We weren't bad to her. No, Hasnah's life wasn't bad. She was paid well – she sent money home every month to her family who lived in Batu Pahat on the west coast of Malaysia. And she kept a little for herself.

I have no idea if she is still alive. I have made enquiries. My father tells me that her people were originally from Sabah,

Malaysia's second largest state. Sabah – the land below the wind, wild and mountainous, surrounded by coral reef islands, not many people choose to visit especially after hearing tales of head–hunting tribes that roam Sabah's rainforest. Still! Other stories recount the arrival of Chinese and Arab merchants, there centuries before European adventurers. How Hasnah came to live with her husband, Mazlan bin Ahmed, in Batu–Pahat, I couldn't say. But Hasnah was *bumiputra*, indigenous to Malaysia; she was one of the *Bajau*, the sea gypsies.

Hasnah had a daughter, Jamila, and a son, Ishak. They must be adults now. Like me. She must have missed them very much, her family. She missed their growing up. But she had to work; they had to have school uniforms – very important to Hasnah. When I left for school in my own uniform she would pat me on the head and say – Nice. She must have seen how homesick my mother was too. After all, Hasnah heard her weep at night. And my mother must have known that Hasnah's family were dependent on her, that Malay women in Singapore earned five times that of their husbands. Couldn't my mother have paid her fare home never to have to work again? My mother was probably unhappier than Hasnah: the unvarying heat had an inevitable effect on her. She had become bloated and constantly remote, dreamy, tired and old as if her life was ending on that congested island that was so small yet so corporate. And so relentlessly hot. At least Hasnah had a husband who loved her as well as her children. He just happened to live hundreds of miles away.

We visited Malaysia. This was perhaps the only holiday we took while we lived in Singapore. It is almost certainly the only holiday I can remember taking with my father. We drove through mainland Malaysia to the Cameron Highlands. The cool mountain air on my skin, such a contrast to the sticky heat of Singapore.

I remember tasting for the first time the sweet juice of rambutan, an opal-coloured fruit encased in a blushing spiky shell – a shy sea creature. And standing at the edge of the jungle, listening to the quarrelsome notes of tropical birds.

Driving through vast rubber plantations along one of a network of roads that spliced land into surprisingly neat sections, the world seemed dark and mysterious. Regular rows of slender trees all marked by welts from which sticky brown-yellow oozed. Sap collected in rusted tin cups that were pinned to tree-trunk after tree-trunk and stagnant pools of water lay at the feet of these trees; I expected to see crocodiles clamber from them. Their dinosaur jaws haunted crushed sleep that visited me involuntarily as I lay curled on the backseat of the car.

My father was afraid we would get lost – his sense of direction might fail him and we'd spend hours driving in squares, one straight, tree-lined road looking exactly the same as another. But we didn't get lost.

Outside of the plantations, winding mountain roads from Kuala Lumpur seemed to forever unfurl before us. We bumped over potholes and swerved to avoid tree roots that had erupted unexpectedly in the centre of roads. When awake, I sat in the back of the car between the triangular, bony knees of my brothers and chanted football songs. Empty bottles of Coke and SevenUp rolled around the car floor leaving thick sugary smears on black rubber matting. My mother gave each of us a red and white striped straw from which to drink so that our lips didn't contact contaminated bottles. Outside, giant bamboo stands, jungle palms and tree ferns and occasional children who stood on corners guarding bundles of freshly-cut bamboo. Loot stolen from the jungle. As we slowed to pass them they waved and shouted gesturing towards their fare, inviting purchase.

Plantation houses and townships – like Tanah Rata still stuffed with the English colonial atmosphere – were also viewed through car windows.

We stopped at *warungs* – small shacks selling fried food, snacks and fizzy drinks. These open-air stalls were mostly run by Indians whose forbears had been imported as slaves to set up and work the tea plantations. Although the estates were conjured from jungle by *orang asli*, native labourers who chopped away the forest with axes and hand saws, crops had to be planted by Indians who were experienced in the agriculture of tea.

My father had his collecting kit; he had become a novice entomologist since moving to the tropics – easier than learning Malay or Mandarin. He still tells me how he tried to pass French O-level six times. And failed. Which, of course, he explains, is why he has never been able to enter university. Unlike you – always goes unsaid. I am not sure how serious he was about collecting; pinning insects to boards, logging their details on small pieces of card, his hand writing meticulous: *Maxwell's Hill; Perak 4500; 20:07:75; P. iswara*. He needed diversions.

And so we stopped at Parit Falls, ideal hunting ground. Behind two derelict tennis courts a path had been created by a feat of concrete engineering; it led into the jungle. But the jungle resisted. Emergent fruit tree roots cracked the concrete as if it were cardboard. Creepers wound along tree branches before dropping down to earth like falling snakes – intrepid visitors were tested by the rope curtain. Basket-shaped rafflesia flowers dropped slippery, decaying petals onto the path making the journey even more hazardous.

We clambered up the jungle hillside, following the increasingly narrow track. Fauna towered above me and I followed close behind my father's legs making sure that he cleared the way. We came to a small corner of Eden – a tropical dell. Sunlight fell between leaves. Shadow-dappled water was made to ripple by the gush of waterfall at the north end of the oval pool. Sandy shallows glowed white and clean and in dense canopy above, tree monkeys sprang from branch to branch. My mother tilted her face upwards, her brown skin glowing in filtered light. Laughing, she tried to follow their chase. Branches shivered and leaves spiralled downwards to the undergrowth below.

I remember thinking that we were the only people on earth.

My family on holiday. We stayed several days in the Cameron Highlands, just passing through the resort. Our destiny an archipelago of islands off the east coast of the peninsula. Jungle trails laced the contours of hills; tea plantations were reduced in size and worked only by a handful of local people wearing turbans; terraced vegetable and flower farms invited visitors to look around; colonial bungalows all with verandahs and brass ceiling fans offered accommodation. At night the temperature dropped low enough to light a log fire and my mother speaks now of the relief she enjoyed during this part of our trip. I wonder if this was because of the climactic change or perhaps, for a short time, she and my father held a truce.

Eleanor's father slowed and stopped in midtrack and read from a small book that Eleanor knew was called *Common Malayan Butterflies*.

– What does it say Dad?
– Shall I read it?
– Yes.
– 'Paths, clearings and streams in the jungle are the best collecting grounds. Some species are to be found congregated at moist spots on forest roads, and on sandbanks of rivers where animals have come down to drink and have contaminated the sand with urine.'
– Will we see any animals, Dad? Any monkeys?
– I don't know. Maybe.

He continued in his reading voice.

– 'Still more species frequent mountain tops; and the tops of

even small hills are worth visiting.' We're in the perfect spot, Elly.
– Read about the Red Eleanor, Dad.
– Again?

Eleanor knew about the Red Eleanor. She knew that it was large and had two tips to its tails as if the wings had melted and were dripping.
– Oh pleeease.
– Really, Elly.

Eleanor did her best to appear crestfallen.
– Oh, OK. If you insist. 'The Red Eleanor is…'
– How do you say it in Latin words, Dad?
– *Papilio eleanus eleanus*.
– Carry on.
– Elly!

Eleanor smiled at her father.
– Right. 'The Red Eleanor is a large black and white Swallowtail which is often seen swinging swiftly but unevenly along jungle paths and roads on the hills. On the plains it is less common. It is said to feed on *Zanthoxylum* and – '
– What's that? *Zan–thox–yl–um*?
– Other butterflies. Or maybe flowers, but I think other butterflies. May I continue?
– Really?! Other butterflies?

Eleanor looked around her.
– Yes.
– Does that mean it's a carnivore, Dad?
– It does mean it's a carnivore, but you probably mean 'cannibal'.
– Yeah, a cannibal, like in Robinson Crusoe?
– Are there cannibals in Robinson Crusoe?
– Yes.
– Oh. Well, yes then.
– Eugh.
– Shall I read on, Madame?
– Yes. Please.
– Thank you. 'It is said to feed on Zanthoxylum and citrus and to have a life-history similar to that of the other citrus-feeding Swallowtails. *P. eleanus* is not found in Singapore; but the rather similar *P. iswara* occurs in the catchment area wherever patches of primary forest remain.'
– Have we seen a Red Eleanor yet Dad?
– No, I don't think so. But we caught an *iswara*. In Singapore. Remember?

Her father closed the book, keeping his thumb between pages, and continued along the path. Eleanor could remember catching the *iswara*. She remembered its struggle, trapped first in the net and then in the jar. The insect fought hard, butting against the glass, the occasional coloured scale dropping from its wing display. Eleanor looked through blown glass which distorted the butterfly's perfectly symmetrical coloration. Flapping. The death lasted a few seconds. Silence; Eleanor had seen this minor passing away many times.

Eleanor's dad stopped suddenly.

– Look, look!

Her dad pointed to a tangle of undergrowth – there poised on a leaf, its legs like stilts, was a delicate black and white butterfly, patterned for camouflage against the bark of a tree. Wings opened and closed slowly as if drying paint.

– A Blue Glassy Tiger!

Eleanor looked at her father's face now lit up, eyes fixed on the insect.

– We haven't got one of those, Elly. Where's the net?

Eleanor had been trailing his net behind her. He strode ahead with his killing jar held on a piece of green twining, banging against his thigh. Eleanor knew that he had, in the back pocket of his jeans, a pair of tweezers which he had bought from the Chinese shop earlier that day. He always lost tweezers. Never anything else. And in the shoulder bag hidden in the car boot a wad of cotton-wool balls and a small brown bottle. Her dad had showed her the bottle and read out the name printed on the peeling label: Ethyl Acetate.

– Don't go anywhere near it, Elly. I'm serious. It's poison.

Ethyl Acetate. Sounded like the name of an old lady. Eleanor had mouthed the words and wondered if other people's fathers kept poison in their bathroom cabinet. It had to be the chloroform that killed the insects Eleanor had decided.

The Blue Glassy Tiger was still balanced on the leaf, antennae exploring. Eleanor suddenly felt as if she knew what it was to be a butterfly. Most species had only one day to live; Eleanor knew this. And she knew what death was too. Because her pet rabbits, Bugsy and Malone, had been killed by wild dogs trespassing from the golf course. Eleanor wondered for a long time afterwards what it was to die and to be dead. Her brothers told her that eventually everything died and they showed her how to kill an ant using a magnifying glass. She concentrated a spot of sunlight through the glass onto the articulated insect. The ant shrivelled up like a sweetwrapper on a bonfire. Eleanor thought she heard crackling. And then she felt sad because the ant was no longer able to speed around, efficient in its business.

All of a sudden, she wanted her father to stop collecting

butterflies; to stop killing them in the cotton wool jar; to stop taking them home in little wraps of paper like envelopes; to stop setting them on blotting paper and leaving them to dry; to stop putting pins into their bodies just below the thorax; to stop coating them – using earbuds as a paintbrush – in a liquid that smelled of garden fences. She wanted him to stop.

Her father's hand was reaching out behind him although his eyes were still fixed on the butterfly. Eleanor knew that he wanted the net. And she knew she could move and cause a disturbance. But her father would realise what she was doing and so she released the rotan handle of the net that she had been gripping and it fell to the floor of the path behind her, hushed by a cushioning of leaves. Using a sandaled foot she pushed the net into the undergrowth.

– Dad, I must've dropped the net.

She whispered. He didn't turn around but continued to stare at the Blue Glassy Tiger, its wings still pulsing open and shut, open and shut to display its subtle pattern like the glow of colour left on the retina after an exploded firework.

– What do you mean?

He hissed. He began to turn around slowly.

– I must've dropped it on the way.

MARTIN CORRICK
Sunshine House
Extract from **The Navigation Log**

Peter took no notice of Reggie Basset's warning. He edged into the back of the hall and stood in a corner. A crowd of adults and children overflowed the rows of benches. Seated on stage was a plump man wearing a blue fez and a robe secured with white cord. This must be James Masterman. His robe was a reddish dun colour that suggested the rolling steppes of Central Asia. He was wearing open-toed sandals without socks. The hall grew quiet. Masterman stood up and grasped the lectern with delicate hands. Gold-framed reading glasses hung on a string round his neck and on his right wrist was a copper bangle. He spoke in a confident, high-pitched voice.

"Let me ask you this." He paused. "What is a school?"

There was a silence punctuated by one or two coughs. Peter leaned his elbow carefully on an extremely hot radiator. In the centre of the hall a man put his hand up.

"I will tell you in one word," Masterman said, leaning forward. "A school is a prison."

The man put his hand down. Masterman stepped from behind the lectern and stood on the edge of the stage. The audience looked up at him. Masterman held out his hands. He spoke in an impassioned tone, his gaze sweeping the audience.

"A school is a prison. I will confess to you that I am myself damaged. I am damaged by the schools I attended as a child. My spirit was imprisoned. My mind was imprisoned. My imagination was imprisoned. My body was imprisoned." He paused and looked round the hall. "It is my life's work to escape from this imprisonment, and to enable others to do so." He paused again for several seconds. Peter heard somebody whisper, "You'll have to wait, Maisie." It was very hot.

"I will state my intention quite simply," James Masterman said. He walked back to the lectern, stretched out his arms and said loudly, *"I want to set our children free!"*

There was nervous applause. A woman in the front row, Peter noticed, was wearing a dun-coloured robe like

Masterman's. A child started to cry and was fiercely shushed by its mother.

Masterman took hold of his reading glasses, placed them on the end of his nose and peered at the audience.

"Let us consider what an ordinary school does," he said, in a sober tone. "A school takes a child from his home and community. A school divides the child's day into regular segments. A school divides the great panoply of knowledge into arbitrary and mutually exclusive domains. A school is *essentially* divisive." He paused, then said the last sentence again with a different emphasis: "A school is essentially divisive."

Peter felt a nudge. It was the melancholy figure of Reggie Basset. "Hallo Basset," Peter whispered, "I thought you didn't believe in libertarianism."

Basset gritted his teeth. "I've got to get a message to the Principal," he said. "Disruption has been threatened."

"Yes," said Peter. "You told me that before."

"Well, what have you done about it?"

"What do you mean, done about it? Nothing."

Around them, people were beginning to get restless. "I say," a woman hissed, "we can't jolly well hear, with you talking."

Basset seized Peter's collar and placed his mouth close to his ear. "The fascists are gathering," he whispered. "They may pounce at any time."

"You'd better squeeze through, then."

Basset pushed past Peter and edged his way through the audience. Masterman was talking about the spiritual needs of the growing child. Basset got to the front. The Principal was sitting in the centre, next to the robed woman who was presumably Mrs Masterman. Peter saw that Basset was undecided. Masterman said something about the need to sustain the child's natural curiosity. Eventually Basset stooped and shuffled towards the Principal, thus attracting the attention of everyone in the hall including James Masterman, who stopped talking and watched Basset's progress with evident interest. One or two people at the back stood up to get a better view. Basset knelt before the Principal and said something. "What?" said the Principal in his precise voice, "Fascists?"

The word whispered round the audience. "Ah, fascists, now there'll be trouble." Several more people stood up. A man in front of Peter said, "All right, Maisie, we can go now."

Masterman raised his hands. "Be tranquil," he cried. "We need not fear these rabid ideologues."

Peter wondered how many of those present would understand the phrase. He looked round at the crowd. Probably everyone, come to think of it.

Masterman gave a large, gentle smile. "It is interesting, is it not," he said, "How fierce a response is generated in some quarters by the simple word 'freedom'."

From the wings appeared a man in black, wearing a balaclava. He had an object in his hands. He tossed it towards Masterman. Peter saw that the object was a firework. Someone shrieked. The Principal stood up and shouted "Look out, Masterman!" There was a flash, a bang and a cloud of smoke. Masterman fell over, hitting the stage with an enormous thump. Dust rose and mingled with the smoke. People started shouting and scrambling towards the doors at the back of the hall. One or two climbed on to the stage and ran towards the wings. Peter was pinned against the radiator by the crowd. There was no sign of the man who had thrown the firework. At centre-stage lay Masterman. The woman in the robe stretched her arms across the footlights towards him, crying "Oh, oh, oh, oh," in a thoroughly unsettling way.

The Principal conferred with others and then climbed on to the stage. "Ladies and gentlemen," he called out, and then again, more loudly. People turned to look. The robed woman stopped her cries. "Please be seated. I am sure there is no more danger. The offender has absconded. The police have been summoned. Is there a doctor here? If so, would he come forward."

The crowd talked it over. Most sat down. A young woman wearing cream-coloured trousers stepped forward. "I'm a doctor," she said to the Principal. "Are you?" he said, looking at her. She climbed on stage and kneeled beside the fallen radical. Two policemen pushed into the hall. One of them addressed the crowd from the stage. "Now then. No cause for alarum." Peter was pleased to hear this antique usage. "Kindly sit down. We have to take names and addresses." Several of the audience looked uneasy.

In the Eagle, Peter and Reggie Basset conducted a lengthy post-mortem.

"I've still got a terrible ringing in my ears," Basset said.

"I'll tell you one thing, Basset," Peter said, "you may have been deafened but I've horribly burned my backside on that bloody radiator."

Basset's wrinkled face was pinched into deep gloom. He stared into his empty glass. "To be honest, old chap, I've decided I'm not cut out for this teaching lark. I'm too much of an introvert."

"Oh I don't know," Peter said. "It takes all sorts."

"That chap Masterman, well, he's a performer. So is the Principal, in his way. They can dominate. I can't."

The door opened and in came the Principal, escorting the lady doctor. Peter stood up.

"Ah," the Principal said. "Anderson. And Basset." He turned to the woman. "Two of my new students. They are evidently interested in progressive education."

"I'm not," Basset said, but the Principal was ordering drinks.

"Do have a chair," Peter said to the doctor. She smiled and sat down.

"Is Mr Masterman recovered?"

"Oh yes, he's fine. It was just shock." Her dark hair was tightly curled. "Did Mr Troughton say your name was Anderson?"

"I'm Peter Anderson. This is Reggie Basset. He's having second thoughts about being a teacher."

She laughed. "I'm Polly Morris."

"Only a step from polymorphous," Basset said.

"Quite so," Polly Morris said. There was a silence. The Principal returned from the bar, handed Polly a gin and tonic and sat down with his whisky.

"Have they captured the villain, sir?"

"No, Anderson, they haven't. And unlikely to do so."

"A pity. Mr Masterman was just getting into his stride. Perhaps he can visit us on another occasion."

"Perhaps."

Peter looked at the Principal and decided not to succumb to superior rank. He tried again. "I presume you're interested in progressive ideas, Dr Morris?"

"I'm interested in institutions." She had delightful eyebrows.

"Institutions?"

"Yes. How they work. What they do to people."

The Principal moved his shoulders. "Useful things, institutions."

"Of course," Polly said, "but they have unfortunate tendencies. Your college toilet paper, for example."

"Our toilet paper?" The Principal sat up straight.

"Yes. It's a peculiarly harsh kind, don't you think?"

"We save our money for teaching."

"That's precisely my point. An institution has a tendency to do things for its own reasons, and ignore the needs of the individual."

"In this case, the end-user," Basset said. Peter saw that he was drunk.

"Are you researching the subject?" Peter asked. "Institutions, I mean."

"It's just an interest. Most of us work for institutions, don't we? It's nice to understand how they work."

"Well," said the Principal, placing his hands flat on the table,

"I expect you two have essays to write, eh?"

"The great panoply of knowledge," Basset said. His head fell slowly forward until it rested on his folded arms.

Polly Morris laughed. "I think the excitement has been too much for your friend."

"It's his doubts. He's been worrying about whether he has the necessary qualities for a teacher. He was daunted by Masterman's command of his audience."

Basset yawned and said, "Arbitrary and mutually exclusive domains."

Polly laughed again. "At least he seems to have been listening."

"Would you care for another drink?" Peter said.

"That's kind of you. Then I really must be going."

The Principal stood up. "I must get back to my wretched institution. We are so grateful for your help, Dr Morris."

"Not at all."

"I take it that you'll deal with Basset, Anderson." The Principal turned and strode away.

"He seems a little irritated," Polly Morris said.

"It's not been a good day for him."

"No, I suppose it hasn't."

"I don't suppose you'd care to go somewhere for some supper?"

"Well – had you somewhere in mind?"

"Gazzi's, perhaps. It's only round the corner."

"What about your friend Mr Basset?"

"He'll be fine. He always finds his way home."

"If you're sure."

They walked round the corner and up the High Street. It was a warm evening. A silver balloon swayed slowly above the Heath. High-flying aircraft had marked the sky with abstract designs.

"My brother's a pilot," Peter said. "We're twins."

"Identical?"

"Yes."

"How interesting to have a perfect copy of yourself."

"Nothing perfect about him."

She laughed.

"Do you get on well?"

"Fairly."

"But he's a pilot and you're a teacher."

"Here's Gazzi's."

Peter held the door and she walked in. Gazzi came up with his usual eagerness. "Dear madam! Sir!" He clicked his fingers. "A table for two – the corner table – Frederico will show you – "

Frederico took their coats. They sat down, Peter cautiously.

"Are you all right?"

"Oh yes, I'm fine."

Frederico had begun to strum a banjo and was approaching their table. "It's a lively place," Polly said. She gave Frederico a straight look.

"I was going to say that my brother and I are quite different."

"No flying for you."

"No," Peter said. "But that's not what we're here for."

"Oh dear – squashed."

"No, I mean – "

"It's perfectly all right. I was being nosy. I'm sorry."

"No, look – "

"It's always difficult to know what to do with one's life. I wasn't at all sure about doctoring. My parents are both doctors, you see. It seemed such a dull thing."

"I really didn't mean to squash you. I'm nervous about the subject, that's all. My brother being the heroic fighter pilot and all that, and me thinking maybe it's wrong to fight."

In such a manner, as the sun went down, the candles were lit in Gazzi's restaurant and Frederico plunked gently on his banjo, Peter Anderson and Polly Morris negotiated their careful way into the beginning of an understanding. On the way back to his room Peter whistled as he walked and at one point suddenly broke into a run for no reason whatsoever. He opened the gate into the basement area and nearly fell over Reggie Basset, who was sitting on the steps and smoking a cigarette.

"A fine thing, leaving a chap like that," Basset said.

"I'm sorry, Reggie."

"You're not."

"No, you're right. I'm not."

"You went off with that doctor woman."

"Her name's Polly Morris. She's only just qualified."

"What's that got to do with it?"

"Nothing."

"How old is she?"

"Not sure."

"Older than you, though."

"Maybe."

"Bloody certain to be."

"Doesn't matter."

"You'll see."

"Sod off, Reggie."

"Still, we spoilt the Principal's plan," Reggie laughed.

"I thought you were too sozzled to notice."

"I'm never too sozzled to notice. But seeing as you're offering, I'll have another of the same."
"Go to bed, Reggie, you silly sod."
"How's your backside?"
"What?"
"I thought you burned your backside."
"Oh yes. So I did."

Polly Morris lay awake. He was young, that was for sure. She turned over and hugged her knees. He was a serious young man, but not, hopefully, a melancholy one. No point in spending time cheering up gloomy men. He was clever enough. He was youngish. He was going to be a teacher. His brother was another matter. She got up abruptly, went to the window, pulled back the curtain and peered into the dark street. The gleam of the river was just visible. On the roof of Barnaby & Mason's the heads of the ARP wardens were moving against the sky. One of them threw a cigarette-end down into the street, a red dot curving down and ending in a tiny burst of sparks. She laughed to herself and went back to bed.

Highgate College, Hampstead, NW3. 30th September 1939. Dear Polly, I very much enjoyed our evening last week and I wondered if you might like another evening out before long. We might go and see a film. Friday is a good time for me but of course I will fit in with your hospital duties. Best wishes, Peter Anderson

Highgate College, Hampstead, NW3. 30th September 1939. Dear Mr Masterman, I was present at your interesting talk in Hampstead last week and I much regret that you were unable to complete it. I hope you have fully recovered. I have read something of your Free School and I would like an opportunity to see how theory is put into practice. I have no experience but I'm keen to learn. I will be happy to come to Norfolk at any convenient time. Yours faithfully, Peter Anderson

Flat 2a, Melbourne Street, W2. 1.10.39. Dear Peter, Thank you for your letter. I laugh when I think of the Masterman talk and our meeting in the Eagle – I hope your friend Reggie is feeling better. I'm afraid that I have to be at the hospital at weekends, but I could probably manage an evening between Tuesday and Thursday if that was suitable. Let me know. Best wishes, Polly

Highgate College, Hampstead, NW3. 2nd October 1939. Dear Polly, Thank you for your letter. What about next Thursday, 8th

October? I could collect you from your flat at 7.30 p.m. Best wishes, Peter

Flat 2a, Melbourne Street, W2. 3.10.39. Dear Peter, Thanks for your letter. Yes, that's fine. I'll expect you at 7.30. Best wishes, Polly

Highgate College, Hampstead, NW3. 9th October 1939. Dear Polly, I'm sorry that something went wrong between us last night and somehow we didn't get on so well. I am sure it is my fault and I apologize. I hope you might be prepared to have another evening out with me sometime. Best wishes, Peter

Flat 2a, Melbourne Street, W2. October 9th 1939. Dear Peter, Well, something went wrong last night, didn't it, and we ended up gloomy. I don't know how it happened but I think it was my fault. I was in a bad mood. Anyway I'm sorry. Best wishes, Polly

Sunshine House, Winterton, Norfolk. My dear fellow, come any time – I'm sure we can find something for you to look at. James

Flat 2a, Melbourne Street, W2. 10.10.39. Dear Peter, Thanks for your telephone call – it must have cost you a fortune! I couldn't think who it might be when the night Sister said there was a call! Anyway, I'm glad we had the conversation. Funny about our letters. I'll see you on Tuesday. Best wishes, Polly

"Come and meet my wife," Masterman said. "She's in the bath." He opened the bathroom door and clouds of steam rolled out. "Irma, my dearest poppet," he called out, "We have a visitor."

Peter could see no more than vague shapes. "Hallo!" he called out. "Nice to meet you!" He stepped back, bumping into Masterman. "Go on in. She really wants to meet you." Peter stepped into the mist. "I can see you," a voice trilled, "turn left at the clothes horse."

The mist cleared and Peter looked no further than the face of the figure reclining in the bath. It was the robed woman who had cried so distressingly at the fascist attack.

"Hallo," Peter said. "I'm Peter Anderson."

"Oh, you're a lovely boy, aren't you! I'm sure you'll have terrific fun here!" Irma was much younger than Masterman, Peter saw, perhaps no more than thirty. She had a little round laughing face, a big mouth like a clown and her blonde hair floated on the water. She was not entirely submerged.

"It's a very big bath," Peter said, a remark that he would

remember with horror for the rest of his life.

"Here, help me up," Irma said, stretching out an arm. Peter took her hot, soapy hand in his and pulled. She emerged from the water and stood before him.

"Now, dear boy," she said, "behind you is my towel."

"She's so utterly lovely," Masterman said from the doorway. "Don't you think so?"

"Oh certainly," Peter said. "Tremendously."

"She's a complete sweetie," Masterman said, leaning on the edge of the door. "She's a hot potato, all right. In fact, dear boy, perhaps you wouldn't mind leaving us alone for a few moments."

"Oh," Peter said. "Oh, all right."

"No need to shut the door," Masterman called after him. Peter walked hurriedly out into the garden. Three small girls were burrowing in a heap of earth. They were, although filthy, fully clothed.

"My train's at five-fifteen," Peter said.

Polly licked her ice-cream, looking steadily at him. "Stop flapping," she said. "We've got all afternoon. Tell me more about Irma." There were wrinkles at the corners of her mouth.

"Are you laughing at me?"

"Of course not."

Behind her, a bronzed oarsman stroked a skiff across the Serpentine, his girl reclining in the stern seat and steadying a wide-brimmed hat with her white-gloved hand.

Two of the younger boys were trying to tear a branch from one of the gnarled Cox's Orange Pippins. Peter watched from a rusting garden seat. Masterman was suggesting to the boys that their action would threaten the future supply of apples. "Fuck off, Masterman," the bigger boy said. "What's it to you?"

Masterman came and sat down next to Peter. "What energy they have! What aggression! This sort of physical play must have been so essential to the training of our ancestors, the hunter-gatherers."

Peter wondered what relevance tree-wrecking might have to, say, working in a bank, but said nothing. Radical methods must be given a chance.

Masterman lit a cigar and leaned back. "What an utterly delightful autumn it's been," he said.

"Well, apart from the war," Peter said.

"Oh yes, there is that. They're putting barbed wire along the beach. I suppose we'll have to abandon our midnight swimming."

The smaller of the two boys walked over, sat down next to

Peter and stared at him. "Who are you?"

"My name's Peter Anderson. I'm probably going to work here for a bit."

"God, are you?"

"And who are you?"

"Ian Lambert. My mother's an actress."

"Moira Lambert?"

"Oh God, you've heard of her."

"She's a very famous actress."

"Oh God, how tedious when people say that." He looked about seven years old.

Masterman drew on his cigar. Childish screams came from various corners of the orchard. A light easterly breeze blew in from the sea across a high bank of dunes. The tower of All Saints stood in black outline against the horizon.

"There are natterjack toads here, you know," Masterman said, his eyes closed.

"Really?"

"A rare species. They dwell in the slack pools behind the dunes. And there are seals in winter."

"Can you read?" the boy asked.

"Yes," Peter said.

"You can read to me then."

Peter looked at Masterman. He appeared asleep.

"All right."

"Come on."

Peter followed Ian Lambert into the house. Masterman opened an eye and watched them go.

The boy went upstairs into a dormitory, climbed onto one of the unmade beds and pulled a blanket over himself.

"Shouldn't you undress?"

"No."

"Oh. Well then. What do you want me to read?"

"Oh God, choose whatever you like."

Books were scattered here and there. Peter picked up the nearest and opened it. "For four days we have been unable to leave the tent – the gale howling about us. We are weak, writing is difficult, but for my own sake I do not regret this journey, which has shown that Englishmen can endure hardships, help one another, and meet death with as great a fortitude as ever in the past."

He stopped reading and looked at the boy. Ian Lambert had his thumb in his mouth and was gazing at Peter with large eyes. "Go on," he said.

"It's not very cheerful."

"Oh God, I know that. I've read it a hundred times."

Flat 2a, Melbourne Street, W2. 5.11.39. Dear Peter, You're a rotten letter-writer, aren't you? A week of silence. – No, I don't mean it really, but I wondered how you're grappling with the Monster Masterman. I'm pottering along as usual at Barts. We get huge frights but so far we've coped. Some nights it's bad.

Hard to say what you feel, isn't it. Such intense feelings when we met, but then I don't know if – oh bloody hell! Anyway it isn't more than a couple of hours to Liverpool Street, is it?

My friend Mary has a friend in the Royal Philharmonic, an oboe player, and they meet in the boiler room every lunchtime.

I ought to say this, that I'm 28, and I think you must be about 22 or something, and what does that mean? Oh I don't know. I do wish you were nearer. There's all kinds of bomb shelters and sandbags everywhere. We've got some boys from France, but not many. I bought a new dress yesterday, a red one, very fashionable! Mary and I went into town last night – men in uniform everywhere – they get so bossy in their caps and belts and everything – they suddenly loom out of the dark at you – I'm rambling on, sorry. Love, Polly

PS – firework night!

Irma was curled up beside Masterman's chair, engrossed in a large book.

"Read Rousseau," said Masterman. "Read Whitman, read Ruskin. And of course, read the immortal William Blake." He poured himself another sherry and caressed Irma's hair. "That is where it all begins, doesn't it, my poppet? With Blake."

"I see," Peter said.

"'Man was made for joy and woe/ And when this we rightly know/ Thro' the world we safely go/ Joy and woe are woven fine/ A clothing for the soul divine.'"

"Songs of Innocence," Peter said.

"Excellent!" Masterman beamed.

"Well – "

"'Sooner murder an infant in its cradle than nurse unacted desires.'"

"I don't think I know that one."

"'The road of excess leads to the palace of wisdom.'"

"Blake again?"

"Exactly!" Masterman lowered his voice. "And then along came Jung."

"Yes."

"Are you familiar with his work?"

"Not exactly, no."

Masterman expanded. He slid his hand into the top of Irma's blouse and looked down at her fondly. She looked up and said "'*Alles, was wir an den Kindern ändern wollen, sollten wir zunächst wohl aufmerksam prüfen, ob es nicht etwas sei, was besser an uns zu ändern wäre.*'"

Masterman was delighted. He leaped from his chair. "Listen to that," he cried, "She's word perfect! My sweetie! Precisely Jung! 'If we want to change something in a child, we must first see whether we shouldn't change it in ourselves.' So terribly true, don't you think?"

"Yes – I'm sure it is."

"What an utter darling!" Masterman knelt beside Irma and kissed her neck.

Peter said, "It's like motes and beams, I suppose."

Masterman looked perturbed. "Not at all the same thing," he said. "That's religion. Mere superstition. This is the philosophy of the new education. I think, my dear, we will have to recommend some reading, don't you?"

"Of course, my love."

"Dear boy, you must read up on power and punishment. Neurosis. Questions of morality." Masterman looked at Irma. "For example, what do we mean by the word 'naughty'?"

"Or 'dirty'," Irma said.

"Psychic conflict."

"Approval."

"Creative sublimation."

"Release."

"Sexuality."

"And of course masturbation."

"Yes," Peter said. "Yes. I suppose so."

"You'll soon realise," Masterman said, looking at Peter with a confident smile, "That 'the tygers of wrath are wiser than the horses of instruction.'"

"Blake."

"You're one of us."

Sunshine House, Winterton, Norfolk, 10th November 1939. Dear Polly, Yes, sorry about the letters, it's all a bit disorganised here, but of course I'm thinking of you all the time. What does age matter anyway? This is an odd place, and I think some of the children are in a bad way, but it's difficult to know what's what. Lots of them are from rich families – one is the son of Moira Lambert – he's seven and he hasn't seen his mother for two years – he's a nice boy but demanding. It's a fashionable place.

The parents like it. Some of the children like it. Most of them, I suppose. I seem to have got taken on, but I don't know for how long. I can't get away until the end of term and even then Masterman wants some of us to stay here. Some parents leave their children here all the time. I can't work out whether he's a fraud or what – he's very convincing sometimes. Ho hum.
Love, Peter

The first snow came in the middle of December, drifting almost undetectably off the North Sea and settling lightly on marram grass and barbed wire and upon the raw, ridged concrete of the new lookout towers. The soldiers on watch beside Sunshine House stamped and beat their gloves together and cursed and stared out across the dark water. That night Peter was woken by Ian Lambert climbing into his bed.
"It's only me," the boy said. "It's cold."
"Let's go and find Matron," Peter said.
"Oh God, not Matron."
"Yes."
"You can't make me."
"Oh yes I can."
"That's not fair."

DOUGLAS COWIE
Back and Forth

When Bob called I was trying to zip the back of my dress, one arm curled behind from the waist up, the other bent down from my shoulder like a question mark and reaching for the zipper. The left shoulder slipped down, restricting my reach, as I picked up the phone.

"Hello," I demanded, more than asked.

"Suz," he whined, "When can you come pick me up?"

"What the hell are you talking about? It's eight o' – where are you?"

"At school. But you have to come pick me up."

I sat down on the bed. There was no way to get the dress zipped and talk on the phone at the same time.

"I don't really have to do anything. Why do you want me to come get you?"

"For the funeral."

"Mr Weaver's funeral is Wednesday, Bob."

"I know. So you have to come get me tomorrow morning so I can be back because otherwise I'll miss it."

"Whoah. Slow down a little. Have you talked to Mom or Dad?"

There was a pause. I could hear the muffled sounds of singing and talking in the background.

"No – not exactly." He belched.

"Are you drunk?"

Another pause. "Well, yeah, a little I guess. I'm grieving, you know."

"Bullshit." I walked over to the chest of drawers and opened the jewellery box.

When Bob was twelve and I was eighteen, Mom and Dad split. Not that it didn't affect me – it did – but being away at school helped lessen the blow. Bob, first-hand witness to the final days of arguing and accusations, took it hard. Luckily Mr Weaver was there to help out, spending the whole fall going to his football games, taking him to dinner and movies. He became Bob's grandfather. When Bob graduated from high school, Mr Weaver insisted on having a huge party for him. My overworked mother was happy to let him do it.

"Bob – "

"What?" He sounded exasperated, as though I'd been interrogating him for hours.

I rolled my eyes. "Yeah, I'll come get you. But you can't stay here this time. You're staying with Mom. Or Dad. I don't care which. Not here, though. I'll try to get there about noon." Bob had a habit of coming into town unannounced and using my apartment as home base for a weekend of frat boys in the city.

"Suz? Thanks."

I wondered if anything I said had actually registered with Bob. "You'd better call them both, on second thought. They'll both be at the funeral."

The line was already dead. I hoped he'd have the sense not to call just one of them.

Near sunset on Saturday, Mr Weaver's boat had been found drifting pretty far from Waukegan harbour by the coastguard. Mr Weaver himself was slumped over the stern, a rod holder draped over his shoulders. They figured he must have had a heart attack while reeling in a fish.

I awoke at seven Tuesday morning and took a quick shower. By seven-thirty I was on my way down to the garage, simultaneously trying to unwrap a breakfast bar and pull on a jacket. It was almost October. The leaves had mostly turned, as had the weather, and a low ceiling of grey clouds spread across the sky. My tan Civic crossed the border into Indiana at eight.

At nine, shortly after I'd reached Michigan, the Talking Heads ground to a garbled halt as the tape player chewed them into crinkled oblivion. I cursed, punched the eject button as hard as I could, and threw the cassette, with the tape still wrapped around the guts of the player, into the back seat.

I pulled in front of Bob's fraternity house at eleven-thirty. A few plastic cups littered the front porch of the square brick building. The lawn was neatly mowed, and a bucket hung from a tap that had been driven into the trunk of a large red maple. Five white Ionic pillars supported the second-floor balcony. I wondered if Bob or any of his brothers knew what Ionic pillars were. It had begun to drizzle around Battle Creek, and now it was raining for real.

"C'mon," I said aloud as I looked towards the house. "I'm not coming inside to drag your ass out of bed."

I pressed the horn a couple of times and reached over to

wipe the steam away from the passenger window. Instead of helping, I left it streaked with my fingerprints and just as opaque as it had been. I took off my seatbelt and reached over to unroll the window. Nobody emerged from the house. I leaned on the horn again.

A minute later, a tall, skinny kid wearing khakis and a long-sleeved T-shirt appeared on the front porch.

"Hey!" I yelled. "Come here a minute!"

He kicked a couple of the cups aside, and in a sort of fake jog, shuffled down the lawn, a cigarette dangling from his mouth, his backward baseball hat looking as though it hadn't left his head in weeks.

"What can I do for you?" He exhaled a cloud of smoke into the car as he spoke. I watched ashes sprinkle onto the seat.

"Do you know Bob? Bob Hillburgh?"

He arched his eyebrows. "Yeah, so?"

"Go wake him up."

"What? I'm not gonna – "

"Drag his butt out of bed and tell him his sister's here for another five minutes, and then she's leaving."

Ten minutes later, Bob stumbled down the front lawn, leaving a trail in the wet grass as he pulled along a small duffel bag by one broken handle. He clearly hadn't showered. His curly brown hair twisted away from his scalp in several directions, and his clothes had definitely been slept in.

"Hi." He grinned sheepishly as he got into the car. His breath smelled of whisky.

"Don't get any closer." I put my hand up as he leaned over to kiss me on the cheek. "You could have at least brushed your teeth."

"Yeah, well, long night." His swollen eyes followed the ribbon from the cassette deck to the back seat. "Stereo trouble?"

"Shut up." I slammed my foot down on the clutch and threw the car into gear.

Bob fell asleep for an hour or so. I didn't feel like trying to find a radio station, so I listened to the rhythm of the windshield wipers as I drove. We were cruising at about eighty – too fast now that it was really raining hard – when he awoke.

"Pull over." It came out in an intense whisper.

"Bob, there's a rest stop fifteen miles ahead. You can wait."

"No."

I glanced over at him. He was breathing slowly and his face had turned the same colour as the concrete road racing beneath the car.

"You've got to pull over now." He was still whispering and shaking his head slowly.

I cut across to the right lane without looking and pulled onto the shoulder.

The car was still rolling as he opened the door, leaned over the stony pavement and opened his mouth. Neon bile poured out. I jerked up on the parking brake and pressed Bob's seat belt button. He fell out, catching himself on the door before he could tumble into his own vomit. He staggered out and supported himself against the hood of the car with his left hand. A mixture of bile and rainwater dripped from his mouth and chin.

He finally got back into the car after about five minutes of dry heaves and vomiting. His hair clung to his forehead and cheeks. He peeled his wet shirt off and pulled a clean – or at least dry – Michigan Wolverines sweatshirt from the duffel bag.

"Empty?"

He arched his eyebrows into a scowl.

"We're still stopping at the rest area," I said.

He put the shirt over his head and I re-entered the highway.

Bob stayed in the car at the rest stop. I bought him a Powerade from the machine. He grunted a sort of thank you and shook it half-heartedly. He really looked bad. As I sped down the onramp towards the spray of traffic, he took a tentative sip, expecting, I suppose, that it would produce a repeat performance.

Another half-hour down the road, however, he'd managed to finish the drink, and the colour began to show at least signs of returning. His cheeks were now off-white, as opposed to the sheet-white they had been. Rather than sitting curled into an unmoving foetal ball as he had been, he straightened into the seat and began to shift his weight from one side to the other. He stretched his legs out as far as he could and leaned his head back against the headrest, running his hands through his wet hair.

"I'm in trouble," he said suddenly.

I glanced over at him. "Do I have to pull over again?"

"No, no, I'm through with that. I mean real trouble."

I didn't understand, so I didn't say anything. A minute or two of silence passed. The rain seemed to be lightening up a little, but the roads were still very wet. A truck passed and threw a screen of water across my windshield.

"Carrie's late."

I tightened my grip on the steering wheel. "Who's Carrie?" I swallowed hard, and noticed that I was squinting at the road now, as though it required special concentration.

"My girl – this girl I know."

Bob started to loop the tape, which still hung across to the back seat, around his index finger. I knew what he was trying to say, and I knew he wanted me to say it for him. This was Bob's pattern: get half a sentence out, then hope somebody else would face the hard part so he didn't have to. I sighed and adjusted my position in the bucket seat. We passed a billboard welcoming us to "Nuge Country."

"Well, I'm afraid she's – she might be – " His voice trailed off. He stared out the passenger window. "Pregnant."

I didn't say anything.

"Well?" he said after another mile of silence.

"How do you know, Bob?"

His eyes remained fixed on the passing roadside. "She's late."

"Really late? Or just a few days, or what? Bob, you've got to know these things." I looked over at him. His chin was pressed against his chest, and his eyes were closed. "Is she sure?"

"I guess," he mumbled. "She called me yesterday afternoon. The thing is – " His left leg began to tremor. "It was her first time." His knee was now tapping against the glove compartment.

I changed tones. "Were you using protection?"

"Not exactly."

"Bob, you're an idiot!" I tore the tape, wound completely around his finger now, from the cassette. "I don't even know why you're telling me this."

Apart from the occasional sigh – I think Bob was trying to get me to say something more – neither of us said anything until just before the Indiana Toll Road.

"Mom's or Dad's?" I asked.

Bob didn't say anything.

"C'mon, I have to know which road to take. Are you staying with Mom or Dad?"

He just looked at me. I knew what that meant.

"You little shit," I muttered.

Bob didn't move. He sat curled into the seat, his head pressed against the shoulder harness of the seatbelt. Steam spread across the window each time he exhaled.

We were back at my apartment by five o'clock. Before I could ask if he wanted to go out to dinner he was on the phone with one of his high school buddies.

"Yeah, I'm stayin' downtown. Yeah, meet you there. Don't forget your ID." He hung up.

"Sure, you can use the phone."

"Sorry," he mumbled. "I'm goin' out with Jeff tonight."

"You're going to a funeral tomorrow, you know."

"Thanks, *Mom*."

I gave him a key and went down with him to tell the doorman to let him in when he came back. Before I went to bed I threw a pillow and a blanket on the couch.

For the second day straight, Bob reeked of whisky. He lay on his back on the sofa, one arm dangling over the side so his hand rested on the carpet. His mouth gaped open and he was snoring.

"Bob!" I yelled.

He awoke and squinted at me, then groaned.

"Get into the shower. I hope you brought some decent clothes."

He had brought a dress shirt and a tie wadded up in the duffel bag. I didn't offer to iron them. He looked like hell, I thought as we stepped out of the car at the church. It was cloudy, but not raining. Bob wore sunglasses, and left them on as we walked into the church.

The church was carpeted in a colour that wasn't quite orange and wasn't quite brown. Oak pews lined the brick-walled sanctuary, and someone had attached flowers to the arm rests of the first fifteen rows. A pile of bulletins with the phrase 'Thy Rod and Thy Staff, They Comfort Me' printed on the front sat on a small table in the narthex. Of the twenty or thirty people lining the aisle as they waited to view the casket, only a few wore black, although almost all were wearing dark colours.

"Oh, thank God you made it, Robert." Mom saw us immediately. She hurried across the narthex from where she'd been talking to Mr Weaver's other next-door neighbour, the skirt of her suit brushing audibly with her long strides. "Both your father and I called you. You're going to be a pallbearer."

I smirked. Bob grunted.

"Take off those sunglasses inside, Robert," Mom said.

His eyes were swollen and moist and ringed with grey.

"Go say hello to your father."

He started over to where my father was talking to a few people.

"Tell him about Carrie," I said, unaware I was saying it until it was too late. Bob scowled at me. I wondered if he'd given her any further thought since shortly after the rest area.

"Who's Carrie?" Mom asked.

"What?"

"Who's – " A former neighbour caught her eye. "Oh, look, Mrs. Newell! Go say hello, dear."

Bob looked like he was going to drop the casket as he helped carry it from the church. It sagged a little on his corner. I could see his arm quivering and the corners of his eyes pulling towards his ears with the strain. He was rubbing and stretching his shoulder when he came back to the car.

There wasn't a burial. Per his will, Mr Weaver was going to be cremated. We stood outside the church for a few minutes while I talked to a few neighbours I hadn't seen in a while and Bob stared at the pavement.

Mom had to go back to work after the funeral, but Dad, not tied to a fixed number of vacation days, took Bob and me to lunch before we started back for Ann Arbor. I followed close behind his Mercedes 500 as he wove in and out of the slower moving minivans and SUVs towards the family restaurant that had been our 'place' in the years before the divorce. The familiar strip malls followed one after another along each block, most of the same stores still in business, although a few delis and pizzerias had been replaced by franchises.

"Bob," I said as we turned into the parking lot, "I think you should tell Dad."

He unclicked his seatbelt. "About what?"

"About Carrie, you jerk. Do you think pretending to forget is going to make your problems disappear?"

He sighed, and rubbed his head with both hands. "I guess – " He opened the door and stepped out. "I guess he could help. Tell me what to do or something."

I put the key into the door and locked it. "I think you have to decide that for yourself, Bob, but you should tell him anyway."

Dad had gotten a table while we were parking. For the first time in memory, I didn't recognize any of the servers. When we were little, we always sat at the same table, and were waited on by the same tall, prematurely balding waiter. Today our server was Jenny, a high school girl who snapped a piece of gum as she took our orders.

"How's school, Bob?"

It was a natural enough place to start. Neither of us had seen Dad in several months, and the seemingly benign question would be an easy way to avoid the fact that we had been gradually turning into acquaintances.

Bob took a sip of water, looking over the rim of the glass at me as he did so. I pulled my napkin from under the silverware and spread it across my lap.

"Good and bad," he said. Dad raised his eyebrows. "Classes are going pretty good – "

"Pretty well," Dad interjected.

"Right, 'pretty well,'" Bob repeated. "Classes are going pretty well, but I might have a bit of a problem."

He was looking at the bare table in front of him, pushing two packets of Sweet 'n' Low back and forth between his glass and the edge of the table. I stretched my foot across and pressed it against his calf. He exhaled deeply and looked at me. "I may have gotten a girl pregnant."

I don't know what I expected. An outburst would have been in character at one time, but we were in public, and Bob wasn't a teenager anymore. I looked at Dad, trying to judge his reaction before he said anything.

"Bob," he said after Jenny had placed our drinks on the table, "Do you know for sure?"

"No."

"What does she think, the young lady?"

Bob removed his straw from the wrapper and dropped it into his Coke. "She was scared when she called me, she was late, but it'd only been a week." He flicked the wadded-up wrapper at his water glass. "She took one of those home tests, and she – it was her first time."

"Was it yours?"

I could feel my face heating up. I opened two packets of sugar and dumped them into my iced tea. Did he really want to know the answer to that? "The issue," I said before Bob had to reply, "is what Bob's proper course of action should be."

Bob's cheeks thinned slightly as his jaw relaxed. "Yeah." He squinted, and smiled slightly in a gesture of thanks.

"I don't know what to tell you on this one, Bob," he said flatly. "First, you're not even sure. Second, if you're old enough to get yourself into this mess, you ought to be able to come up with some of your own answers."

The conversation ended. I ate as quickly as I could, mumbling one word answers to his enquiries about my job, my new apartment and my social life. I knew he didn't really care. Bob ate half his food and shifted the rest from one side of the plate to the other while he waited for Dad and me.

"Look," he said as I chewed my last bite, "I've really got to get back to school. I have an early class tomorrow, and I haven't finished the reading. Sorry to cut it short."

Dad asked for the bill. "It was nice to see you both," he said in the parking lot. He didn't offer a hug or shake Bob's hand.

"Yeah," I mumbled. "Give me a call if you're downtown around lunch sometime." I think he knew I really didn't mean it.

We drove in silence for most of the ride back. Bob slept for the first half, then sat, staring at the roadside as he had on the day before. It remained cloudy, but the rain held off.

"I thought Dad might have been useful for once," he said as we passed the first Ann Arbor exit. "I really am worried, you know. About what to do. About Carrie."

I pushed my hand through my hair and moved into the right lane, slowing to exit. "Bob, don't forget that she's got more at stake here than you do. You might start thinking about her instead of what to do about her. How well do you even know this girl?"

He didn't answer. I turned left onto his street and slowed as we approached his house. He grabbed his bag from the back seat. The same kid who'd ashed on my seat shouted an obscenity by way of greeting from where he sat smoking on the front porch.

"Thanks for coming out here and driving me back and everything." Bob opened the door and got out.

"Bob," I called as he started to shut the door. He paused. "What are you going to do? You'd better think about it."

He shut the door and walked up the lawn.

When I got home the message light was blinking twice. The first message was from Mom, asking me to call her when I got home. The second was from Bob.

"Suz!" He was yelling into the phone. I could hear music and people shouting. "Suz! Good news! She's – Carrie's – Well, she's not – you know." Somebody turned the music up louder. "Hold on!" He yelled away from the receiver. "Gotta go, Suz."

I picked up the phone and dialled his number. Voice mail answered. I waited for the tone, then hung up.

FFLUR DAFYDD
The Heroics of Hair

There were three of us, of course. I say 'of course' because it contains such an obvious truth I am surprised it ever escaped my notice. We certainly weren't musketeers, but something about us painted the same pictures. We were undeniably on our guard, but each one of us for a different reason. We were singular and solitary in our defence.

Nevertheless, each one knew why the other was there. It was the kind of understanding that paved the way for a perfect, unruffled silence.

It was all about numbers. All my life I have spoken two languages, seen things through four eyes, and heard six different meanings. My very existence has revolved around plurality. So much so, that when it happened, it seemed like the only logical conclusion. That a part of me would eventually grow and accelerate until it could speak a thousand tongues, until its depths equalled that of a million, fathomless oceans.

And this, you may, or may not believe, was my hair.

About memory I am most particular. Part of me chooses to see it as it was, to colour the events with the subtle shades of retrospect. Another part of me chooses to see it as it is, injecting time back into the moment, until I am there, in the same seat, the same skin. As if I have never left.

There were three of us at the hair clinic. The first patient was called Mrs Little. Both her personality and her hair were disproportionate. Her hair was a cascading, swirling mass of violet curls that had undergone several treatments. She did not seem to realize that it was rather her personality that was in severe need of amendment. "It's not a blue rinse you know," she spat over the waiting room's copy of *Curl Up and Dye*, "my father married a mermaid."

The second patient was a small, timid looking young man, who had but a few strands of hair, distributed sparingly over his glistening scalp. His silence denoted that like myself, he liked to play safe, to reveal nothing. But he failed. Loss was written all over him. In his hands he clutched a copy of *The Mabinogion*. I found it haunting that a man so distressed by his own inadequacy should consciously choose to torture himself with such contradictory images; of heroes and heroines who had more than enough hair to go round. I wondered if leaf by leaf, tale by tale, all he saw was his own, once golden locks, flaying away.

And there, sitting at the far end of the waiting room, was myself. Or rather, is myself. I look down and see my lower body in the plush red seats, the white skin of my palms against the black of my dress, my hair coiling about my shoulders like serpents. I have never known anything like it. My hair has burst forth with the greatest energy I have ever known. It is endless, boundless, seizing my whole head with its weight. It is thick with fury. Unlike Mrs Little, or the young man, I know exactly what the problem is, or at least, at the time, I think I do. It wants retribution for what I have done to it. Over the years it has been captivated, pinned, punctured, chopped, grazed, coloured, twisted, crimped, straightened, steamed. It has been transformed so many times that it does not recognize its own face in the mirror. It has lived out my disasters in a way my body never will.

Three strands of hair. Three different lives. Three different ways of looking at things. Mrs Little is insistent that hers will be first. She has already informed us that when she was a little girl, she was dropped on her head. They couldn't prove that this was anything to do with the state of her hair – but according to her, she knew more than any doctor ever would. Her mother always kept her neatly tucked into the basket at the front of her bike – a tight squeeze at the best of times. Sometimes she would even have to share her space with the daily groceries, and the ride was so bumpy that when they got home, it was difficult to tell the baby from the dairy products. On her way to the supermarket one afternoon, it happened that her mother was crossing a junction. It was only when she got to the other side that she realized that the basket was empty, and that little Violet Little was rolling across the road like a marble. Both mother and daughter claimed to have never recovered from it.

Somewhere in the distance, a phone is ringing. A girl appears from beneath a desk, bearing the slightly dishevelled look of one shaken from her dreams. She answers the phone with two greetings, the first, muffled and dissonant, drowns in the flurry of her speech, the second, powerful, concrete, surfaces to her lips like a giant fish swallowing a bait.

"What was that first thing she said?" asks Mrs Little.

It is not, for a change, an annoying question. It shows an intrigue in language that probes beyond the usual dullness of her imagination. Mrs Little becomes technicolour, subtitled, surround sound. I explain to her that the first greeting, *pnawn da*, means 'good afternoon' in Welsh. She is silent, mulling over my words, retracing the sound on her own lips.

"That's nice for them isn't it?" she remarks. The picture fades to black and white.

Split ends. It's funny how certain things remind you of certain people. Her name was Nerys. I remember asking her what she was doing. I remember her disdain that I didn't know. Then she explained it all. Millions of little fork-ends with defiant grooves. All you had to do, she told me, was pull at one end, until it peeled off like a sticker. Leaving one solitary strand. I asked her what was wrong with having two strands, all growing from one root. She told me I was being silly. I told her that not everyone is scared of duality. She told me that my hair was a mess anyway, split ends or not. I told her that was all very well but she wasn't getting the point.

We were not friends.

We are all waiting in our own different ways. Mrs Little is seizing time by the bull-horns, shaking its gigantic frame with fury. "This is absolutely ridiculous," she barks, pinging the reception bell repetitively as if it were a novelty toy, "I've booked this appointment since last month, you'd expect them to get it right, wouldn't you." No one answers. No one confirms that time is something linear, progressive, exact – not to be toyed with by yesterday's facts. Mrs Little is surprisingly unaffected by our lack of reaction. After all, she is a born performer who knows that above all, the show must go on.

The young man is distinctive in his silence. I feel the absence of his speech heaving beneath my skin, so much so that I want to shove my hand in his mouth and fish around for words. For fear of looking insane, I restrain. He has put the book down. He is looking at something else now, only it is something that neither I nor Mrs Little can see. Although I do not know him, I am intensely jealous of this exclusive vision.

Time clicks into place. The nurse announces that there has been an accident, the doctor is on emergency call. Mrs Little sighs. The young man bestows a heavier silence. I am embarrassed that I have no visible trait of my own, and so I adopt one. I sneeze five times.

Transformation. An intrinsic part of life. This explains why I am no longer the first-row choirgirl with a high ponytail and a cheerleader smile. Or the crying, dreadlocked girl on the youth club stairs. Or the long-haired blonde face down and unconscious outside the rugby club. The faces may change and yet the skin is the same.

My mother said that if you stop washing your hair it starts washing itself. Miraculously. Almost as if it sprouts tiny hands. If you ask me, it's a case of being rational. If you neglect something for long enough then it is only a matter of time before it starts looking after itself, before it finds new ways of doing things. There is nothing rare, precious, supernatural, or miraculous about it.

We are all hiding a secret of which our hair has become a symptom. I have taken great pains to ensure that mine is banged up, nailed down, fenced in. Secure. I get the impression that Mrs Little's secret is a little simpler. Something I could whip out of the breast pocket of her silk blouse if I were quick enough. As for Owain, there is no telling. In the shuffling of his feet he is precise, ritualistic, quietly confident. Like a criminal after the perfect crime.

I couldn't believe it when the words came. To me first, Mrs Little later. I felt triumphant. His name was Owain. He wanted to know if anybody wanted to join him for a cigarette. I nodded my head, Mrs Little turned hers away. Not that I'm a smoker. I am prone to the occasional cigarette, usually only when I have seen the act of smoking ridiculously glamorized in a film. Mrs Little held out an accusatory finger which led our eyes to the non-smoking sign, beneath which there was a picture of a child asleep in an ashtray. I found it a peculiar image, which somehow served to say all the right things at once. If only humans were as articulate.

"The cheek of it," grunts Mrs Little, "you don't say a word for two hours and the ones you do say are filthier than a thief's hands." Here she goes again, catapulting the unsaid, the unnecessary, hoisting it into the air.

"I thought a sophisticated woman like yourself would have understood that to smoke with one's companions is an act of gentility," retorted Owain, placing an unlit cigarette playfully between his lips.

Owain and I were united. We were a team. We smoked one

cigarette after another, he talked, I listened. He told me that when he was seven he pushed his sister's pram down a steep hill. She cracked her head open on a pot-plant holder. He said that he had asked her if she'd wanted to go for a ride and she'd said yes. She'd consented and therefore it wasn't strictly his fault. But she was one year of age and could barely differentiate the word 'ride' from the word 'mother'.

He presented the inconsequential parts of his life and this was enough. We did not talk about what we were doing there or how we were feeling. When he started his impression of Mrs Little, that was it, I envisaged him kissing me against the white walls of the clinic. When he told me of the time he nearly missed a wedding because he was in the wrong one, I could see us choosing furniture together in Habitat. When he told me of the time he'd tried to leave a lecture theatre and accidentally walked into a cupboard, I caught a glimpse of him in the garden with our firstborn and saw myself making pancakes, while simultaneously waving lovingly at him through the french windows. His comic timing was inspirational. Our wedding photos were fantastic.

The more I laughed, the more he wanted to tell me everything.

"I'm married, you know," he blurted. The assertion threw me. I felt entirely exposed, as if he knew what I'd been thinking, as if he were flicking through me like a book.

"How is your wife?" I asked. The question bounced off me, the voice no longer my own.

"I haven't seen her in two years and technically she no longer exists," was the answer.

"It's all going very well then."

"It's complicated."

"What's complicated about it?"

Hesitation. Officially, I was still a stranger.

"She's a man," he replied, and walked back into the clinic.

I have often tried to colour my hair in an attempt to be different. The first incident was for the benefit of a carnival float. My sheer blonde became nothing more than a black mess in the bath. I received severe looks from the school headmaster over the steam of his hot dog, which provided all the incentive I needed to get rid of it. And I did. But it wasn't quite the same. Nothing ever is.

The second incident occurred when I purchased three packets of chestnut hair dye because I thought it would make me look older. It made me look pink. The blonde wasn't growing back. In fact, there surfaced a bland, duller colour in the root, as if the hair had been saddened by what I had done. I was always a wizard at destroying the best things I had.

We had been waiting for another hour. Owain and I had not exchanged a word since our smoke. It was as if it had never happened, I began to suspect a fanciful daydream. Mrs Little's smug smile was the only thing that confirmed that we had been given a chance to form an allegiance and we had failed. The potential for conversation, stolen glances and private jokes had amounted to nothing. And of course, she had to comment on it. "Didn't have much in common then did you? Then again, she's not really your type is she? Never mind. You can always talk to me."

He didn't.

It was a moment for the mind, ticking over, churning and changing things, bringing a whole rotating mass to a shuddering halt. As far as numbers were concerned, I satisfied myself with the fact that I knew a tenth of one story, 75 per cent of my own, and contributed a third to the waiting room's population. Mrs Little, however, although representing the same share, seemed to have taken charge of 95 per cent of the atmosphere.

Hair products. Shampoo, serum, wax, spray, softener, shiny finish cream, best for baby, best for you, hot-brushes, long-brushes, wash and go, leave-in conditioner, leave-out conditioner, I'd done it all. I knew *when* to do it, too. When suddenly, he'd forgotten how beautiful it could be. Your hair looks nice, he would remark, smoothing it with his palms, drawing me in with the thread of his eyes. Then another, more distant voice, speaking through it, nuzzling the golden locks in the crook of his shoulder. They didn't know it was a fraud, that naturally, primitively, it looked more like sinew than silk. At times like these it posed as something else. It was entirely laden, smeared, weighed down. As if it was drugged. It had no idea what it was doing. And neither, it would seem, did I.

"This is ridiculous," exclaimed Mrs Little for the seventh time that day. Owain lifted his eyes, I nodded my head. It was something on which we could all agree. Mrs Little had previously pronounced that she favoured watermelons. Being bored with the situation, I had agreed with her that it was indeed, an exquisite fruit. Owain declared that it was his preferred flavour. Similarly, we were all in concordance about the wait. It proved to me that people are not altogether as different as I might have them be.

THE HEROICS OF HAIR

Mrs Little remained unusually quiet after this. This inconsistency made me see her, for the first time, as she really was. Her lips were bursting with secrecy. I realized that the things she had been saying were mere compensation for the things she could not disclose. It was also evident that she was on the very verge of revelation. Something was moving through the dark tunnels of her mouth, spiralling its way towards the light.

"I have killed people," she said.

It was such an alarming and confusing assertion that I had no idea what to say and merely tried to encourage her confession by stating, "It's OK," which under the circumstances, and in the human awareness of knowing right from wrong, was the wrong answer. It wasn't OK at all.

"I love my husband," she continued, strangely soothed by my foolish answer. "Call me old fashioned, but when a woman loves her husband it is a love that will suffice forever."

Owain shook his head in disagreement, but Mrs Little ignored this, mistaking it for a nervous twitch.

"Now, men, they don't know what they want. Fair enough. They want to stray. They want to sleep with other people." By now, there was no stopping her. She didn't even seem aware that there was anyone else in the room. "But he wasn't sleeping with other people was he? No, that wasn't good enough for my husband. He wants glamour, he wants excitement. He wants something different from the rest." She paused.

I began to visualize unspeakable things.

"He doesn't think like a normal man. He doesn't think to spare his poor wife the shame, the degradation, the embarrassment of – " and with this she burst into tears.

"Of what?" challenged Owain, impatiently.

I put my hand gently on her arm. She was shaking.

"Whores," she spluttered, "dirty, disease ridden, gold-digging whores, that's what. Leaving their stench all over him. I told him, if he was going to sleep with all those whores then I was going to have to kill them. Every single one. And do you know what he did? He laughed."

"You should have killed *him*," said Owain. I had now gathered that sensitivity wasn't his strong point.

"He's getting what he deserves, believe you me."

The air was still. No one dared move.

"Well, you want to know what happened? I'll tell you what happened. I followed him to every whorehouse that he went to and I did what I promised – I killed them. I killed them all and I left him there to deal with it."

It was like discovering a coffin on your doorstep.

"How?" Owain asked. His morbid intrigue fascinated me.

"With this." She pointed to her hair. The violet hue suddenly looked threatening.

She buried her face in her hair, pulling it over like a veil. There was something at the back of my mind I was trying desperately to retrieve, the tip of the iceberg, the last piece of the jigsaw. Suddenly, there it was.

"Where is your husband now?"

"In prison for murder." Her voice crumbled in the air.

Ever since I was three years of age, I have twirled my hair around the little finger of my left hand. At this age, it was done habitually, accompanied by the sucking of the index and middle finger of my right hand. My own trait. My own way of dealing with things. I was also aware that this mannerism had no place in what was referred to by my parents as the 'real world', and so one day I vowed to stop. Just like that. I was trying my best to move on, to change the order of things. However, to this day, parts of this mechanism remain, as if they are built-in, deep under the skin. I have no qualms about grabbing the smallest strands of hair from my head and rotating them violently around my finger in the most inopportune moments. Like my graduation ceremony, the day I left him, the time I was caught for speeding. The day I got married again. I am even doing it now. It proved to me that some things simply do not go away.

Owain admitted that his story was nearly funny, but it had taken him years to accept the comedy. There had been no indication that there was anything wrong. She had been smiling when she cut the wedding cake, she had made love to him on their wedding night. She was a stickler for nostalgia and had kept the chocolate wrapper he left in her car the first time they met, the drive-through vouchers they had procured on their first date, a strand of hair she had found on her pillow. Everything spoke of devotion.

The transformation had not been gradual, it had been clear and simple. One day, she had caught a view of herself in the mirror and she had seen a man's eyes. That was it. She wasn't destined for femininity any more than Owain was destined for a full head of hair. That was the way it was. His beautiful, charming Heledd Francis ceased to exist. She became Howard.

It hadn't turned his hair white, it had simply killed it, ripped all life from the root. Because of a love that had nowhere to go. Mrs Little said she understood. She said that it was the kind of love that wore hiking boots, climbing on and on in all manner of hazardous conditions.

"You're better off without her love," she sympathized, cradling Owain in her arms as if he were a tired child. It wasn't what he wanted to hear. He withdrew from the embrace. Her next assertion, however, made such immediate sense that it startled us both.

"If you ask me, a woman who wants to be a man is no kind of woman in the first place."

My grandmother was a peculiar woman, a funny fish, as my father used to say. There was something unnatural in the way she loved my curls, and yet mercilessly ripped them through harsh combing. Similarly, she had said she loved its luxurious thickness and yet had made me cut it every summer. When I had exclaimed, "But it makes me look like a boy," after a cruel remark at a birthday party, she had merely replied, "Nonsense": a word that, for her, subsequently closed all conversation. She, on the other hand, boasted a brand new perm every six months, even when her hair turned white.

It would have been rude not to partake. It would have been both a betrayal and an insult. They were keen and attentive like competitors in a talent contest, who, having already performed, were free of worry as they judged the others. There was simply no turning back.

This is what I told them. That for several years I had been married to two men. Mrs Little gasped, as if my crime somehow superseded hers. Owain's eyes encouraged me to continue. It was a situation I had got myself into simply by loving too much, by demanding that I have everything. The first, Medyr, was my life and soul, the very core, and nothing would do without him. Gwern, the other, for whom I harboured a carnal obsession, was the lust of my life, and nothing would do without him. It was exhausting business, running back and forth from home to home, from bed to bed, changing my heart like a pair of socks. And yet, all these years, I had managed it.

I made Gwern's breakfast, kissed him goodbye, and by twelve I'd be at Medyr's side, stroking his hair. I didn't deserve any medals, but as I was living it, coping with it, such things seemed possible.

Until that week. Gwern and Medyr had met at an agri-food convention. They had exchanged phone numbers. They intended to meet, accompanied by their wives. Or should I say, their wife.

In this game, I'd rolled a six when all I needed was a one.

"Can't you just choose between them?" said Owain, as if the obvious had never occurred to me.

"Shut up and let her finish," howled Mrs Little.

It was over. Game over. There was no more to tell. Nothing to go back to. If I was to leave then I must leave them both. Which is what I had done. Which is why I was there. Like Mrs Little's conscience, Owain's heart, I came up against a hard, brick wall, which denied me the way forward. At least, until I knew where it was I was going.

The three of us stopped talking for a long time. The air was dense with contemplation.

"I'm going home," stated Mrs Little, the most sensible thing she had said all day.

"So am I," affirmed Owain, rising to his feet.

"Me too." I didn't even know where that was.

We parted like children after school, knowing it was not, by far, the end.

It's all about control. Treated with care, with the right attention, my hair can become the thing I long for it to be. Chignon, French twist, top knot, bouffant. It can find ways to be orderly, it will curve into place. Soft between fingers, shiny as a button, full of small, glistening eyes. There's a lot to be said for a good conditioner.

A week later, Owain, Mrs Little and myself received a letter from the hair clinic confirming that our treatment was complete. That afternoon, we had been monitored closely, and had undergone an experimental therapy process termed as 'Self-Conditioning Therapy'. It entailed that intense human interaction acted as therapy, and that our problems, (or 'issues' as the therapists liked to call them), in effect, solved themselves. The hair, they argued, would follow suit. They needed three of us, of course, to ensure the cross-section of character that they undoubtedly achieved. It was a hit, a sensation, a breakthrough. We dissolved into celebratory glasses of champagne. We were phenomenal.

We had paid £1, 243 for this privilege.

Mrs Little didn't need money where she was going. She was arrested almost immediately afterwards and for a long time she was more of a household name than Heinz. In front of the cameras she was obnoxious, arrogant and rude, and yet I could not help but feel some deep-rooted affection for her. I listened to her say the most implausible things ('crimes of passion should be rewarded,' and 'I'm only guilty of love,') yet her words spoke straight to me, sweet and precious like a secret voice.

"Haven't we already heard her say enough?" teased Owain, turning off the wide-screen television. My visions of him had not altogether been unreal. We had bought it together at Comet in the January sales.

There were many reasons why I was not jailed for my crime. Firstly, because Gwern and Medyr were influential managing directors who did not want the matter to come to the attention of the press. In some sordid way I was disappointed, for crime gave me the edge I had searched for throughout my life. Secondly, because of a little fact they had neglected to mention: they were lovers. Their pet name for me had been 'boomerang'. They invited me out to lunch, to celebrate their engagement. I had taken Owain. I had thrown a glass at Medyr's head and punched Gwern in the nose. For dessert we had tiramisu.

Owain received several letters from Howard that year. I tried not to notice. Walking past I always managed to read the top of the page which read 'My dearest Owain', which I thought inappropriate in the least. She/he professed her mixed feelings, her regret, her longing for his companionship. Eventually, when he had moved the last of his belongings into the house, I was granted permission to read them. Each letter requested a reply that she obviously never received. The seventh letter read 'I have heard from a neighbour about the new woman in your life, and by all accounts she will try her best to trick you'. The words hung awkwardly from the page. Then, gradually, a laugh broke out that seemed to be coming from my own body. A trickster indeed. I relished the fact that someone thought me cunning and dangerous enough to be evil.

On the screen, Mrs Little's hair was a character of its own. The disordered curls rolled into the fine, ribbon-like swirls, the colour radiated the deepest, darkest violet. It became her stronghold, her forte, her trademark. In fact, this week I even overheard a girl at a hairdressers tell her friend that she was going to get a 'Mrs Little'.

Owain, like myself, is realistic about the proprieties of what is termed as 'trouble hair'. It never showed any signs of recuperation, but the fact that the few strands that he did have, have remained strong, is in itself a sign of survival.

My hair is what it has always been. Excessive. Extravagant. Elaborate. Owain tells me it has the power to invade countries, to take over the world.

For now, however, it is content to put its feet up.

Hair speaks a thousand tongues. The root pushes through the skin, not out of fear, or desire, but out of the basic human need to be cultivated, to live. To be heard. You can soil it, you can punish it, you can train it like a monkey and tame it like a lion. But you can never push it down so far that it doesn't know what daylight looks like. It knows that life is there. Today I am wearing bunches. Owain has a slight fringe. Mrs Little is promoting afro-hair shampoo.

There isn't a stray strand to be seen.

DEBORAH DAVIS
Court Pastoral

PROLOGUE

The stage is black. A silent movie begins. This may either be performed by actors or could be a film composed for, and projected onto, the walls of the stage.

Belinda *sits at her dressing table applying kohl above and beneath her eyes. The opening notes of a jerky piano tune reflect the oddly fast, jerky image. Belinda completes her make-up, pats her bobbed hair and stands up to reveal a knee-length flapper dress. She smiles straight at the audience/camera.*

Belinda *sits at a table in a night club flanked by two young men in tuxedos. The piano tune gathers pace as* **Belinda** *flirts first with one tuxedo, then with the other, both of whom are dancing attention on her. Finally,* **Belinda** *turns to* **the Gentleman** *seated opposite her, smiles sexily, and with a great flourish throws a pair of dice onto a board game.*

A little way into the game, **the Gentleman** *stands up, extracts a pair of scissors from his top pocket and snips a lock of hair from* **Belinda's** *polished, bobbed head. The rise and fall of the piano reaches a frenetic pitch and comes to an abrupt full stop when the lock is cut.*

Belinda *jumps up. She covers her eyes in a greatly exaggerated way and starts to weep just as the piano tune resumes with a low wail.*

Triumphantly, **the Gentleman** *holds up the lock of hair to the chorus of tuxedos.* **Belinda** *runs away, constantly turning back to look accusingly at her aggressor. The stage returns to black.*

Light travels in through a bow window picking out a writing desk, finely bound leather books, piles of parchment covered with calligraphy and an unusual quantity of quill pens. A raised bed sits on the centre of the stage facing the audience. The style of the bed is eighteenth century. A portrait of the profile of a Roman senator wearing a garland hangs above it.

Alexander Pope *(29) emerges from the gloom, sitting up in bed wearing a white silk turban. He is holding a quill, as if in mid-sentence, but he has clearly nodded off.* **Pope** *suddenly jerks awake and looks around him. He checks where he has reached in his composition. He looks up at the audience, confused.*

POPE Am I dreaming? I can't distinguish fact from fiction at this time of the morning. I am attempting to complete my regime of twenty-five lines before the cock rises. 'Tis the only way to fit Homer into my busy schedule. Since Belinda proved to be a hit, I confess I have had fame and its attendant duties to contend with as well. 'Tis an occupation in itself. Did you see Belinda? Did you take note of her dress. Perhaps that was also a dream. She was considerably more déshabillée than I could have conjured up in my waking head. Now I find you here. Naturally, I have always suspected that you would express a desire to pay me a visit. I confess that it has been one of my dreams. But today. Today. No. I shall not boast, not even to you. You shall come with us. Mr Gay is to be my guide on this great journey down the River Thames. Incidentally, I have arranged for him to be woken by three alarums to avoid his natural tendency to doze through life. He is skilled. Of that there is no doubt. I have great hopes in his talent. But in truth, apart from a few frivolous lines, he has yet to set the world alight. His other great passion is society, particularly that of women. 'Tis not easy to answer to one muse, let alone two. [**Pope** *lifts up a piece of parchment*] This is the work in progress. Translating *The Iliad* is more arduous than it was to conjure up that light confection of Belinda's lock. Although 'tis not an emanation from my imagination, the job requires a certain skill. Little Mr Pope, they call me. The genius of the rhyming couplet. You shall judge for yourselves. I note that you are considering the brush strokes on the back of this parchment. That is my grotto. [**Pope** *lifts the coverlet and climbs out of bed with great difficulty. He is wearing a long white nightgown. Pope stands up and manages to balance by holding on to the bed. He could easily pass physically for a twelve year old boy*] For the moment 'tis but a work on paper. But if Homer proves to be another hit, I shall acquire a villa and plant fig trees, an orange grove, herbs of every variety, an arboretum. And of course my grotto. But of that, more later... [**Pope** *peeps at the audience from* *odd angles (underneath his elbow, over his shoulder, between his legs) as he dresses, as if he is meeting for the first time, and flirting with, a much talked about stranger*] You shall watch me complete my toilette. Then we shall take our petit-déjeuner together. And then I shall open my letters. Or should I say one letter in particular. For I believe today... Yes I am certain. It all points so decidedly in that direction. But enough of that. Let us not tempt the Gods to deride my tightly clasped dreams. [**Pope** *struggles to wrap silk around his bare legs like a nurse applying a bandage*] Even at this time of year 'tis necessary to apply these silks. I am apt to lose the heat quickly in these unreliable limbs.

[*A knock at the door and* **Martha Blount** *(27), plump and pretty, enters with a tray of coffee and a pile of letters, each inscribed with the name: Mr Alexander Pope.* **Pope** *is dragging on a pair of velvet breeches.* **Pope** *has to twist and turn like a worm crawling on the floor to achieve this simple act*]

MARTHA   Mr Pope. Stop this minute. You have only to tinkle the bell to summon the girl.

POPE   Fair angel of light. Miss Patty. I love no woman but you. To love you is as if one should wish to eat angels, or drink cherubim-broth.

[**Martha** *struggles to help* **Pope** *to stand, their lips almost touching. There is a definite sexual frisson between them*]

POPE   Have you come to pour balm on my poor parched lips?

MARTHA   Stop your nonsense, Mr Pope. 'Tis far too early in the morning. We must look sharp.

[**Martha** *helps* **Pope** *to dress in a white shirt and silk cravat*]

MARTHA   It is not every day that Hampton Court opens its gates to my two favourite poets.

POPE   Can you see who else has come knocking on my door?

MARTHA   Mr Gay is not due for at least another hour.

POPE   No. No. I speak not of Mr Gay. Look my sweet handmaiden. Can't you see them?

MARTHA   Who?
POPE   Posterity, dear lady.

[**Martha** *looks out blankly at the audience*]

MARTHA   'Tis your imagination running away with you again, Mr Pope. I can see no one. However, I have spotted the signature of a certain aristocratic acquaintance amongst your letters.

POPE [*Serious*]   Give them to me direct, Miss Patty.

MARTHA   Her handwriting is, I believe to be distinguished from the common run by the beauty of her script.

[**Martha** *holds the letters at arm's length from* **Pope**]

POPE   This is a cruelty of unimagined dimensions.

[**Martha** *dances away from* **Pope's** *grasp*]

MARTHA   And consider her presentation. Do not those couplets that describe your name and residence reflect the skill of a mistress of the lyric form?

[**Pope** *grabs* **Martha**]

POPE   Stop, or I shall banish you to the further reaches of Mr Gay's shabby lodgings. There you will languish 'til he finds the time in his busy schedule to write his comic masterpiece.

MARTHA   The fates could not devise a more cruel destiny.

[**Pope** *manages to seize his letters and whisks through them until he finds the one he is looking for*]

POPE   Yes, 'tis Lady Mary's handwriting. I have been waiting for this token these last three months. Look. She has finally taken possession of her new realm at Constantinople. Let me read her dear, sweet hand. Today is indeed destined to be a very special day in the life and times of Mr Alexander Pope.

MARTHA [*Anxious*]   Does she finally make her declaration to you?

POPE [*Reading*]   She describes her journey with admirable tedium.

But here perhaps she gives the lie of the land. In Vienna, 'tis the established…

[**Pope** *looks up and realises that the audience is listening*]

POPE [*To the audience*]   Perhaps you would prefer to listen for yourselves.

[**Pope** *produces a tape recorder, like a magician who has pulled the rabbit out of the top hat.* **Pope** *smiles mischievously at the audience and switches the machine on.* **Lady Mary Wortley Montagu's** *voice – deep, flirtatious, lively – travels across the stage.* **Pope** *looks up excitedly*]

TAPE OF LADY MARY'S VOICE   In Vienna, 'tis the established custom for every lady to have two husbands, one that bears the name, and another that performs the duties.

POPE [*To the audience*]   A hint of hope, do you not agree?

TAPE OF LADY MARY'S VOICE   And these engagements are so well known that it would be a downright affront, and publicly resented, if you invited a woman of quality to dinner, without at the same time inviting her two attendants of lover and husband, between whom she always sits in state with great gravity.

[**Pope** *switches off the tape recorder*]

POPE [*To the audience*]   Don't be surprised to see artifices that have not yet been invented.

MARTHA [*Irritated*]   What inventions are you referring to Mr Pope? I can see nothing but the quills in their containers and the portrait on the wall.

POPE   I am not speaking with you, dear madam. [*To the audience*] I have I can assure you more than enough invention to imagine the tools of the future, although the quality of their sophistication may surpass even my great skills.

[**Pope** *walks forward to the front of the stage. Whilst the set is cleared, he puts his fingers forward to play an imaginary piano.* **Pope** *is in fact typing an e-mail and the words appear on a computer screen projected onto the stage*]

POPE   To Lady Mary Wortley Montagu at Constantinople.
SCREEN   To: ladymarywortleymontagu@constantinople.com

POPE/SCREEN   This letter is a piece of madness that throws me after you in a distracted manner. I don't know which way to write, which way to send it, or if ever it will reach your hands. If it does, what can you infer from it, but what I am half afraid, and half willing, you should know.

[**Pope** *tries to send the e-mail, but the subject category flashes on the screen*]

POPE   Subject. My subject?

[**Pope** *thinks and then types*]

SCREEN   Subject: love

[**Pope** *clicks on an imaginary mouse*]

POPE   There. It is done.

SCREEN   Sending

[**Pope** *turns on the audience with great force*]

POPE   Now, do you have the imagination to see me?

[**Pope** *places a gold turban on his head, treating the audience like a mirror.* **Pope** *turns to stand in profile. He looks the image of the young Roman senator in the portrait on his wall.* **Pope** *limps off stage with the help of a cane*]

REBECCA DEANS
The World of Insurance is Looking Up

Sarah was woken up with a punch that Sunday. Eight o' clock and the sun wouldn't let her sleep, insisting through the curtains, peering into her eyes. The only way to avoid it was to get up and get herself into the bathroom. She sat up briskly, more easily than she expected. Normally they spent half an hour slumbering, half listening to the radio alarm before they rolled out of bed.

This must have been the first night in ages she'd actually got some sleep. Strange that his absence made her sleep easier; he always used to say that cuddling up together was the greatest thing. Sarah would smile and try not to think about the constriction around her chest. He always held her too tightly.

That night she'd been on her own and she could already tell it had done her good. She could feel it. When she got into bed without the Saturday half-bottle of wine inside her, Sarah thought she'd be awake all night. But two pages into *The Tenant of Wildfell Hall*, a book she'd been meaning to read since it was adapted by the BBC, and the light was off.

Sarah reached over to the door to get the dressing gown that Jules grudgingly shared with her. Sarah preferred a larger, longer robe. She felt protected by the rolls of towelling, ruched by the long belt that trailed along the floor as she walked.

The bathroom was cold. Jules had left the window open. It wasn't like him, security-conscious Jules, who had just recently fitted an expensive burglar alarm. Not as if Sarah ever put the alarm on. She was too afraid of setting it off.

Sarah got into the shower quickly. Despite the cold, she enjoyed it. It must have been the first morning in a long time she hadn't had to scrape away the sweat of the two of them. She shampooed and conditioned carefully, with no one to comment on the time she spent in the bathroom doing her hair. She left it wet and wandered downstairs, dressing gown open and no make-up.

It was strange breakfasting on her own. Sarah looked in the fridge for inspiration. Jules had bought in lots of eggs and bacon but she fancied something light. She caught a glimpse of herself in the polished chrome SMEG refrigerator door: nice brown hair, pity about the thighs. Sarah hated the fact that Jules had a fridge that acted like a mirror. She always felt it was jeering at her each time she opened it and had something to eat. Jules said it was high design and showed taste. He didn't need a normal white fridge. That was common.

Sarah settled on muesli. It was time she started looking after her body. She was having trouble getting into a size twelve. At school, she'd been quite athletic, even representing the school team for the eight hundred metres. She never won anything, but it was fun taking the bus all the way to Tipton and back. She liked to talk to the sixth-form helpers about their plans for university, about music and gigs. She got on well with them. Now she'd hate to look at herself in PE pants, let alone parade around in them.

She left her pots on the breakfast bar. What Jules didn't know wouldn't hurt him. Sarah flicked through a pile of letters left there. She noticed the headed paper of several firms she had heard of. Jules must have been doing some work on Saturday morning before he left. He certainly had some important clients for his insurance business. Sarah had never told him that; she found it better not to mention the firm. Jules often asked her to become a junior partner, but Sarah wanted to get her career going on her own. And she didn't want to work in insurance.

As Sarah went upstairs, a picture of the Business Studies intake for 1990 caught her eye. It was in a horrible frame, dark brown plastic with a gold line that had tarnished because it wasn't really gold. Sarah hadn't bought that picture. She felt the whole idea was a ruthless attempt by the department to make money. At the start of the year, everyone looked so young and so fresh. She didn't want to remember them all like that. A better record of their student days would have been a picture taken two weeks later, when all the friendship groups were set and the first sexual partners found. When at least half the students had changed the colour of their hair.

Next to it was a picture of Jules with his mates at the bar. Sarah was with a couple of friends and appeared to be with them but that was a coincidence. She just happened to be there. She hadn't even noticed him then. Sarah and Jules' affair hadn't started until the reunion five years after graduation.

She carried on up the stairs. As if in order, the next picture of them together was at the reunion. This was in a green Ikea frame. It clashed a bit with her pink gypsy-style dress, but then

Jules really never was one for colour. Saying that, he looked stunning at the do. He was wearing a pin-stripe suit that she knew was expensive from her stint at John Lewis. Things had gone quickly since then. They'd hardly been apart.

She went into their room and put on a CD. Jules had bought it for her after she'd told him about the burglary at the flat she had lived in when she worked on Camden market. He'd scoured the second-hand shops until he replaced the valuable CDs: the Happy Mondays, the Beloved, the Sundays, all that 1989 stuff. Jules was strictly into soft metal, which made the gesture sweeter. He liked to tell her stories about the stadium gigs he went to while at university. Sarah didn't like to say she would have been at illegal raves. Now his Def Lepard nestled easily with her Prodigy.

She opened up the wardrobe, looking for clothes to go with the music. She found the flares she'd worn all Summer of Shoegazing. She put them on but it felt like dressing up in someone else's clothes. Even a printed cotton top didn't make the outfit look right. It was the hair. At university Sarah had long black hair with white streaks à la Cruella de Ville. But that wasn't suitable for the workplace so she'd let it grow out. It was now shorter, its natural colour. Jules preferred it that way.

She looked through more old clothes. A red satin dress with spaghetti straps that she wouldn't even wear to bed now, a long button-down skirt. Jules didn't understand why she kept them. He always threw things away as soon as he bought replacements. Sarah thought that was shortsighted because clothes often came back in style. Jules said if they did, he'd buy them again.

Sarah found a bright orange tracksuit. That was hers? She put it on and looked in the mirror. She looked like a sixty-something glamorous granny. All she needed was a sweat-band and leg warmers. Still it was early. No one would see her.

Sarah let the morning draw her out of their converted-factory apartment. She walked round the corner. Better not let the neighbours see her start her jog. She needed space to decide whether she would actually run or not. Maybe she would find it was too much after a couple of paces, instead become a woman in a horrible tracksuit walking for the paper on a Sunday. When she was seventeen, Sarah always used to get her driving instructor to pick her up round the corner, so no one could see her pull off nervously.

Out of sight of the flat, Sarah broke into a run. It wasn't yet a struggle, but she could tell that soon, if she wasn't more careful about taking exercise, she would lose any of the athleticism she had somehow kept. She wasn't out of breath, but each time she took a stride, parts that she had forgotten wobbled and her knees jarred. She wished she hadn't opted for fashion trainers.

This was her Sunday and she was going to run to the park, and back, talk to some ducks or something. Sarah ran on past a group of kids playing in a woodchip park with yellow, blue and red swings and slides and rocking horses on springs like Zebedee. She saw the mothers, sitting around, chatting. She could never grow into their leggings.

She ran past the indoor reservoir topped with unreal green grass, the sun getting higher and yellower in the sky at every footfall. Past the wrought-iron gate made by the local iron foundry for Lord Shipley's house. The grounds had been left to the council and made into a park. The English garden was a remnant of the time when the area was richer. She took the left path, past the herb garden, out of breath with phlegm gathering in her throat.

No one was around, save the park keepers dealing with the weeds around the fence and a couple of kids on their bikes, looking shifty. She decided to do some exercises, like in PE, some star jumps, 1, 2, 3, maybe that would be enough. It hurt her back. She carried on running, jumping to touch the deep green leaves of the rhododendrons surrounding the path.

Perhaps, instead of this, she should brave aerobics again. But how she had hated it before when she'd gone with Sue from work. All leotard competitions and too much techno. She particularly hated the parts when the instructor would remind them all why they were getting exercise. "Get your bum firm for your man, girls. We don't want to let him see you sag. Hold that stomach in. Don't want to look fat when we're sun bathing. Come on, run for your man." She'd make them run round in circles for a while, to shift that fat, erase that cream cake. At least Sarah had known she wasn't doing it to please some bloke. Jules always seemed to want to put weight on her.

There was a lake in the middle of the park; a large lake with two small islands that people rowed to when the weather was fine. Sarah noticed the burger bar waking up to the day's trade, the boat-hire man checking out the boats. As they lived so close, Sarah had thought they'd spend a lot of their time in the park, on the lake, at the outdoor table-tennis tables or on the tennis courts. It's what made the flat so special. But they'd only come that first Sunday when he'd shown her around.

She approached the café by the lake, a white wooden building with a slight tinge of moss. When Jules and Sarah were there, the outside chairs and tables had been full so they couldn't have a coffee. It was a pity; Jules had said the owner was a character.

Today there was a group of people there, eating a great fry-up and settling their stomachs with Tetley tea. They looked young, like students from the sixth form or university. Sarah couldn't tell the difference any more. They were probably on their way home from clubbing, just got the first train back from the city. Their hair was messy and their clothes were too sparkly for the spring light. Sarah realised she was staring when one girl looked pointedly back at her. But Sarah kept on running.

She ran back through the industrial estate, a grassy area that had been landscaped by the local Groundwork Trust. Sarah remembered when she was a child, going with her grandad to a place like this to pick wild flowers. Surprisingly, there were quite a few rare plants colonizing the grass verges around the units. On a Sunday, no one went through the estate and it was peaceful, the carpet factory wasn't chugging out black smoke through its towering silver chimney and no lorries went past.

Sarah slowed down. The world still throbbed in her head and in her stomach. She stared at the two horses tethered in the field by the footpath. They always seemed to be there, these black horses with flashes of white on the head and belly. They weren't well treated. She could tell from their coats, which were clogged up with mud. She wondered if they ever felt shy and exposed there, stuck always in the public view, in their permitted circle of ground. Perhaps they'd like to do their business in private. It must be tiring, she thought, to be a stuck-outside horse.

She patted one of the horses absent-mindedly and was surprised when its mouth opened, revealing grotesque and yellowed teeth. She started to run again to get away from the horse, knowing it was tethered to the ground, but not believing it. The flies that had surrounded the horses seemed to follow her. She never understood how a simple insect could fly so fast.

And when she got back she saw Jules' car in the drive. She hadn't expected him back so early. He said the conference would be a twenty-four hour thing. Like a bug, thought Sarah.

Jules was sitting in his chair: a squat black leather affair in prime position to monitor both the outside world and anyone who came in. It contrasted strongly with his slim figure and blond hair. There were five or six remotes on the table by the side of him. Sarah sometimes wondered which one was for her.

Tired today, or maybe less vigilant, he was head down into the business section. "Hi, love. We finished early. You said you wanted me home." His blue eyes peered up over the rim of his glasses. "Are you all right, love? You look a bit flushed."

"I've been for a run."

"A run." A raised eyebrow and a smile. "You used to love running. Why don't you do it more often?"

Because there's always ironing to do. Because you wouldn't come with me. Sarah shrugged and sat down on the sofa, trying not to smell her feet as she took her trainers off. She removed a piece of straw from her trainer, thought about leaving it on the carpet, then realised she'd better put it in the bin. As she got up again, her stomach felt funny. She would have to get more sleep or eat more fruit.

"I missed you, but it was a good conference. The world of insurance is looking up." He moved towards her, reached out as if to hold her hand.

"Great." She made a beeline for the cafetière he had already filled. "Look, there's something…"

Jules got up and walked towards the kitchen area, pushing his blond hair away from his eyes. "I know." He came up behind her, hugged her, breathed deeply, moving his hands down to her belly. Sarah let him hold her. Her eyes flitted around the minimalist sitting room, settling nowhere.

SARAH A. FAIRHURST
Hakataramea

You can see the farmhouse standing on a ridge about half a mile away from the road. The house is abandoned now, and the grey cab of a truck in the yard stands out against the low outbuildings like a bald head. But it is strangely flattened at the back as if its maker palmed away all its intelligence, pushed it up into a mean point and left it that way. Unfinished somehow.

That truck killed a man. Rocked off the jack when he was changing the back axle and crushed him right outside his kitchen window. But the kitchen is the preserve of the wife. It's her place to stand there at the sink whilst he performs this last task of the day. She was making his dinner, or so the story goes, the version of it in my head. What else? It's evening, cold and fine. The sky high and milky after the departure of the sun. That particular Central Otago sky over a bare land, dominating the land with its expanse.

She's in there. She's got the radio on, playing sentimental songs via the satellite on Bald Mountain. Soft rock and romantic ballads. It plays; baby I want you, baby I need you. It plays, baby, when I think about you, I think about love. There is nothing to intersect the sky. She makes their dinner and at some point she looks up wondering what's keeping him so long.

And does she see his legs stretched lifeless under the capsized truck, does she know instantly that he is hurt? Yes. It happened this way. The radio and the dinner her main concern, a flare of irritation at him still outside. It is like this.

A song finishes and the DJ's voice cuts in over the closing bars. Why do they have to do that, cut in like that? It is her favourite song.

She is pouring the potato water down the sink. Steam flows from the lip of the pan and clouds the window. She is careful of her bare wrist, holding the tea towel over the bakelite knob of the pan lid and pouring the water off. The potatoes are slightly overcooked, she shakes them back into the bottom of the pan, they are breaking apart into a sludge of starchy water. She decides to mash them and looks up. It takes one raw instant to comprehend that the truck has keeled over, not hugely, no visual drama of excess, but this new quiet leaning to the ground.

What does she do? She grips the kitchen sink. It is some anchor to her, this gleaming plane of steel, the way the clean grooves of the draining board fan across its broad surface. She holds onto the stainless steel sink and looks from her lighted windows to the light outside. The truck is in silhouette against the wider sky. It has the mathematical purity of her worst school nightmares. There is the sky, waiting to be drawn on. There is the dark hypotenuse of the tray of the truck angling to the ground. And in shadow she sees his legs emerging from under the truck as before but the rim of the truck is cutting across his groin. Oh, she runs out, she runs outside to confirm what the half-light tells her, that the truck is pinning him down.

She runs to his legs, she is shouting his name, Bruce, Bill, Brian. Shit. There is no response. She runs around the truck to the other side, gets down on her knees in the dust. The dust feels like satin under her hand, already cool after the sun has gone. She makes two splayed handprints in the smooth dust and then obliterates them scraping aside a stone, careful with her damp hands. She cranes down under the dark of the truck, under the dust caked chassis. The huge bulb of the differential is bearing down on his crushed skull. He is already dead; she knows it instantly. His head is twisted to one side; his cheek and his open mouth pushed to the dirt. It is all wrong. She would lift his head from that dust, feels the grit of it in her own mouth. The way his open mouth is full of dirt, proof of his death.

Other things. His skull under the differential. The metal bearing down on his broken skull. She sees it like a bowl, a broken bowl, the shards falling away from the round. She feels that she might piece it together again, place the fractured lines one against the other, that they would interlock and he would be mended. In her mind she does this over and over again, holds the curved bone in her cupped hands, rights it. Later she will elaborate. In a recurrent dream she beds his broken skull into a box of sand and the sand accommodates the perfect round of his skull until it is healed. But not now. His hair is matted with blood where it has burst through the split skin of his head. It's dark under there but she can see it clearly.

She stands up again. Turns round. Her eyes take in a scoop of the clear evening sky and come back. The jack is lying in the dust, on the other side, next to his olive green work pants and his unfurled left hand. It must've popped out when the truck came down. It's broken. She can see the dull shine of the new break, a rough pitted disk of metal, and on one edge an ugly eclipse of rust that marks the old fracture. It must've been like that for ages.

There is the weight of the truck. She can't move it. She touches the tray briefly to make sure it is firm, aware that she is touching his skull through the body of the truck. There are all sorts of things in the tray, a sawn off sleeper, old binder twine, bits of straw. They haven't even slid down to the end. She gets right down in the dust, lays beside the truck and reaches under to his head. She puts her hand over the skin of his face, over his nostrils and his loose mouth. He is dead.

She hooks her finger into his open mouth to get the dirt out. She is running her hooked finger along the inside of his under lip trying to drag out the dust. She can feel it balling into wet clumps against the flesh of her finger. Clotted blood and saliva and dirt. She lies for a time in the dirt. It gets fully dark, the first pale stars come out and then a rash of stars. Her hand is stretched to his dead face under the truck. After a time she smells the dinner burning and withdraws her hand and sits up. The blood is drying on the pads of her fingers, when she moves them she can feel the slight resistance of it before it cracks and gives way.

She goes inside, to the harsh electric light and switches off the oven. She leans against the kitchen sink and waits there with her dead husband lying outside. A pall of smoke flows from the open oven door and finds a level in the room. She opens the window above the kitchen sink to release it and leans there. The smoke drifts to the open window and disperses. She turns on the tap and holds her hand under the flow of water to get the blood off it. The water flows in a silvery plaited column from the hooked steel tap. She stands there a long time, watching the water.

Later she rings her mother. She says you'd better come over, Brian is dead. She stands in the hall and leans against the cold wall. The back door is open. She is cold. The show of grief begins with her mother's shocked voice catapulting into disbelief. She has to counter it, she says, I dunno, Mum, the truck rocked off the jack. Somehow, I don't know. She says, yeah, Mum, you'd better ring the ambulance. But it's too late now. She pulls her cardigan around her and stands in the hall.

This is what you have to say regarding this woman and this man. Not long after they were married he took her up to the pass overlooking the McKenzie Country. They went at dusk. He was showing her his special place. There's an old musterer's hut up there, older than you think, the corrugated iron still grey and unrusted in this high mountain air. He wanted to show her it, maybe fuck her there. The road runs straight, due west following the broad course of the Hakataramea valley. If you turned the other way you could follow this same road to the distant sea. It is the one pure line drawn on the landscape, the apt human inscription. The road follows the land. Running straight along the generous valley floor. Off to the right the unseen river runs, hidden by a gentle lip of rising land. It is a sere country, a brown country.

She watches his freckled arms and his loose hands on the steering wheel. He is sandy; his forearms burnt deep brown beneath the sun-bleached hair. He wears the sleeves of his work shirt rolled loosely up; he wears his khaki work pants. The folds of his clothing and the folds of the land are in accord. She looks beyond his shoulder to the smooth repeated fall of the foothills bounding the valley. They are in accord.

She leans forward to get a cigarette. Her purse is jammed into the open glove compartment above a litter of papers. When she gets her purse the dry papers lift and tremble in the wind. She lights her cigarette and chucks the lighter back on the papers to anchor them.

You should clean this up, she says.

Nah, he says, that's your job. You're the woman, he says, and grins at her.

They nearly blew away she says and leans forward again to look at the papers. They are the registration papers for the truck, pink bills of sale for timber, for petrol, for pesticide. There is a fine drift of dust on them. She takes them out and slaps them against her hand, shuffles them into a straight-edged pile and puts them back. The papers feel light and brittle in her hands; all the moisture is sucked out of them. Feels like she could crumble them up into flakes just by closing her fist.

Look at this mess, she says and prods at the car jack lying on the floor at her feet. There is a piece of blue raddle lying there; it is the dye he uses to mark the sheep. She drags the sole of her shoe across it, drags a long cobalt streak of the dye onto the underside of her shoe. She can feel the irregular chalky lump of the dye under the ball of her foot.

I dunno, she says and slumps back and exhales cigarette smoke. She looks at the sky bleached white under the long westward fall of the sun, how it is narrowing toward the foothills, loosing its ascendancy to the steep-sided hills they are approaching. She looks at him again; he's still grinning. What's so funny? she says, and punches his arm. She punches like a girl, with the pale underside of her wrist showing. He reaches out and grabs her wrist and pulls her toward him across the vinyl seat.

There are lines in the seat where the fabric has been stitched. The vinyl has worn away from the stitching to reveal the cloth backing. Each furrow is scored with a raw umber line of greasy dust that edges to a paler chalk where the deposit is newer. It is the archaeology of the front seat of the car.

She licks his earlobe and feels the fine down of his ear on her tongue. For awhile she holds her tongue there, in the soft hollow of the lobe of his ear. He drives with his left arm around her. She can feel his earlobe vibrating against the curve of her tongue from the motion of the truck. But that was in the days when she hardly knew him. She would not reveal herself so readily now.

Her mother is coming with her father down fifty forty thirty dark miles of road. The same road. She knows how it is. Her parents speeding in their big car. American car. The car fishtailing in the dust, throwing up a long roiling plume of dust. And her parents' tight faces in the window, lit by the faint green glow off the dashboard, off the slick rim of backlight on the bonnet of the car.

The headlights cut into the dark and light up the wire fence line either side of the straight road. Light the pale yellow roadside grasses. Each grass stem and fence post has a stroke of shadow that wheels and falls away behind the car into the larger darkness. A maelstrom of shadows.

There are a few sheep sleeping on the road where it's warmer. There always are. They are lurching to their feet at the far end of the beam of light where it breaks down into patchy flakes. They are shaking themselves, shitting, beginning to run. Her dad slows down for the sheep as they run before the car. He has to cut down a gear to avoid the sheep. He's savage, swearing at them to get out of the way. The headlights shine on their arses rising and falling before the car and on the stiff flickering repeat of their hind legs, running.

Her mother wills the sheep to get off the road with her stomach in a slew of apprehension. Hoping to lessen his anger with her silence. But they will run yards like this, panicked in front of the car before they finally veer off to butt against the fence. He jerks the window down and screams at them to get out of the fucking way. He'd like to stop and slaughter them all, boot them, kick them senseless. The night wind buffets into his face and his open mouth. Then he has to shut his mouth against the wind. Cold air swirls into the car and around the back of her mother's neck. Hasn't she ridden countless times with her father, and her mother who says nothing?

One thing she knows right away waiting for her parents. She

knows she will leave the farm. She stands in the empty house. In the hall and then in the front room. The ranch sliders are sheeted black in the darkness. She looks into their black panes and sees the room and herself reflected in the light from the hallway. There is a row of canna lilies she has planted hard up against the glass. Even in this poor light she can see the sheen on their bronze leaves.

She doesn't go out to the truck again, but she has this time waiting with her dead husband. She stands in the formal front room with the tips of her fingers resting on the back of the sofa. The sofa has a heavy brocade pattern in swirls and curlicues of sea green. Without moving her fingers she can feel the soft raised nap and the colder tighter thread of the sunk pattern. Her own form is blocking the light from the doorway. There is light fraying along the sleeve of her cardigan but her face and the bulk of her body are indistinct. The reflection of the room is just a transparent slick across a gulf of darkness. She can see right through it.

She watches a single prick of light hanging midway in the window. It grows in magnitude and divides against the felted darkness of the land. It is the headlights of her parents' car moving swiftly along the valley floor, past the dark breach of pines on the further hillside, past the boundary fence stalking down out of the hills. She watches the fence line, briefly illuminated as the car slows to cross the cattle stop. She can hear the faint burst of sound as the wheels run over the loose iron bars.

She watches their rapid approach. The headlights travelling down the main road and then slowing to sweep into their farm road. The light shines through the bars of the gate whilst her father stops to open it. Drive through. Close it again behind him. He's close enough now to see the details of his clothing, his red checked work shirt, the stretch of his belly. But she's watching the huge rayed shadow of his legs moving in front of the stationary headlights.

The car is low-slung; she can hear the rhythmic screeching of the chassis as her father drives up the rough road to the house. He drives with one wheel on the grassy verge and the other on the raised hump in the centre of the track, avoiding the ruts. The headlights cut across the short-cropped grass of the home paddock and then pitch into the sky as the car climbs the terraces. The dogs are howling; she can hear the links of their chains running out over the kennel floors as they rouse up to bay at the approach of her parents' car.

Her mother is in the room with her arms outstretched. She

goes into her mother's arms. Baby, her mother murmurs, my baby. And strokes her pale hair. She leans into the curve of her mother's neck but feels no adequate response. She is surprised at her mother's tears, feels that she is playacting, running through the required emotions with her pinched face, her attitude of grief. When she herself feels bone empty. She takes her husband's broken head in her mind's eye and continues to feel void.

You're shocked, her mother says. It's like her mother is talking to herself, comforting herself. I'll make tea, her mother says. To override the sound of her father jacking up the truck. As if now she must be cosseted from it.

Her mother says, stay inside. Don't go out there. She wonders what she is trying to spare her. It is all taken from her hands. Her mother goes into the kitchen and shuts the window. She hears the muffled thump of the frame against the sill, and feels the air compressed into the room.

The next time she sees him he is in his coffin. They have wiped the blood away and closed his mouth. There is a hierarchy of death. The undertaker and his assistant attend him. She is his visitor. She visits her husband's corpse. She bends over him to see if that is cosmetic on his face or if it is just the way he looks in death. His head is wrapped in a gauze bandage. She wants to touch it to see if the bones grate or whether they have made a template of his skull out of cardboard or something, something to give it shape. In a later dream she unwraps the bandage and the bones of his skull fall away clean as the shell of an egg. And reveal nothing underneath. His skull is like a lotus flower, a water lily. It opens onto nothing.

Her mother is behind her. Even to rest a finger on his cold face she feels she is violating some social code. Betraying herself somehow. She checks herself from any aberrant display and does not touch him.

They bury him in Hakataramea cemetery. She throws the canna lilies onto his coffin; her mother throws cut flowers. Listen. It is the sound of the earth thumping onto the broad metallic leaves of the lilies, onto the coffin lid. It is the sound of the zip whistling in the church hall adjoining the cemetery, the pitched and rising hiss of the steam escaping. It is hot; the sun bears down through the fabric of her black dress. She walks from the cemetery and she can feel the individual chips of gravel shifting under the thin soles of her best shoes.

This happened. A man and a woman lived on a farm. He was a farmer; she was a farmer's wife. She went to school in Oamaru and got a taste for people in numbers. But she married a farmer anyway. Sometimes they die like this, by overturned tractor, or truck, or fall of rock, by accident.

They buried him. She left the farm and left it empty. On her way from the valley she passes the overhang of the Moa Hunter caves at Duntroon. But she doesn't go there. She doesn't see the red ochre drawings of the Moa Hunters, the arcane and the sinuous line. She doesn't see this red supplanted by a later black, a sailing ship; and that this too is overwritten by a ruder graffiti. Brian loves Judy forever, Bruce and Michelle, Norelle, Linda, Shona. Forever.

L. B. FISHER
Dress You Up

Nicole's tape player clicks. Song over. Tova remains squatted with her right hand spread out on top of her head. With the other, she wipes the line of sweat from her upper lip but lets her hair mask her face. The crowded room is silent; there's no applause like she expected. No one comes rushing towards her in amazement, and envy. She opens her eyes and notices that the hole in her stockings has spread from her calf to her upper thigh. She raises her chin and sees her shirt lying on the carpet a few feet away, the arms crossed in front as if awaiting an explanation. Her twisted bra strap digs into her shoulder. Tova holds her position for a moment longer, and then stands.

Nicole Haberman decided to have a dress-up party for her twenty-first. Tova thought that there might be other Madonna wannabes, but she knew that she could be the best. She had a plan: Tova told Nicole she'd perform a song with a surprise ending, one that no one would ever forget. That was bound to cause a stir and guarantee the party a success. Nicole, with thick glasses, greasy hair, and terrible party food, agreed, because otherwise who would come, and if so, how long would they stay? When people called to RSVP, Nicole told them about Tova before they could say no. Well, she gave them a morsel, but said they'd have to come to get the rest.

Tova was an Orthodox Jew from Flushing, Queens. She lived with her parents, three sisters, and two brothers in their three-bedroom apartment on Jewel Avenue. Tova commuted three times a week to Yeshiva University in the city, and spent the rest of the time helping out in her father's bookshop, Ivrit Books. On Mondays, Tuesdays, and Thursdays, she met Rachel, Yael, Feigie, and Naomi at the subway stop. Orthodox girls didn't travel alone. They moved in groups until they got married. Then, they were taken around by their husbands.

Tova had been at Yeshiva for a year and had three more to go. She was twenty, like the rest of her pack of girlfriends. In a year they would begin going to social events organised by their school where they would be introduced to prospective Orthodox boys. After they had met a few times, they would begin to pair off. Tova would become engaged to a man she hardly knew, and probably didn't love. She would be pregnant within a year of marriage, and have at least five more; hopefully a total of six or seven children. She would be faithful, a dutiful wife. She would live in Queens, not too far from her parents or his. She would spend the day caring for the children, cleaning the house, preparing meals. She would accompany the family to synagogue on *Shabbos* but otherwise she was obligated to take care of the home. If her husband made a decent living, they might take a holiday once in a while, to relatives in Baltimore or maybe even Israel. They would be good members of the community, like her parents, like his. Tova would live this day after day, month after month from 21 until either she or her husband died. Rachel, Yael, Feigie, and Naomi couldn't wait to get started, to embrace and enact the real traditions, *mitzvahs*, of a religious woman. Tova felt differently.

Tova was sure she was adopted. She had blonde hair and hazel eyes. The rest of her family was brown and brown with dark rather than fair skin. She was the first child, and her parents probably thought they couldn't conceive, so they adopted quickly. Tova thought she was Danish, or Dutch, or maybe from California. This is how she reasoned that she was able to turn her back on her religion, life, family. She wasn't innately Orthodox, which is why she couldn't completely accept that she was part of the chosen people. Which is why she couldn't be expected to continue the charade.

At the bookshop, Tova was in charge of deliveries. Sometimes publishing houses would send samples, thinking the bookshop was just like any other, not just a Jewish text shop. Tova would sit in the back room and read as she went through the new stock. She learned about women living alone in their thirties, in one-bedroom apartments in downtown New York. She glanced through travel guides instructing how to travel through Europe on twenty dollars a day or less. She read about falling in love. No arranged anythings. Just meeting someone someplace and he being your *besheret*, fated one. Samuel from their synagogue had been Tova's only boyfriend, when they were ten. Since then, because of her reputation, Tova hadn't had any other suitors, which is why her parents thought Yeshiva would be better than the local college. A new environment, some new people; almost starting over in a sense.

Once, Tova had asked Samuel for a kiss. Tova was obsessed

with chocolate. "Greedy child," her mother used to say, but Tova didn't care. She couldn't get enough. She heard from David S. that Samuel had a bag of Hershey's kisses so she went straight to the source. Samuel waited until everyone was out of the coatroom in Jewel Avenue Synagogue, Tova thinking so he wouldn't have to share, and then he pressed his lips on Tova's right cheek. "A *Hershey's* kiss!" Tova yelled, and stamped on his right foot so hard that she killed his big toe. Dead. He had no feeling in the toe and from that day on dragged his leg. Since he had trouble walking, Samuel, once a nice-looking, athletic boy, became an overweight, needy man. Word spread through the community and Tova had *mamza*, un-kosher child, branded on her forehead. The boys steered clear, the parents said what a problem she was, but the girls liked hanging around with the supposed community rebel. They pretended they were trying to change Tova, even though she'd never acted out since then. The punishment that she received from her father, at ten years of age, taught her to never again behave that way, to never do anything out of turn. She began working in the bookshop on weekends or after school, studied, helped her mother, and got older. Tova was never exceptional in school, but she did well enough to get into Yeshiva, to give her parents hope that maybe one of the rich New York City boys might take to their daughter's exotic looks and sound background.

The week before Nicole's party, Tova flipped through her clothes. She stood in front of the closet, closed her eyes and listed aloud: "Four long skirts (denim, black, brown, cream), two long-sleeved shirts (floral, white), two three-quarter sleeved shirts (yellow, blue, white), two dresses for the high holy days." Most days Tova wore her white tie-up canvas Keds. But on Shabbos she wore the same black penny loafers she'd had since her feet had stopped growing when she was fifteen. Tova pushed each wire hanger against the next wishing Madonna's outfit from Borderline would appear. She wanted to wear a short skirt, fishnet stockings with a hole in the knee, a half shirt, black tie-up boots, and a huge bow in her hair. She wanted her stomach to show, her elbows and part of her upper arms to be seen. Tova would have to go shopping, and not on Jewel Avenue.

Naomi was going as her mother. She was borrowing the apron she wore around her waist at the restaurant and the *shmata* she wore on her head. Rachel and Yael would be Sara and Ruth from the Bible. They were re-reading passages so they'd look just right, and nobody would have to question their identities. Feigie was going as Michael Jackson. Her mother had an old white glove and Feigie was sewing on rhinestones. She asked her father if she could borrow one of his black hats to finish the look, but he wasn't sure if that was right.

On Sunday, Tova told her mother she was going to help *Aba* out at the bookshop for a few hours in the afternoon. When her parents conferred a few hours later, Tova would say that she ran into the girls on her way there, and they decided to study together instead. They would both forget before the next time they saw any of the girls' parents. Avram was teething. Aton was having trouble understanding biology. Mira needed braces. Liba had whooping cough, and Lea would probably catch it if they weren't careful. Tova took the Long Island Railroad into Penn Station, to avoid the chance of bumping into anyone she knew on the subway platform, and walked down to the Village. On the subway into school a few weeks earlier, she'd heard two girls talking about The Antique Boutique, a trendy thrift shop on Sixth. Tova knew she'd find her outfit there.

Inside the shop, Tova felt on display. She wasn't out of place because she was too young, or too old, but too different, and not in an interesting way like many people in the Village. Since she started looking like a woman, people always deferred to her – on sidewalks, subways, buses – anywhere. People looked at her and stayed at a generous distance away. The expressions on their faces were always so interesting: frightened, intrigued, trying not to stare, and Tova liked to role-play. Sometimes she made her eyes bulge and stared at passers-by as if asking for help. Other times she kept her head and shoulders pointed down, acting like a proper Orthodox. Or, she glared right back, sometimes flashing a stealthy smile that made them look away immediately.

As Tova looked through piles of clothes strewn randomly throughout two rooms and a long basement, people blatantly avoided her, even the staff. After forty-five minutes of browsing and holding up in front of mirrors, Tova had her outfit. She wrestled with the idea of trying it on to make sure it all fit, but the scrutiny told her to forget it. Anyway, there was always the chance that she could see someone from the neighbourhood. Her reason for being in the Village was that she was on a field trip with school, and she had to catch up with the group so excuse me for running away.

Tova walked back to Penn Station in fifteen minutes, stuffed the plastic bag in her knapsack, and was home in time to help with dinner. When they sat down for the meal, her mother never even asked about going to the shop. She didn't have to lie, so she tucked that one away to use for another time. In her mind, Tova was still in The Antique Boutique. She saw herself in used 501's, a tube top and motorcycle boots, writing prices on tags with an indelible marker. She knew what the other girls would say if they saw the shop – "What a disgrace!" – and Tova felt the opposite. "How cool," she couldn't help saying over and over in her head as she touched the used clothes that could've belonged to anyone.

"Why do you keep so tight-lipped, Tova?" Feigie asked a few days before the party. They all wanted to know what her outfit looked like, and if she really was going to lip sync to a Madonna song. "Where did you even get the music? When did you hear it?" Tova's family had a radio that her father only used for the news. He'd stand right in front and repeat sentences he felt were important louder and with clarity. "Not ours, theirs, he says!" he'd yell and point his finger into the air. They had a television, but it remained stored on a bookshelf in the kitchen. Tova had never heard Madonna sing. She had only seen her dancing in her videos in the shop next to her father's. Tilden's TVs was located next door, and he permitted himself to put some of the televisions in the window on MTV to attract younger patrons. On Tova's way in and out of the bookshop, she would wait for a Madonna video. She would stand on the street staring at Madonna dancing around a parking lot, spray-painting a man's car, going into a bar with her pout, then smile, seductive and then authoritative looks. She could do whatever she wanted. Tova had never heard her voice, but she memorised every clip of each video she had seen, and all the titles.

"Naomi Rokach is going as Madonna too," Rachel said. "She got a new black skirt to wear, and a red bow for her hair. Her father even said she could wear some lipstick. Will you wear lipstick, Tova?" Tova said nothing. Naomi Rokach was the princess of Flushing because her family was supposedly one of the founding families of Tel Aviv. There was even a Rokach Boulevard in Tel Aviv, which they had a framed photo of hanging on the wall in the lounge. The rules soundlessly stated that Naomi should be the only Madonna because of her status, but if she wasn't, then she should be the best. Tova knew better, and only said one thing.

"Listen, girls, remember not to tell your parents about any of this. I want it all to be a big surprise. No slips of the mouth. *Sheket*. OK?" They laughed since Tova was imitating one of their professors who always said, "No slips of the mouth girls in the back," when they would talk during a lecture. This was always followed by, "*Sheket!*" and never *bevakashah*, or please.

You couldn't say shut-up without please, but this professor did, and Tova loved to mimic her, use the words as her own.

Nicole called the party for six-thirty. Her father and brothers would go to one of the neighbours, and her mother and sisters would help prepare. They lived in a terraced house on Main Street. Mr Haberman was a lawyer and represented the entire community, whatever the allegations. The day before, Tova had bought the single of Borderline. The family was lounging around the apartment since it was Shabbos. Tova had said she was meeting a few of the girls to go for a walk around the neighbourhood. Tova knew she didn't have as much time as before, so instead of going into the city, she had taken the bus to Little Neck, where she had read about a record store. The advertisement said it was open ten to six. Tova got there at two-thirty, found the single, paid, and left. Tova's feet felt numb on the bus ride home. In 21 years, it was the first time she had consciously violated the laws of Shabbos. "We are *shomer Shabbos*; we guard the *Shabbos* like something so very valuable. We rest. We do not expend energy like non-Jews on this day," she heard her father articulating. On the way off the bus, Tova took the remaining money out of her knapsack and left it on her seat. It wasn't hers any more. She was a new person. There was no turning back.

Tova dressed in the bathroom, the only door with a lock. It took just over an hour to get everything right, but looking at herself in the mirror, she knew she had it. And the twinkle that always seemed to emanate from Madonna, was now surrounding Tova. She couldn't help but smile. The rest of the family was in the lounge so Tova wouldn't be able to hear the song until the party when she performed. It didn't matter, she reasoned to herself. She did a pretty good job miming words when she was praying, so she'd do the same while she re-enacted all the memorised moves.

In the bedroom, Tova put on her ankle-length navy overcoat that she only wore on the high holidays. As she walked through the lounge, her bangle bracelets jangled. Tova paused, looked to see if her father's eyebrows were raised, or if anyone was looking at her as she left the house in her holiday coat. But no one missed a beat. "*Shalom!*" she yelled behind her as she closed the front door.

"So loud that child," she heard her mother say to no one because Tova knew no one was listening, so she opened the door up and slammed it shut again.

"Bye!" she yelled.

"And immature."

The girls met on Jewel and walked together to Main. The coat was coarse against Tova's arms, stomach, and legs. As they walked, Tova felt her skin getting hot and itchy. She kept both hands in her pockets, one clutching the tape, the other in a fist. "Take off the coat, Tova," they all pleaded throughout the walk.

"Patience, *yentas!*" Tova said, forcing a smile, but really trying to keep herself composed.

Inside, the front room had balloons randomly taped to the walls and pop music hummed in the background. Everyone marvelled at each other's outfit. Nicole dressed up as an Israeli, wearing sandals and a long-sleeved shirt with a dove and *shalom* on the front. Naomi Rokach was Madonna, or Madonna in a long black skirt, and black loose fitting knit sweater. But, she had a red bow around her head that matched her painted lips. She also wore new white tie-up boots, and kept raising the front of her skirt to give everyone a peek. She thought she was the only Madonna at the party. Tova kept her coat on.

At seven-thirty, when everyone was giddy from the soda and snacks, Nicole took the tape from Tova.

"All right. I promised you a show, and though there's two Madonnas here, one of them, Tova, is going to perform a song. But Naomi, if you decide after that you want a chance, you can sing to the same song as Tova."

"I think my outfit speaks for itself," Naomi said as she settled into the upright recliner. The other girls nodded their heads in agreement. They just wanted to see Tova.

Nicole pushed the dining table against the back wall to make room. Everyone assembled into a horseshoe, squeezed together on the couch, carpet, or chairs. Tova was waiting alone in the unlit living room. She looked up at the chipping paint on the ceiling, and clasped her hands together as if she was ringing water from a dishrag. When she heard the first note, she opened the door leading to the lounge, and let her coat fall off her shoulders.

ADAM FOULDS
Eight Poems
Postcard from Switzerland

'The odd thing about the young Jew was that although he seemed to be rich and was cultivated, he had no friends in the town.'
V.S.Pritchett, *Handsome Is as Handsome Does*

The mountain adjusts its perruque of cloud
and glances in the lake's ornate mirror.

The waiter brings coffee in a silver jug
and bows, neatly, to the notion of me.

Drinking tisane, the thin pretty woman
by the fountain loves her lapdog with scraps

of three languages. Something in the way
she lights her cigarette – held to her lips

in a stave of painted nails, the other
hand raising sidelong a sputtering match –

reminds me that I'm glad I am so scarcely
here, stirring my coffee slowly, gazing,

precise in a politesse that hides
the traveller's absence from his presence.

Chagall's Marriage Paintings
for Ruth and Mike

Lives, climates and fathers
melting of like quick snows
leave a dust of home
on his greatcoat, a needlepoint
constellation in her blown veil.
Poems and fears process
into nowhere, into now,
and lift with them,
falling awake, up, and carrying on
over the river, the moon, over
the parents' sleeping town,
the flowering chimneys.

Tanka: the Heron

Through flexing clouds and
surface quibbles you tune in
to throbs, steady glints,
then hurl down your water-knife
and gulp slick, twisting ingots.

TWO POEMS

1. Flight
(after a print by Kuniyoshi)

i.
Tokiwa Gozen
fleeing from
the Taira troups
through the snow
shields her two
young sons
beneath her cloak.

ii.
The silk roars
and swerves
around them,

iii.
its pattern
suddenly vast
in shocks
of the wind,

iv.
their needy breath
tugs at the cold,
enormous air,

v.
their feet slip
on icy ground,

vi.
three cranes rise
crying *kaa!*
to settle
farther off.

2. Just Before The Epilogue

A cold invitation to five a.m.
and a deserted field.

Horses shift in harness
under a snowing sky
of blood and watered silk.

Brief conferral and the curt nod
of top hats top-heavy with snow,
now discarded with folded gloves.

Twenty fair paces
and the first gun levelled.

Did his hand tremble
when that pigeon spluttered up
from between them and made
for the faraway trees?

Moments later the bullet tore through
his fine lapel and left verticle,
'Our Father' or some other name
trembled on his lips.

Twenty paces off a satisfied man
considers the rouged snow
and sudden voices. A rose of dove-grey
smoke unfurls beside him.

'The perfect phrase is French,
perhaps: *La fumeé ébouriffe.*'

Frost

It shames our humid dramas
the grasp

of gross
conversation,

our needing each other,
wretchedly, in detail,

clamorously for
and against each other,

to step into this frost,
this world wrecked

and at peace
without colour.

The fields are dazzling
low and shut,

the sky
a scoured absence.

You can walk away,
treading the breaking grass,

into space and the vivid
empty cold.

EIGHT POEMS

Thickly, your breath
leaves you in clouds

your loud thoughts
leave you

the rumpled
human odours.

You can walk
away

devoutly
away

until your hands
begin to stiffen

and the wind,
humming the fences,

crushes a sharp pebble
of real cold

into your forehead.
When your name is called

across the glittering
birdless air

it takes a moment
to mean you

who have nothing to do
with trees that survive

the assaulting wind,
plain as charts,

locked
in frozen soil,

whilst your blood, bewildered,
draws back –

your hands –
you look drowned

in this cold
as you walk

to the house,
movements

tightened
by the wind

relieved now
to return.

EIGHT POEMS

But kicking your boots
against the step

you know something
has entered you

out
there

:

cold space
hard light

your mind scraped
with brilliance

as with anger
that relents in you

only
slowly

in the warmth
inside, the voices.

On Ends of Affairs

The girl I love said It's negative vertigo – suddenly you're at the bottom of this great drop and they are high above you, already moving away. Is the coffee ready?

The coffee was ready. I poured two cups and wondered to myself if her being short had anything to do with her choice of image.

Next time, however, I think I know what I'll say, she told me and smiled, just as I tasted the bright snap of coffee flavour hot in my mouth.

Something

I forgot
to put in the letter
which I thought you might like:

I was walking to work past the cathedral through bright winter sunshine, that light you just want to drink like cold water, feeling alive with the clean city morning, although hungry and looking forward to my coffee and rolls. A fat woman was taking photographs of her daughter feeding the pigeons from a plastic cup of grain. She had long hair, the daughter, quite pretty with obvious assets. I took in the scatter of freckles over her cheeks and her slightly crooked teeth. She was laughing at her mother as she fussed with the camera and tried to focus. Meanwhile the pigeons started arriving for the food: a few shabby customers jigging over, others spilling out of the trees, then a long strip of them peeling off the cathedral and skittering down. The mother was taking photos by now, saying Hold the cup higher a bit higher look at me. The daughter, still laughing, was cringing away from the birds. Then one tried to land on her head, flicking her hair with its wings. She yelped and threw the cup down, backing away, as her mother laughed and took photos and the pigeons chased after the cup, their beaks ticking at the plastic, at each other, at every last seed.

SOPHIE FRANK

Extract from **Disappearance**

CHAPTER FOUR

More men go missing than women. Most of them are between the ages of thirty and forty-five. These people are never, or rarely, missing to themselves. Infrequently have they lost their way. Usually they have planned an exit route out of a life with which they are dissatisfied. They know where they are going, and why. Commonly, they are in the process of finding their true selves. They are like snakes, shedding an old skin to uncover a new one. They are always missing to others. Often they are trying to escape from the very people who miss them most. Since to grieve fully one needs a body, the missers will be caught forever in a no-man's land of not quite mourning.

If you are the one doing the missing, then, unless you are withholding information and there is more to the story than we think, the first days are hell. You will replay each and every conversation that you had with the missing. You will ransack your mind for hints and pointers as to why he left. Or rather, as to why he left you. Which links us to the nub of the problem, the howling ugly truth – which is that *you are the one who is left*. You are not the one doing the leaving.

More pain is to come as you realize that this is a break up like none other. There can be none of the usual ghastly yet finalizing, explanatory conversations in which grains of truth are weeded out of flowerbeds wet and slimey with clayey mud. There can't even be any mudslinging. This end contains no rows or fights or witnessed tears. Oh no – you alone must deal with an odd sort of loss, an abandonment that isolates you from 99 per cent of the rest of the world. Very few will ever truly understand what it is to be a misser.

Women with even the slightest suggestion of a sadomasochistic sensibility turn the loss in on themselves. Maybe you didn't like his friends enough, cook well enough, fuck enough, have long enough legs, laugh enough at his jokes, support enough and so on. Most of your questions whittle down to a single line – did you love enough? You will feel that you did not. You will keep asking yourself why? You will feel powerless, victimized. It is never good to feel this way. Over years you will reclaim your lost power but you may spend decades so doing. Why did you lose it in the first place? Who made it leave? It wasn't you.

If you have children, they too will blame themselves for the father who has gone missing. For me, this was the most painful aspect about Gary's disappearance. Children bring all loss back on themselves. Even if their pet hamster dies, it's their fault. (They didn't give the animal the correct food; they left the cage in a draft). A simple question – "Why did Daddy go?" – elicits an inadequate reply of, "Don't know." Children want a certain parent, not a floundering one.

In time, you will conclude that to walk out of a life without telling your nearest and dearest where you are going is an unutterably selfish action. It is the action of a coward.

You will grow to hate the man whom you once loved. This is only natural. If you truly loved him, you will now truly hate him. This is a sad conclusion to an altogether excruciating journey, since it denigrates the very love that you held dear. You will come to feel that you never really felt any love at all.

Lovelessness leaves you feeling empty, hollow and vacuous. I am not called Claire, which in French means thin, pale and transparent, for nothing. Someone saw this emptiness coming. My mother named me whilst I was floating in the saline waters of her womb.

We went down to Cornwall for a holiday. It was to be a holiday to celebrate the year that we had just spent. When we were planning the break he said that he wanted it to be just the two of us. He wanted to be alone with me. Maybe I put my foot down too firmly on the fact that the children had to come with us. Maybe I should have managed things so that it was just he and I. But Gary relented (damn it, his daughter was only one year old – didn't he know that we couldn't leave her?) and we set off at six in the morning.

The roads out west, to Hammersmith and beyond, were empty. The kids scoffed smelly cheese and onion crisps on the back seat of the car for breakfast. We cleared the empty Menai Bridge before rush hour. The journey down the finger of England which points out into the blue sea was easy. We didn't argue. Did we?

Six hours later, we saw an italicized Hotel Florence sign, spiked into a grassy bank, fronted by virulent pink busy Lizzies.

We turned off the road and swirled up the driveway, into a tunnel whose walls were composed of thick green foliage. Gravel spurted out from under the tyres – 'Pop Pop'. Dominic and Leah pressed their noses to the side windows but could see nothing except the waxy leaves of laurel bushes until, at the end of the road, the leaves stopped and a pink stuccoed building rose from a pale yellow forecourt like a giant dolls' house.

Hotel Florence had been built at the turn of the century. Despite elaborate ventilation systems (a new one had been installed with every decade that passed) it smelt of roast dinners and chips. It had one foot standing in the 1950s (a rotating entrance door with brass handles, a gold and scarlet printed carpet) and the other foot firmly positioned in the 1980s (it offered a video in every room, an answering machine service, a health club and so on). At night, an outdoor pool glimmered like a green topaz against a bed of navy blue velvet. Indoors, a smaller pool, designed for lazy adults, had a jacuzzi sunk into its shallows. There was also an oak-panelled games' room with a full-size pool table, darts' board, an indoor badminton court and three table-tennis tables. Outside there was a croquet lawn. I can still hear the clip clop of wooden mallets.

At the reception a young girl, straight brown hair divided by two gold kirby grips sat behind a mahogany desk, before a wall of keys. One of us signed into the leather-backed visitors' book. The girl twisted to fetch a key down from one of the hooks. She pressed a knob on the wall beside her. A ferociously loud buzz rang out over the silent foyer. Next a young lad appeared, whose trouser legs were several inches too long and which draped over the tongue of his shoes.

"Take them up, can you?" The boy nodded, smiled at us, and picked up the two heaviest suitcases. He pressed for the lift to come. There was a rattle as the elevator dropped a couple of floors, followed by a clank as the cage jumped to a halt. The boy slid open the criss cross bars. We all went inside. The bars zigzagged back across. We shot upwards. Leah clung onto Gary's legs.

With its colossal bed, a soft ivory coloured carpet, a huge TV screen, a long wrought-iron balcony with sea views and a bank of French windows, our suite was the hotel's premiere accommodation. Two doors led off from the main room – one into Dom and Leah's room, the other into a gold-tapped, marble-tiled bathroom.

The bed was a four-poster, ebony columns carved into barley sugar twists and a canopy from which fell white gauze drapes. Lying on the bed, with the curtains pulled across and billowing in the wind, one felt disconnected from anything that was going on beyond its edges. It was a room within a room, a world within a world.

(Obsession over minutiae is a common by-product of the grieving process. Later I obsessed about this bed. I wanted to discover its origins. It must have been an ancestral bed, in which generations of a family had been conceived, born, and died. My hunch was correct: I was told that it had come from the local manor house which had been left to the National Trust in the late 1950's. Rumour had it that the bed had given rest to Elizabeth I and later, to James II. I enquired as to why the National Trust hadn't kept such an historic piece of furniture and the answer was that it had not been theirs to keep. Sir James Harold might have left the Estate to the National Trust, yet he had singled out the bed to leave to his son, Charles. In time Charles fell out with the Trust whom he saw to be defilers of his family's heritage. When Charles died, he deliberately snubbed the Trust. He left the bed to the National Trust's arch-rivals, the hotel chain that owned the Hotel Florence, desecrators of the headland).

The hotel was situated on the top of a cliff top, two miles out of Clovelly. Access to the village was denied to motor vehicles. On the first day of our holiday we parked the car in a shadeless field that a local farmer had rented out as a car park for the summer season. We walked down into the village.

From eight in the morning until seven at night, Clovelly's lanes were packed with sightseers. Its cobbled alleyways were thick with families trying to patch up their differences by licking away at Cornish ice cream cones, and with elderly American visitors, limbs rendered even more rheumatic by the passivity of coach tourism, who struggled out of the buses and moved towards the water. All paths led down – down four hundred feet to the small harbour whose protecting wall arched in a curve like an arm embracing the shoreline. The thick harbour wall had two levels to it – an upper and a lower walkway. The lower dropped down into the inky, oil filmed harbour water, the upper ramparts sliced straight into the sea.

The harbour was used mainly by pleasure boats. There were several yachts docked in its waters, their tanned owners messing around on deck, their Golden Labradors sunning themselves on the harbour wall. At low tide the boats flopped onto their sides like cast-off toys and the harbour bed revealed various detritus – broken bottles, milk cartons, plastic packaging, tampons, and nappies. At high tide the boats sprung upright. They bobbed and danced and jiggled and the dark glint of the harbour's still waters contrasted against the white spume and aquamarine blues of the sea beyond.

We ate lunch – fish and chips in a pub on the harbour front. Gary stuffed a matchbox under the white plastic table leg to stop it from wobbling. Dominic kept kicking at the table, probably unintentionally, irritating Gary.

We went back to the hotel. Dominic and Leah were over-excited and overtired. Gary couldn't relax. He wasn't able to read a paper. He swam. He walked. He played table tennis with Dom. He swam again. "Relax!" "Slow down!" He replied that it always takes a few days to settle into a holiday, and that anyway, surely I should know that he was a man restless by nature, always on the move.

The first night we arranged for babysitters – one for Dom, another for Leah. The girl who came to mind Leah had an easy job. All she had to do was watch TV and get paid for it whilst Leah slept. Dominic's girl took him out to the pool. We saw her sitting on the white diving board, dangling her feet in the bright water, thinking about her boyfriend, whilst Dominic swam and the sub-aqueous lights illuminated his skin blue white.

In the hotel restaurant, at a table draped in a starched pink tablecloth, we ate what was to be our last supper. We slid our tongues into the yolky frilly mouths of mussels, sweet with the amniotic juices of the sea. The hard, shiny tendrils of squid skidded across the plate, in garlic and oil, away from our forks. We ate sea bass with a flaking flesh so white that it turned the white plate grey, and we soaked up all these juices and myriad textures with a quilt of soft steamed rice – a dish so simple, and so untrammeled that when we requested it the waiter, whose English was poor, thought that he couldn't possibly be hearing us correctly, and called over the maitre d' to verify his translation.

After dinner we wandered down to the beach. It was a warm evening. A full moon threw a broad silver beam over the water. We walked from one side of the bay to the other. We found a flat rock and sat on it until it the wind got up and it became too cold to stay still any longer. The tide had come in faster than we had realized. Our rock was surrounded by deep water. We hitched up our trouser legs and skirts to wade through the knee-high water towards the dry sand.

Six hours later, on the last Monday in August, I woke. The bed was empty beside me. I called out Gary's name quietly, so as not to disturb the baby or Dom. No reply: Gary must have gone over to the pool for a swim before anyone was awake.

The children got up. Dominic hurried out onto the balcony

to check out the bright blue sky. He asked where Gary was. "Don't know," I replied, as if I didn't care one jot. There were jobs to be done, and part of why we were here was for these jobs to be shared. Gary was ducking out of the nappy- bottle- getting-dressed routine and we hadn't even been here a day.

I dressed Leah. I yelled at Dom to turn off the TV, I told him to get fucking dressed, to do so fast.

We went down to breakfast. It was eight thirty.

"Just the three?" the headwaiter asked, and we were led to a window table.

"Where's Gary?" Dom asked a second time, trailing the claw of a jam-laden croissant through milky hot chocolate. The chocolate dripped, splashing several brown circles over the tablecloth. "Don't do that!" I hissed. "I don't know. I'm not sure."

Dom rolled his eyes, shuffled back into his chair. "So-rry. Only asking." An Algerian waiter, who had given him a stick of peppermint-green rock the day before, hovered a yard or so away, ready to take away our plates and bring on the full English breakfasts. The waiter sniffed the tension around us. He didn't take his black olive eyes off us.

"Ask him. He might know, Mum," Dominic suggested.

When the waiter came over, I asked whether he had seen Mr. Blue. He hadn't. The food was delivered. Dominic ate in silence, munching through the eggs, sausages, tomatoes and mushrooms. I toyed with scrambled eggs, pushing the yellow rubber from one side of the plate to the other. Dom asked again, this time plaintively, "Where is he, Mum?"

I wasn't angry any longer. I was worried.

"At the pool, maybe. Gone for a walk."

"And forgotten breakfast?"

Gary never missed breakfast.

"Maybe he's gone for a drive? Maybe the hotel hadn't got the paper that he wanted. Maybe he needed to go to the bank."

None of these ideas seemed likely – they might just do for now. They didn't do – not for Dominic who replied, "But where to? Without us? He wouldn't do that. We're on holiday."

After breakfast, we took a detour through the car park. The car was parked in the corner of the yard, exactly where we had left it the day before. I put my hand on its bonnet; the engine was cool. Dom kicked some grains of gravel at the wheel hubs of neighbouring silver, four-wheel-drive.

"So. What do we do now? He's gone nowhere, Mum."

"Fuck him for leading us on a wild goose chase. We'll carry on as normal. We'll go down to the pool. He'll find us there," I snorted.

"Don't swear."

Back in the hotel room I checked for Gary's wallet. I discovered that he had left in the same clothes that he had worn yesterday, that he had taken his wallet, and his keys. The keys weren't such a big deal: I had my house keys on me, and my car keys. But the money might be significant. Maybe he had gone to buy something, maybe not.

Half an hour later, we trailed out of the hotel and made our way across the lawn. Dom ducked in and out of the sprinklers and darted behind the rhododendron bushes, leaping out to scare us. Leah cried. Once she had begun to cry, everything bothered her. The sun shone too bright in her eyes. Dom was too noisy. She hated the chalky sun block that I had spread over her skin. She tried to suck it off and couldn't. Her buggy's wheels jammed in the soft grass and her tiny, soft body shot forward. The safety harness cut into her shoulders. I swore. She bellowed. I yanked her out of the buggy, held her, and rocked her. She dribbled over my clean black T-shirt. The buggy, now unbalanced, capsized. I pulled it upright and pushed it forwards with my free arm. Leah sobbed in my other arm. Dom raced off ahead, out of sight.

At the pool, I could tell within seconds that Gary was not there. I stood beside the deep end, scanning every sun lounger for Gary or for his possessions. All through breakfast, all through the standing in the car park, all through the getting ready in the bedroom, I had held out on Gary being here. I had told myself that he would be.

Things must carry on as normal, until – until such a time that they couldn't. Until such a time that it was obvious that things were not normal – which would be when? At what stage would I have to admit to the fact that my husband might be missing? Not now – not so early as two hours after his disappearance. After five hours? Six hours?

Leah and I walked round the poolside, looking for a vacant sun-lounger. An uncushioned plastic one was still free. I put my bags down on it. Next I tried to put up the sun umbrella. Dominic ran up to me.

"He's not here, is he?"

The umbrella shot down its stalk and bounced up on my thumbnail.

"YOWCH!"

"Where is he?"

"God only knows, Dom. Can't you help?"

He grabbed the white metal pole and held it upright.

"You're not doing it right, Mum. You've got to press that."

He pointed to a catch on the side of the pole, and pressed it. It was a safety catch. The umbrella unfurled gracefully.

I flopped down on the lounger. One of the bags fell onto the ground. A beaker rolled under the next-door neighbour's chair. The seat's occupant, an elderly American lady, handed it back to me and smiled.

"He must have gone for a very long walk," Dom said.

"Where's Mickey? Can you see him?"

Mickey was one of Dom's new found friends. On the other side of the pool I could make out the supine, oiled figures of his parents. I needed Mickey now.

"I said he must have gone for a very long walk, Mum. Didn't you hear?"

A thin, tall blond boy ran down from the hotel's hire office towards the pool, carrying a large inflatable banana. Dom raced towards him, waving. The boys began to play in and out of the water, on and off the lilo.

Leah began to cry. I hitched up my T-shirt and grappled with the straps of my swimming costume underneath it to feed her. The American woman's husband focused on his newspaper. I checked my watch. Ten-thirty. Leah's eyes began to close. Her head lolled back.

She would sleep for a couple of hours. I was grounded until she woke. I closed my eyes.

Had he gone for a walk, as Dom had suggested? A walk seemed unlikely. Anything solitary seemed unlikely. Gary wouldn't want to go for a walk on his own. He'd want to do it with me, or with Dominic. Had he had an accident? Wasn't there something about heart disease running in his family? Maybe he was lying dead in a field, flies buzzing around him. Hadn't I better tell the police now? Leah rolled over. The night before she had slept badly. I didn't want to wake her. Dominic was playing.

Very soon I would look up and I would see the man who had slept beside me last night as he had done the night and night and night to infinity before, with whom I had born a child, to whom I was married, stride over the green grass towards me, about to deliver an excuse for his absence that was airtight. A second voice cut into my head easily, like a hot blade against cold butter, with an insistent request to walk the cliff paths. I battled that voice off. To wander the thread-like cliff paths in a lone quest with two kids would be a stupid thing to do. Besides which, if Gary had fallen, then chances were that someone else would have found him by now.

Stay here at the pool, I told myself. Relax. This is your holiday too.

I replayed details from the night before. Whilst walking the beach, the sand crunching under our feet, he had said that we had done too much driving; he wanted to spend the next day at the hotel. I moved further back in time. I ransacked the last few days in London, searching words, gestures and actions for clues. I couldn't find anything that was in any way unusual. Between us, everything had seemed normal. Better than normal. Above average. Way above average. For the past month I had felt idyllically happy. Little had cut into that happiness. We had been having one of those rare smooth sweeps through life, one of those easy runs that life serves up say two or three times a decade. We were having an easy run.

An hour passed. It was almost lunchtime. Dom bounded up.
"Giv'us some money, Mum. I'm hungry."
Mickey was standing beside him, grinning.
"I want a sandwich. Please..."
"What about you, Mickey?"
"He's got some."
I pulled my purse out of one of the bags. A fiver stuck out of the credit card section. Dom made a grab. Mickey eyed me suspiciously.
"Bring back the change."
"Where's his dad?" Mickey asked.
"Yeah, where is he, Mum?"
"No sign yet," I replied.
"Weird, man," Dom replied. "Come on!" He pulled at Mickey's T-shirt. They ran off up the green hill towards the hotel.

Leah woke. I left Dominic and Mickey eating their snacks. I carried Leah up to the hotel. I went straight up to our room. The corridor was silent, so silent that it looked as if I was the first that day to walk down it. I unlocked the door, and struggling with the baby, a bag, the key, walked into the bedroom. The beds had been made. The wastepaper bins were empty. Nothing else had altered. I slammed the door shut, ran up the silent corridor, and ran down the staircase to the bar. Two men were sitting on bar stools, talking to the barman. They twisted round as I entered. I was half dressed – wearing my swimming costume with shorts. They were dressed in the uniform of golfers – soft shoes, polo shirts.

"Looking for someone, love?" one said. He must have been in his early sixties. At a time when his hair should have been thinning, or gray, he had a thick, sandy coloured thatch.

"My husband." I paused, realizing that more was needed. "He's tall, dark."

"And handsome, I suppose," the sandy-haired one quipped. His friend laughed. The bartender kept a straight, serious face.

"He's not been here," he said. "Only these two gentlemen here. Oh – and a family earlier."

I tried reception. I was stretching out to press the buzzer when the manager, wearing a courtelle maroon jacket, slunk out of a side door.

"How can I help you, Madam?"

His voice was a soothing voice, a tone trained to eliminate stress.

"I've lost my husband. I don't know where he is. Has he left a message? Has he phoned in?"

He checked the message book. He shook his head.

"No, Madam – no message."

"What should I do? What do you think I should do? He didn't say that he was going anywhere. We've only just begun the holiday. We only arrived yesterday..."

The hotel manager stood still. When he spoke, he spoke slowly.

"Madam, I'd wait until evening. Evening is only a couple of hours' away. If he hasn't turned up by then, you might consider informing the police."

My thoughts, unspoken, ran something like this. Question – and if he had fallen off a cliff into the sea? Answer – he would be dead. Question – and if he was lying somewhere after having had a heart attack? Answer – he would probably be dead too. Question – and if I phoned the police now? Answer – I would be setting a seal on Gary's absence, writing the word 'end' in indelible black ink, admitting that he was missing before I was ready to admit to it to myself. Therefore, though my passivity seems strange even to myself, I did what the manager suggested. I went back down to the pool.

I devoted myself to Leah. I played with her, on and on and on. I kept busy. Only sometimes – whilst running to fetch the ball, or in between reading the paragraphs of a story – my thoughts would be elsewhere.

By five o'clock the pool was in full shade. Most of the families around us were packing up to go in for high tea. Mickey's mum came over. She was a tall, handsome woman, with a gold bangle wedged half way up her forearm, a sarong twisted tight around her waist, and blonde hair twisted up in a bun. We had nodded to one another across the water but I hadn't spoken to her since morning.

"You on your own today?"

Dominic must have said something. Her husband was standing on the other side of the pool, bags packed, shoulders drooping, waiting to go.

"Yes," I replied.

"Is there anything we can do? If there is, you know our room number? Dom does. He'll know where to find us."

I gave her an unassertive nod – the type that asks questions, and that allows inroads. She followed with, "Can I help?"

Her question burst me into tears. In some way she gestured to her husband who read his wife's private code and started kicking a football around with the boys. She put her arm around me. She listened to my story, which was simply that Gary had been gone all day. She said that she thought I should go to the police. She beckoned over her husband, again in gestures that a stranger might miss, told him the tale and asked what he thought. He replied in an American accent.

"The cops. I think you'd better give them a call. Let's go up to the hotel."

Mickey's mum helped to stuff our belongings into our bags. The dad shook my hand and said his name was Ian. His wife was called Sarah.

Ian turned to the boys. "Let's fix some tea for you guys." Dom was shivering, cold and hungry. I gave him a towel to wrap around himself and then we all plodded back up the hill. Dominic and I fell a few paces behind Mickey and his parents.

"Where is he Mum? What's happened? Did you two have a row?"

"No, we didn't argue. I really don't know where he is, Dominic. I'm telling you all that I know."

"He might have drowned."

We reached the hotel's rear entrance. From here we could walk through the conservatory and into the restaurant. Sarah said that she would take the children in for tea. I could go with her husband and phone the police. The boys' ears pricked up at the word 'police'. Mickey wanted to know more. His dad told him that he would explain later. Dominic wanted to come with me. I had to make this phone call childless. I told him to go with Sarah. Leah clung to me. Sarah took her from me assertively, and walked off into the dining room.

Ian accompanied me to the reception where he asked to make a private call. The manager recognized me and unlocked his office. I swear that I could still hear Leah crying. I tried not to hear her. I tried to block out even the thought of her crying. I sat at a large desk and dialled 999.

An officer took my name and then a few details.

"We'll come over in the morning. Round ten. OK?"

"Don't you need to do something sooner?"

"No, Madam. Morning will be fine."

I put down the phone. Ian said he thought it was ridiculous, leaving something as big as this until morning. He dragged the phone across the desk and jabbed 999 himself.

"This might be an emergency. What do you mean, waiting until tomorrow?"

The police knew how to handle men like this, or women, since Ian was silent for a long time, listened, and even nodded at what was being said. Underneath my T-shirt, my swimming costume felt damp and cold. It stuck to my back like a cold flannel. Leah had stopped crying. She was too young to leave with strangers, even for just a few minutes. I was desperate to get back to her.

As we left the office, the hotel manager asked us what was going to happen.

"Nothing till morning," Ian replied.

CLARE GEORGE

Extract from **The Cloud Chamber**

CHAPTER ONE

The news of Nunn May's arrest has disturbed me considerably.

I don't know why I am worrying at it so much, when there is so much else to be thinking of – the responsibilities of my new job, our perpetual house moves, the hundred concerns touching the lives of the children. But each day as I walk to the station it comes back to me, and ruffles my calm as I attempt to read the newspaper or prepare my mind for the work of the day ahead.

It has taken a while for my routine to settle back into its old familiarity since our return to London. During the war, University College was evacuated, and scattered all over the country: my own department, the science faculty, went to Bangor in North Wales, and others ended up in Swansea, Cambridge and Leatherhead. We came back in dribs and drabs during 1944, when the risk of bombing was thought to have subsided. In fact we arrived just in time for the summer examinations to be interrupted by the V2 rockets. I heard the boom and felt the shake of the floor beneath my feet when one of them exploded half a mile away, as I began a lecture addressed to an almost empty theatre. In those first days back in the city, the corridors and common rooms were still half-deserted. If I chanced across any of my fellow staff, we would inevitably shake hands in enthusiastic reunion, and insist on meeting for a coffee. Sometimes we even managed to find ourselves some students to teach.

Things were so ramshackle in Bangor – it really was the barest shreds of an institution, and we cobbled things together, teaching whatever subject was needed at the time. Now peace really is with us, and the lecture theatres have filled. We are starting to get to grips with shaping the new life of the university, and I have a whole range of things to sort out. All the courses need to be rewritten, particularly modern physics. Since my appointment to the post of Reader at the beginning of the year, I have been embroiled in endless committees debating the future of the faculty. And now that the scientific community as a whole seems to have pulled itself back together and started to get into gear, a flood of new papers is pouring across my desk. If I do not catch up on my reading soon, the university will have to subject me to taxidermy and stick me in a glass case in the entrance hall alongside Jeremy Bentham, on display as a relic from the past.

All of this was in my mind as I stopped outside the station one morning a month ago and purchased a newspaper from the stall.

"Morning, Dr Duncanson," said Jim, and passed me my copy of *The Times*. We got to know one another soon after I first moved to Watford. Jim was demobbed from the Navy, and on his return to his former patch was determined to recognize all his customers from the old days. He counted me among them, mistaking me for a school teacher he once knew, even though I had never been in Watford before. Once I had explained what I actually did for a living he was most interested. He had, he told me, made very good friends with a number of engineers on his ship, and so every now and again I divert him with stories about the latest developments in physics before boarding my train.

"Good morning, Jim," I replied quite calmly. It was not until money had changed hands that I looked down at the paper, and saw the name.

"Everything all right?" asked Jim, for I must still have been standing there in the same position for several seconds.

I have often noticed that if a thing crops up randomly on one day, it has a tendency to keep popping up again. It was so with Nunn May, for I had seen the man myself just a matter of weeks before, after a gap of more than a decade.

"How very odd," I said, partly in reply to the vendor, and partly to myself.

"Terrible business," agreed Jim, following the line of my sight to the headline. "Beggars belief. They should all be hanged, no questions asked."

It was then that I realized that Nunn May's first and second re-appearances might not be unrelated. I looked up at Jim in alarm. "Good heavens," I said, and then became aware of how oddly I was acting, and took my leave.

His visit had been entirely unexpected. He turned up at my office one lunchtime, with no warning, and when I opened the door to him I recognized him immediately.

"Nunn May! How good to see you!" I said, though I was rather perplexed, and unsure of what to do with him. "Do come in and take a seat. I thought you went to Montreal?"

The academic grapevine has the wonderful capacity to keep

one informed of the every movement of former colleagues. Nunn May and I worked together on the same experiments for a year in Cambridge, while we were both researching our Ph.D. theses. We parted company when I left for London in 1934, but I have always kept a keen eye on the further adventures of the men I worked with there. Over the last decade, I have noticed a distinct trickle of physicists across the Atlantic, which hastened into a flood once the world was at war. Of course the state of British universities in wartime was barely functional, and the whole of Europe was occupied by a hostile force so it was not so very surprising. I have wondered once or twice recently whether any of them would care to return now that it is all over. And here in front of me was the evidence that at least one of them had.

He was, and is, a wiry spider of a man. In his youth he had an air of concentration that bordered on the monastic, and he looked as if he might drift away on a gossamer thread at the puff of the slightest breeze. Now, more than a decade later, wrinkles had given his thin face a weight and dignity it had lacked, and the focus of his gaze had drawn inwards from infinity to something hard and real in the here and now.

"I did go to Montreal," said Nunn May, "and now I've returned. I'm due to take up a position as Reader at King's College – it will be announced any day – and so we will be University of London colleagues. When I found out you were just down the road, I thought I would drop in. Congratulations, by the way, on your new post."

"Thank you," I said. "It's good to have you back in England. Did you enjoy your stay in Canada?"

He looked away from me for a second. "Hard work," he said. "My goodness, it's strange to be back. I tried to imagine what it might be like after all the bombing before I returned, but you just can't anticipate these things. Some places seem to be utterly unaffected, don't they? And then one turns a corner and half the street is gone. They seem to be doing a good job of the tidying up, though."

I thought about it, and tried to remember my own feelings on coming back to London. In Bangor we had a large house with a lovely garden where the children could play, and a view over the Menai Straits. We spent the weekends tramping in the mountains. It was good to get back and find ourselves a little house to buy in Watford, and to return to my office and all my books and resume business as usual, but I could barely believe the city we found when we got here. Everyone was so thin, and so pale. I suppose they were malnourished. It was the case in

Wales too, but there is something else in London. It was only when I was told the stories – of nights spent waiting hour after hour for the bombs to pick out a neighbour's house rather than one's own – that I realized that it was not just the streets that were scarred.

"I think the people have been through a great deal," I replied.

How exactly did the conversation go after that? Since I read the news, I have racked my brain trying to remember. He sat perched on the edge of the armchair in my office and his talk wandered from this to that. I asked after old friends, particularly John Cockcroft, who was with us in Cambridge and for whom Nunn May worked in Montreal. But he did not have much to say about Cockcroft, nor of what they did together. War work, he said. I did not think much of it at the time. Everyone speaks of their war work, and they are usually as vague about it as Nunn May was. They are keen to let you know they made a contribution, but it is all too tiring and dull now for elaboration.

I think he must have asked me about my own efforts. This is a question which sometimes leads to awkwardness, for I was a registered conscientious objector and my duties were restricted to a series of chaotic stretcher-bearing exercises at the local hospital. Nunn May, however, did not seem particularly surprised by this information. Somehow the conversation kept leading back to a single topic, on which he seemed fixated.

"Do you know much about the Canadian Mounties?" he demanded.

I stared at him. "No," I admitted, for my ignorance was complete, expect for being in possession of a mental image of a man wearing a red coat, white jodhpurs and a broad-brimmed beige hat, sitting on a horse.

"Remarkable organisation," he said, "quite remarkable."

"Really?"

"They have a Secret Service division, and its powers are extraordinary, if you consider that Canada is merely a Dominion, and so very far from the centre of things."

I felt my neck prickle, as it tends to in reaction to statements such as this. I am myself what might be termed by Nunn May a Colonial, and I dislike the bad press we inevitably receive. But he clearly did not notice, or did not think it important, and continued:

"I had a friend who was a Frenchman. Throughout our time in Montreal he was naturally very concerned about his family in Paris. As soon as the city was liberated, he went straight back to visit his relatives. After all the worry – virtually no information since Dunkirk, not even any news of whether they were alive or dead – it's only natural. Or at least that would be the conclusion of any rational being."

His tone required agreement, and so I made sympathetic noises and gestures.

"Not so for the Mounties. It seems they got on the plane with him and followed his every move. As soon as he had returned to Canada, they got hold of him and told him every detail of his stay in France. They told him which streets he'd walked down, which coffee bars he visited – the whole thing, day by day. Don't you think that's incredible? That they should be interested, for a start."

I agreed that this was indeed remarkable. I could not really believe that a mounted police force would be responsible for the surveillance of a scientist, and for a moment doubted his sanity.

"I wouldn't be surprised," he said, "if they were watching me too. In fact, it wouldn't be the slightest surprise to me if they were aware of my visit to you right now."

I was assailed by the image of the door flying open and uniformed men galloping in on horseback.

"Well," I said, "I don't suppose they would find very much here to interest them."

"But that's the thing, it seems there's nothing which escapes the interest of the Canadian Mountie. He would be sure to take down the contents even of your biscuit tin." And so he continued, for some considerable time, until my mind drifted from his paranoid ravings and I started to worry about my supervisions, and the lecture series I'd planned to make a start on preparing. I think I particularly remember that part of the conversation because it made me feel uncomfortable, but then everything about the man was disconcerting. The way he wouldn't sit down properly, and the manner in which his thoughts jumped all over the place.

There is one other thing I remember him saying. I was commenting on the eerie silence which had subsumed many areas of physics over the past years. I showed him the pile of journals on my desk. "I'm having a time of it trying to catch up," I said, "but it's such a relief things are getting back to normal, don't you think?"

"Back to normal?" said Nunn May. "Do you really think things will ever get back to normal in physics again?"

I looked at him in surprise.

"By normality, I suppose you mean the way things were in Cambridge?" he said.

"Well – " As Cambridge was what we had in common, it seemed as good an example as any. "I suppose I do. I mean, things have been so secretive. A colleague of mine's a geographer, and the committees wouldn't let him publish a thing during the war in case it helped the Germans mount an invasion. It was only about rock formations, and that sort of stuff. Now, everything he's written in the last six years is all coming out at once."

Nunn May was not interested in rock formations. "And you suppose that everything will go back to being just like those colloquia we used to have at the Cavendish?" he challenged me. I smiled involuntarily. I was just a research student in Cambridge, and these occasions, at which the leading physicists of the day debated the finer points of quantum theory, were capable of inspiring terror. "I remember making a terrible bodge of presenting that Heisenberg paper," I admitted.

"Well, exactly. That Heisenberg paper. You do know that it was Heisenberg who led the German atomic bomb project, don't you?"

Of course I did. It was not a thought on which I liked to dwell. Back when Nunn May and I were students, Heisenberg visited Cambridge from time to time. I sat next to him at a lunch party once and found him very pleasant company.

"Do you remember how we all used to get together," said Nunn May, "in that funny little room in the Attic, and Heisenberg told Chadwick exactly what he was up to?" He was getting excited. "And Chadwick told Bohr, and Bohr told Kapitza, and Kapitza told Curie. And it didn't matter in the least that one man was a German, and another English, and another Russian, because science was all that mattered. Wasn't it?"

It was indeed. I wanted to say, and it does still, but then I thought of my wife and my three children.

"I have to break it to you," Nunn May told me, "but those days are gone for ever, old boy."

He said it with such an air of certainty – an arrogance, almost, that he was wiser in these matters than I. I considered feeling a little affronted, for I was senior to him in Cambridge. But I decided I knew nothing of what had prompted those words. Perhaps he had lost friends or relatives in the fighting, and was feeling bitter towards all mankind, as I had in the dark days after the death of Alan, my youngest brother.

"Well, obviously," I said, "the war has changed many things. But we must have faith in the future. I'm sure it can't be too long before we can start to build trust in our fellow human beings again."

And at that moment I could almost feel the chill from his skin, as when a man walks from the cold air into a warm room and brings the frostiness of the outside world with him. I examined his face and thought perhaps he was more changed than I had originally thought. He was very pale. There were shadows under his eyes.

"No," he said, quietly and very surely. The pompousness had gone and was replaced by simple weariness. "Duncanson, I've seen those men. I've seen what the war has done to them. Things will never be the same again. I would to God believe that you are right, but I cannot."

And then I think he enquired after my family, and I updated him on the various children we had produced since I last saw him, and somehow the talk got back to the Mounties once again.

Three weeks later, there was no mention of the Mounties in the newspaper article which reported his arrest. Instead, it told me exactly what he and Cockcroft worked on during the war. As I read it, I felt my stomach lurch. The Montreal laboratory was an outpost of the Manhattan Project. The men who worked there were amongst several hundred scientists scattered across the North American continent, pursuing the development of a weapon capable of ending the war. Nunn May was privy to the project's deepest secrets. On the day of the Nagasaki bomb, he stole a platinum foil coated with a fissionable uranium isotope, and had it flown directly to Moscow.

The authorities discovered his treachery when a young Russian cipher clerk named Gouzenko defected from the Soviet embassy in Ottawa with one hundred secret documents from the military attaché's office stuffed inside his shirt. They included details of everything Nunn May had revealed to them about the development of the atomic bomb.

Why did he come to visit me? We worked together every day for a time, but we were never great friends. He was never the sort to drop in on one for tea, so why would he do so now? Was he trying to obtain information from me? If he was, then he must have gone away disappointed. Was he trying to tell me something? His failure to perform any such mission was absolute.

On the day his arrest was reported, I took the newspaper home with me to show to my wife, but she had already heard the news on the BBC, and was as astonished as I.

"I never met the man," she said – my time in Cambridge with Nunn May was before our marriage – "but I do seem to remember you mentioning him once or twice. He was a communist even then, wasn't he?"

He was indeed, as many were. I always seemed to be getting mixed up with communists for one reason or another, and found it troublesome. They would persist in trying to enlist me. When I finished my Ph.D. and had to find myself a job, I seriously considered emigrating to Russia and finding myself a job in a research institute out there, as I was told that there was an urgent need for Christian witness under the harsh regime. In retrospect, it is a decision I am very glad not to have taken.

"What's a communist?" demanded our son Peter, for the term had been bandied around all day. We did our best to explain it to him without undue political bias. He seemed intrigued by the idea, and I suppose the idea of equality of all possessions is attractive to a ten-year-old, who owns nothing. "Does that mean everything would belong to me, as well?" he said hopefully, and we said that in so far as he was represented by the state, we supposed in theory it would, but that in practice it did not seem to have worked out that way. I trust we have not sown the seeds of anything which might later prove problematic.

We decided that I could probably expect a visit from MI5 over the next few weeks, or perhaps even, if their vigilance was as great as Nunn May supposed, from the Canadian Mounties. Nothing has materialized as yet.

"Do you think you should contact the police?" my wife suggested. I have thought about it, but have not done so. I can't believe his visit to me had any sinister motive. I can only conclude that he really did come to renew an old acquaintance and congratulate me on my promotion. The Secret Services would hardly be interested in such an odd conversation, and anyway the man has been caught red-handed. I have no desire to add to his troubles. It is hard not to hate him for his actions, but what can one really know of what leads a man to do such a thing, or what mental tortures he has suffered along the way?

I sit now at the window of my office and look down at Gordon Street below. A few houses along, the flat my wife and I rented just after our marriage is occupied by a family whose home has been destroyed. The authorities contacted us a few weeks back in their attempt to get them out. Instead we found some clothes and blankets and visited them under a pledge of secrecy. We saw a scene of squalor and misery rare even in these days. A bus conductor, two women, and three schoolchildren were camping out in a large dilapidated room without light, water, or fuel for a fire. Their sullen and dirty faces were swollen with colds. All the furniture they had was an orange-box scraped dry of all but coke-dust, two saucepans and an unmade bed, a spirit stove on which bacon was frying, and a green teapot shaped like a racing car on a strip of newspaper many times ringed. It was very hard to believe that it was the same place we discovered together, fresh from our wedding, my wife rushing around the place carrying all her possessions and making a dozen happy decisions about the way we would live.

I look at the armchair on whose arm Nunn May sat, and I feel a shiver run through me. What has he done? What, for that matter, have any of us done, these last years, struggling through the darkness, trying to do the right thing? It is the future which matters now, and with God's help we must make the best of it we can. But when I look at that chair, all I can think of is the past.

The above is the first chapter of The Cloud Chamber, *a novel about nuclear physics and pacifism set in the 1930s and 1940s, based on the life of the author's grandfather, Dr W. E. Duncanson. Whilst it features real events and fictionalized versions of real people, the conversations are imagined.*

LEONIE GOMBRICH

Extract from **The Assumptionists Part III**

The roads around Harley Street are rich in chemist shops, their general shelves sparkling and glassy as the perfume counters in Liberty or Harvey Nicks, their pharmacy departments less restricted to the National Health White List than most chemists around the country. There is about them both a sense of clinical chic, of access to richer, rarer cures than the State will provide, and a whiff of ethical degeneracy, as if here are to be found under-the-counter contacts accessing chemicals with dubious safety records and one-kidneyed villagers in Turkey and Pakistan. Rachael was introduced to the district by one of the hospital doctors whose private practice was nearby. Soon she had been picked up on rota by three different pharmacies within less than half a mile and her behind-the-counter work had begun to outweigh the time she spent in hospital dispensaries. She welcomed the shift in emphasis from the acute to the chronic; she'd witnessed enough overdoses for the time being and she was happy to be surrounded by shampoos. Her own hair took on a better condition. It was while working at a chemist's in Wigmore Street that she happened to meet – to be intercepted by – Yvette.

She looks like the passing headache type, mused Rachael when she first saw Yvette cross the long, light-spangled shop from its big, glass doors towards the pharmacy counter – with that neat grey riding coat and those spanking black boots. So I'd think ibuprofen with codeine. But now I'll find it's Canesten or some anti-bacterial ear preparation. Or perhaps she's only stained a cream-coloured carpet. Rachael met Yvette's clear, purposeful gaze from six or seven paces away. It had been apparent from her first days behind the retail counter that it is not possible to predict a customer's chemical needs from their appearance, but Rachael could not make herself give up the game.

"Excuse me, are you the pharmacist?" Blonde Yvette with her metal twist of hair, fresh as a magazine page and even smelling like *Elle* or *Marie Claire*. "Have you got a moment? I've got an unusual request." She presented Rachael with a card. Yvette considered everything she did or thought to be unusual, and was making a career out of the fact that it was always comfortingly familiar to her peers. For more than two years she had been putting together television projects which, however tormented the subject matter, emerged as cosy as bedsocks and Night Nurse to the impressively overworked television executives who handed out contracts, and increasingly, to thousands of viewers across Britain. What was more, she had a habit of generously allowing employees and colleagues to be unusual by proxy. Her accessible smile was a constant invitation to the timid and the hide-bound to treat themselves to some brief but memorable moments in her orbit. Confident, cheerful, clean: Yvette was the sort of woman everyone looks for when they are desperate to find a new administrator, co-ordinator, nanny. People who had worked with her wanted to work with her again. Her nascent success, like her appearance, was heartening as a *Blind Date* love match. No one had a bad word to say about Yvette.

Rachael, however, was used to unusual requests of a different order. "How can I help?" she asked in a distinct but lowered voice. *YT Schemes Limited*, written on the card above *Yvette Turlington, Producer*, meant little to her, although the act of displaying it seemed designed to impress. In Rachael's experience, pumped-up advances often heralded somewhat dubious theories of treatment and disease. What disorder did this woman think she had, think she could be cured of, if only a drug might be found which was inaccessible enough? What scientific whimsy had she discovered on the internet with which to plague the local pharmacist?

Not Yvette. Her interest in the workings of the body stopped at the skin which is, after all, the traditional limit of beauty. "I'm a producer, you see. We're an independent company, working largely in television. I'm here because I'm developing a documentary series in which there's considerable interest at the BBC. What I'm after, initially, is just a half-hour meeting, perhaps, so I can explain a little more fully? It's a major, *major* series."

"About pharmacies?" Rachael was cautious. This was not her chemist shop. "You may want to speak to the proprietor, I think." She could not know that it was her own solemn presence and dark features which had caught the producer's eye; Yvette had come to woo.

"Not pharmacies, no, because what we're doing focuses on people, rather than organisations. We've been looking at modern women as a force in society, but not threatening. Strong. Still sexy. We'll be looking at mums, too, and women in traditional female rôles –"

Prostitutes? thought Rachael; almost simultaneously, she pictured her own tense, fussy mother, and blushed at her thought. Of course not!

" – but seen in a post-millennial light."

She looked at Yvette blankly, having missed the last phrase; but Rachael's gaze always seemed more penetrating than dumb.

She's just perfect, thought Yvette. So, so scientific. Only, maybe some glasses would be good. I'd love to see the hair down.

"What I want initially," Yvette leaned forward, brushing lozenges with the end of her coat-belt, "is just a brief chance to chat a little more with *you*. I'm interested in *your* rôle, *your* outlook, *your* career path and the choices you've made – Please!" She held up a calm hand, as if Rachael would leap the counter and charge at her. "Don't answer me now! I understand that you need to know much, *much* more about the concept, the circumstances, what any involvement means for *you*. And equally, I'm not here to make any commitment on our part until you and I have spoken further. You know the Susan Faludi book about the modern male?" Rachael shook her head, no. "*Major* book, loads of press. Doesn't matter. We're not answering that. We're not answering the men's movement *per se*. The point is, this isn't about a battle, about this or that. It's about interest, real interest in what women are doing *now*. Plus," Yvette smiled, "we're having *such* fun putting it together. Really brilliant women."

"Yes," said Rachael. There were two other customers in the shop. She could feel one hovering, a middle-aged lady with a ferocious regiment of gold buttons down her bosom; she thought she glimpsed a scrap of scrawled paper clutched in her hand. She wracked her brain. "I suppose pharmacy school was about seventy percent female – is that the sort of thing you're interested in?" Nobody mentioned it much, she thought, except that if we'd wanted to meet more boys we should have done metallurgy instead.

"Well, *perfect*," Yvette encouraged, "and I'm sure our fact-checkers would very much want to consult with you. But can *we* meet? Talk? Would you have a moment later today, perhaps? I'm very sorry to impose..."

"No, it's fine," said Rachael. "I'm just a little surprised. But I suppose I could be free by six, if that's any help."

"Oh, no, six is *splendid*." Yvette, triumphant, grasping the prize she'd never doubted. "Look, why don't you come to my office? It's literally five minutes away – I'm on my way there now – and we'll go on from there. Yes? But do let me have your number, too, just in case and sorry! I don't even know your name!" Rachael was wearing a name badge.

"It's Rachael Truman," and Rachael was glad to be able to hand her the pharmacy's own card, with the green cross embossed upon it.

"Great, Rachael. Six. Yvette." Yvette extended a cool hand over the counter, grasping Rachael's with a little laugh. "Pleasure to meet you."

"Well, you too," Rachael had to smile. "I'm sorry," she said, turning to the gold-rivetted lady, whose crisply sprayed hair quivered in a cunning swoop over the cotton wool pad affixed to her right eye. "How may I help you?"

Taking two steps backwards with an approving smile, Yvette made way for the progress of the Cyclops, and after pausing for a couple more moments at the door to watch the specialist in action, she left the shop. She waved goodbye between the trusses and the heart diagram as she passed in front of the tall windows, but Rachael was too occupied to see.

N. JOHNSON

Extract from **Buddy Meansville**

In July '69 Nixon helped Gunner Deutsche move to Fresno. Now I know not many people would be too happy about that, but in the opinion of Gunner Deutsche it beat going to Washington's Olympic Peninsula. You see, Washington's Olympic Peninsula is what you could call Tripwire Vet country and Gunner Deutsche is suspicious that so many Tripwire Vets go live there that it can no longer actually be Tripwire Vet country. Because a Tripwire Vet is a person who needs to be alone.

Gunner Deutsche has lived in America for about twenty years, and it was only last year that he left the country for a while. That's a long time to spend in one place. Now Gunnery Sergeant Jerry K. Deutsche is special, not just because he is a German, but because he is totally invisible. You really can't see him at all. It is rather as if somebody has come along with a big eraser and rubbed him out. Gunner Deutsche wasn't born invisible of course as that would be stupid. He turned that way when he was seven and in Germany along with lots of other people at the time, although Gunner Deutsche was the only one to go properly see-through. Everybody else just went a light transparent yellow.

Gunner Deutsche has never known when to stop even at the best of times.

When WWII ended and people got something other than potatoes, things went back to normal. All except Gunner Deutsche. He must have eaten one potato too many, because he never regained his colour, which is a pity because he often feels he makes people uncomfortable, especially as no one can tell if he's smiling or not.

So, Gunner Deutsche has been setting up a nice little place in Fresno for a couple of months now. He's got yard-sale furniture and a real live TV set on which he watches the *Mary*

Tyler Moore Show. He's also got a little photo of Nixon on his front wall and he refers to him as Dicky. People who see it get told, "Dicky got me out. He's a guy you can trust."

After the first month Gunner Deutsche's military money ran out and so he got a job translating manuscripts, which is good because it means that most days he doesn't have to leave the house. In fact he spends nearly all of his time working at his yard-sale desk.

On the right-hand corner of the desk is something that Gunner Deutsche reads everyday. Somebody has gone to a lot of effort to carve words into the polished wood desk, and it is written very badly because it had been so difficult to make a mark against the grain. Whoever had patiently gouged away at the surface must have written something terribly important for it to have warranted such an effort.

What it says is this,

Ralph Elliot Blows Goats

The distance between Gunner Deutsche's house and the local store is not as far as he would have liked. It takes about twenty minutes for him to walk it, and although it can get very hot in Fresno, for Gunner Deutsche that is not really an issue because he has spent the whole of last year 'very hot'. In fact he can't remember what it feels like to be anything else. He has heard that sometimes in the winter in Fresno there is a frost at night. This is something he is looking forward to immensely.

On this particular excursion Gunner Deutsche wishes to buy more polish for his yard-sale furniture however just outside the store is a large umbrella shading a neatly laid out stall. It is the kind of umbrella that is very good at making things cool, but would fail completely to keep you dry. In Fresno keeping dry is not really an issue. This is an attribute that Gunner Deutsche also fully appreciates.

Sitting at the stall is a group of neatly dressed ladies. They all want to be Jackie Kennedy even if it means having their husbands shot at, and nobody that enters or leaves the store is going to get past them. They are all wearing pin-on buttons with writing on them. Some of them are wearing two. Gunner Deutsche thinks that perhaps after last year he has some knowledge of how to get around people, but without distracting gunfire he finds himself at a loss. He tries just looking away, but to be honest when you're invisible nobody can ever tell what direction you're looking in and anyway, these are very determined ladies.

"Sir?" says one with three buttons. She must be the most dangerous. "Sir, would you help us in our campaign?"

"Sir, your support is needed."

"All we need is a signature and a small donation."

"Sir we're going to take this to Washington."

She has hardly noticed that although you can see Gunner's clothing, and baseball cap, you cannot see his face. She is busy watching out for his signature and his wallet.

Gunner Deutsche doesn't want to look. He says, "Look I ..."

But this lady is well trained, she's not about to let Nixon himself talk, even if it's in agreement.

"Sir if you were in Vietnam right now you'd want our help too."

"Whu ..."

"The boys need us, sir."

Gunner Deutsche looks down at her. Her three buttons display proudly the words,

POWs NEVER HAVE A NICE DAY

All over the stall there are pictures of very thin looking men with bored expressions.

Gunner Deutsche thinks the slogan **POWs NEVER HAVE A NICE DAY** is the most idiotic thing he has ever read. He thinks that if all of those ladies were wearing buttons saying **Ralph Elliot Blows Goats** then they would be making a more worthy statement. **POWs NEVER HAVE A NICE DAY** doesn't say anything at all.

"We're going to bring our boys home, sir."

And so Gunner Deutsche signs his name and leaves a dollar, and he is given a pin a little too forcibly and the ladies say, while looking out for their next victim,

"Thank-you for your contribution. Have a nice day, sir."

That is what they say, "Have a nice day, sir."

Not, "It's good to have you back, Jerry."

Gunner Deutsche's walk home consists of roads that are as far away from the fields of grape vines as possible. He doesn't like how green they are, or the way they hang, but there is something about their presence that makes him feel acclimatised. Sometimes the vines get so close to the road that Gunner has to run down the middle and pull his cap down real hard so he can't see so much. But a funny thing happens when he peers out from under the peak and runs. The shadow of the cap blocks half of his view and it bounces up and down in such a way that it is really similar visually to the way things look when you run under the blades of a Bell UH-1D. And Gunner Deutsche runs and runs and never makes it out from under that chopper. But this time he feels a little different. He feels like something is coming. Something is trying to find him, and it is coming.

And Gunner is right, something is coming. In fact, it has already arrived. It is waiting on his doorstep in a T-shirt saying,

WHEN I DIE BURY ME FACE DOWN SO THE WORLD CAN KISS MY *ASS*

and when it see's Gunner shape under the shirt, pants and baseball cap and the familiar absence of face it starts hollering a song that's not been sung for a few months.
   First the worst
   Second the best
   Third the one with the hairy chest
   Fourth the Goerring
   Fifth the Hess
   Sixth the golden prinnnceesssss

Gunner stops. He thinks about stripping and running through the undergrowth,
   but he has only done that once.
   but he has only done that once.

In the jungle you can't see wire amongst the foliage. That's what the Viet Cong counted on. Only once has Gunner Deutsche counted on it too.
   "GUNNER!"
   "GUN-NER, Heyyyyyyy. Man you're sexy in civvies."
   "Hello Reno."
   "Jeez, when I heard you were living in this dump I didn't know whether to shit or go blind, man."
   "Oh? Where did you hear…"
   "Come here man, come onnnn, give me a hug man. Tell me, why don't we kiss any more?"
   "Reno what are you doing here?"
   "Shit I knew you'd be happy to see me."
   "Uh…"
   "Are you gonna let me in?"
   Now Gunner really doesn't want to do that. His house is clean and Reno looks exactly the same way he did last time Gunner saw him, which was in the middle of the Nam jungle. Plus Reno has a very large camouflage bag over his left shoulder that makes Gunner rather nervous.
   "Heyyyy, Gunner, what's the matter, don't you think I'm worthwhile company?"

"Of course you're worthwhile," says Gunner, and no-one can argue about that, because Private Joseph R. Reno's life is worth an awful lot. It is worth at least two Sikorsky HH-53C's, an EC-121, an OV-10 Bronco, three Douglas A-1 Skyraiders, a Lockheed HC-103P Hercules and a converted Sikorsky CH-53. The amount of lives he is worth is at least 26, and the amount of money he is worth is over quarter of a million US dollars.

Imagine being worth all that.

But you see actually Reno is only worth what is frequently referred to as chicken shit. At least this is what Sergeant Balamonti called it when he found out that Private Joseph R Reno was only a marine and not a part of the Air Force at all.

See this is what an airman's life is worth,

Two Sikorsky HH-53C's, an EC-121, an OV-10 Bronco, three Douglas A-1 Skyraiders, a Lockheed HC-103P Hercules and a converted Sikorsky CH-53

And this is what a marine's life is worth,
Chicken shit.

What happened is this,

Private Reno was at a round-eye strip show. A crewman from an F-4 Phantom was also there and between them a fight broke out over who it was the round-eye stripper had just winked at. Well, Reno has a very good right hook and he had had considerably more Kentucky bourbon and so by the end of the night only Reno was fit to return to duty the next day. This would have been not particularly uncommon, if the air crewman had not been part of operation Igloo White. So when they saw the state of their unconscious bruised fellow crewman, the rest of the crew of the F-4 Phantom decided that because their mission was so important, Reno would take his place. Besides all he had to do was drop the ASDISs out of the plane. How hard could that be?

Well now, Reno did just fine at dropping the seismic intruder devices but unfortunately the navigator did better. He'd predicted almost exactly the whereabouts of a Viet Cong base. And F-4 Phantoms fall hard when hit with AAA fire. The plane nosedived and Reno squashed at the back was the only one to survive. The pilot perhaps would have made it, if one of the ASDISs shaped perfectly for penetrating the soft earth, had not pushed perfectly through the back of his soft neck.

The minute he was down, Reno heard a crackling. A nearby Rockwell International OV-10 Bronco aircraft was radioing through, it was saying that it was keeping an eye on Reno and that help was coming real soon. Within about 30 minutes Reno watched a Sikorsky HH-53C chopper taken out by the same AAA fire that got the F-4 Phantom, as it lowered a 250ft cable to pick him up. When the OV-10 Bronco got shot down too, the Air Force sent a Lockheed EC-121 Warning Star and two Douglas A-1 Skyraiders, the second Sikorsky HH-53C had come from a long way and so a Lockheed HC-130P Hercules was also sent to refuel it along with another Douglas A-1 Skyraider to protect it.

Well, so close was Reno to a North Vietnamese missile installation that what was not shot down by AAA fire was brought to earth by Soviet supplied SA-2 missiles. In one last desperate attempt to rescue what they thought was one of their own men, they sent in the middle of the night a converted Sikorsky CH-53. However by this time Reno was making his own way across the ground back to base and the chopper on landing at the F-4 wreckage was seized immediately by awaiting Viet Cong.

And that's how Reno found out how much he was worth. Isn't that nice of people to go to all that trouble for him. It's a shame they had to find out he wasn't the man they thought he was.

So Gunner says, "Come in Reno. How have you been?" And he watches close to hysteria as the large camouflage bag scrapes along the walls. He can also smell something bad and can detect soft brown chunks transferring from the soles of Reno's boots to his light cream carpet.

"You got any beer?"

"Coffee."

"Oh. I guess that'll do. You heard about Brooks?"

"No."

"Dead. Jeez what is that? You got Nixon on your wall? What the frig?"

"Dead? How? I thought he was in the rear?"

"Yeah. Dumbshit tried to find out why his mortar wasn't firing. I mean what kind of dumbass…"

"I think the coffee is ready."

"Oh great, I got my own mug."

Reno starts to fish about in his belongings and Gunner Deutsche gets a real bad feeling in his stomach.

"Hey Gunny, you mind if I crash here for the night?"

And so it was that Gunner Deutsche ended up with the world's most expensive pile of chicken shit staying on his couch.

The next day Gunner Deutsche lies in bed until past 11.00. The vineyards seem closer than ever and he is trying to work out how to face what is downstairs. When he does go down he finds Reno in the kitchen with the pancake mix and a case of beer. He is asked,

"How d'ya like your eggs?"

And gets them scrambled anyway.

"Go sit down, I'll bring you a beer."

"No, no beer thank you." Gunner Deutsche takes his plate into the front room where the TV set is on and Reno joins him.

"Well hell, go on and eat."

Now Gunner thinks there may be four different foodstuffs on his plate but it is hard to tell.

"You crack the eggs before cooking them?"

"Heyyyy, you don't like my eggs? I'm famous for my eggs."

"No doubt."

"You shoulda seen the chickees outside the store this morning. Whooo hooooo."

And that's when Gunner starts to wonder where the beer has come from.

"They got this table, money for POWs or somethin'"

"Really."

"Yeah, you imagine that? I told 'em if they really wanna help, why don't they go over themselves."

"Oh?"

"They said I didn't understand so you know what I did?"

"No."

"I said fine, I'll sign her petition and when she bent over the table to get a pen, I bit her ass."

"What?"

"Whhoooo yeah, a real peach it was too. I said, that's the best thing a chickee like you can do for a POW."

"You bit her ass?"

"Hell, she enjoyed it."

"I can't believe you bit her ass."

"You think she'll call on me?"

"Sorry?"

"I gave her your address in case she wanted to go out some time."

"What?"

At this point somebody knocks on the door. It is somebody in uniform staring at Gunner's chest. Boy he'd have a shock if he looked up.

"Sir, are you Joseph R. Reno?"

"No I…"

"That's me officer. This here's Gunny Deutsche, s'his house."

"I need to speak to you, Mr Reno."

"Private Reno."

"Private Reno, do you admit to biting a … Mrs Kapowski?"

"Sure I did officer, right in the ass."

"I know where you bit her. Private Reno you can't go around doing that. It's indecent assault."

"Oh jeez, all I did was…"

"I know what you did. Would you step over to the car for a minute?"

Gunner watches the police officer walk Reno over to the car where a young twin-setted lady stands.

"Madam, do you recognise this man?"

"Yes sir, he's the one who bit me."

"Well hel-lo chickee."

"Sir, if this young lady wishes to charge you, you could be in real trouble."

"Not when the judges get a load of that peach. Turn around chickee and see if this cop can blame me."

"Wha… ?"

"Private Reno I have to ask you to…"

"Private Reno?"

"Sure chickee, just got back from Nam."

"Really?"

"Yeah. Kinda plays with your mind you know? Leaves all sortsa psycho… psychoo-log-ical res-o-nan-ces."

"Oh?"

"Say, I think you ladies are doing real swell work you know. POWs NEVER HAVE A NICE DAY. I mean, that's a hell of a slogan. You ain't gonna send me down are you lady?"

"Well I... I don't know Private."

"Cos you know if the officer here was to caution me, hell, I wouldn't do it again."

"No... no. Officer caution this man."

So Reno finally walks back to the house with a grin that just about nearly splits his face, pulls the lid off another bottle of beer with his teeth and belches contentedly.

"How come you're not in jail?" says Gunner because secretly this is what he wants.

"Chicks. They love me." And the weird thing is, he actually believes it. It may be because that's what they all said last year. "She'll be back."

And Gunner watches as Reno pulls personal belongings out of his bag. A couple of skin mags, another pair of olive drab pants, a copious amount of orange silk parachute. Somewhere at the bottom is a load of greasy peanuts and a few pairs of socks. He says,

"Let's turn this place into somethin' a little more homely."

He means he wants Gunner Deutsche's beautiful clean house to look more like the hooches in Nam.

"No Reno."

"You like her?"

Reno opens one of the magazines to a woman stapled down the middle. Her legs are at a 180 degree angle. That's quite a thing to be able to do.

"No Reno."

"Awwwww c'mooon."

"Reno."

"Yes?"

"I'm not smiling."

Reno places the magazine over Gunner's picture of Nixon.

"You're kidding. You look at this and not smile?"

"Reno, I'm going to have a shower. Miss Orange County stays down."

Reno is left alone in Gunner's front room. And you know for the first time he gets a little nervous about Gunner's visibility, or lack of. He thinks that perhaps before Gunner steps into the shower he might decide to sneak downstairs naked and rip up his skin mags. That's a pretty frightening feeling. Knowing that there could be someone you can't see watching you. It makes your skin over sensitive, it's a feeling that Reno is very familiar with.

Reno remembers the day Gunner made it back to base that time. He could see a piece of wire being blown through the air and it passed him like a hot wind. And you know the worst thing was, was that it was expressionless.

A couple of marines saw Deutsche in the jungle that day. Or at least saw the effects of Deutsche, they couldn't actually see him. It was such a memorable image that twenty years later they will tell a writer who will make a Hollywood film. The film is going to be about an alien who falls to earth in the Vietnamese jungle, but because he's an alien he has all sorts of superior technology including an armour that makes him invisible. While he is invisible he kills off most of the cast one by one.

The alien doesn't win though. We've all found out that superior technology isn't always a dead cert.

And you know the film isn't all scary. Sometimes it is funny, because there is a bit where the hero stabs a Vietnamese man with such a long blade that it goes right through his stomach and out through the other side to the extent that at least half of the knife is buried into a wooden beam behind him. And the hero says,

"Stick around."

And that's funny see, because the Vietnamese man, he's stuck to the beam.

"Stick around."

Isn't that funny?

When the day hits 14.00, Reno flicks a large gob of egg off his lap and says,

"How 'bout we go shoot some pool? This town got a pool hall?"

"I need to work."

"Bull. C'mon, we can get some more beer. Be like the old days."

Well now this is exactly what Gunner is trying to avoid. He says,

"No"

"C'mon. Maybe we could find a couple of dinks to shoot on the way back. It'll be fun."

"What?"
"Joking. C'mon whadyya say?"
"No, that's what I said. I said no."
"Ahhh hell. The thrill has gone, huh Gunny."
Reno puts one finger over a nostril and blows out real hard. A massive hulk of booger flies and lands half on his empty plate half on Gunner's coffee table.
"Yes, OK. OK lets go shall we?"

The pool hall is smoky and dim. It is pretending to be imitating pool halls from the twenties when really it has just not been updated. No one can see any face in here so Gunner is not special. There are large rotating fans on the ceiling that circulate the fog.

They go like this,

wackawackawackawackawackawackawackw

But that's not what Gunner Deutsche and Reno hear. What Gunner Deutsche and Reno hear is this,

wackawackawackaw

Reno is winning.
He says Gunner owes him six beers, even though they never put down any stakes.

ackawackawackawac

Gunner Deutsche doesn't need to run in his baseball cap.

ckawackawackawack

And Reno says,
"Jeez I hate these dumb fans. I mean they don't do anything."

"I hadn't noticed them."

awackawackawacka

"They just spin the hot air about. That's it. Dumb things."
"What do?"

kawackawackawacka

"How can a person concentrate on their game with those dumbshit things going."
"I didn't realise they were there."

awackawackawacka

"No. Neither did I."

kawackawackawacka

And Reno says,
"Gunny? Anyone know what you look like?"
"No."
"When's the last time you saw yourself?"

awackawackawacka

"When I was about seven."
"You not curious at all?"
"Uh, I don't know."
"See I got this plan."
"Yes?"

ackawackawackawac

"But we need a load of clay and plaster."
"Yes?"

awackawackawacka

"Jeez, I gotta piss like a racehorse."

Reno puts out his Lucky Strike. He started smoking out of boredom in Nam. He keeps it on out of boredom of not being in Nam. But now he's got a plan. He actually forgets about the beer Gunner owes and drags him out of the pool hall. He says that he passed a hardware store on his way to Gunner's house.

By the time they get there sweat is making diamond shapes on the backs and under the armpits of their shirts. Even invisible men can sweat if the conditions are right.

The hardware store sells an awful lot of things that you don't expect. There is a sale on plastic garden ornaments at the moment. Two squirrels for the price of one. Reno spends a long time looking at the beavers, he wants to buy them for Gunner's living room. Make it more like the old days... Three boys are milling around a display of knives that are kept under glass. They wish there wasn't an age limit to buying these things. Rather they wish they were over the age limit to buy these things.

The store is deep and it has twists and aisles and displays everywhere. Gunner and Reno get lost in the jungle of DIY, they want help but they have yet to find the till or the owner, and then they hear them.

"Just surgical spirits, Mrs Kapowski? Must work Mrs Kapowski you look younger every day"

"My mother's invention, apply after a sauna. Nothing tightens up the skin like it."

Gunner and Reno recognise the voice.

They recognise both voices.

And everything

Stops.

Mrs Kapowski leaves the store with the three boys and Gunner and Reno are alone with him.

Gunner thinks all the way up to the counter that he's gotta be wrong. The voice holds a trace of it. That's not much.
    And then they see him.
    Behind the counter.
    A gook
    A dink
    A squinteye
    Don't kill them all
    See this rabbit
    Only kill certain ones
    Looks like any rabbit
    Kill the bad ones
    You gotta live
    Kill only the bad ones
    This is your survival
    Make sure you kill only the bad ones
    You boys know how to skin it?
    But you gotta kill em
    Tasty

Anyone thinks they can't handle a bit of rabbit stew?

        My dinner
        Lai down the rules now

The man behind the counter recognises them, too. He recognises Gunner especially. He looks at Gunner under his baseball cap and he thinks this,

Tinh

That's it. One word.

Tinh

You can't quite explain that. But the man behind the counter is feeling tinh and he is thinking tinh. Because tinh is ... it's complicated but it is something you feel, an irrational emotional response, and it is something else.
The Bogeyman.
Keep your mouth shut or it'll take your soul.
You can't see it, but it's come for you and it'll trick you into opening your mouth and steal your soul.
It's evil.
You can't see it.
See no evil.

He goes, "ohhh," and then clamps his lips shut.
"We're gonna need wood and clay and plaster."
Nod.
"You do that?"
Nod.
"You speak English OK?"
Nod.
Gunner and Reno watch the tight-lipped man rush towards a stack of wood. He bends over to grab the expensive stuff and something falls out of his shirt. It's silver and it says his name.
John Sung Yim.
"Jeez you're one of us? I coulda sworn you were a gook."
"Reno..."
"I mean he's still a squinteye but he's not a gook. What's your rank? Where dya fight?"
"He probably doesn't want to..."
"Course he does, still wears the dog tag."
"I still wear..."
"Just in case you die naked."

"Can I help with that?"
Shake.
"Don't be worried about Gunner here I'm surprised you didn't hear about the way he looks in Nam."
The man behind the counter starts to relax a little, but he's a little panicky for different reasons now.
"I come from New York, I'm no gook, you kike."
"Heyyy private dink, I'm a goddamned wop don't call me no kike."
"Just so you know."
"Didn't mean to cause offence, I guess I just can't tell the difference."
"Is this the size you want?"
"Not quite," says Gunner. "We need them about the size of my head, maybe just a little bigger."
"See Gunny that ahhh, that don't help him much."
"We'll take the ones under the second shelf then."
"OK. OK."
"So you know Mrs Kapowski? Know where she lives?"
"Leave it Reno."

Now something is going to happen to Mrs Kapowski, and it's not going to be pleasant. You see Mrs Kapowski is going to go to the local swimming hall because there is a sauna there, and she is going to sweat a good ten pounds out of her and then smother herself in surgical spirits. It is something she has just started to do recently. She thinks it is true that it is the ultimate way of looking young.

Today is different. Today Mrs Kapowski is going to step out of the swimming hall freshly spirited up and the three boys from the Sung Yim Hardware store are waiting for her. They are still wondering what to do on a Thursday afternoon, more specifically what you can do without a knife on a Thursday afternoon.

One wiff of Mrs Kapowski and they come up with a rather spectacular idea. And it is while Mrs Kapowski is unlocking her car and worrying about appearing freckles that the boys light a match and woooommmff.

Everybody knows what sound it makes.
That sound is woooommmff.

I can't tell you what sound Mrs Kapowski is going to make because I'm not going to be there. But I can tell you what Mrs

Kapowski is going to smell of. It is something between roasting pig and boiling chicken. That doesn't sound so bad, so I suggest buying a couple of legs and some cheap part of a pig and trying it at home.

And the sad thing is, is that if the boys would have held off for just one more week it wouldn't have happened, because next Thursday the swimming pool is going to be closed down. It is going to be closed down because the council can't afford to build two pools and it is unfair to let only one colour of people go swimming. You see when you do that all the other people who are different colours to the ones who are allowed in, get upset. But having everyone swimming together just isn't working. It seems people are happiest when they are colour coordinated in the swimming-hall department.

So here is Mrs Kapowski all lit up and nowhere to go with a whole pool full of water just fifty cents and a footwash away. In Fresno when it is hot outside people don't go outside too much. They go to the movies or to the department stores and they go there in cars. It is not as if there are streets of pedestrians around to put Mrs Kapowski out. Mrs Kapowski has never put out at the best of times. She's not going to put out now.

PANOS KARNEZIS
Deus Ex Machina

She came on the morning train, on Monday. Loaded on the cargo car together with a bale of hay and the bottom half of a scrapped boiler which had been hastily cut with an oxyacetylene torch to make a watering-trough. A king-size mattress was nailed on each of the wooden walls to protect her from the sharp bends of the track. She had a canvas bag roped to her croup between her legs to collect her dung, but by flipping her tail to swat the flies she had displaced it, and it had served no purpose at all during the trip. The porter noticed immediately he opened the door, even before his eyes had time to get used to the dark interior of the car. She came at 14.07 on the 11.03, and no one knew about her until then.

An hour earlier, the station master finished reading yesterday's paper, cut it into square pieces several pages at a time, and walked to the small shack across the track. Pinching his nose he hung the pieces from a nail next to the toilet bowl and quickly got out again, closing the door behind him. Back on the platform, a young man in a suit sat on a bench and put his cardboard valise next to him.

"Are you sure I haven't missed my train?" he asked.

"Yes."

The big clock above their heads showed 13.10.

"But it's over two hours late."

"That clock is running fast."

And pretending to check his watch, the station master climbed the bench and turned the hands back three hours. There was a whistle at the distance and the young man stood, straightened his jacket and picked up his suitcase. A minute later a train passed through the station at full speed and threw him off balance. From the concrete floor he watched the open freight cars leaving the station in a cloud of air and gravel.

"It's iron ore," the station master explained. "From the mines of the penitentiary."

The station master sat on the bench and took off his cap. He took a collapsed cigarette pack from under the lining and offered one to the other man.

"What do you sell?" he asked after lighting their cigarettes.

"Encyclopaedias."

"What sort?"

"Medical."

The station master shook his head.

"People don't get sick much around here. Maybe it's the fresh air. Or maybe because they die young – while they're still healthy."

"Why do they die, if they're so healthy?"

The station master took a draw from his cigarette and swallowed the smoke. "I haven't thought about it before."

They watched the train disappear over the horizon, bumping up and down on the uneven tracks. There was silence again. A brief wind turned the blades of a water pumper and brought over the smell of the shack from the other side of the track. The young man spat, disgusted.

"Virgin Mary. What's that smell?"

"Sanitary facilities."

They carried on smoking.

"Our station is on the top of the Public Works list of renovations," said the station master after a while. The salesman didn't reply. Above their heads, the carousels of gears ticked the minutes inside the old clock. The station master listened to it with attention and pride: it never missed a minute. "But the customer's always right," he thought, amused. A fresh cloud of diesel emerged from the hills and soon another train approached. This was a passenger train and was slowing down. The salesman combed his hair and took his valise, but put it down again when the train stopped at the water tower outside the station.

"This isn't your train either," said the station master and stretched his legs. "How much are the books?"

The salesman fell back on the bench.

"Much less than you'd expect. And you can have one volume free. Either the anatomy atlas or the digestive system."

While the train was taking on water a woman climbed down and ran to the shack. But as soon as she opened the toilet door she closed it again. She covered her nose with her handkerchief and returned to the train. Her dress was a shrub of stamped roses and she wore a hat.

"How about the reproductive system?"

"That will cost you extra."

They fetched the plank they kept for unloading barrels but it was no good. When she put down a hoof, the wooden boards arched, oscillated, and made a hollow sound so that she backed into the railcar, neighing. She refused to walk down it. In the end, they took stones from the collapsed wall of the yard and built a solid ramp under the board from the car to platform one, strong enough to support an ox. But she didn't trust them any more.

The peasants who got off the train stood on the platform and made suggestions as to how to get the horse out of the car. Then they silently observed the spectacle, eating what had remained of their provisions. Their straw baskets of shopping from the town were at their side, a pair of cackling hens hung upside-down, a demijohn of wine, a braid of garlic.

A man in a white hat, a summer suit and an Italian leather briefcase also climbed down from the train and wandered among the crowd. The station master assumed he wanted to use the facilities.

"I'm afraid the toilet's broken, sir."

"I don't understand."

"Better wait until the next station, sir."

The horse neighed in greeting and the small circle of men stepped aside with respect when he said he was a solicitor from the capital on business.

He suggested feeding the horse sugar and they did. In fact, the whole stock of sugar cubes from the village chandler. And only then did they get her to listen to their commands. Finally, when she stood on the platform, they were all so impressed they forgot that they had missed lunch, they didn't notice the smell of her dung, and they ignored the fact that they would be drinking their coffee bitter for at least a week. For what they saw was a racing mare, an Arabian from Damascus that had won thirty-two races in her youth – although they didn't know that then, and still had a perfect set of teeth. She stood naked but for the halter and a rubber-stamped luggage tag with the name of the village written on it tied around her neck. Her back and flanks made the men cheer, the women sigh and the children want to touch. The book salesman compared her mane to the tassels on the velvet curtain at the National Theatre. But no one acknowledged his simile, because they'd never been to the capital city.

"What's her name?" the station master asked.

"History," said the solicitor.

"Hell!" said a boy. "They called her after a book!"

As if it were the beginning of a religious procession, the crowd started down the street with the mare in front. The solicitor was on one side holding her by the halter and on the other were the encyclopaedia salesman and the station master who'd forgotten in the commotion to semaphore the train out of the station. The train engineer was there too, determined to see who would turn out to be the lucky owner of the mare. Further back walked the train passengers, both those who were returning home and those whose destination was some other place along the line. The crowd passed by the church and walked through the forest of crosses in the listing graveyard. They turned left at the ramshackle telegraph office where the wasps had made their nests in the chinks on the plaster and the rats ran in and out the bullet holes from a battle of little importance back in the days of the civil war. They made a brief stop at the civil guard station with the withered flag in order for the corporal to check the papers of the solicitor, and search for contraband or inflammatory material that could destabilise the government under the horse's tail and inside her anus, before he joined the procession himself.

When they arrived at the house, the solicitor knocked at the door. Silence. He knocked again. The door opened and a young woman with hands covered in dough squinted at the sunlight. She looked at the solicitor, annoyed. Then looked at the horse, then the crowd.

"Where's your husband?" asked the station master.

"He's not in. Some people work for a living."

A boy found Isidoro in his plot of land and told him they were looking for him. The young man stopped working and leaned against his hoe. The words "Property of" were painted on its handle, but the name had been ground away with emery paper. He took a brief look at his plot. It was small and on such a steep slope that now that he had worked the earth deep, the soil had rolled to the bottom of the hill and he'd have to carry it back bucket by bucket.

"Isn't that old Marko's hoe?" asked the boy.

"No, it isn't."

"It must be. The blade's broken at the corner just like Marko's, and – "

Isidoro put his foot on the blade and pushed it into the earth.

"What's this about?" he asked.

"The horse."

"What horse?"

"The horse that's so important it travels by train."

Behind the bar of the coffee shop the landowner sat on a low stool. His eyes just emerged above the counter in front of him.

He watched the door, every man that walked in, and then the traffic outside. In the shadows his eyes shone like a swimming crocodile's. He wiped his forehead with his handkerchief and put his fingers deep into the brine of an open tin. When the waiter came back he caught him eating the olives.

"Why don't you sit at a table like everybody else?"

The landowner wiped his fingers on his trousers.

"The doctor said I should stay out of the sun. And in any case, I've saved you a table."

The waiter took the bucket and mop while the landowner searched the shelf for newspapers.

"Where's today's?"

"The train hasn't come yet."

A customer walked in, leaving the door open. The wind from the direction of the train station blew into the shop.

"Close that damn door," shouted the landowner. "My clothes will smell of shit."

The customer obeyed silently.

"They should demolish that toilet at the station," continued the landowner addressing no on in particular. "In fact, they should demolish the lot. It's a public danger."

"It's required by law to have sanitary facilities in public places," the customer offered.

"Why do I waste my life in this shit hole?"

"You're the richest man in miles."

"What's the point when all I can smell is shit and can't get my newspaper on time?"

He leaned against the wall and rested his legs on the gas cylinder of the stove. The waiter finished mopping and the sun on the wet floor made the round tables look like lilies in a pond. The landowner gazed beyond them to the square glow of a window where a cat licked its paw. Suddenly the cat jumped off and the face of a horse looked at him from the other side of the glass. Then a crowd of human faces covered the windows and it became dark inside the shop. A well-dressed man walked in. "Send a boy to find him," he said to the crowd who had stayed outside and were watching quietly. "I'll wait here."

The landowner turned to the waiter.

"Who is he looking for?"

"The man you sold that useless patch of land to. Up in the hills."

Later, when Isidoro came, the solicitor told the crowd about the mare. How she used to belong to an army general, a relative of Isidoro so distant he wasn't sure whether he was from his mother's side of the family or his father's, God rest their souls. In fact he was the cousin of Isidoro's wife's aunt, an eternal bachelor, a warlord during the Occupation, a major in the civil war, a pagan repenter who had been told on his deathbed the pearly gates would remain shut like a constipated arse unless he demonstrated humility and the altruism of love. The general fulfilled the former by donating his fortune to the benevolent fund of his local parish, and then scratched his head, thinking, "Son of a bitch, those priests are worse than politicians." Finally, he remembered he had once had a family; a father, a mother who had a sister – Yes, that was it; an aunt who had three children he used to play War of Independence with when he was a little boy until he had almost impaled one of his cousins in an attempt to re-enact one of the most moving pages in the history of the Revolution.

The general called in his solicitor and gave him orders to trace his relatives.

"I have to put him in my will."

"Which one, sir?"

"Any bastard you can find as long as he's a man, because only a man can care for my beloved History, the only female I loved in this life."

He signed the inheritance papers, and two days later peacefully passed on.

"And now she's yours," the solicitor said to Isidoro. He opened his briefcase and took out a typed page and a pen. "Please sign here."

"I know nothing about horses," said Isidoro.

"You are twice lucky today," the encyclopaedia salesman said. "I have everything you need here."

"You sell human anatomy books," said the station master.

"It's the same thing."

The wasps appeared at sunrise after the horse had been in the house a matter of days, even though the shutters of the cellar were closed. They found her from her smell as insects do, methodically searching for a crack in the wood until their persistence paid off. Then, encouraged by the warmth, they explored the rest of the house. It was a small rubble house with only two rooms; a bedroom, and a kitchen where they eventually made a banquet out of the food on the shelves and the meat in the meat-safe, flying in and out through the open window. The cobwebs on the lintel caught a dozen of them, but that was merely an inconvenience because of the strength of their numbers. Diamanda was aroused by the sound of their wings and, under the delusion of sleep, she believed it was the noise of a radio. But only for a moment, because soon she was awake enough to remember they couldn't possibly afford one.

She tiptoed to the kitchen door, opened it, and her eyes needed only a few seconds to take it all in: the yellow spots on the leg of lamb, on the bread, sucking the oil and bathing in the jar of molasses, building sandcastles in the sugar dunes, sipping from the drops of lemonade on the table. Taken by surprise, the thick cloud of wasps circled the kitchen with the panic of clandestine lovers, hitting the walls and trying to fly away not through the open window but through Isidoro's shaving mirror. Diamanda quickly closed the kitchen door and woke up Isidoro.

"What is it, woman?"

"I don't know why I ever agreed to marry you, but I know now why I should divorce you."

It took Isidoro several hours to calm her down. Every time they heard steps or the hammering of donkey hoofs on the cobblestone path outside their house, they stopped until the sound had faded away, and then carried on arguing.

"Fine feathers make fine birds," said Isidoro and killed another wasp which had escaped through the kitchen window only to re-enter the house through the bedroom. "People used to pity me for what that cheat the landowner did to us."

"A plot on a slope we need ropes to get to!" exclaimed Diamanda.

"Anyway," said Isidoro, regretting he had brought up that matter. "Now with the mare, I get free drinks and snacks, and people talk to me like old friends."

"All they want to talk about is the horse."

"It's talk isn't it?"

Diamanda closed the bedroom window. The wasps had managed to escape from the kitchen and were circling the house. In the garden the cat was clawing the air.

"What are you going to do about the tools?" she asked.

"That horse was a God-sent gift. It will help us buy our own. Then I'll put them back in Marko's shed."

"How's the horse going to help you do that?"

"I'm thinking of racing her."

"You know nothing about horse racing!"

Before Isidoro could continue there was a knock on the door. It was the landowner. He walked in not waiting to be invited, shaking his handkerchief to get rid of the wasps.

"What do you want?" Diamanda asked.

"I have business to talk with your husband."

"The last time you talked business with my husband we almost ended up in the poorhouse."

The landowner turned to Isidoro.

"I understand your uncle, son."

"My uncle?"

"The general. I'm a bachelor, too. I can use some company."

"You should get married," said Diamanda.

The landowner made an expression of displeasure.

"I want to buy the mare," he continued. "I will look after her well."

Isidoro stood up. He was still in his woollen one-piece underwear and looked more stout than he really was. He felt as if a dream had come true. He felt lucky like the time he had won his necktie in the church raffle. He felt proud.

"She's not for sale."

The landowner left without saying another word.

Diamanda sighed. "We'll live to regret another of your decisions." She opened the kitchen door a crack; at least the wasps had gone.

It was the same evening when the landowner sat with the priest in the coffee shop. They started by drinking coffee, then had a beer each, then the landowner suggested they had a couple of brandies.

"Why not?" said the priest.

"Will you be all right for matins?"

"If you'd ever been to one you'd know it's only old women these days, and they're all deaf. I could recite the Cup results and they wouldn't know the difference."

They drank the brandy. A group of loud children were playing in the street. Then a woman came and sent them home, cursing and throwing stones at them as if they were dogs. After they were gone, the men in the coffee shop could hear the music on the radio, the women on the steps of their houses could chat in peace.

"The man who couldn't afford a donkey now owns a race horse," said the landowner.

The priest nodded in agreement.

"Who would believe it?"

"This country is on course for disaster, Father. The poor are too proud for their own good."

The priest ordered another round of drinks.

"There's a lot to be said about the evils of pride."

"By the way, Father, do you know about Marko's tools?"

For the rest of the week the wasps would come every day at dawn and circle the house for a way in. But they couldn't find one, because Diamanda had put mosquito nets in the windows,

Isidoro had blocked every crack on the walls with plaster, and the cooking fire was kept on day and night so they couldn't get in through the chimney either.

On Sunday the rooster crowed earlier than usual. In bed Diamanda thought: "This means a clear, sunny day. Just what the wasps love." It had rained the night before and soon the humidity added misery to the heat. Inside the house the smell of horse manure and urine from the cellar had taken over. Isidoro got dressed standing at the window, looking toward the hill where his plot was. Money was running out, spent on hay for the mare and the encyclopaedia payments. But he wasn't worried. He put on his only coat even though it was a warm day and did up all the buttons. He opened the door and jumped out. Before the wasps had time to attack him, he hid his head inside his coat. "This is the siege of Constantinople!" he said and started walking fast, while the wasps fell on the coat like rain.

Half a mile down the road he stopped and listened: silence. He took off the coat, hid it in the bushes while watching for neighbours, and in his short-sleeved shirt got back onto the road and headed toward the square. There was plenty of time until the meeting. On a side wall a lizard basked in the sun's rays and he clapped his hands to watch it run away. "Fast, but not as fast as my horse, lizard," he said. He looked up and although he was far away, immediately recognised the priest from his black cassock. "Damn," he whispered and crossed himself. "It's bad luck to see a priest early in the morning."

"I didn't see you today at the church, Isidoro."

Isidoro kicked a stone.

"Well, I'm busy these days, Father."

"Lay not up for yourselves treasures upon earth, where moth and rust doth corrupt, and where thieves break through and steal."

Isidoro shrugged his shoulders.

"I'm poorer now than I ever was, Father."

The priest stroked his beard.

"You know, old Marko's lost his set of tools."

Isidoro avoided the priest's eyes.

"I know nothing about that, Father."

"But if you ever do, you'll make sure Marko gets back his hoes."

"Why is Marko bothered? He's old. He doesn't work the fields anymore."

"A sin's a sin, son."

"Yes, Father."

"You used to be a good Christian, son."

"I am, Father."

"I'll investigate that."

After the priest had gone, Isidoro spat on the ground. "Priests aren't happy unless they see you in a pine box," he told himself. "I'm not a thief. All I need is one race, one win. And I'll buy Marko and everyone else ten hoes each."

In the coffee shop he greeted the other customers and took a seat to wait. It was 10.30 and the 07.35 was due at any time. He ordered coffee and then decided to buy everyone else a drink with the last of his savings. When he turned to give his order, he saw the eyes of the landowner fixed on him from behind the counter. "That bastard crocodile is everywhere," Isidoro thought calmly. "But today's my day."

The other men asked him questions about the horse, and he answered all until the train whistle interrupted them. A few minutes later the first passengers crossed the square. Isidoro watched, impatiently, trying to determine who was his man. Soon the square was empty again but for a boy playing with the stray dogs. Isidoro grew impatient. "He won't come," he thought. "What a jinx, that priest."

The boy was the first to see the little figure walking from the road that led to the station. He was dressed in dark clothes, patent leather boots, a hat. Isidoro walked out to meet the stranger and led him to the table. Everybody stood as if he were a guest of honour.

"Thank you for coming," said Isidoro.

"I'm afraid we don't have much time. The train's leaving soon."

"As I said in the telegram," started Isidoro, "I have a horse. A race horse. I would like to get into partnership with someone who knows about racing."

"I was surprised to hear that someone owned a race horse in this – "

He didn't finish his sentence.

"Yes, History is a great horse."

"Did you say History?"

"Maybe you've heard about her. She's a champion."

"Everyone in the business knows about History. She was a champion indeed. A very rare mare."

"Well, I own her now. Inheritance, I won't bore you with the details. I'm thinking of racing her."

"Racing her?"

"Racing her, yes."

The man had some brandy and smiled. "The fact is," he said, "that horse has no racetrack value anymore. She's too old." Isidoro and everyone in the coffee shop went silent. "And she's not a workhorse, either."

The stranger stood and checked his watch.

"I guess she's only good for walks now. I hope you'll enjoy riding her."

As soon as he left, a laugh began from behind the counter. It started like a cackle as if a hen was in the kitchen, but only the landowner was back there, sitting on his low stool and holding the folds of his belly like an accordion, spitting olive stones with every breath of laugh. Everybody else was silent. The waiter collected the empties and returned to the kitchen to wash them in the sink turning on the tap all the way in order for the running water to cover the laugh. But it was quite unstoppable now, louder that the wind in Isidoro's land where only rock grew, or the drone of the wasp cloud and the sound of Diamanda's insecticide sprayer. It was worse than the smell from the station every time it blew towards the village, and worse than the pestilent air inside Isidoro's house.

When Isidoro found the knife on a table, the laughter became the sound of dynamite in his ears, and he could already see himself in the iron mines of the penitentiary, shovel in hand and a civil guard behind his back with a rifle, lazily smoking and keeping an eye on him. He slowly walked towards the little man behind the counter who fell off his stool as he tried to back off. The landowner had nowhere to hide. The only way out was past the young man who shuffled his feet, still coming.

Some believed that he would've killed him then, if it weren't for Diamanda who walked into the coffee shop that very moment and seeing what was happening, stood between them. "Isidoro," she said. "You are about to sign another contract without having read the small print first." Isidoro stopped. His face was flushed. He looked at his wife and then dropped the knife, ashamed.

The priest sat at his desk with a cup of coffee, a plate of meat, and the oil-lamp next to his notebook. He didn't have much to do for the next day; a one-page sermon, a few lines for a lamentation, and a letter to the bishop in the county capital. It had been a strange few days. But now old Marko's tools had been returned and he had given Isidoro absolution and a promise not to notify the civil guard – but only after the foolish young man had agreed to the donation. As far as he was concerned it was a fair punishment.

He started the sermon. Writing about the rich, the poor and those in between, he became so absorbed that at some point he imagined he was Archangel Michael and his pen was his mighty sword. He had to stop then, because he realised he was committing the deadly sin of pride. To get his mind off it, he picked a slice of cured meat he'd kept for himself before sending the rest to the poorhouse. He tasted it.

"Sweet!" he exclaimed. "A God-sent gift. That horse saved Isidoro's soul and will feed the poor, too." And he proceeded to eat everything on his plate, stuffing his mouth as if he hadn't had anything for days.

SIMONE KNIGHTLEY

Extract from **Sightlines**

ONE

'Memories are motionless, and the more securely they are fixed in space, the sounder they are. To localise a memory in time is merely a matter for biography... a sort of external history, a temporal tissue, which has no action on our fates ... For a knowledge of intimacy, localisation in the spaces of our intimacy is more urgent than determination of dates.'
from *The Poetics of Space*, Gaston Bachelard

The tale she likes best starts like this: a child is sent on an errand to collect eggs from market, and told be sure to carry the right vessel, don't veer from the path but be aware of all about you.

So the child sets out singing and takes a blue painted wheelbarrow, looks straight ahead and doesn't notice as the eggs roll one into another, crack and pour through the gaps in the wheelbarrow's wormy planks on the way home through the wood.

And the child is told next time, take a basket. Next time, the child is sent to collect a quart of milk. So the child sets out singing and takes a green woven basket, looks straight ahead and doesn't notice the milk trickling through the wicker bottom onto the dusty track below.

And the child is told next time take a basin. Next time, the child is sent to collect a brace of pheasants. So the child sets out singing, takes a red enamelled basin and looks straight ahead while the pheasants fly out of the basin and into the wood.

The destination is always the same. Yet repetition seldom occurs in this story. Madeleine, Eloise's grandmother and teller of tales, carefully arranges before her a world of brittle and fluid textures, introducing infinite solutions to the safe passage of domestic ingredients; dried peas, flour, poultry, salt and medicinal herbs, measured in quarts and bushels, pinches and pecks. The teller and the listener slide seamlessly across decades choosing alternative arrangements of the everyday. The routes

Eloise chooses stretch from Teutonic forests to Maida Vale and back. Shifting decades so that an entire century can be covered while her Sunday bathwater cools. And before the brown bakelite Bush television set, with its beige carpet insert and logo in silver relief, is transformed into a flickering icon by The Singing Nun.

"*Dominique, nique, nique, sont allez tout simplement,*" she sings, projecting framed audio-visual holiness onto the round-cornered screen. And confirming to Eloise, like school photographs, that the blessed exist smiling in two-dimensional black and white, with few grey bits in between. Then the icon stops fizzing until *Thursday Playhouse* when Madeleine is held spellbound by plays in which nobody dies in pain.

The house is a kaleidoscope. Arranged on four floors, the middle two have been divided by hinged screens of leather cloth fixed with brass-studs so that its Edwardian proportions are fragmented into several small chambers. Previous occupants, seduced by the miracle of electricity, had fixed tall mirrors and wall sconces to the screens, forming a sequence of faceted corridors that seem to spin off in different directions between bathroom and bedroom. The light fidgets like a glitterball across yards of mirror – as if stolen from a scene in Orson Welles' *The Lady from Shanghai.*

On school days, waiting for the bath to fill, Eloise traces her own pale sometimes fat, sometimes thin disjunctured form flitting between bathroom and bedroom, duplicated by the play of angles and perspectives. Madeleine has added further to the imperative to capture light. Weekdays she pieces together lozenges of scarlet, orange and yellow made from broken crockery, and arranges them along the edge of the bath like adolescent teeth. She cuts panes of glass; flat fragments stained in watery-jewel colours by Eloise with a cut-price box of water-colour half-palettes and a hogshair brush. Then she seals the edges with *gutta percha* and props them in front of the bathroom windows to soften the edges of the day.

On the window-ledge, opened at Eloise's elocution lesson for today, a book printed in a pseudo-antique typeface is proposing: 'Nature is the visible translucence of a divine agency.'

This evening the pink-tinged bathwater has swallowed Eloise's limbs. Her wilful hair, caught in waist-length plaits has been twisted at the ends into two fat paintbrushes. They are rippling the horizontal surface in the bow-legged bath. In the scullery, Madeleine has brought a grey-flecked enamel tub of water to boiling point on a grey-flecked enamel stove. She tips first scalding then cold water into a bucket, a jug at a time, and brings it to the bathroom.

Unable to live without flowers you paint scarlet
and ochre pansies on wicker footstools, unravel
my plaits, comb through small birds nests and
knead my sunday scalp with warmed Pomade,
I plink-plink "You are my Honeysuckle"
instead of scales. Until Grimms' Fairy Tales
come via Teutonic forests to Maida Vale.

The bedchamber, shared by grandmother and child, is decorated on each of its flat surfaces with irregular painted shapes the colours of aubergines, oranges and the sea, that roll in a continuous flow over the edges of tables and chairs and disappear underneath. Two silvery pillars of faux-snakeskin hat-boxes are stacked to the ceiling either side of a large climb-up bed, where assorted velvety robes slither from the bed onto the floor. Hung from one screen is a sketch for a painting called *After the Bath* and a pencil drawing of Rilke. Some winter evenings Madeleine, pulling her past from a collection of wooden trunks with tarnished clasps, performs awkward arabesques while Eloise flutters about their makeshift stage like a twitching parakeet. Their audience, characters from a collection of pop-up books, is lit from behind by slices of light filtering through the shutters from the world outside. And a Chinese yellow rug, stretched diagonally across the floor and scattered with spilled sequins, glitters like a stretch of beach with thousands of whitebait thrown from a seventh wave.

Three score years and ten going on nineteen,
pulling your past from a dressing-up trunk:
ostrich feathers, paste tiaras, taffeta, kid –
and me, all satin pumps and tutus,
Palgrave's Golden Treasury teetering on
my deportmenting head,
preparing for betrothal to our future king.

The bathwater is getting cold. The child is tracing with her finger in the pink foamy water, the shape of a woman at first kneeling by a stream and then standing, washing herself. Now Madeleine pours fresh water into the bath, warms orange pomade between her palms. Nudges her convex stomach against the back of the pale head lolling backwards over the rolled edge. As she kneads Eloise's scalp, the child asks her to tell a story about her young life in France. About her friendship with Henri, the painter she met in Nice at the beginning of World War I. Entering the story and focusing the view, Madeleine continues to knead.

"Well, let's begin with my family. And where we lived. Our home was in Chiswick. My grandparents were shopkeepers. On Father's side, Silas Jones 'Hand-Sewn Boots and Shoes' was in Fulham. My mother's family were called Lausseur. They had several greengrocers' shops in London and more in French towns around their family home in Nice. In 1903 when I was nine, my sisters and my brother and I left with our mother to go to school in Nice."

Eloise slides further into the flesh-tinged water as Madeleine takes a comb from her lap and starts to untangle the knotted, loosened hair. Now she tells Eloise that during the first few years of their new life in France her grandparents had often taken her on trips to the ethnographic museum at the Old Trocadero and the World's Fair in Paris. And how at one of the salon exhibitions, she had become 'simply overwhelmed' standing in front of a huge oil painting of fruit and vegetables in a green woven basket.

"The marks and colours were so exciting it made me gasp, feel weak in the lower part of my stomach, if you please. I was mesmerised by how the reds and yellows overlapped so you couldn't see where they began or ended. And where the white merged into red or blue or orange it left a smear of paint that almost seemed to move across the canvas. As if it were alive. Then Mother gave me a watercolour paintbox. For my tenth birthday actually, so I was about the age you are now. Well. I was convalescing after a bout of whooping cough. Mother was always so busy organizing everything. The shop, business sort of things. It seemed to take a lot of her time. And she was always writing to her mother. My first attempts were made in between spluttering fits. Naturally they were naïve and clumsy. But I saw straight away that the more I stumbled and made mistakes, the more interesting the results were. I was fascinated. And then I suppose I became even more self-absorbed than I'd already been."

Girls I'd seen wore black-painted nails,
mimicked Cher, launched their voices
through hoover pipes in the lavatories after school,
instead of homework.
Instead of homework I painted The Praying Hands
in Rose Madder and Hooker's Green Light
from a cut-price box of watercolour half-palettes,

mimed to a Dominican Bride of Christ:
'Dominique, nique, nique, sont allez tout simplement...'
and wondered why the day never reached our
eau-de-cologned world.

Eloise wonders aloud, "And did you know that your mother was going to take you and your brother and sisters away to France? Had she told you that by then?"

"I think we all guessed that we were going to leave our home and our father. We hadn't been encouraged to make friends with other children or to think about a future life in London. My sister Josephine had been learning to embroider. She spent months decorating the same bedsheet. When it was finished we saw that she'd sewn along the top edge the words '*Restez ici ou vous êtes tranquille*'. Eloise, swishing her paintbrush, translates effortlessly, "'Stay here where you are safe...' I think you've said that before."

"Yes, I think I may have. In any case, after I got better I'd spend afternoons after tedious French lessons trying to make interesting marks by 'accident' on butcher's paper we used in the store. Sometimes there was a small area where I felt something exciting had happened, and I'd cut it out and stick it with flour and water paste into a little sketchbook with other scribbles that nobody would ever see. When I'd filled the sketchbook I read a little pamphlet about still life painting, and then of course I thought I knew everything: that it was best to start off with two objects arranged against a simple background and to draw them in a heavy line with a brush dipped in Indian ink and so on. But I kept thinking about the painting I'd seen at the salon. And I realized it had been made without those rules. To begin with, there seemed to be no obvious line separating one thing from another. And the spaces between the objects weren't real spaces.

Eloise's synapses shift. She writhes up from under the water, wrapping her arms around her and flipping off water like a seal-pup. As Madeleine wraps a towel around her and she steps from the bath, Eloise says, "Miss Button our art mistress who wears three colours even when she's sleeping, says that straight lines don't exist in nature. She says it's not helpful to see the world divided up by straight lines. Like we have for four hundred years, she said. She says we should try to think of rhythm when we draw, so that its more like music, or dance. She showed us a picture by Cezanne. She said it was a hymn to a mountain. Then she showed us a plant with its roots dangling underneath and said it showed the rhythm of living things, and how they're never still."

The teller and the listener simultaneously flash back to the afternoon they have just spent planting pansies and sowing ten-week stocks from seed. Back in the bedroom, Madeleine, wearing a turquoise robe embroidered with orange parrots, is warming chemises on a narrow wooden rack by the fire. And arranging trailing stems of white periwinkle with viburnum opulus in vermilion glass jugs, that catch the light like vast jewels, shrieking back at the colours she calls *mouse* and *drab* on the flaking paintwork. Eloise climbs up onto the bed. Madeleine sits beside her, breath smelling of violet cachous. They pick up the threads of their story.

"And now can I have the Raw Ratatouille story please?"

"Ah yes where are we now? My chaotic groupings of vegetables! Well, the next day I set about making my own still life arrangements with vegetables from one of our shops. Arranged them on the work table in my room and then spent day after day, alone for weeks, trying to draw them if you please. Even now when I look at a calendar I see Thursday and think aubergines. I'd spend all week planning how I would learn to paint. On Mondays after piano lessons I'd go straight to the shop, choose my vegetables and ask for them to be put aside until the weekend. When I think about how extremely solemn and self-important I was for months on end... Mama called several doctors during that time to explain what she called 'my malaise'."

Eloise says, "Let's see if I can remember: Mondays were purple onions. Tuesdays, yellow gourds. Wednesdays, red capsicums. Thursdays, purple aubergines, and Fridays, striped courgettes, yes?"

"That was it exactly," Madeleine smiles. "We'd been in Nice for only a few months. My French wasn't then good enough to read books on even the most basic art theory."

Madeleine then tells how she persuaded her mother to arrange lessons for her in watercolour painting. And how for several years afterwards she tried to paint 'always the same subject. A brown milk jug, full of anenomes if you please... And without much progress I'm afraid.'

At the beginning of World War I Madeleine was nineteen and working in Nice as companion to the daughter of a widowed professor.

"Victor Kastner, Professor Victor Kastner," prompts Eloise. "He lived in a house called Chateau Peyraut."

"Well yes, that was his summer home. Your pronunciation improves all the time by the way. Well, one evening at the Professor's winter home," Madeleine continues, "Mama and I were introduced to a middle-aged man. A painter called Henri. He was a friend of Professor K's. We were told that he was a well-known artist. And that he planned to stay in Nice for a while to recover from an illness."

"What kind of illness?"

"It would have been impolite to ask. What was most interesting to Mother was that his family were shopkeepers. It seems they owned a general store in Bohain, selling seeds and grain. I shall always remember," she says quietly, stepping further into her reverie, "because sometime later he made me a sketch on headed notepaper to show light effects falling on solid objects. It was a drawing of a lamp in the studio, showing the brilliance of the halo around it. And the notepaper had the words 'fodder and garden seeds, cattle cake & manure' printed under his family name. But what was more interesting to me, was that he said he'd been in London before the war began to see Turner's paintings. He joked that he'd been unable to buy aubergines, in Pimlico of all places, if you please. Of course I wanted to ask him about his own painting. But I was too shy. So I clumsily told him about my lessons in watercolour painting at *L'Ecole Normale*. About how our subject was usually 'Wild Flowers'. And he asked what I found particularly interesting about the classes. I remember so well, blushing and stumbling over my words. Trying to say that it was the flowers' *wildness*, and the impossibility of being able to capture a likeness, or a colour, that interested me most. All very embarrassing! In any case when it was time for him to leave he told me that 'the wild' was something that he too was particularly interested in 'capturing' as I'd so charmingly called it! And he invited Mama and myself to visit him at the rented studio he was sharing on the Quai St Michel, if you please."

Eloise looks over at one of the closed trunks in the bedroom. On it there is a sepia photograph of the young Madeleine leaning against a rail in front of an hotel on the Promenade des Anglaise. She has often looked at the image of her grandmother as a beautiful and sumptuously dressed young woman. She knows that the background includes a view of the suite of rooms that had become Henri's studio.

"It was on the ground floor of the Hotel Beau Rivage. He'd chosen it he said, because it made him happy to see 'that particular quality of light' every morning. Of course I'd never been inside an artist's studio before. It was full of objects from another world: easels like giant's skeletons, plaster casts of feet and hands. The floor was streaked with paint and charcoal and there were unfinished canvases propped against the walls."

"And there was a raw ratatouille by Henri called *Pink Onions*," Eloise shrills.

"Ah yes, that too."

"Tell me some more about what was in the studio. What it was really like to be there. Do your senses thing, that you do when you describe things you really love."

"Well I remember the sound of dripping taps and the smell of oil and putty. And there was a spirit-lamp with some brownish sheets of glue next to it. And some bags of powdered colour. And bits of torn cardboard with pencil studies on. And some very tattered shop mannequin they'd borrowed for anatomy drawing. And everywhere the most gorgeous strips of rag smeared with paint. Mama was horrified I could tell."

"And the sound!" says Eloise.

"Hollow," Madeleine says, as if surprised. "It sounded hollow. Like I imagine a laboratory to sound. Taps dripping into a deep sink. Echoes. Mother was perfectly bewildered."

They have come to Eloise's favourite part.

"And what about the question you asked Henri?"

"Ah yes, my gauche question. Well there was an unfinished portrait on an easel, of an English girl. A Miss Lansdowne. We knew her slightly as it happened. But the flesh colours were all wrong. Her face had been painted in short fat marks the colour of absinthe. Naturally I found it completely confusing. So I very shyly asked Henri about it. Eloise pictures 'absent green' the colour Madeleine has chosen for her new ballet tutu, now folded neatly into a dressing-up trunk."

"And he said 'green doesn't mean grass'," shouts Eloise, thrilled.

"Calm, Eloise. Please. Yes, and then he said, 'You say you're interested in the wildness of nature. Would you allow me to introduce you to the way we've been looking just lately at '*the wild*' in painting?'"

Eloise almost leaps off the bed with excitement and screams, "The wild beasts. We've got to the wild beasts!"

"I think that's enough for one evening. Perhaps we'll have the last part with Daisy after school tomorrow." And she produces a packet of blue rizla papers left behind by Daisy Treadlight and takes two leaves of thin tissue. Daisy Treadlight: actress/cleaner, size eighteen, yellow frizz-perm. Lives three floors down. Shares Madeleine and Eloise's garden and dusts and mops their three storeys twice a week for company. Daisy, Daisy. She is bread and golden walnuts kneaded into it. She is carbolic soap, lemoned elbows, mender of plumbing, saviour of fledglings and keeper of rainbow-coloured cocktail cheroots she unwraps on Wednesdays in winter and lights from the fire while she's toasting crumpets for Eloise to spread with salted butter. Sundays she joins Madeleine and Eloise for breakfast. They wear Japanese robes and tiaras and eat boiled eggs and soldiers off green china, on red checked linen. And Daisy sucks Ambrosia Creamed Rice from a spoon with an impaled monk while Madeleine tells tales. Now Madeleine makes two little dickie-birds with Daisy's blue rizlas. They stick to her fingertips. Two torn white birds. Now her arms swoop them high into the air and trail them back around the room until Eloise becomes a dreamer of winged life.

On Monday at school Eloise sits at the front with a girl called Esther, who smells warm and has a faint moustache. Eloise's first day at the new school, Madeleine had introduced herself to the headmaster as Eloise's guardian. She'd arrived wearing a turquoise and yellow fake-jewel-trimmed cloak with an ocelot necklet and turquoise cowboy boots with spurs, and was unable to explain why Eloise was not 'in uniform'. Now Daisy takes Eloise to the school up the hill in St. John's Wood.

Daisy, Daisy who'd once threatened
to wipe the floor with the postman
for saying I should "mix" with other children
on the first day at another school, when I'd sat
at the front and those Germolene-pink knickers had grinned
through the cut-out chairback, and boys
had offered me boiled sweets to look inside.
And I'd run behind the long wall and scraped
my perfect knees along the entire length of pebbledash
until they bled like veal.
And they'd stared at my legs,
and found a white cloth to wrap around
the dull skin of solitary children.
And no one noticed that my mouth was full of bats
that my eyes wept tiny fish,
or that I held a whole bird in my hands.

Mr Levinsky, the fresh new history teacher has written on the blackboard, 'who we are and what we are is rooted in a belief in a shared history' and asked the class to write down what they think this means. Eloise is thinking about Miss Lovedge, who Daisy calls 'the lesbian.' Because she once took Eloise to Sunday School wearing one glove inside out. And just as Eloise had prepared herself to swallow the body of Christ, the vicar asked her had she been baptised? And afterwards she'd wondered 'why the wafers?' and what Miss Lovedge had meant when she'd said, 'God's the father of us all'. Eloise, too shy to speak, wonders if this is the answer the new history teacher is looking for.

It is Eloise's eleventh birthday. Three storeys of scents rise up through the house to the attic playroom where she is lying across a pile of overstuffed floor cushions. The floor has been coloured a warm yellow. Several lilac-coloured doors conceal a series of dripping pipes and the leaking water tank that sounds a waterfall each time the lavatory is flushed three floors down. She is playing with miniature furniture made for her by Madeleine and Daisy: sofas made of varnished bread, chairs from cotton-reels and pipe-cleaners, bureaux from match-boxes with brass press-studs to ease the drawers out with... and sewn with 'mesmerised' thread. In the basement Daisy is proving bread for sandwiches. On the ground floor Madeleine is baking a birthday cake. And from the first floor drifts the ubiquitous incense Attar of Roses.

After lunch Madeleine goes up to the playroom and continues her story.

"We took sketchbooks on a picnic outing to Mont Alban – the hills behind Nice – to encourage me 'to really look at the wild'." Eloise's attention shifts inward from the table to *the wild*. She is peering between the leaves of a giant rhubarb into a repeat-pattern of green and gold forest, full of polka-dotted giraffes and sienna-striped cats climbing purple vines. Madeleine is saying, "Then we climbed up to a spot overlooking the valley. The light there is known for its sharpness. But that day the valley was shrouded in mist if you please. In any case, we sat to make some quick sketches. And as we drew, Henri lifted his head for a moment, and the mist lifted with it. It felt to me a moment of complete magic."

Eloise's thoughts stray to the small pile of parcels left on the ground floor this morning by the postman: A small watering-can from Madeleine. A box of rainbow-coloured Alice bands from Daisy. And her favourite, a wind-up tortoise from her uncle named after Ivan the Terrible. Catching the word 'magic' and turning it in the air, her memory-store snaps open at the telescoping feeling she gets when her head grows huge. And becomes trapped in the chimney. And her body goes on growing. And her arms and legs make for the window openings either side of the house while her feet slide along the pavement, one up, one down, the street. And they stay there until somebody speaks and makes her shrink back to her previous size.

Now Madeleine is telling Eloise about Henri's notion that

'quick sketches of a landscape show only one moment of its existence'.

"'Placing it in time' he called it. And he talked about how Turner had achieved his 'timeless effects of atmosphere' through ideas about light and colour that had come from philosophers. He said that his own ambition was to simplify forms, to picture feelings of stability and harmony that would comfort the viewer like a soft armchair if you please. 'Reality plus pictorial invention' he called it."

Eloise re-focuses her attention on Madeleine.

"We discussed the war of course. And whether I should go with my family back to Silas Jones in Fulham. And whether Henri should leave Nice when he was well again... "

"And what about," Eloise asks, "how you make 'the shapes of feelings?' And what about changing feelings into colour?"

"And what about your birthday tea, yes?" Madeleine goes to the kitchen while Eloise stands on tiptoes to draw the outline of a dove in charcoal on the wall washed with cerulean blue. It's the kind that rubs blue off on you. Eloise is inching along the wall and a stream of birds are forming at the end of her outstretched arm, when the doorbell rings.

Two voices drift up from the ground floor. One is that of a man. It is a voice she doesn't recognise. Two pairs of feet are climbing the stairs. Eloise lays her painting down and clasps her hands hesitantly. The visitor, in his late twenties, is standing on the threshold of her playroom. His head is touching the slope of the roof. His hair is pale yellow and white like hers. His eyes are circuiting the walls of the attic like marbles in an egg cup. Madeleine introduces him, "Look you have a visitor, Eloise."

A soft-spoken voice says, "Hello Eloise."

The child looks up at him. He is holding a huge polka-dot patterned paper parcel under one arm, and a smaller one in his hand. His eyes point to a place above and just to the right of her.

"Happy birthday, Eloise," he says, stressing the third syllable of her name. "This is for you."

Madeleine is saying, "Goodness, what a surprise," over and over again.

Eloise doesn't understand if it is the visit or the gift that is so surprising.

"We usually call her Alice now. The name they call her at school. After *Alice in Wonderland*. You prefer it, don't you, Alice?" The child smiles shyly. The rash of confusion breaking out on her skin begins to glow. Her feet become glued to the floorboards.

But when she hears herself saying, "Thank you," quietly, not, "who are you" loudly, and "why are you here with a birthday present ... ?" she propels herself forward to take the wrapped parcel. Nervously, she unwraps the huge package in front of Madeleine and her birthday visitor. Inside is a huge shell-pink doll made from varnished rubber. It is something like a mirror image of herself. But with a shiny complexion and stiffly-jointed limbs and closed eyes that snap open as the doll tips towards her. It is dressed in a colourless starched frock with crisp lacecap sleeves like a dead hydrangea. And buttoned-up to its throat. Its bloodless lips are stretched into a taut rubber smile.

Madeleine gasps, "Why it's a life-size doll!"

Eloise smiles in bewilderment at the visitor and asks, "Is this the size of life?" Then she props the doll gently against the wall and slowly sits back on the heaped floor cushions to look at her stiff, colourless twin.

There is a present for her grandmother too. Madeleine takes the round parcel in her mottled hands. She peels the paper like the skin of an onion. And she gasps and blushes with delight. Her gift is a white bone-china teapot with a red and gold Japanese dragon motif in relief. With flames twisting around its fat body like the torsion of a Michelangelo Sybil. Madeleine is delighted with its exoticism. She is unsure whether it is a dragon or a snake. The visitor tells Madeleine to hold the teapot up to the light. At its base, the face of a young oriental woman is trapped in the porcelain, as if under ice.

The visitor says something very quietly to Madeleine, who nods and smiles and leaves the playroom. She is taking her marvellous teapot to the basement to show Daisy and to pick flowers for the special birthday tea-tray she will bring to the attic for Eloise's guest. The visitor sits cross-legged beside Eloise on the floor and immediately begins to tell her stories about his travels across the sea. They are the stories told by sailors who have travelled the world for years. Haiti, he says, was his last stop. And he describes an image of palm trees and lizards and fish that fly and fifty types of banana and birds that glow in the dark. And he tells Eloise that when he and his fellow sailors were bored, they'd take spiders as large as soup plates for walks on leads. And Eloise is spellbound.

The frequency of his voice changes. He stands and walks towards the door. Gently lifts the latch. And clicks it shut. The floor shivers as he walks back towards the child. His body obscures the skylight for a moment before it sinks back into the cushions and strikes the floor. The voice is quietly, softly, telling the child to undo her plaits, take off her dress. At the edge of her vision, the life-sized doll's eyelid snaps shut like a camera lens.

Its articular head pivots away from Eloise as the visitor turns her body to face the wall. Her mouth slides from a plea to a silent scream. Splits through its skin at the outer edges. Becomes the shape the feeling makes.

The stream of birds have flown from the blue wall into Eloise's throat and are trapped there. Screeching. Writhing. Silenced. The colour begins draining from the kaleidoscope house. The basement twists in its housing away from the light. Madeleine, advancing ceremoniously with the tea tray, has arrived at the foot of the stairs. She pauses at the closed door. Suddenly the warm constancy of her heart, the circuit of her blood, mounts up against freezing, sterile sanity. The tea tray clatters to the floor, as the ground rises and slams into her face. The dragon-snake teapot smashes. Gunpowder tea stains the walls. The dragon-snake unwraps itself and slides across into the child's consciousness. Enters her throat. Enters her belly. And spits fire into the heart of the stream of birds.

Two floors down: Daisy Treadlight. Smell her. A warm buttered toast smell. She's sewing a sampler: 'Home is a time and place of innocence', it says in wonky cross-stitch letters. Now she stabs her needle into the punctured cloth. Crashes up to the ground floor. She is screaming POLICE into a square, black bakelite telephone with a circular white face. Her robes tasselled sleeve is tangled in the wire. Above this, The bathroom smells of spilled bleach and warm semen. There is an opened bottle labelled Parazone. Or is it DRINK ME. And a luminous pale yellow fluid trickling across the floor. The bathtub, streaked with scarlet, has become a sarcophagus with dripping taps.

And in the attic, Alice has become mute.

JULIA LEE
Diapason
Gift-Giver

You have walled her away inside of you,
where we cannot touch her; protecting her
from our jokes, ensuring there are no burrs
that might stick in her skin, let the blood through,
show us she is red and real, and not just
a part of you. Gifts from her turn into
Hector, dragged round the walls of Troy as you
try in vain to protect them. And she must
be displayed, but her secrets may not
be exposed, as her secrets would let
us see inside of you. That self will not
be shown, walled inside your little town. Yet
with her, some gate or wall must give. Destroy
these walls, let her break them down, let go of Troy.

JULIA LEE

Finessed

He was a dummy,
laying down his cards,
slipping out the door

*and here's where Mr Iverson had to be very clever
and commit a crime
almost as foul as the one he was later to commit,
something only a cad could do –
he cheated at cards*

down the passageway to the study door

*he contrived to deal his partner such a good hand –
and the others such a poor one –
that Mrs Vincent had no option but to bid*

he knocked

*as Mrs Vincent had made the first bid – two spades –
Iverson became dummy, and was able,
under the pretext of going for a cigarette,
to knock on the study door*

he raised the bronze statuette

where he was able to murder his brother-in-law

it was quick –
quick and messy

*for no other reason than to burn the papers, of which –
ironically – copies had already been made*

Edward's eyes slid into his head
and he crumpled to the floor

*and to return to the bridge table
in time for the next hand.*

'Bach'

going back to the land of my youth,
not my fathers
(which would be
'A chara' or 'A mhuirnín'
or
'dear'
because I am a mongrel),
and saying it to a boy who is
half-Welsh –
and who won't have me –
and who doesn't even know what it means.

Intimacy Imperative
for J.M.

I stroke your so-blond hair out of the way,
rough and tangled on my fingers, a heap of flax on the pillow.
I will not spin it to make gold, nor to find your name.

Your arm is rolled around me like a wall around a harbour.

There is someone else here,
but between us it is understood
all of the intimacy and none of the desire.

You took my hand on the A3 underpass
    under the glare of the yellow streetlights
    as I sat and stared at the night;
    and as I watched the lights flicker past
I could see my reflection in the glass,
    yours behind, ghostly, expressing what might
    be fear, or lust, or longing, or a tight bend
    approaching. A sudden sense of farce
    hits me. I have no idea what you intend
    by this: two people floating through the dark,
    one warm connection and nothing else; we're
    not talking. As I try to apprehend
    a meaning from your face, a sign to mark
    his change, your hand leaves to find fourth gear.

Epiphany – Utah

This is a chosen land
which purges me of my sins
in its heat
strips my mind bare
forces me to think
in straight lines,
and in those lines, repent.

It is a great salt desert of my purging sins,
rolling to the mountains,
from which will come
rivers in flood.

America
(after Allen Ginsberg)

America this is a protest against everything you've become
America this is your long lost daughter speaking
America I'm exiled
America its not true you have no space for lefties,
but I can't live with you;
I can't live with your (lack of) gun control
I can't live with your militias,
I can't live with how intolerant you've become.
I can't live with Prop. One-eight-seven
which refuses to accept
'the wretched refuse of your teeming shore'.
And, yes, that includes Mexicans.
America, I come down and read shit at the breakfast table.
America I see your much vaunted religious freedom
for the crazy and the bigoted and the gunowning
but not the atheistic.
America, I love you;
but I love you without your people in
America I love your pine trees, I love your beaches and your food –
America, I love my mother.
America, I don't want to bash you –
everyone else did it first –
America you're still a land where the stupid and the crazy are
                                  outnumbered by the clever and the sane
Please remember this.
America, etc.
America, I'm living here.

Pauses for Worship

I flick through the 'Special Enthronement Edition' of
                                        'Diocesean News'
full-colour, it shows the Bishop entering Yarmouth in a lifeboat,
nervous in a lifejacket.

Putting it down, I notice how little one can see of the choir from
                                                  here –
my hypothetical critical parishioner cannot see my mouth
                                          move, or not move,
if she sits here.

My friend says:
take a humanistic view of it. Offer repentance to society
                                    during the confessional prayers.
Offer thanksgiving for what you have, through whatever agency.

She is shortly to be a woman of the cloth.

I say often, 'there but for the grace of God go I' – but why
                                      outwardly profess faith,
and make accommodations inside?

She says:
have you thought of praying about it?
We have a God who loves us who doesn't mind.

That afternoon, I consult an atheist.

Over the starfruit in Sainsbury's,
half-an-hour too late,
I feel at peace.

Over the Lake

As I was walking to work, –
fairyland,
a mystical forest,
not too defined,
no single tree,
instead, flat shadows on a background of hazy light.
It is as if someone has pulled the cut-outs away from the screen,
letting the light diffuse and blend the edges,
until the forest could contain anything,
wolves, witches' cottages,
anything our imagination can place in the unknown.

D.W. LEWIS
At the Post Office (after Chekhov)

"Smoke signals are loud-mouthed compared with us" Seamus Heaney

"She choked to death on a feather you know." The voice was a hoarse flutter. Gripping the handle of her shopping trolley as tight as her arthritis would allow, Eileen hacked her throat clear. "Terrible way to go."

"Aye," replied Marty.

For a moment they ruminated on the thought, gobs moving abstractedly, two septuagenarians at cud.

The old cronies stood on the pavement, facing the traffic. Behind them, half torn from its moorings, the wire grill over the post office window rattled in a chilly lick of wind. Every fortnight the pair queued inside to collect their pension money; the meeting a tacit rendezvous during which they would discuss the weather and the afflictions of their declining peers. Afterwards they would re-emerge into the soggy light, make a hesitant goodbye and depart on separate ways. But that morning they had paused, shuffled into position and waited respectfully for the funeral cortege to pass.

A workman holding a STOP sign had forced the lead car to a halt in the middle of an oily puddle; a remnant of the skiffle of snow that had coated the country overnight. Inside the hearse, on top of the coffin, an arrangement of red and white carnations spelled out 'Mummy'. The word floundered in the murk of the puddle.

"They're late," said Eileen, straining to read her watch. "With the roadworks it's a good ten minutes to the top of the hill."

"Aye," agreed Marty.

"It's the kids I feel sorry for. Who's going to look after them? I doubt that father of theirs will be able to keep them out of care."

Marty nodded. The shirt collar slopped around his wizened neck. He wore a grey suit that was several sizes too large. A few years ago his body had filled the suit; now the cloth hung in folds around him like undrawn curtains. His ma had never told him that eventually he'd shrink into his clothes.

"It's his fault she's lying there in the first place. He always was trouble. Even when he was little he could charm the leg off a donkey. Oh, he was the cutest of babies. Then, when he was old enough, always a girl on each arm. Such a handsome man... but sly with it."

A pram nudged out of the doors of the post office, clattering down the steps to the pavement; a woman pushing a baby, dragging an elder child in her wake. Glancing at the couple she stooped to yank the toddler's hood over his head. She sensed that rain was on the way, that great hulks of cloud were scudding in from the west. The pensioners turned back to the road. The hearse, wintery breath pouring from its exhaust, had half-shifted its elongated black body from the puddle. Marty peered at the mourners' car behind. He could barely make out the shadowy figures in the back. The husband would be in there, red-eyed and snotty as the children.

"She never seemed to mind when they were courting," Eileen began again. "But once they were married it was a different story. I'd never have thought it possible, but she kept him in line all right. He stayed faithful to her throughout. Clever woman to manage that."

"Aye," said Marty slowly.

"Do you know how she did it?" Eileen lowered her voice and rummaged in her handbag. "She spread a wicked rumour around the town. You must have heard it, she told it to anyone who would listen. 'My husband is sleeping with Patty O'Neill,' she'd wail, tears in her eyes. 'That rebel bitch Patty O'Neill is in love with my husband.' What with Patty's *activities*, nobody would touch him. The girls wouldn't even take a drink off him. They didn't fancy a hiding, or worse..."

At last Eileen pulled a half-smoked cigarette from her bag. Marty sighed as she huddled up and lit the butt. No matter how hard he tried to stay clear of things, the *craic* always seemed to get back to him in the end. He had a reputation as a polite man, a quiet man, a man who had refused to talk, a man who had 'never said nothing'. As a result people told him everything.

"This went on for years," Eileen crowed, clamping the fag to her cat's arse mouth. "The husband couldn't figure out what was wrong with him. He thought he had bad breath. Everyone else knew rightly..." Eileen spluttered on the smoke, half laugh, half cough. "A wicked rumour isn't it? Pity Patty couldn't see the funny side. I can understand her being angry, but a lynch mob? ... Tar and feathers, in this day and age!"

A car horn sounded from down the street, hooting once, twice, three times. From the top of the hill, in sonorous response, the clock tower tolled back eleven long notes. The workman turned the sign from STOP to GO and the traffic rolled ahead slowly, tyres swishing through the snow-water.

"They didn't *know* she was an asthmatic mind you," Eileen concluded, dropping the butt and fumbling shut the clasp on her bag. "You can hardly blame them for *that*. No, in my book the husband is the guilty one."

Marty counted past the cars in the funeral procession. One, two, three... less than a dozen, much less than usual. The wreath had been removed from the lamppost overnight. He wondered if half way up the hill the mourners would turn their heads and gaze at the dark streaks of creosote on the pole and pavement, or if they would keep their heads bowed, eyes downcast. Marty watched the last of the line of cars start the slow climb to the cemetery.

"Pray God he doesn't marry again," he muttered.

KENNETH MACLEOD
Swimming

I steered the little rented car onto the grass verge at the side of the road and parked. Without a slipstream fluttering through the open window the inside of the Fiat was uncomfortably hot. I was wearing only shorts and sandals and to get out I had to peel myself carefully from the warm plastic of the driver's seat.

According to the map and directions printed on the invitation I was about twenty minutes away from the farm. I stood in the road, swinging my arms, trying to loosen up my injured shoulder. Above me the sky was empty and depthless, while on either side the bleached, stubbled fields seemed completely still, devoid even of the hum of insects, as though all life had been burned away through the duration of summer. Only an occasional dark huddle of trees spoke of coolness and sanctuary. The countryside reminded me strongly of Poland, sixty miles away to the East.

I left the driver's door gaping open and walked around to the boot. Inside there was a sleeping bag, a wrapped present, and my suit. I slipped off my sandals. Despite a thick callousing of skin on my feet I could feel the oven warmth of the road radiating painfully against my soles. I removed my shorts and stood naked in the heat.

My skin was dry and tanned, but the sun seared my back as I dressed. With the addition of each item of the suit my body felt more constrained. It seemed strange to be wearing trousers in the daytime; to have the dark abrasive material wrapping my thighs and the belt buckle pressing hard against my belly muscles. The top button of the shirt poked into my Adam's apple like a prodding finger and the gold tie was noose-tight around my neck. As I shrugged into the jacket it seemed to weigh down my shoulders and arms. Finally, I sat on the tailgate to put on socks and expensive leather shoes that pinched.

When I was finished I slammed the boot shut and used the dark reflection in the rear windscreen as a mirror. It was nearly

5 p.m. I was glad that I was young and thin and fit, and that the worst of the day's heat would have dissipated before I could begin to sweat. I got back into the car and started the engine, letting the door swing shut of its own accord as I bumped down off the verge and accelerated through the gears, steering carefully on tyres that were sticky and sluggish against the melting road.

I first met Jens Hilke in Berlin the year after the Wall came down. I remember it as being at a party or possibly a bar, but whatever the occasion, we were both drunk. Like all educated Germans he was polite and genuinely interested in my opinions of his country. He wanted to know what I was doing there and when I explained about quitting my job he asked me if I'd ever considered going into Public Relations. My answer was careless with drink.

"The problem with PR people," I said with feeling, "is that they're all arse-lickers. Every last one."

For a moment Jens looked stunned. Then he cracked into huge, helpless laughter. It turned out that he was in the middle of a PR degree at the Humbolt University.

After that we became friends.

The road up to the farmhouse was bumpy and dusty and full of potholes, so that I feared for the Fiat's exhaust. From what I could see the building had a rough, red-tiled roof and grey stone walls that soaked up the sunlight. There was a high courtyard wall that obscured the view as I approached, but it was clear that the farmhouse was large and, I guessed, very old. The outer wall was chipped and pockmarked and I wondered if there'd been a firefight there in 1945. My first impression was that it would have made an ideal field headquarters.

I drove in through an archway and found myself in a cobbled yard that was already nearly full. Around twenty cars had managed to squeeze in and find a parking space – mostly black or silver BMWs and Mercedes' Benz, but with an occasional brightly coloured family saloon present amongst the ranks. Where the back wall should have been there was a large wooden barn, its doors pinned open, and beyond that a glimpse of trees and grass. I wedged the Fiat into a corner and got out.

The sound of conversation and music reached me dully in the still air. I fetched the present from the boot, then walked the length of the farmhouse and into the barn. I stood in the doorway, blinking as both the sights and sounds around me became more distinct. The air was wonderfully cool.

"Jamie?"

It took me a moment to make out and recognise the small round figure who had detached herself from one of the groups.

"Frau Hilke! Lovely to see you. How did it go this morning?"

"Oh Jamie!" In her joy she clasped her hands together. "It was beautiful. Very, very beautiful. I was very moved. I cried, just a little."

I kissed and hugged her carefully, trying not to disturb her broad hat.

"You must be very happy and proud, for them both."

"We are. We are." She hugged me back hard and then drew away.

"Now Jamie," she said briskly. "You must enjoy yourself. Make sure you drink plenty of beer and *sekt*. Herr Hilke is paying for it and he doesn't want any going to waste. I hold you responsible. Jens and Sarah are out the back. You can put that present over there on your way through, and come and see me if you have any problems with anything. Finding a wife for yourself, for instance. Above all, darling, enjoy yourself. *Alles klar?*"

"*Alles klar*, Frau Hilke. Thank you."

We kissed again and she moved away. My eyes had adjusted to the light and I looked around.

Clearly the great barn had been emptied and cleaned for the occasion. There was still a smell of cut grass and machinery, but now straw bales had been replaced with white-clothed trestle tables piled with food and drink for the buffet. There was a bar area with three barmaids in traditional costume and a small band in one corner playing light German folk music. Around 70 guests, about half the expected total, were standing around conversing in groups.

I made my way through the people and placed my present with the others stacked beside the wedding cake. Then I stepped outside.

It was an idyllic setting. A small meadow lay behind the barn, bordered by trees and a stream. On one side large wooden tables and benches stood in the grass. Above them, strung out in a spider's web, dozens of coloured Chinese lanterns dangled from poles, waiting for darkness before being lit. In the centre of the pasture two men were tending an open fire over which the carcass of a full-grown pig was being roasted on a mechanical spit. Behind them, in a corner of the field, I could see a group of loudly-calling children riding on a wooden cart. Squinting in the sunlight I made out the figure of Jens walking beside it, and I strolled down through the dry grass towards him, breathing in the scent of pollen and wildflowers along with the sharp tang of cooking bacon.

Jens saw me approaching and came to meet me, arms outspread. He was short and slim and blond, and as always his open features were marked by kindness and good humour.

"Hey Scotland!" he called.

"Hey, Sarah's husband!"

We embraced and slapped each other on the back.

"Look at you, Jamie. You look like a model in that suit. Never seen you dressed up before."

"What about you, married man? What about all this?" I raised my arm to take in the meadow and the barn.

"Ach! Parents! You know how it is. They get carried away. But Sarah loved the setting, and so do I. Beautiful, isn't it?"

"Very. It's absolutely lovely."

"And we'll have a lovely time too, I hope."

"Without doubt." I clapped his shoulder. "And how did it go this morning? In church?"

"Ah *Mensch*! God I was nervous. Really. My brother had a flask of schnapps on him and believe me I needed it. Ha! Several times. I was practically drunk at the altar!"

He leaned close.

"But seriously. It was quite an experience. You should try it yourself. And Sarah. Wow. She was an angel."

"She'd need to be, to marry you."

"Really. I can't describe it. She seemed so calm. So certain."

"And you weren't?"

He laughed out loud.

"My friend, what groom is? Women are different in these things. You know that. When I saw her in church I thought, 'My God. I don't know her. Six years and I don't know her at all.' It set my knees shaking."

"And now?"

Jens shrugged and smiled wryly.

"And now we're married. And I love her. And I have the rest of my life to get to know her."

"Yes. But do you even know yet which country you'll be living in?"

"America. I got the job. We'll be staying in Sarah's old apartment until we can get something better."

I began congratulating him all over again, but he changed the subject.

"Listen," he said. "How long can you stay?"

"Until tomorrow night. I've got to be back at the beach on Monday morning."

Jens nodded.

"Baywatch on the Baltic! Of course. I want to hear all about it. But I'm going to be really busy tonight. Sarah and I will have to spread ourselves about a bit as the happy couple. Make sure everyone's having a good time."

"Don't worry about it, man. I'll look after myself fine."

"Good. There'll be plenty of girls for you and you know Tobias and some of the others already. But about tomorrow. There's a group of us planning to go swimming in the afternoon. There's a lake about an hour's drive away that's supposed to be really beautiful. What do you say?"

"Sounds great."

"*Wunderbar.* A real lifeguard for the girls to make eyes at."

"Just as long as none of them need rescuing. I plan on having a bad hangover tomorrow."

"Spoken like a true Scotsman. Maybe we can even find you some Highland whisky."

"Schnapps will be just fine, thanks."

"Well, we've got plenty of that." He smiled and touched my arm. "Now Jamie. Come and say hello to my new wife."

Sarah was leading the cart horse that was pulling the children. She had a garland of flowers in her long blonde hair and had taken off her shoes. It was hard to believe that I hadn't seen her for eighteen months, not since I'd been backpacking around the States and Jens had arranged for her to put me up. She brought the wagon to a halt when she saw us.

"Jamie! Hi."

"Sarah. Congratulations. You look lovely. A lovely bride."

She let me kiss her hot cheek.

"Thank you. We're glad you could come."

"I wouldn't have missed it. You two are a perfect couple. It's wonderful."

She smiled an acknowledgement and turned to Jens.

"I think it's time we got back inside. Can you send Volker out to take over here? And maybe Jamie would like a beer?"

Her Californian drawl managed to soften the harsh German consonants.

"Sure!" Jens wrapped an arm around my shoulder. "We'll get you a cold beer."

"Great."

We left Sarah with the children and started walking back to the barn, two men dressed ridiculously in suits walking through a field in high summer, making jokes and very happy.

I woke the next morning still drunk and with a desperate urge to piss. I struggled clear of the sleeping bag and lurched across the meadow in my shorts. The grass was sparse under the trees and when I relieved myself the stream of my water drummed on the dry earth.

Out of the seven of us who had bedded down around the embers of the fire, I was the first awake. From the wristwatch of the girl who had been sleeping next to me I saw that it was eleven o'clock. I'd slept for four hours. The girl, Katja, stirred when I touched her, burying her face deeper into the shade of her sleeping bag. It was sunny again, but not as hot as the day before.

In the barn the buffet tables had already been cleared, although empty beer and *sekt* bottles littered the floor around the makeshift bar. I was surprised to see that the photo-projector was still switched on and whirring at intervals. The night before it had thrown snapshots from Jens' and Sarah's family albums onto one big wall while we'd danced underneath. As I passed by now it hummed and clicked and a four-metre-high picture of Sarah flashed up. Her giant eyes, opaque with photo-flash, seemed to follow me as I moved on bare feet across the concrete floor.

It was a relief to find my suit neatly laid out on the back seat of the car. I couldn't remember having taken it off. Reaching into the boot I fished out sandals and a T-shirt, then rummaged in the glove compartment until I found my sunglasses. I put them on and immediately felt better.

Most of the cars from the previous day were gone, having made the trip back to Berlin in the small hours. I knew that around twenty people – mostly relatives – had been invited to stay in bunks in the converted farmhouse. I followed a small path around the side of the building and found them, already breakfasting in some style, on a terrace overlooking a well-kept garden.

As I threaded my way through the tables I returned the greetings from Jens' older brothers and their families. The best man, Tobias, and another friend, Uwe, slid out a chair for me at their corner table.

"*Morgen Jungs.*"

"*Morgen* Jamie!"

A bottle of Dopplekorn stood among the breakfast things. As I sat down Tobias poured me a glass of the clear, fiery liquid.

"*Prost.*"

I drained the glass and the two East Germans followed suit. They were red-eyed and obviously hadn't slept, but they began talking eagerly about the party.

It was a long, long breakfast of Bucks Fizz, coffee and half-croissants. One by one the others from around the campfire joined us, rumpled and surly at first until the Dopplekorn and caffeine took effect. Katja, the girl with the wristwatch, seemed happy to greet me with a kiss and sit with her hand on my thigh. The ashtray filled up, was emptied, and filled up again. There was a lot of laughter. Finally, at two p.m, Jens and Sarah appeared and those of us who felt well enough got into cars and set off for the lake to go swimming.

I lay on my back on the diving platform, enjoying the sensation of water droplets drying on my body and the warmth of the wood soaking into my spine. The four of us, Jens and Sarah and Katja and I, had swum out to the platform, thirty metres offshore. From here we could look down on big lazy fish resting in the structure's shade, and their smaller, more active cousins darting and flashing in the sun. The sandy bottom, three metres down, was clear in every detail.

Katja and Sarah sat with their legs dangling over the edge, talking quietly. Occasionally they would turn and wave in response to squeals from the man-made beach, where Jens' nieces and nephews played under the eyes of their parents. Jens was sunbathing beside me, feet twitching as he hummed his unofficial wedding anthem, Monty Python's *Always Look on the Bright Side of Life*.

I propped myself up on my elbows and gazed out over the water. Apart from the beach, the banks of the wide lake were overgrown with reeds, grasses, and tangled thickets. In some places the branches of fallen trees stuck out of the water like broken claws. The woods were a wildlife preserve, closed to the public.

My gaze returned to the girls. They were both topless – Katja dark and full, Sarah pale and slim – and very beautiful. Sarah laughed and tossed her hair back, glancing across at me.

I rolled over and nudged Jens with my foot.

"Hey man. Want to go for a swim?"

"Yeah. Sure. Why not?"

We stood up, stretching. My hangover was gone and I felt clearheaded and fit after months of sport and outdoor work. Even my shoulder moved easily in the warmth.

"Race you to the middle of the lake," I said. "I'll give you a forty-second head start."

"Make it a minute. And get rid of those."

Jens took off his swimming trunks and indicated mine, grinning. I winced.

"Give me a break. I'm Scottish, remember? We don't share the German partiality to public nudism."

"Try it. You'll like it. Very free. And the girls don't mind, do you girls?"

I looked over my shoulder to where the other two had broken off their conversation.

"Get them off!" Katja yelled.

Jens laughed.

"One minute Jamie. You promised."

He jumped from the platform into the water.

Cat calls and wolf whistles came from behind me. Grudgingly I stripped off my speedos.

"Hey look, the moon's come out!"

"Lucky he's not got spots like that on his face."

"So that's what a Scotsman keeps under his kilt."

The sixty seconds passed very slowly.

Once in the water I caught and overhauled Jens' breaststroke easily. I kept swimming for some minutes, as the lake became deeper and blacker and colder around me. I kept my crawl loose and easy, not pushing myself, enjoying the movement. Eventually I stopped and began to tread water, waiting for Jens to catch up.

"God. You're in good shape, Jamie."

He was red-faced and breathless.

"I've been training. And anyway, I've got age on my side. Five years makes a lot of difference."

"Well, I'm feeling old right now."

"Take your time and get your wind back."

We floated quietly for a while, the only sounds the lapping of water and distant shrill cries of fun from the beach. At length Jens spoke.

"So how do you like FKK?"

I was confused for a moment, until I remembered the initials were used to signpost German nudist beaches.

"Oh that. Yes, well. Different. Definitely different."

"Freer though, wouldn't you say?"

I considered.

"I don't feel free as such. More like vulnerable. I hope there's no hungry pike around."

Jens' laugh echoed out over the water.

"I think Katja would be pretty upset if that happened," he said.

I grinned.

"Let's hope so."

"You like her?"

I shrugged.

"How should I know? She lives in Kiel and she's an architecture student. Apart from that I've barely spoken two words to her. We just sort of wound up together, towards the end."

Jens shook his head.

"I don't know what they all see in you."

"Well, I'm not German, for a start. Anyway, what are you so jealous about? The woman of your dreams has actually gone and married you, God help her."

"Yes. Life is good." He made it sound like a forced admission.

I laughed and lay back flat in the water, spread-eagled.

"It certainly is," I said to the sky. "I wish it could be like this all the time."

Jens said something in reply, but with the water in my ears it was just a muffled vibration.

I let myself float, staring upwards until I felt as though I was falling into the blue. My stomach lurched and I straightened up.

"Aren't you going to miss all this when you go to America?" I asked, looking around at the lake, the beach, the woods. "I mean, it's beautiful."

Jens nodded.

"Yeah. Of course," he said. "Some things. My family. My friends. The way the land looks. All that. The same things you miss about your country."

I grunted acknowledgement.

"But Sarah and me have been apart for so long. I mean, OK, we were engaged for five years, but you saw what it was like. We were only together about three months out of every twelve, what with my studies and her work."

"I know it wasn't easy."

Jens laughed.

"It wasn't," he said. "It really fucking wasn't. But we're together now. And we want to build something together. A home. Careers. A family. All that. And the way things have worked out it's easier to do that in the States than here. And I really love San Francisco. It's a great city."

I nodded.

"Oh yeah," I said. "Definitely. And you've the mountains and the ocean practically on your doorstep."

"Exactly," Jens smiled. "I was forgetting that you'd stayed at Sarah's. When was it? Two years ago now?"

"Summer '96."

"Oh yes. So it was. You enjoyed it?"

"Very much. It was good of you to organise it. And Sarah was great. Really looked after me. It's just a shame you couldn't have been there too."

"Well, my friend. I wish I had been."

"But Sarah was very kind."

"I should hope so. And how did you find the couch?"

"The couch?"

"To sleep on."

"Oh!" I gave a short laugh. "No. The couch was fine. No problem."

"It's just that I know how uncomfortable it can be," Jens continued. "I've had to sleep on it before. We had a row once and she banished me to the thing. Woke up with a bad back."

I laughed again.

"The couch was fine for me. Really. I can sleep anywhere Jens. Compared to where I sometimes bunk the couch was a luxury. It was very kind of Sarah to let me stay."

"Well, Jamie. You'll have to come out and visit us when we get the new apartment. And we'll have a new couch as well. Just for you."

"Thanks. That's very kind." I paused for a moment, then went on. "Actually man, you and your whole family have been very kind to me. I've been meaning to say how much I appreciate it."

Jens raised an eyebrow.

"Seriously. You've been a real friend. And your family's been great. Christmas dinner. Nights out at the theatre. All that stuff. I want you to know I'm really grateful."

"Jamie. It was nothing. It was our pleasure."

"Well, you're generous people, thank God, or I might've starved. And I want to wish you and Sarah all the best. Really. You make a great couple and you both deserve to be happy."

"Thanks Jamie."

We grinned and shook hands awkwardly in the water. Gripping his palm, I saw Jens momentarily for what he was: a husband, half of something whole, a future father. I felt a sudden tug of shame and foolishness.

There was a short pause. Uncomfortable, I twisted in the water, looking towards the diving platform and shading my eyes against the sun. We were quite far out, floating near the centre of the lake.

"Hey. How deep is it here? Do you know?"

"What?"

"The water. How deep is it?"

Jens shrugged.

"Don't know. Deep."

"I bet it's not that deep. It'll be shallower than you'd think."

"Well. There's no way to tell."

"I bet I could reach the bottom."

Jens snorted.

"Come on Jamie. It's too deep."

"No. Seriously. I reckon I could."

There was an impulse welling up inside me. I took a big breath. Then another.

"I'll bet I can. I'll bet you a bottle of *sekt* I can bring back a handful of mud from the bottom."

Jens looked doubtful.

"Jamie…" he began, but before he could continue I bent at the waist, straightened my legs and disappeared below the surface in a duck dive.

I kept my eyes closed and my hands trailing at my sides, moving with the stiff-legged motion scuba divers use. I felt pressure building behind my face and swallowed. I went down about six meters, twisted around and opened my eyes.

The water was cloudy with algae and a mist of particles that diffused the light to a dark green. I saw small pieces of twigs and leaves suspended, slowly turning, around me. Looking up, I could just make out Jens' form silhouetted against sharp flashes of sunlight fragmenting on the water. I doubled over and swam deeper.

It became much colder and darker. As I descended I used my arms to pull me down and let small bubbles of breath escape my mouth, releasing precious air to lessen my buoyancy. The chill spread over my body, numbing my skin and sinking through to flesh and muscles. I was down around eleven meters, but was having to fight to drag myself deeper. I relaxed and let my feet swing back underneath me. I hung there, weightless but heavy, lost in the limbo, unable to see the bottom and with no sense of it being near.

My heartbeat was slow and steady and I knew I could hold my breath a long time. The blackness was nearly complete. My hand was a dark shadow in front of me and the surface a lighter shade of ink above. The cold trapped the air in my chest. Half a minute went by.

In the darkness I gradually became conscious of a sensation mounting within me. I began to feel as I had the previous day, when I'd parked the car by the roadside. It was the same feeling of constriction, of foreboding, I'd experienced putting on my suit. I became aware of the pressure of the gases within me, and of the thousands of tonnes of water around me and over me, wrapping my body, bearing down. In my mind's eye I saw the lake bottom, littered with debris and washed by strange currents, covered with long tangled weeds and the twisted fingers of dead tree branches. I saw these things just below me, then around me, reaching out, swathing me, and for the first time in the water I felt fear.

I don't remember starting upwards. It was the change in temperature that brought me to myself, the warmer layers of water on my cold skin. I realized I was kicking, and the further I rose, the faster I went. The darkness was lightening, becoming greener and brighter. Bubbles of air streamed from my nose. My throat and skull and bladder felt swollen with the urge to breath. I forgot everything, lost in an extreme of physical sensation.

I wasn't aware of breaking the surface, of taking in heaving, shuddering gasps of air.

It was a few moments before I came back to myself. Jens was beside me, one of his hands gripping my arm, supporting me as I lay limp in the water.

"Jesus Christ, Jamie! Are you all right? Do you need help?"

I took more deep breaths and managed to shake my head.

"No. I'm OK," I croaked. "Just give me a minute."

Nothing was different. The lake was warm and sunny and quiet.

I kicked my legs experimentally. Already the strength was returning to my body.

Jens let go and I managed to tread water, carefully, on my own.

"God, Jamie. I was really worried. You were gone for ages. What happened?"

"Nothing happened." I smiled shakily. "It's just cold down there, that's all. Cold and deep."

Jens looked doubtful.

"Maybe we should go back," he said.

I shivered and looked over towards the beach. I could make out the splashing of the children playing in the shallows.

"In a minute."

I lay in the water, waiting as my heart and breathing slowed, trying not to think about the depths beneath us, the debris waiting to drag us down.

Jens saw me shivering.

"There's schnapps on the beach," he said. "The girls will be waiting for us."

"Yes. They will." I thought of Katja and felt a small spark ignite in my chest. I collected my strength.

"Come on. Let's go then."

We turned and started swimming slowly, back across the lake.

PAULA MAIN

not in gods or angels

TODAY'S THE DAY

So I steps out from behind the bushes (don't laugh) and says tae him, "Scuse me son, but you huvnae seen ma fitba huv ee? Only it's got all the signatures of the Celtic Football Team on it, and I wouldnae want tae lose it, know what I mean?"

A direct hit. None of that puppy-dog shite. His eyes light up, though he looks wary. It takes a bit of work these days tae wrestle the bogeyman image out of their heads.

So he says tae me, "No, I huvnae seen it." He pauses beautifully; eyes cast downward, feet shuffling, lips slightly parted. He follows the script word for word as if he'd read it. Little cock-teaser.

"You wouldnae want tae help me look for it would you? I'll show you all the names and let you have a wee shot."

He wants to say yes.

"Who's your favourite player? Gould? McNamara? Lahrssen?"

"Aye, Lahrssen," he says, just audible.

His eyes scan the horizon, then drop again. He's trying tae gauge how far fae home he is. How isolated we are. How far he'd get before I'd catch him if he ran. Lucky he doesn't know I can't run 'cause of my leg.

"Lahrssen is it, eh? Aye, top fucking player, Lahrssen," I says. Need tae keep steering. These are tricky times.

"Tell ye what," I says, "if ye help me tae find my fitba I'll see if I can get you intae the game against Rangers next week. My pal works at the ground. We might even be able to go backstage when the game's finished 'n huv a chat wi' the players. I could come back wi' you now and ask yer mam? I'm sure my baw's just over there. I gave it a hard enough kick."

The little bugger yielded. No need to give details, except to point out that this was the first time I'd wanted to kill afterwards. Probably why the poor bastard survived – I scared myself half tae death.

Killing first crept intae my fantasies about five months ago.

I'd taken delivery of some new videos from Amsterdam – the kind you cannae get in this country. Inside was one of them snuff movies. Blew my fucking mind. Since then – no turning back. It ensures a delicious, savage orgasm every time I wank. All that other stuff I've been doing for years. Not through choice you'll understand. I think God must've sent me tae the wrong world. Somewhere in the universe there's an entire planet dedicated tae people like me. A place where loving children is the norm, and those poor bastards who like women are locked up for their unnatural acts. Loving women, tae me, is obscene. I don't want tae be deviant. I don't want tae hurt anybody, it's just how I feel. It's an addiction like any other. Mibby those of you who smoke, or drink, or take drugs will better understand. I try tae stop, I hate myself afterwards, and I always say never again. But when I get the feeling it's dirty and it's pleasurable and it's who I am.

Can you imagine what I look like? I have two heads, each covered in a profusion of boils and welts that seep and weep uncontrollably. I leave a fluorescent green trail of vile poison as I slime along the ground. I have horns, and a large fork, and, of course, a tail. I keep bits of half-eaten children about my person at all times, and from every devil-red pore escapes the malodorous hum of rotten intent. That's how you can tell what I am. Spiders have eight legs, giraffes have long necks, paedophiles look like the devil incarnate. Right?

WRONG. Heartfelt apologies good citizens of the world. We have no such markings. We're the chameleons of the human world. Like aliens we assume human identities. And most of us are free tae roam and act. I look just like you, or your father, or your next door neighbour. Just the same. Just the fucking same.

I wake this morning wi' that undeniable feeling and my past experience tells me it's serious. I don't know why it comes when it does. Sometimes I go for months and feel nothing at all. Other times I feel it mildly and I just need tae shut myself away for two or three days and wank relentlessly until my cock's raw and the feeling's sated. If my magazines and films don't work (through over-use) I walk tae the local primary school and watch the football or rugby games along wi' parents and uncles (and other like-minded folk); or I go tae the swimming pool and exercise my right to be naked wi' young boys in a public place. In the showers and cubicles I get a glimpse of the pale goodies they have to offer. The faces and bodies serve as fresh, visual substitutes for my porn fantasies when I return home.

I cancel all appointments for the day. I've been wanking like billy-o all week but the feeling hasnae left. If anything it's got stronger (and with it this 'new-improved' feeling) and I know I won't be able to function or concentrate in the real world until it does, so there's nae point trying.

I make myself a huge breakfast: bacon, eggs, tattie scones, black pudding and haggis. I make double what I can eat and eat it all. I'm thinking mibby I can draw attention away fae my cock by satisfying my belly. But it disnae work. For an hour afterwards I feel too bloated tae move. I don't want tae leave the flat cause I'll regret it if I do. That's what happened wi the last kid, John Morrison. I got his name fae the papers. Little fucker reported me, even though I told him nobody would believe him, and that if they did he'd be taken intae care and then I'd come back and kill him. The fucking lengths you have to go to these days. Kids've got nae fucking fear or respect. I felt bad afterwards – always do. Once satisfied it's like waking up fae a bad dream; or like the morning after a wild, drunken party. I replay what I remember and think, fucking hell, did I *really* do that? It's as if I've been possessed. I always say never again. Never fucking again, I'm finished wi' all that shite. And I absolutely mean it – until the next time.

I wash the dishes and pull myself off wi a soapy hand. I make the bed, bubbles tingling as they burst on my dangling cock. My cock grazes against the rough blankets as I bend tae tuck them in. I brush and dribble against the leather couch. I tidy, hoover, polish the living room. Daydream. Feel. Stand by the window. Lick my finger, squeeze the spunk from my little eye, insert it into my mouth and suck, rolling my finger around my tongue – tasty, though a poor substitute for the real thing. Feeling getting stronger. Unbidden images slice into view. Shit! Stop. Cock back in. Clean the bathroom. Water the plants. Put the rubbish out. Stop. Rub through jeans… cock out.

I get myself comfy on the couch. Pick up my favourite magazine and press play on my favourite fantasy. I give full attention to working my groin. One minute. Two. But it isnae happening. I want more. I'm scaring myself. I bring myself tae the point of fantasy murder and then stop, unclimaxed. I know I won't be satisfied by wanking today and I'm terrified and trembling and fucking hard from it.

Mibby I could just walk tae the corner shop to get some fresh air and exercise, I've been in all day *and pass by St Ninian's on the way, just in time tae catch them on their dinner break, the little lads and lassies, running through the gate, wind in their hair, squealing, shouting, playing…*

OK then, mibby I should take a ride around town on the bike, gie myself a break, try tae dissipate this rising tension *even better, duck out of town, drive out to Auldgirth or Thornhill, just in time tae catch the latecomers ambling back across the fields after dinner at home, not a care in the world ...*

I stop kidding myself. I dress in my leather trousers – the ones with the extended poppers – and nothing else. I pull on my leather jacket and routinely switch off plugs etc.

I'm like a kid about to go tae Disneyland: a paedophile about to go tae Kiddyland. I grab a pound coin from on top of the telly as I leave. I'm too excited. My cock strains against the leather, dribbling a slug-like trail from its eye.

I leave the flat in a state of intense sexual agitation.

ONLY COLLECTING DANDELIONS OR SOMETHING

Margaret follows a strict routine each day that cannot be compromised. Most of the time her husband, family and neighbours don't notice but occasionally it's unconcealable and they ask her what she's doing. She's adept at telling lies, knowing they mustn't ever be told the truth. If they knew they'd think she was either mad or joking and she is neither. She is, in fact, a witch.

She discovered she was a witch when she was just eight years old. She had been collecting dandelions in the old shed at the bottom of the garden when she just *had a feeling* that she shouldn't pick any more. It was summer and the garden was full of them and she'd collected quite a lot already – enough to fill her doll's bathtub that she was using for the occasion. This dandelion that she had in her grip seemed to be saying to her 'something bad will happen if you pick me' and she'd hesitated, and thought about it, and decided that she wanted just one more, and so she picked it, its sticky juice soiling her hand, the green threads of the stem breaking unevenly. She put it in her bathtub with the others. There, that was enough.

When she'd woken up that morning, and bounced downstairs, she'd expected to find her mother busy at something in the kitchen, as she usually was. Instead a piece and jam had been left on the table for her, along with a glass of milk. Margaret supposed her mother was over at Kitty's or Mabel's or another neighbour's house. She didn't mind. It meant she'd be able to slip out without washing her face.

Five minutes after collecting dandelions she heard her Aunt Sandra shouting on her from the top of the garden and wondered what she was doing there. Margaret didn't like Aunt

Sandra. She was mean, and she didn't like children cause she didn't have any herself. She wasn't fun to play with – she thought playing meant spelling games and adding-up games, all the things you had to do at school already and she always insisted on cleanliness, even when Margaret was playing outside. Margaret hid round the side of the shed, standing on a pile of grass cuttings her dad had left last time he'd cut the grass. Her bare knees scuffed against the rough shed and a spelk got stuck in her knee. By now Aunt Sandra was halfway down the garden and Margaret knew it wouldn't be long before she found her and made her do something she didn't want to do, or go somewhere she didn't want to go.

Aunt Sandra approached the shed looking grim as usual. Margaret peeped out from first one side and then the other, squealing, nervously excited.

"Didn't you hear me calling you child?" Sandra snapped as she appeared, grabbing hold of Margaret's small arm. She pulled her roughly up the garden towards the house while Margaret protested that she wanted to carry on playing in the garden.

"Well you can't," Aunt Sandra said dourly. "There'll be no playing in the garden from now on because from now on you won't have a garden to play in: you're coming to live with me."

They reached the house and Aunt Sandra let go of her arm. Margaret, now curious and rubbing her spelked knee, followed Sandra into the kitchen.

"Where's my mummy?" Margaret asked, outraged that she'd been dragged from her den on the authority of Aunt Sandra.

"Gone," snapped Sandra. "Run off with the coal man, just like I knew she would from the day your father met her."

She handed Margaret a drink of lemonade. "Now drink that and then we can pack some things. Don't bring too much though. I don't want my house messed up by your rubbish. Hurry-up."

And that was that. It seemed Margaret's mother had in fact run off with the coal man, and her dad, unable to cope, had sought solace in the arms of a beautiful vodka bottle. When Margaret was collecting her things to take to Aunt Sandra's she'd gone back to the shed where she'd left her colouring books and had found the bathtub with the dandelions. The last dandelion she'd picked lay on top, looking bigger and thicker and meaner than the rest. She recalled the feeling she'd had when picking it and guiltily knew that this was her punishment. From now on she mustn't disobey what things told her. She'd listen and be good, and hopefully one day her mum would come back and her dad would come back, and she would be allowed to live with them again and it would all be all right.

So now, aged 34, Margaret sticks to her routine, only it's become far more complex and intricate – but it's magic, and magic mustn't be tampered with.

Each morning she gets out of bed on the left side, even though she sleeps on the right, and clambers over her new husband Derek on her way to the bathroom. She rinses her face, using her hands and cold water only, six times. She turns to the left and dries her face with her large, pink, bath towel that she also uses for washing her hair and bathing. She brushes her teeth with her blue toothbrush, holding the toothpaste in her left hand, then rinses her mouth out by bringing the water from the tap on the toothbrush eight times (odd numbers are used for other things entirely). She puts her toothbrush and the toothpaste back in the holder, the attached toothpaste cap not properly shut, turns to the left and exits the bathroom.

Occasionally mistiming her steps she arrives at the top of the stairs and, left foot first, descends, her right foot satisfactorily landing on the second last step before she reaches the bottom.

Her first chore of the day is always to wash the dishes of the previous evening's dinner. She collects all the used cups and plates and stacks them neatly beside the sink. She fills the green basin with hot water and Fairy Liquid and puts her rubber gloves on. She washes eggcups, then china cups, then mugs, then saucers, small plates, big plates, teaspoons, forks and knives before dealing with anything bigger like pots and pans. Then she makes breakfast for the boy.

This has been her fixed routine for one and a half years. Every day, faithfully, since her first husband Jack died, knocked over by a car while going to the shop to buy a sherbet dip for their son with a pound coin the boy had found on his way home from school.

She'd called him the boy ever since that day. Before that he'd been called Tee-Tee, not his proper name of course but the one her husband had used on him since he was a baby and which had been adopted by the family since. She didn't blame the boy. She entirely blamed herself. That was what happened when you turned your back on witchcraft. It had returned to dog her in the same way as when her mum had left.

Before she'd met Jack the amount of time she was spending on her witchcraft was increasing. She'd become responsible for all kinds of world events: from who won Wimbledon (she'd had to sit side-on to the telly and stroke her hair with her left hand three times before Bjorn Borg served a shot) to helping Britain win the Argentinean war (she'd done spells by rolling up herbs in tissue paper and storing them in a special bag).

When she met Jack and married him she became happier than she'd ever been. He was a good man: kind, loving – all the adjectives you'd want to apply to the one you love. They'd been delighted when she became pregnant and the boy had been born. Her growing happiness had led to a dwindling of her practising magic. She simply forgot about it. She only kept to a basic routine of walking round a certain tree a certain way, and not stepping on the cracks in the pavement on Buccleugh Street, but apart from that it had left her life.

The day the boy had come home and produced the pound coin he'd found, desperate to go to the shop to buy his favourite sweet of the moment – a sherbet dip – was the day that the old feeling had returned to Margaret. She was at the kitchen sink in her blue pinny washing dishes. She wanted to indulge him 'cause he'd just been to the doctor's. Jack said he would go to the shop for the sherbet dip while the boy changed out of his school clothes, and she just *had a feeling* that if she washed the knives before the forks something horrible would happen to Jack on the way to the shop. She was reluctant to listen though because she'd been so happy without witchcraft and so she ignored the feeling, thinking, what could possibly go wrong from here to the corner shop? She relaxed, washed the cutlery in any old order and let him go to the shop with the boy's money. As soon as he'd left the house she knew. She paced back and forth, anxiously awaiting his return, trying to do counter-spells to redress the balance. None of it worked. The policeman was as kind as he could be but her happiness had been destroyed and she obediently returned to trusting her magic heavily.

When she met Derek she took him on more as a companion and financial provider than as a husband. She counted herself lucky to have found anyone at all at her age, let alone someone willing to take on another man's six-year-old son. Derek positioned himself, very firmly, as the head of the household. He was to be consulted on all matters and the final say in any decision was definitely his. He was opinionated and persuasive and Margaret soon deferred to him on every concern. Including the boy. Derek took an active interest in the boy, and the boy became sullen and distant. Margaret wished Derek would leave the discipline and affection to her but Derek said they were a family now and the boy had to accept that.

He was good to the boy in his own way. He tried. He took the boy on adventure days out and always bought him a present on the way home. They even went camping in the Lake District.

'Male bonding,' Derek called it. He shared responsibility for the boy, which Margaret was grateful for. She thought all the attention and treats would eventually win the boy over but it didn't. If anything he was even more moody and silent after a trip out with Derek. Last time they'd gone camping he'd caused a terrible commotion just before they set off. His little hands gripped hard onto Margaret's skirt and it had taken all her grown-up strength to prise him off. He sobbed his heart out as the car drove down the driveway, his little face pressed against the glass, smearing it with saliva and snot. Margaret didn't understand. The way the boy acted anyone would think Derek was beating him up *or something*. She thought it must be because he missed his dad. Anyway – he'd have to put up with it. She couldn't cope on her own.

WATERMARKED

Open the door onto a world of vivid visuals. The grass shot-through with green; the sky with brilliant blue cyan. Pillar boxes red. Heavy hues. Luscious. Leafy. Languid. A beautiful day, and the air, muted, as if in a gasp. Sounds, suspended on this special day, linger, watching, awaiting their cue.

Step down the watery steps, oh so slowly. Through the floating iron gate. Peel the cover from the bike. Insert the key. Today's the day.

A child will die. Tommy feels it in the doughy sweat on his skin, in the pulp of his bones. He straddles the bike, kicks it into life and sets off down the road. He heads straight for St Michael's school – his very own – passing others on the way, playgrounds quiet now after riotous breaks.

He's no longer in his body but sits at the back of his head, watching through windowed eyes. People go about their daily business. They don't notice that the world has stopped and he's got off. Any minute, he's sure, someone will stop him, take his arm gently and say, it's okay friend, you're safe now, it's finished, we'll take away these bad feelings and replace them with normal ones, you'll be just like us.

But that doesn't happen. He's watermarked, and today's the day that a child will die.

He waits at traffic lights, engine purring. He pulls off, an excited buzz settling in his stomach. He looks to the left and sees the most gorgeous boy leaving school a little early. Too late to turn left he circles the block.

Panic sets in with the boy out of sight. His stomach flutters. He wonders if he's peed himself he's so wet with anticipation.

The boy's image is burned into his eyes, the peachy fresh, honeyed skin, the freckled nose. He turns the next corner. Blond everything. Fluffy soft hair and succulent skin. Next left. Look for him. Amber. Red. Where's he got to?

The van smashes into him full impact, side on. Screeches as it desperately tries to stop.

Tommy drops limply to the ground, money spilling from his pocket. A freeze-frame. Now people stop to look at him. The frame judders into motion and people move towards him.

Tommy opens his eyes, a taste of metal in his mouth. A mess of people crowd round him, peering and poking, unintelligible. Tommy tries to move his head to respond, to get up, but there's something very wrong with his body. He can't move or feel anything. For a few moments he's dazed, then memory crashes in on him. He remembers the chase and groans. It wasn't meant to be like this at all.

Mangled and tangled in the frame of his bike, someone is trying to lift it off him, someone else is saying no, leave it for the fire brigade to cut him free, someone else says shouldn't we put him in the recovery position, someone else peers closely at him, says don't move, help is on its way, you'll be all right pal, someone further back says don't crowd him, there's too many people here, leave him in peace, someone else says he's losing consciousness, when's the ambulance going to come, and someone else steps through a gap in the crowd, bends over and stares. The blond boy.

The child looks at him, brow creased.

The hum of the crowd, discussing, arguing and directing one another fades into a background drone and Tommy and the boy are left contemplating each other. Tommy dips in and out of consciousness. The boy fazes in and out of focus. Tommy sees an angel, brilliant, whitened, haloed by blinding light. The angel hovers close by. Smiles at him. Forgives him. It's all right, mouths the angel, it's finished now, it's over, give me your hand, come with me. The angel reaches out his cherub hand, his body reaches to meet him, to kiss him and keep him. Tommy is slipping...

The angel withdraws his hand, breaks free from the light and disappears. Tommy is left alone and hurtling towards black.

BLACK

Today's the day that a child will die. Tommy. Six years old. Frozen at the age of trauma.

Nothing must be done to harm the children. *Please.*

TOMMY THOMPSON'S STORIES

One day I went to the doctors. I had a sore leg. I left school early and my mum picked me up. Don't cross the road by yourself Mrs Elliot said. Wait till your mum comes. I will I said. Mum is late. I waited at the school gates for fifteen minutes. Then an ice cream van came. Don't spend all your money on sweets Mum said. I won't I said. I bought a sherbet dip, my favourite, and a lollipop. There was a loud bang on the corner. Lots of people ran over to see. All the people were talking. There was a gap I went in. A man bumped into me. Watch out lad he said. I will I said. I went in another gap. A woman said call the ambulance. I went under a big mans legs. A man was on the ground sleeping with his motorbike. My dad has a motorbike. On Sunday we went for a run round the block. Hold on Dad said. I will I said. My Dad drives fast. He puts a rope round me so I don't fall off. We went to the main road and then we went to the sweet shop and we got mum some Coke and we got her sweets and dad got a Mars bar and then the weather was not nice so we went home. and then we went to a pub and I had some pie to eat then I went home. And then went to bed. Dad read me a story. It had a magic castle and a bear in it. We have an apple tree in the garden. My mums friend Joyce came over. We had a barbeque in the garden my Dad cooked it. It is sunny for a change. Yes said Mum. My hamster played in his ball in the garden. I don't like hairy things said Joyce. No neither do I said Mum. I played on a swing then Dad came and said do you want to help me cut the apple tree down because it's twisted. I would like to help. I would like you to help Mum. I will Mum said. Put the sticks in a pile. When I finished we put some fire on it then we went to bed. The man's bike fell on him. His leg is twisted like the Apple tree. He has a dog's bone sticking out in a rip in his trousers. There is a pound coin by his head. I bend over and pick it up. The man opened his eyes and looked at me. I wasn't pinching it I said. I was picking it up for you. He shut his eyes and I put the pound in my pocket. His eyes look funny. Like when Jerry hits Tom on the head and Tom falls over and has stars and birds on his head. He is still looking at me. He has a sore mouth. I have to go and get my mum I said. My Mum is shouting on me. I thought I told you to wait at the gates Mum said. I did I said. Well what were you doing over there. We got the bus to the doctors. I sat at the front and pretended to drive. They put the man in an ambulance. The cover was over his head to keep him warm.

JAMES McKENZIE
dogfight

It was Danny Sessions who first came up with the idea of a dogfight. Around mid-October, when it started getting dark early, the four of us were hanging about the back of Deakin's Motors; checking door handles, trying to get inside one of the second-hand cars to smoke a fag and see if anything had been left behind. Sometimes we found old cassettes or something under the seat. Tom reckoned he found ten quid once, but nobody saw him. And one night Pete stuck his hand down the back of a driver's seat and pulled out a pair of dirty pink knickers. He chased the three of us around the car lot, swinging them above his head and chucking them at anyone he got close to.

Danny and Pete were creased up laughing. They were wearing these thin jackets and when they weren't laughing they were shivering.

This is fucking silly, Pete said. My bollocks are trying to climb up inside me.

As we walked between the cars the two of them took it in turns to breathe out hard and we watched as their breath condensed like shiny grey wool in the air.

Hey, here, look at this, Tom said.

We turned around thinking he'd found another door open but he put his mouth up close and breathed onto the side window of a fairly new Ford Capri. Deakin's must have bought it recently. In the thin wet film Tom drew a big cock and balls with his finger. He was just starting on the woman's spread legs by the time his breath disappeared again. Pete looked at him and shook his head. Danny kicked the wheel of the car and then leant back onto the side of another.

What the fuck we doing here? he said.

Soon after that we stopped going down to Deakin's, didn't play much football and hardly ever went up Robber's Hill. We were looking for something else to do. When we had any money we went down the King George. If we got there early enough we sat in the armchairs around the open fire and talked about... well, sometimes we talked about Sarah Brakewell. Her dad, Ted, owned the pub, so she was often serving. And as long as Ted didn't come down, we usually got a free pint or two.

Sarah let us know that Ted didn't like us sitting up at the bar when he was about. That's because apart from Danny, who was nineteen, we were a bit too young to be drinking in the George. Tom and me were fifteen, Pete was sixteen. Once or twice though, Ted came down in a good mood and caught us sitting up at the bar. Then he said, Sarah, love, find out what these lads are drinking. And we were all, Thanks Ted, cheers mate. And that was Ted gone up in our estimations for the whole night.

What about dog fighting? Danny said.

Over by the pool table, Tom was getting thrashed by Pete. Every now and then we heard Tom shout, as a ball went off somewhere unexpected, or he accidentally potted one of Pete's balls. When he finally managed to get one of his own down, the white ball went bouncing around the cushions and ended up spinning towards the bottom pocket and went in.

Tom looked across at me and Danny and said, I don't know what the fuck's wrong with me tonight, I'm playing crap.

Pete was smiling. Tom played crap every night.

At first I thought he was joking. We were sitting in the two armchairs and he was smoking a cigarette. The chairs had high backs that curved around at the sides and then sloped down into soft arm rests just wide enough to rest your pint on. We called them thrones, and on nights when everyone was standing around, gripping their pints and eyeing up the only two armchairs in the pub, thrones is what they felt like.

What you grinning at? Danny said. He had his feet up on a wooden stool and was flicking ash onto the carpet. What, you think it's a crap idea?

Pete and Tom must have heard his tone because they stopped playing.

The fire was too hot. I was covered in a blanket of warm air and the back of my shirt was sticky. Danny picked up his pint and brought it towards his mouth but he carried on staring at me.

No, sorry, Danny, I said. It's just I thought you were joking.

Yeah, well, listen, it *will* be a laugh. We can make some good money out of it.

We can breed a real big mother fucker! Tom shouted across.

Then Pete joined in. Hey, my aunt Sue's got a Jack Russell, vicious little bugger it is.

The back of Danny's chair was all they could see from the

pool table. But without turning around, and as if the conversation were finished, Danny said, Don't be a twat, Pete.

But Pete went on. Well, come on Danny, none of us have got a dog. And even if we're going to breed one, it'll take fucking ages before it's ready.

We can buy one, can't we? Tom said. He looked at the back of Danny's chair.

Have you got any idea how much a dog like that'll cost? Pete said. Have you Tom? And have you got any money? Eh? No? Shut the fuck up then.

Danny leant forward and craned his neck round the side of the chair to look at both of them.

Why don't you two ladies stop squabbling and come over here? I'm not talking about getting a dog, I'm talking about organising the fucking thing.

Tom gave Pete a pissed off look, threw his cue down onto the pool table and walked over to where we were sitting.

A pint or two later it was all settled. The venue, the prize money, the entrance fee and the profit.

Fine, all we need to do now is find the dog owners, Pete said. And went off to the bar to chat to Sarah.

That boy's beginning to fuck me off, Danny said, tapping his shirt pocket for his cigarettes. He knows what happened the last time.

Over at the bar, Sarah was pouring a pint and she was laughing with some older guy who was sitting on a bar stool next to Pete. Her head was tilted and from where we were sitting her throat looked long and thin. Her hair was swinging gently from side to side. Sarah laughed like that sometimes, like she was auditioning for a part in a movie. She finished pouring the pint and put it down in front of Pete. He must have said something because then she gave him a big smile. Pete and Sarah had known each other from first year. Danny reckoned she had slept with him. Pete wouldn't say and when I asked Sarah, she said, You shouldn't listen to what Danny Sessions says.

Sarah…Break…well, Danny said, picking up his pint off the chair arm. I bet she did. He smiled and took a swig of his beer.

He'd said it a hundred times before.

We went out to look at the barn that weekend. Tom's uncle had a farm just outside the town in the fens and as we walked along the road, by the edge of the cornfield, Tom's uncle told us that he'd put up two new steel sheds at West Acre.

I been meaning to rip that barn down since, he said.

He didn't say anything else on the way there, but as we stood outside the barn, he said, A couple of boyos from Giles End reckoned they could use it for scrap.

Tom hadn't told him what we needed the barn for. He said if we made any money from it, there'd be something for his uncle too. Tom's uncle just nodded, chucked the padlock onto a patch of grass and slid back a big wooden door.

Except for a disused tractor blade, the barn was empty.

Ain't much light in 'ere at moment. But won't take much to rig something up.

On the roof, the birds were scratching about. Under the cracked grey skylight the mud floor was faintly lit up. There was a strange smell; in the air was a damp tang of manure. I looked around.

Don't you worry about that, boyo, Tom's uncle said, I had dung in here, be gone soon. He turned and went to over to the door.

Lock up, Tom. I'll have a word with Fred Sayers, he's got an old generator in one of his corn sheds, at Banley Gate. Maybe yous can get it going.

Pete joked about him as we walked back into town. You-boyos-had-best-be-careful-with-them-there-four-legged-wilde-beest.

Tom was looking happy. We all were. Danny was walking along with a stick in his hand, whacking bits off the roadside hedges. We figured out a way we could make a bigger profit on the bets and decided to charge three instead of two quid entrance fee.

After all, Pete said, Them boyo's has gotta pay for their enertainment.

As we came up Chancellor's Lane, Tom told us his uncle's farm had been in their family for six generations.

Well fuck me, Danny said. Who'd want to spend their whole life in this shit hole?

Tom stopped smiling and looked at Danny.

Never mind six of the fuckers, Danny said.

We planned the dogfight for the last Saturday in October. But by the second Saturday of November we still only had one dog owner. It was a guy Tom's older brother knew. He had a pitbull and said he wanted to make at least thirty quid. I told Danny we'd have to get ten more people to come.

Me and Pete were sitting up at the bar and Pete had been telling Sarah these dirty jokes. Danny had gone with Tom to see a couple of mates about a 'financial deal'. Tom said Danny told him not to say anything about it, I knew there was no point in asking Danny. He always tapped his finger on the side of his nose and said, Need to nose basis.

Sarah was in a good mood. Pete told her about the guy with the pitbull, and that we still needed to find another dog.

Well, she said, there are plenty that come in the King George. What about Susan Priestley?

Pete coughed like he was about to spit out his pint.

Na, Pete said. We want *somebody* to put money on the pitbull.

Sarah had a nice face. She was a bit overweight, but overall, proportionally I mean, she had a good figure. When she moved about behind the bar, I looked at the shape of her breasts. They seemed so womanly and she was only seventeen. But it was always her hair that figured most in my fantasies. It was long and brown and hung down onto her shoulders in two thick waves. It looked really soft. It was really soft. A couple of times she'd let each of us touch it.

Danny said that Pete was only the first and that really she wanted to fuck all of us. When Pete went off to the toilet, I asked her what she was doing on Saturday. I told her I was going into town to the new Radley shopping centre.

Sorry, I can't, she said. I've got to help my dad clean out the cellar this weekend.

Perhaps another weekend? I said, thinking we could set a date.

Yeah, perhaps another weekend, she said, and moved over to wipe down the other side of the bar.

When Pete sat down again, we drank our pints until they were nearly empty and Pete told her to give us two more halves. She filled both of them to the top. On a good night we could do that quite a few times.

Are you going to come to the dogfight then, Sarah? Pete asked.

I don't know, we'll see.

You could set up a bar, make a killing, Pete said.

He always seemed comfortable with Sarah. They were smiling at each other again.

Should be lots of that, I said.

She said she'd think about it.

It was later that night, I asked her if she was a virgin.

None of your bloody business! she said. And took three empty glasses off the bar and over to the sink.

When the other two came in they were pissed.

Alright Sarah? Danny said. You're looking gorgeous tonight, sweetheart.

Tom smiled stupidly and sat down on a bar stool.

You're not looking too bad yourself, Sarah said. How's work?

Fucking back breaking, I'm gonna give it up and go to London.

Danny worked on the building site at the bottom of Lincoln

Road. Whenever he'd had enough of it, he talked about this bloke he knew in London – someone who could set him up with a good city job. Pete challenged him on it one night after we'd had a few pints.

Why don't you go then, Danny? Sounds too good to miss.

As soon as we got outside the pub, Danny turned round and head-butted him. The blood was pouring out of Pete's nose in the back of Reggie Taylor's car. By the time we got him to the hospital it was already turning black, but it wasn't broken.

Danny pulled up a stool, picked up an empty glass from the bar and told Sarah to pour him another half. He turned to me and Pete. Move over then boys.

OK, Sarah said. But you're going to have to pay for the next one.

Danny leant forward and stared at her. Alright love, alright.

The following week we found another dog owner. Danny had been put in touch with him through a mate on the site. The guy had a young Rottweiler. He said it would rip the guts out of any pitbull. We thought it didn't have a chance but I said we'd have to get people to bet on it. If that didn't work, we'd fiddle the odds some other way.

The sun was shining the day we walked out to revisit the barn. Pete was away at his grandparents. Sarah came along to see where the bar could go. She said she just wanted to have a look, nothing definite. We were supposed to be putting some wooden planks across the back as benches, doing a couple of repairs on the wire cage we'd got hold of. That's all.

Inside the barn the air was crisp. We wanted to hold the event before it got any colder. Tom's uncle said that if there was any snow on the ground, we could pretty much forget it.

Dogs or no dogs, no bugger'll come, he said.

Tom swore he hadn't told him what we were doing.

Sarah was standing over by the bundle of wire and light bulbs that we'd got along with the generator. She was wearing a bomber jacket and a black thigh-length skirt.

It's great, Sarah said. You could have a really good party in here.

Danny leant over and whispered in my ear, I'd fucking party with you any day, Brakewell.

We looked across to where she was standing.

Right then lads, coats off, let's get to work, Tom said.

Whatever you say Thomas, Danny said. You're the boss.

Sarah smiled coyly. Coats off? It's a bit cold, isn't it?

Come on, darling, Danny said. If the work don't warm you up, then this will. His hips were thrust forward and his hand was grabbing hold of his crotch.

If Sarah was wary of Danny, she wasn't showing it. She looked across at me and Tom and said, I think he'll need some help boys.

She took off her jacket and reached up to hang it on a nail in the corner of the barn. The blue cardigan she was wearing rose up above her skirt and there was a thin band of skin bridging the two. Danny elbowed me in the side and pointed to her arse. He held out his flat hand and ran his tongue from the middle of his palm up between his fingers. Whenever Danny grinned he looked like a weasel.

Watch this, he whispered. Sarah love, why don't you and Tom sort out those lights on the floor while we put up the benches.

Tom didn't know what was going on. What about fixing the cage? he asked.

Never mind the fucking cage! Danny said.

We watched as Sarah bent over and started unravelling the wire.

When the benches were up and the lights unravelled, we started on the cage. Sarah had taken off her cardigan, her long sleeved T-shirt was clinging tightly to the shape of her breasts and I thought she had lost a bit of weight too. At one point Tom was doing something inside the cage and Danny locked him in. It was only made of chicken wire and a few planks of wood

Oh yeah, right, Tom said, Looks like I'll have to break down the side.

Danny raised his eyebrows and smiled humourlessly. I wouldn't do that if I was you, Thomas.

Eventually Danny let him out.

I didn't know what was going on at first. I was back over by the benches, retying one of the ropes, when I heard Danny saying in a slow mocking tone, Yeesss.

And Sarah, trying to sound angry, saying, No!

Then Danny shouted, Come on lads, give us a hand! And he was pulling her towards the cage. Me and Tom ran over and we picked her up. We were laughing. I think even Sarah was laughing. She was struggling like mad but we were all laughing, and as we got her towards the cage door, I went forward to hold it open. Then she slipped or Danny pushed her but the next thing the two of them were on the ground and Danny was trying to pin her down.

Get hold of her hands! he shouted, and me and Tom held down one each. Sarah was sounding more worried. Every time she said, Danny! It sounded like a question, an answer and a protest all in one.

Then I saw that her skirt was all the way up her leg.

Danny! she said.

Her hair was spread out against the mud. I remember thinking that the two were indistinguishable. You couldn't tell where the one began and the other ended, I saw the whole of the barn fill up with her soft brown hair. I don't know which but she was wearing a nice perfume. I caught a whiff of something sweet and woody. The muscles in her neck were taut and as her arms struggled against Tom and me, it seemed like she was pushing one breast up into the air and then the other.

Danny had his cock out. I saw the tip of it poking out from his fist. There was a line of black hair running down from his stomach to the thick curly bush just below his hand. He was struggling with his jeans with one hand and with the other, he was trying to pull or rip her tights off.

Danny! she screamed. Her chest was rising and sinking in panic and this time there was no mistaking the fear in her voice.

I moved my knee up onto her wrist so that I didn't need to hold her down with both hands. I brought my free hand up to her hair and ran my fingers through the ends. She was kicking out at Danny and then I thought I could smell something sour coming off her skin. I put my hand on top of her shoulder and slid it under her T-shirt and bra. I could feel her nipple, the skin on her breast was smooth.

Her head jerked towards me, What are you doing! she said.

I snatched my hand away. Without even knowing it, I'd let go of her arm and now her fingers were digging into Danny's cheek. I stood up, surprised more than anything, though I thought I was going to be sick. Danny got up as well, he was shouting and swearing but he wasn't trying to hit her. Tom still had hold of her arm.

Let go of me! she shouted, and pulled her arm away from his grip.

She got to her feet without taking her eyes off any of us. She pulled her skirt down and straightened out her top. There were bits of dried mud and a few fine strands of straw hanging from her hair. I wanted to help her take them out but as soon as I moved towards her, her face snapped round in my direction.

Stay away from me!

She moved over to her coat and took it off the hook. She was shaking. When she reached the door she turned around.

If any of you come anywhere near the pub, I'll let everyone know what happened. My dad will fucking kill you.

The three of us stood there in the middle of the barn. It was quiet but for the birds making a noise on the roof. The barn door was open and in the far distance you could hear, like the waves of the sea, the rising and falling of passing traffic.

Danny kicked the cage door closed and the whole thing tilted one way and then another.

Fuck it! he said. I'm leaving. He meant it this time.

What about the dogfight? Tom said.

Fuck the fucking dogfight! Danny said. He had that look on his face – the one where he could lash out at anyone. You chicken shits couldn't organise a piss up in a brewery. He was looking straight at me.

I only saw Danny Sessions once again after that. He came back from London for a weekend. He was in the White Horse wearing a new leather jacket he'd bought with the money from selling Pension Saving Plans. Reggie Taylor said the only savings plan Danny Sessions knew about, was saving people from their own money.

When Pete got back from his grandparents, Sarah must have told him what had happened. I saw him coming down Hollinghurst Road about two weeks after it happened. At first I thought he was going to walk straight past me. Then he stopped. Alright Pete? I said. His face tensed like he was biting his own teeth. He punched me below my eye. He stood over me while I was crouched down. I braced myself for another but when I looked up he just shook his head and said, You stupid cunt.

Tom started working on his uncle's farm so he's not about much. I've been hanging around Deakin's again and I got to know some of the third years. I said I'd show them the ropes, take them up Robber's Hill and down the path that leads onto the back of Fraser's supermarket. When it gets a bit warmer.

JANE MONSON
Shouts from the Skin

Crossroads: Part I

My mother was in bed when I left for school;
my efforts to shake her out of sleep,
to get her to stand up, hug me, kiss me
and say, 'Bye sweetheart, see you after school,
enjoy your last day',
collapsed onto her warm, damp skin,
and made me leave her room
with a pain in my chest,
that climbed inside my neck
as I stepped out of the front door
into the snow,
along risen streets and slowed roads,
and over the red metal bridge
to Stapleton Road station.

I'd caught the same train for years
and always with my brother,
but he had cried in bed that morning
with an upset stomach,
and as the single carriage stopped at my feet,
moved off ungainly towards Clifton Down,
my shoes bouncing around the opposite seat,
my hands warming under my thighs,
I pictured the two of them
with shut faces,
black hair a mess around their head,
sunk into the pillows,
dreaming.

At half past one
I stopped eating and listening,
looked at the clock above the blackboard
and heard inside my head:

JANE MONSON

'What would me and Danny do without mum?'

In the minutes before the next lesson,
I had planned the rest of our lives.

When the final bell of the day rang,
I felt like an adult disguised as a child.

Some of the walk home was lit in patches
by street-lamps and corner-shops,
but in the darkness of high walled paths,
I listened to my steps
sifting and grinding unbroken ground,
crunching low and deep
around bends of crooked bricks;
my shoulder rushing against the snow
that frothed between cracks and ledges;
my startled breathing
when broken limbs of creepers
sprung out,
and caught on my face.

Turning onto the hill of our road,
I told myself I was getting closer to school;
that the numbers of the houses to my right
were getting younger,
that my footprints were appearing in front of me instead,
untreading the bleakness,
but outside 52, the street stopped moving
and the wind slowed down upon my face:
two doors away, in the empty space outside our house
was a car, its blue light crowned by an inch of snow,
its wheels dunked in slush
that edged down beside the kerb,
like a stiff dirty river.

Danny opened the door, shivering in his pyjamas.
Beside him, a man over twice his size in uniform,
closed the door behind me
and stood in my way,
to explain that 'mum was in hospital, with a broken arm or leg,
and would be back tomorrow or the next day.'
While he was speaking,
another man appeared in the hall from the kitchen,
without a word,

and I grabbed the banisters,
clamoured up the stairs,
'no she's not, she's dead, she's dead',
yelled into Danny's room where our clothes were kept,
tore the drawers onto the floor
rammed socks, tee-shirts, knickers, tights,
and a nightie into a bag.

Part II

We were as close as we could be that day:
my mother in a mangle
of bicycle bars and car tyres,
me in a classroom
staring at a clock,
while her head leaked blood into her hair
and stopped inside her hood to dry.

At half past one, her watch I wore for years after
was still working,
and in the moment
before the driver
went from his car to her side,
it was ticking while they were still;
moving with the clock on the wall,
when the classroom went quiet,
so I could hear her.

The Dream and the Visit

In the clearing of a Welsh forest,
the sky slumped and cried over our hoods,
our red plastic boots sucked in and spat out mud
around pond-sized puddles,
and we stopped in front of a hill;
stood frozen and dwarfed
before a hoard of grey cracked slates.

As we looked up, our hoods fell back,
and our eyes opened wide
at the maze of origami gaps,
and shadowed planes;
surfaces that shifted out of the dry,
soaked up the dark
and kept growing:
a myriad of gleaming layers and edges
that split cataracts of rain,
and tilted and clapped in secret places.

Inside the pine-stung wind
my mother took these words from my mouth:
'This feels war-like,
I've seen this before;
no, I've dreamt this before.'

Then turning towards the forest again,
we walked out of our dream
back across the needled path
with entangled thoughts and unsure smiles,
her arm around my waist.

Easter Island

Over by the water that collects in shallow dips,
thousands of lady crabs shake themselves
into miniature waves;
the soft pattern of eggs
dropping from their scarlet shells,
like crumbs from lifted skirts.

If the tide is fair
the land will bloom again
into fresh red crabs,
that keep the island's face
shifting and edging
over stones, inside grasses, across roads;
and changing
wax-red in the moonlight,
flashing white briefly
in the glare of head-lights,
glowing wet-red under the sun;
and moving
as it has always moved,
neither forwards
nor backwards, but sideways.

JANE MONSON

'Weston-Super-Mud'

Unhindered by its slurring tide
you flung clothes to the wet sand,
grabbed my hand and left everything unguarded
in the rain;
your frantic need to strip and swim,
the reason we ran so fast.

Behind us
the laughing mist:
a ghosted row of boys
who lined the wall between the town and the beach;
their shouts spat into the wind,
their whistling fingers
serenading your ashen hair,
and my callow flesh.

And then it all began to disappear:
first clothes, then wall, then boys,
then feet, ankles, calves, and knees:
the closer we got
to where the sea gurgled a beginning
or an end,
the more the sinking ground
would hide it from our eyes,
and when we stood still
searching for a wave of sea,
the more we could hear and smell
rotting, just outside us.

Pulling me over to you
my wind-sore hand bunched up in yours,
we slid away from the horizon;

the unsettling mixture
curdling on our legs,
lounging in our throats,
scratching at our eyes.

Walking back,
the wind crept sharp and cold
everywhere,
fixing our filthy,
naked skin.

JANE MONSON

Danny's Birthday Balloon

Lilleith went through cars like cigarettes.
On Danny's 14th birthday she drove us to a field near Bristol
in a red Citroen Diane, that juddered over smooth roads,
and made Danny swear and laugh above the engine's racket
into the soft brown frizz of her hair.

I snatched at views,
as they changed from smoking chimneys
to thin wintered forests,
tilting snowmen, collapsing in gardens;
the distant chill of cows, fences, ditches, fields,
keeping my eyes from the sky.

When we arrived, the ground around us
was hidden; altered; its surface blistering in colours,
that bubbled up and down like frogs' throats
with each storm of air.

We waited, in the grip of cold, noted hour,
and when the dry-ice breath of strangers lost its charm,
I imagined passengers smoking, leaning over the edge
and gasping: 'The air is so much better from a balloon'.

Families were everywhere, keeping warm,
hurling their arms around themselves or each other in punches.
I followed a small girl fighting for breath inside her padded suit;
red cheeks puffed up as plums,
her stubby run intended for giant striped skirts;
the rubber eyed fronts of her wellies
flung in and out of blooming stomachs.

I copied her kicking;
watched frost spit from balding tufts of grass,

until Lilleith shouted, 'Bye Danny, Happy Birthday.'
and I looked up and saw my brother being led to his balloon
where men and women were standing,
waiting to be lifted into a basket,
the wind-stuffed silk, heaving slowly from the ground
and my brother, rushed into a room of woven walls,
fire exploding over his head.

Pushing his glasses against his face,
he waved us away from him, back to the road we'd use
to follow the birthday boy and a flock of strangers,
the canvas roof of the car rolled down
so I could stand on the back seat
blame tears on the wind,
shout as though I was ecstatic about my face being stretched,
my hair lashed into knots,
my eyes opening and closing in slow motion with my fists,
scream, because my brother was flying into his birthday
somewhere without me;
curse, because when I'd hold him in my arms again,
he'd laugh out the sky in my face,
and cover me in strange air.

JANE MONSON

Tea in Ireland

Outside, by the holly bush
that arched and shaded the land
they had called Sarah,
he knelt and sunk his hands
into an old coal bucket full of water,
and wiped the last of the clinging ash
from every crease and corner of his skin.

As she stood over her uncle's greying head
the wind murmured inside her hood,
and grainy scatterings of her mother
changed direction on the water's surface,
while the rest
reeked of Irish soil,
and made a black line under his nails.

The tea cooled quickly in her palms.
"Shall I pour it now?"

Shutting his eyes,
drawing his breath in
as though he was about to sneeze,
he raised his head
towards the mist-slung mountains;
his hands trembling over the bucket
his face breaking into circles
the circles breaking into ash.

Stepping behind him,
standing over 'Sarah'
still wet from paint and rain,
she turned her wrist
and slowly
drained the cup.

The fawn-coloured liquid
smelt like her mother's breath,
and a kick inside her heart
shot through her skin to her fingertips,
upset the careful strand of tea,
so that it bent and broke everywhere.

She felt him move nearer,
heard the cup smash across the upturned earth,
saw a mess of cold, dark, milky puddles
look back at them,
and vanish.

JANE MONSON

Our Day Trip

Hidden behind the cushions
our family of hands
scratched at the sofa for a way out.

Somewhere amidst the tobacco bits,
the biscuit crumbs,
the Matchbox toys,
and pencils,
was enough for a day trip.

Reaching for the pot of coppers
above the fireplace,
I staggered as it slid and leaned in my arms.

Kneeling on the living-room carpet
the three of us counted and made up towers;
each one piling towards a pound,
crashing to the floor at halfway.

The moment we could buy tickets to the sea,
we snatched at coats, ran from the house
towards the bus station,
echoed through the tunnels,
and pulled your hands towards the city.

When we emerged into the centre
under the sun,
one moment you were laughing,
and then you were gone;
taken from us again.

Your hand yanked out of mine,
your body crumpled on the ground;

the stitches on your chin
re-opened;
a smack of red
on a wall surrounding a flower bed.

As sandwiches, juice, pills, cigarettes,
and money spilled from your bag,
a punk spat at you: 'Stop grovelling!'
and I screamed in his face
that you were having a fit,
until the cleaners came running
from the underpass toilets,
to hold our hands and ask our names.

Danny hid under my arm.
I looked over his head
and saw shoppers, drunks, performers and travellers
shoving and rushing each other,
in and out of a concrete spider.

The Artists

My mother and I
nursed an artist,
Errol Le Cain.

He was an illustrator of fairy tales;
he gave me *The Snow Queen*,
and I kept her
tucked under my pillow.

I wanted him to teach me
how he painted the wicked
so delicately;
he taught me to stop shaking
the spoon in my hand.

I remember the colours of the room:
woven browns and blues
maroons and creams;
oriental tapestries
fading behind incense and candle-smoke,
he never stopped burning.

Those colours and smells
were reflected in the silver eye of the spoon;
they were instead of the food.

Errol was hungry;
kept watching the spoon
dipping the soup and lifting to his lips.

My mother and I stood by;
anxious reflections
appearing and disappearing
in between mouthfuls,

until he could taste nothing,
but the words,
no more
thank you.
I've had enough.

SANDRA NEWMAN

Extract from **The Church of the Unexpected**

"This Isn't My House and You Aren't My Parents"

- 1 -

1.	My name is Chrysalis Moffat.
1.1	I was born in Peru.
1.2	When I was three, I was brought to the United States.
1.3	Here I was adopted by rich white people.
1.4	Insofar as that is possible, I became just like them.
2	I am brown, and my face looks like a South American mask because my parents were South American Indians.
2.1	My body, too, is foreshortened, plump; next to Anglos, I look rudimentary.
2.2	PC people make a point of saying I'm beautiful, even to my face.
3	Although I am so brown, I give an impression of whiteness.
3.1	People often remember me wearing white clothes when I was not wearing white clothes.
3.2	They also think my surname is White.
3.3	It's a supernatural phenomenon, I think.
4	My father gave me the name, Chrysalis.
4.1	He was a biochemist.

Discuss

No one in my family is interesting or praiseworthy; only my father. Born in rural poverty to alcoholic parents, he worked his way through Berkeley, received his Ph.D. and was expected to have a brilliant research career in microbiology. Instead of pursuing it, however, he volunteered for Vietnam.

My father fought in Vietnam for four years.

Although he would refer to the evils of that war, this was more polite, I believe, than sincere. Nor did he seem – though this must surely have been the case – to have fallen in love with jungles, technicolour murder, freewheelingness – to love the smell of napalm in the morning. In all he did, he was rather the simple, honest man. He was, preeminently, a man who loved dogs.

He got down on the floor and rolled with dogs; he swung children round and round by the hands, playing 'airplane'. Mom and Dad were always laughing behind their bedroom door, when we were very small.

You got the sense that, when all else failed and the world had weakened utterly, succumbing to corruption and mean-spirited trivia, still there would be Father, taller than everyone else and irreducibly blond.

He looked like John Wayne.

2	On the drive to my Uncle Jerry's, we used to pass my father's work.
2.1	It was called BSI: Something Something Institute.
2.2	It had a chicken wire fence and a checkpoint hut with an orange barrier.
2.3	No buildings were visible from the road, only set-piece maples.
2.4	Eddie and I would try to get the guard to wave.
2.5	Mom would sing out; "Hello, Bull Shit Incorporated!"
3	Early on, we realised there was something about Dad's work.
3.1	He was always going to Chile or Guatemala, conducting studies.
3.2	We couldn't know what he studied; that was a state secret.
3.3	The date of his return was likewise secret.
3.4	Where in Chile too.
3.5	Every five years, federal agents would appear to do a background check on my father, interrogating all the neighbours, the cleaning lady, and his friends. – Had he made any large purchases? – Was he cheating on his wife? – Did he ever take illicit drugs or drink to excess?
4	But I don't know, I only know he died when I was ten.

FATHER: ELEMENTARY

A   soldierly, upright:
he strode, and grinned, and gave
manly firm handshakes.
A is for Astronaut, like them,
like many Army men, he was
B   Permanently boyish,
brash, bluff, broad-shouldered
like a B-movie hero.
Or,
just,
BIG.
Moving on to
C   he was a cowboy.
A cracker born in Cody, Texas.
"Howdy, podner, I'm headin out t'the corral," he'd go,
corny for us kids.
We'd cackle,
cry, capsize
curl up with glee
because he was never there.
Conspicuous by his absence.
"Comin home real soon, chicken – "
D   Now he's dead.

But these big heads that watch over our childish night skies, a nightlight left on to the end of time in a darkened bedroom, mysterious like a Mayan hieroglyph or rune;
        indecipherable and throbbing
        nauseous
        headachey
        with its lolling top-heavy heap of cheap significance.

AT THE DINNER TABLE; 1971

Dad looks like John Wayne. He has grown his hair out of its familiar crewcut and dyed it black to stop the women in Peru asking him for autographs. People in Peru don't know John Wayne is old. Those movies are all brand new there.

  Mom is laughing and laughing. Dad sits up with his hands folded. I think he looks very fair, like when Eddie and I fight and Dad makes us sit down in 'court' and come to a 'settlement'.

Next to me, Eddie is making faces because we haven't had dessert yet and he knows there's chocolate chip ice cream.

"I'd kill to have been there," Mom crows, "the ladies in their ponchos mobbing the shady operative – Señor Wayne! Señor Wayne!" Then she does my father, talking into his wristwatch; "Operation Kookamunga, abort!"

"Lannie," says Dad, "I am not a shady operative."

"Señor Wayne! I see all jour movies!"

"Lannie. Nobody's laughing."

"Laughing? It's an effing laugh riot!"

Mom starts coughing and finally looks in her lap, distracted. Eddie pipes up:

"Mom? Are we having ice cream? I can get it, I can reach."

"Just one minute, Eddie, honestly."

And 'cause it's the dinner table, Mom has her tequila glass to hand, to grab to her mouth and her head bucks

chucks it down hard

two-handed, one

palm spread over the glass bottom to shove the liquor home

and hold the dry glass for a moment, leaving it time to shine and be seen

we are waiting too:

because there wasn't enough tequila, just wasn't enough, and the light swimming up the glass was a mockery of the tequila needed. Give her an effing sun that gave tequila not light, that gave inebriate night; the stiff moon floating like a pickled worm to another tequila sunrise and

by the tequila of that day, the shades of all the operatives would be washed out, the secrets dissolve in their vaults, unread, and through the blue weight come swimming

the promised things.

"Lannie. The children are waiting for dessert."

"This Isn't My House and You're Not My Children"

- 2 -

1	My mother was an art historian.
1.1	That's what she put on forms.
1.2	And she held a Master's in art history from Berkeley.
2	Really she was just rich.
3	It was family money.
3.1	Her father had made a killing in real estate.
3.2	Pictures of his suburban developments hung in the dining room when she was a child.
3.3	My mother used to think he built the houses himself.
4	Her family were rich people all day long.
4.1	They held their children as if they were vases; the dog was groomed by a company.
4.2	Salad fork for salad, full dress for breakfast.
4.3	They were, in these respects, profoundly, paranoiacally, arriviste.
5	My mother was just, common.
	– She was never persuaded to like shoes.
	– Her knees were skinned, somehow. Somehow she had mussed her crew cut.
	– She always looked as if she had just washed her face.
6	Girls who wore make up were weak, according to my mother.

STORY

When she turned eighteen, my mother's birthday present was a mansion. It was strategically chosen for its location on a dull stretch of California coast. Her father thought the town to be ripe for development. A gift, then, bought in my mother's name for tax reasons.

"But I can't even *live* in it," my mother squalled. "I'm going to college, *remember*?"

"It's an *investment*," said her father. "For your *future*."

They had the hackneyed screaming match, in which father laid down the law and daughter wept; mother fretted, saying patient reasonable things.

Around them were the beautiful acquisitions – like a jury. High ceilings and marble and even the placid air with its scent of autumnal roses; my mother fought bitterly, at that age, against their sway.

"I'm going to burn it down!" she screamed finally. "I'll invite you all over and burn it down!"

Her parents died in a car accident one year later.

She lived in that mansion for the rest of her life; Eddie and I grew up in it.

Her mother, Lily, who really was like a white funereal flower, and trembled, used to say that tomboys grew up to be the nicest big ladies.

Her father used to say, "Lannie's going to blow everything we've worked to save, you wait and see!"

1	After her parents' death, she moved into her mansion.
1.1	No one else lived there; there was no gardener, no maid. There was no furniture.
1.2	The derelict guest wing leaked, and moss grew, demarcating the parquet.
1.3	It was 35 rooms, two towers, a private beach, and a cultivated wood.
1.4	In the wood, she found a pointy-eared white mutt she called Remember.
1.5	They used to sleep together on the beach on summer nights.
2	Her brother Jerry got away with the bulk of the family fortune.
2.1	She hated him, she called him 'King Jerry', she was implacable.
2.2	There were court cases all her life; she never forgot that money.
2.3	The rest of the family backed him because my mother rode a motorcycle.
2.4	She never forgave them either, though she attended polite family gatherings.
3	When she was at Berkeley, she rode two hours to get to class.

3.1 She was penniless.
3.2 She sold all the mansion's antique doors.
3.3 She had three million dollars tied up in a law suit, but wouldn't borrow in case the bank "stole" her house.
3.4 When the money came through, she bought three cars.

4 Her mattress on the floor was surrounded by cigarette butts.
4.1 She'd taped cardboard over the broken windows on the ground floor.
4.2 In the courtyard lawn, one of her boyfriends had dug his name.
4.3 "It brought tears to your eyes," my Dad said, "Lannie was such a slob."

For a while, he was only one of many rotating boyfriends. Then he put his foot down. He turned up at her house one weekend, wearing a suit, to say, "OK, Lannie. Now we're going to buy furniture and then you're going to marry me. I had about enough of this runaround."

He was standing on her cracked white step, in sunlight, bearing a sheaf of flowers. The engagement ring was hooked on the first joint of his pinky; a diamond solitaire she wouldn't like. His stance was easy, friendly. They knew each other well; and he wanted, badly, to put the flowers down and touch her face.

She said, "No!"
But he was right.
Then he was in Vietnam.
Then he was in Chile at a secret destination, conducting studies.
For the rest of her life, my mother always had a mutt who would follow her down, down our private beach and out of sight, on summer nights.

BEGIN AGAIN

1 When my parents married, they were both 21.
1.1 They
   – smoked marijuana
   – drank
   – rode her motorbike down to Baja
1.2 When there was no party at the weekend, they threw one.

1.3   Wet hair; sun-tender skin; sand in the toe of a canvas shoe.

2   No one had seen anyone so much in love.
2.1   They had inside jokes. She rode him piggyback to bed.
2.2   Dad once broke a man's nose for calling her a slut.

3   He was doing his doctoral work.

4   She bought art and sold it to friends of the family.

5   There was always money; there were always friends; there were pre-booked tickets and dinner reservations.
5.1   "There was a little place with a patio where we used to have breakfast. I don't think I cared then if the whole world exploded."
5.2   "People were different then. You did what was expected of you, even if it was no fun. You didn't try to run the world."

Mother sat beside the pool and Father swam. We were not yet born, and Mother sat in her wet bikini bottoms on the concrete and green light swam in tiger stripes in mimicry of the tiger stripes that swam down father's back in muscles as he swam;
   it is water but it all comes to a point like the last note of a perfect rock anthem and
   here you are kneeling on wet concrete with both hands thrust down into the water as if you could catch something
   he goes off to his copters and jungles
   Sergeant Doctor Jonathan Moffat
   Jack, baby
   She used to call him John Wayne

Sometimes when she gets into the car in the sun for the minute while she waits for the plastic's heat to mellow – she slackens and breathes on a sudden note of sexual excitement, shuts her eyes surprised
   and smiles
   as if she's pulling out of a supermarket parking lot in Canada
   as if he's really here

   Your head is bigger than my head
   Your arms are bigger than my legs
   Your hands are bigger than my breasts
   You
   got right
   through me

man, so I
lost so much weight
I was so
I don't know *(She put her knuckles to her mouth she put the phone receiver to her lips, the cold plastic and its holes*
a nozzle
nuzzle the nozzle and
cry
baby
Are you ever really coming home)

My father used to say, if he'd had any sense, he would have stayed and protested against the war. We had no concept what hell guys went through there. War is about death, he would say, always remember that. Death.

He liked to say these things because he was a decorated veteran. He said them at dinner to people who had not been to war. My mother admired him as if it were a chore.

"It's not something to envy," said my father. "Not at all."

He said when we were grown up, there would never be any wars again. That's what he was working for, and with God's help, they'd get it licked.

The manner of his death was a state secret. No personnel attended his funeral, and Mom was advised not to advertise it in the paper. They buried an empty coffin. We saw Mom in a dress for the first time.

After that, often in the mornings we would find an uneven trench dug in the sand of our private beach. Mother had been out there pacing, and drinking, all night. Although it wasn't his job, the gardener used to go down and clear the butts from this trench. He would even seem to try to fill it in again, shovelling with his boot tips. At such times, he looked sad in a private, Hispanic, way, as if he realised that grief was something in the earth and it was vast and it would outlast him. As if Mexicans can cope with these things, are heavy enough and wise, although I know that's stupid.

KATE NORTH
No Particular Method

Icarus the Kite Flyer

From the window your bright fabric directs my eyes
in looping motions
erratic as the wind causing your dream-on-a-string to pull.

Taut arms upwards
open mouth suggesting
the world's pigeons beating in your chest.

I want to curve through the air
reaching for your colours
cling onto a ride that's not mine.

The Birth of Venus

A dart is flying down the M4 this evening.
When she hits home
she'll take the wind out of everyone's sails.
But as she's stripping off, she's growing.

With a smile like a canoe that's
announcing, all sorts of baggage resting in the boot,
she walks through the front door and declares;

I'm growing my hair.
I'm heading to Llangranog.
I'm going to that little cave where I sat with you.
    I'll count all the pearls of the coast,
        trying to keep them here in my lap.

Today I made myself a necklace of pearls.
Significant rounds, sea sliding across my neck.
Give me more for my arms and legs,
    let them be painted,
        I want to glow in the dark.

Sunbathing in Llangranog

I can see me dipping my toes over the side of a squeaky air bloated mat. Arms flapping in and out now, annoying myself, directing the spray onto my lenses. The sun burns through the water through the glass through my eyes.

…now rain shoots up from the Earth's core like tinsel rockets, clouds frown like crabs stranded on a shore, rabbits carry Spanish acrobats on their backs…

I can see you sat, a diver mid-tuck, rocking back and forth like an unstable Polar Bear. Opening each sandwich before you eat, checking for rogue ingredients. Then you spill the egg mayonnaise down your chin, quickly wipe away the evidence and check that no one has seen.

Turning Numb

There was no call at 2 a.m.,
not a siren, a policeman, an onlooker.
She knew where she was with death,
it had been waiting in the queue for years.

Dusk burnt as she entered the nursing home.
Woodbines, *Malteasers*, and updates on the docks;
she carried no surgical steals.

The smell of cabbage didn't bother her now,
nor did the woman who thought she was her daughter.
Though there was always the cold and quiet,
rude silence, interrupting air that should have followed shipping
                                                          forecasts.
Where was Biscay?

Where was her father?
Found
on the bathroom floor.
Waiting
for her to call the white hearse
which she followed in appropriate silence,
except for sucking viciously on a hard boiled sweet.

The Man with Two Left Feet
(for M.O.)

I'll take you dancing.

Please, not dancing.
How I long to waltz
my arm locked across your waist.
Crossing realms reserved for brothers,
sharing pulses designed for lovers.
Each foot placed by my desire for your melody
that toys with my spin.
Getting to hold you like I shouldn't,
grappling with your taffeta wings.

When you ended it...

We were walking across the rugby pitch
short-cut home.
The try posts framed a cloaca bound sun
as you cupped my face with your disinfected hands.

Your mouth decomposed into a compost smile,
my cheeks blistered with red disturbance.
Then, at the try line,
your curtain call tongue spoke.

Look, there's a Magpie –
let's salute him.
I don't believe in such games
and it happened to be a Peacock.

I saw two words hanging in the air

Who was so clumsy to leave them behind?
Like dropping your watch down the drain,
losing your husband behind the frozen peas at Asda
for good.

Maybe they were unrequited
fired into the sky with nowhere to land,
or they strayed from the sentence like a name you forget.
Perhaps they'd lost their keys and nobody was in.

Just in case –
I scooped them into my pockets.
They may have been left for me to keep warm
until I use them at a later date.

First Reading

Shivering in the vestibule
waiting for the show to start;
he fingers the psalms in his hands
stumbling over *steadfast* and *forgiveness*.

At the lectern,
he stands on an upturned crate
to view an audience whose mouths hang like fish.
Everyone's a child in the eyes of a horde.

Hot and empty air hovers,
the chalice brims to his left.
The congregation are getting warm and sticky
in one another's company.

This time he chooses not to read;
he speaks instead
of the proverbs in his head.

Thirty times smaller than I
Jesus' gilt torso is flung in a child's playful leap,
his legs bend impatiently against a decorated crucifix,
waxen toes drip from his limbs
to collect at the base.

Code continually shifts
dispersing to some other place,
there are toes and tears
crosses and cakes
thorns and beds,
words that won't glue to a page.

A man no bigger than my palm is bleeding.
Eight pints of blood in the human body
÷ 30 = 0.26r
The silver saviour on my wall is bleeding
0.26 pints for us
recurring, recurring, recurring.

A Bonanza on the Love Train

What am I doing, can't you see?
I'm doing it now – I'm falling in love.
You're watching me in the phone booth.
I'm Clark Kent stripping off
only I've got an 'L' on my chest,
though I am wearing red knickers.

I've tasted amazing and swallowed it down
a thick chocolatey shake.
L-O-V-E
bring it on, bring it on
I can take it with my tea
everyday.
Love on my tongue
knock it right back
love on a skewer like a kebab
love in a bap
love on toast
I'll make a new menu of love.

Love's all new to me,
but there's nothing I'll do without it.
I've got plans for this one baby.
In the morning I'll polish the clouds.
I'll spend the afternoon skating on banana skins
ripping up copies of *The Good Food Guide*
I can do anything.

JEFF NOSBAUM
Five Poems

Drowning

I focus all of Venice through the breakfast window:
Pigeon on a ledge above an alley of orange stucco.

Inviting, narrow endless ways of trying to get lost
are all appealing to me through the early morning frost.

A maze for stolen moments, paths are arms that wish to hold –
quickly, *kiss*, they whisper to us in the dissipating cold.

Embracing for a furious second fading with the dawn,
we turn a corner, and again, until this tilting maze is gone –

The broad expanse of the piazza opens, gentle tides
of sunlight lapping the Palazzo leave nowhere to hide.

Washed beyond the Basilica, bewildered and yet free,
with gold mosaics lying upon the ever rising sea.

JEFF NOSBAUM

Going to Lake Benoit

My father's father once lived here,
and we return him to his home,
we take him back to wife and lake
as though, somehow, he could feel alone.

It seems my father really is lonely,
but he doesn't say a thing, thinking
about Grampa's ashes, which will soon
be strewn across the lake and sinking.

Eight hours and many miles ago
the sun burned down on empty highways –
a scene of mute reflection – blurring
the asphalt with a hypnotic haze.

The only sign of life appeared
to be the line of telephone wires.
Below though, heading south between
the dirt and white lines, the first two tyres

seemed to wade through the haze as if
emerging from a murky pool:
the tyres propelled a bulky red
motorcycle, shining like a jewel.

This was no mean Harley Davidson,
riding low and driving fast,
unless a retired Harley, squat
and slow, gently coasting past.

The next one came a short time later,
and it was much the same but blue,
and so they came: three, four, five, six,
with each new mile their numbers grew.

A breadcrumb path of sparkling gems,
there was no end of them in sight –
as if a funeral procession
that had turned tail in flight.

We left the last somewhere long past,
there in the road, one final gem.
We near the place he once called home,
but it is lonelier without them.

JEFF NOSBAUM

Picasso's *El Viejo Guitarista*

Christ, long past His prime, lovingly
Draped around His cross, His shoulders
Bent with the weight of such a burden,

Hangs in tattered blue upon the wall.
His fingers, fallen rays of hope,
Are Greco's vision in decay,

Floating above an Aeolian cave.
They pluck six strings, stretched taut and tuned,
Six strings – six threads – spun by Clotho,

By Lachesis measured and given Him.
Their touch tantalizes, drawing up
Emotions, only memories now.

I can see these strings through His fingers
When I look closely. His very soul
Being drawn from His fading body

Into the hole, which I now think
Must be the spear's thrust. Like Thomas,
I want to reach out and touch it.

Screen

the light is blue it's always blue turn off
the light stand near and feel the warming waves
penetrating you enter alone it saves
you pushed it generates a welcome cough
for you it speaks to hear it is enough
to listen –   enough that someone craves
the background whisper of the blue the graves
of photons ghosts to never call your bluff

alone it is enough to be alone
to want a voice not mine but which to call
the choice exhausts exhaustion makes the choice
delaying for a while I will postpone
indefinitely beneath its gaze will fall
and finally will fall beneath the voice

JEFF NOSBAUM

After withholding
for Celia

The release

a cool breeze
catching
at the small
of your back

the weight
falling from you
two steps within
the door as
you let
the luggage drop

a large glass
of water so
cold the surface
has just
begun to ice
when you tip
it past parched
lips

the same muscles
the same motion
the same
satisfaction of
for one brief
moment
having nothing
else
to do

ANDREW PROCTOR
One Step Ahead of The Spider

The smell of piss.
The room is grey under weak fluorescent lights.
I'm in a urinal. It's trough shaped, slightly embedded in the floor and it runs the length of the wall. I'm on my side, stretched full length, my hand under my head. I'm not only fully clothed, but I'm wearing my long felt coat and scarf. There's a blue urinal puck just under my chin.
I listen to the tap drip, echoing around the tiled washroom.
I don't feel injured. I open and close my hand in front of my face.
There's a paper napkin stuck to the floor about a foot away. I gingerly pluck it out of a shallow puddle. On it is a cartoon of two Mexican men and a donkey. Underneath it reads: Carlos and Peppés – Montreal.
Fuck. Fuck. Fuck. I bang my head against the porcelain.
Sax?
There is a God. The case is lying on its side below a row of condom machines.
I check my watch. Five-thirty. They'll be opening the kitchen soon. The bastards probably didn't even check when they locked up. Or worse, they did check. I could have drowned. How would my obituary read? 'Drowned in tragic urinal accident'. My left leg, shoulder and arm are soaked. People pay to have this done to them. I should sell tickets to the can of Carlos and Peppés and smuggle them in.
Am I really awake?
The tap drips.
Things, I suppose, have gotten a little out of control.
I can feel my keys digging into my leg. My wallet lies open on the floor, credit cards and ID exposed.
I'd like to say, 'They told me there would be days like this,' but that would be complete bullshit, because I never imagined that it would be like this. I never thought I would be drunk

everyday (let alone pass out in a urinal), I never thought I would be playing spoof Mexican music at a restaurant that's more like Disneyland than a place to eat, I never thought I would accept so little cash for a gig and I never thought I would pretend to like it.

I sit up.

My head feels like a cork bobbing in the harbour. Still drunk. I hear a trickle of water and leap to my feet just in time to avoid the waterfall of the automatic flushers, but as I do, I bash my head on the upper lip of the urinal. Clutching my head I limp (my right leg is asleep) to the sink. I run the tap and look at myself in the mirror. I have urinal bed-head. Who'd have guessed that was possible? Urinal bed-head. I take my hand away from my head. No blood.

The sink is encrusted with that industrial pink liquid soap and a thin film of brown grime. I rinse the basin, half-heartedly, and then push my head under the stream of cold water. Whatever is in this sink can't be half as bad as what is in that urinal. The icy water floods over my head and the blood rushes to my face. I'm either going to pass out or puke.

I straighten up. No paper towels. Predictable. I walk over to the hand blower but am unable to get the nozzle to face up. The water runs off my head, down my neck and under my collar.

I pump the button on the dryer, remove my coat and sit on the greasy tiles under the warm air. Only my left side is wet, and not that thoroughly. Could be worse. I'm not exactly sure how... uh yes, I suppose I could've woken up completely covered in human shit. Yes. I'm quite sure that'd be worse.

'Roll with it, man. Things will change. Fighting against fate never helped anyone.' That's what a drummer in Moosejaw once told me. I wonder if that means waking up in a urinal is my fate? 'Roll with it, man.' What an asshole.

The lock clicks. The heavy door swings open. A man's ass backs toward me. He is dragging a bucket of water and a mop, which he pulls alongside the door to prop it open. He turns and sees me. This man looks like the most stereotypical Hollywood Mexican fugitive. He could have posed for the cartoon on the napkin. Short, black hair, dark skin and a huge, and I mean huge, moustache. His surprise keeps him silent for a moment and then in the thickest Quebecois accent he asks, "Wud du-el are you doin' 'ear?"

The hand blower clicks off and I stand up. I put my coat on and pick up my wallet and my horn. All the while Pedro rants at me about what he has to put up with. He follows me out into the restaurant. The chairs are still up on the tables. There are giant cacti, sombreros, and even a stuffed donkey (I assume it's fake – but then again, I woke up in a urinal) in the middle of the room.

Julia is behind the bar. She's wearing a poncho and wide brimmed sombrero with tassels that hang down about an inch. She's a beautiful woman when she's not being humiliated by corporate America. She holds up a pot of coffee as Pedro vanishes back into the Señors' washroom. I sit down at the bar and she begins to pour, but then suddenly reels back.

Forgot. I smell like piss.

"You sleep in the toilet?"

"Funny you should ask. Only slightly better."

"Marcel left a note for you."

"Great."

"He called to warn me that you were asleep in the washroom."

"That was considerate of him. Did he mention why he left me in there?" I watch her cleaning and stacking ashtrays.

"Said he couldn't wake you. Said he's sick of unreliable people."

"Unreliable? Did something happen during the gig?"

"Charlie, the last set was ridiculous. I mean, you fell over and then that drummer, what's his name, started ranting into the mic and telling Mexican jokes…"

"Right, right." I look down into my coffee.

She pauses and then says quietly, "Look, I gotta open in twenty minutes and you can't be in here smelling like that. Finish your coffee and go home."

I meet her eyes through the tassels of her sombrero. Her gaze is soft and sympathetic.

"Wanna go on a date?"

"Hmmmm. An out of work musician who smells like piss."

I wince, "Out of work?"

She hands me the note.

Out of work. Hated playing that Mexican shit anyway.

Ten to six. I walk outside. Dark as midnight. It's cold and the wind rips up the Mountain and cuts into me. My breath is visible. No snow at least. I walk down the street a hundred yards. My bicycle lies flat on its side, still chained to a lamppost. It looks so pathetic that I apologise while I unlock it. I stand it up and brush off the seat, which is stupid because the street is probably cleaner than my ass. It's a woman's bike, a banana yellow cruiser with a wicker basket and bright red fenders.

I saddle up and begin pedalling along rue St Laurent. At least it's downhill all the way home. The streets are empty except for a few delivery trucks. At intersections, plastic bags swirl upwards in whirlpools of wind. The stop lights click, green, yellow, red, controlling invisible traffic. The hill steepens and I run all the lights. I like the wind rushing around my body, the big wheels turning over the concrete and the city blowing by me. Up and down rue St Laurent are the clubs, cafés and restaurants where every musician in the city plays. When I was a music student, especially in my first couple of years, this is where we would come to see anybody who was anybody – young, old, local or on tour.

One of the most exciting moments in my life was when I got my first gig at a place called L'Exterior. I subbed in for a good friend who had accidentally double booked himself. I showed up an hour too early and puked between each set.

Mexican fucking theme nights.

What am I doing? I'm weaving all over the road.

A huge delivery truck thunders behind me.

I ring my bell. He cuts me off and I nearly slam into a parked car.

"Ah, Tabernac!" I half-yell, as I huff his exhaust.

One drunk driver is enough. I turn off, onto a side street to avoid the other inebriated idiots on the road.

Maybe they did tell us there would be days like this, but I chose not hear it, allowing the romance of that grainy footage of Miles in a black suit infect me. All my teachers were working jazz musicians and their sheer love for the music, their enthusiasm made us forget about the practicalities. I practised for five hours a day, I wore albums out, studied theory with the devotion of a monk and watched hundreds of video documentaries.

I started gigging in my last year at the University and after I left I continued to gig, and... nothing happened. The same gigs, in the same places, for the same money. Nothing has changed. I took on a few students, and there I was. Here I am. Despite all my practising, I don't think my playing is much different than it was four years ago. No musical epiphanies, no big shows, just the same old restaurants with the same people who just want you to play quietly enough so they can carry on their conversations.

A cat darts out from under a parked car and freezes in front of me. I squeeze both brakes with all my strength. The front wheel locks and as I fly over the handle bars, rolling through the air like a circus tumbler, I think, 'Should've fixed the brakes a long time ago.'

I find myself lying flat on my back in an icy puddle, my right knee throbbing. Man, pay attention. I can hear the wheel of my bike ticking. A streetlight hums like a fly above. My sax is near the wheel of a parked car. I hear that drummer's voice, 'Roll with it man. Things will change. Fighting against fate never helped anyone.'

Fuck. Fuck. Fuck. I bang my head repeatedly against the concrete. This has got to stop. The cat swaggers up and looks down into my face coldly. We stare at each other for while in the lamplight.

I lunge and grab it with both hands, fight to my feet with the thing clawing and scratching my hands and forearms. It howls and screeches. It lands a hook on my face and cuts my cheek. I drop it and it vanishes over a fence.

Dripping wet, bleeding and with the chills, I slowly pick up my bike and my sax and decide maybe it would be better to walk the rest of the way home.

I live in a basement apartment with only thin rectangular windows along the sidewalk for light. It's the first level of artistic ante-purgatory. The place where you wait to be punished.

I unlock my front door. It swings open into the kitchen. I click on the light and then respectfully wait for the cockroaches to retreat for cover. They say that for every one you see out in the open, there's a hundred in the wall. That means the cockroach version of China lives in the plaster of my apartment. I used to try to kill them. I would burst in the door, shoe in hand and pound the floor in the dark like some maniac on acid. I pestered my landlady to have the place sprayed. I bought every insecticide on the market. Nope. The little fuckers will survive a nuclear holocaust. I can respect that.

I sit down in the kitchen and the spider emerges. The Duke. Twice a day he crosses the scratched and stained pine floorboards of the kitchen (I've always intended to paint them). It takes him about ninety seconds. I should know, I've timed him. Many times. He's a poised, delicate creature. He is auburn in colour and has thread-like legs that are so slender they're almost invisible. His body is a small dot, the centre of a fountain of fine appendages.

Dutiful and reliable, I imagine him with a lunch pail on his way to work. He cuts a diagonal across the kitchen, once in the morning and once at night. He carefully approaches each gap between boards, hesitates, feels the width of it, then gingerly steps over.

I've tried to kill The Duke many times. In the days when I hunted the roaches. I saw him as part of that mob. But each time I had him where I wanted him, I couldn't do it. It was the way he crossed the floor. He didn't scramble like the roaches, but walked with pride straight across the open floor, the most exposed part of the apartment, under the neon lights of the kitchen and when my giant shadow leaned over him, shoe in hand, he didn't flinch, but kept his dignity, and just carried on walking, as though he knew the meaning of the word 'gentleman'.

I get a bottle of beer from the fridge, light a cigarette and slump into a kitchen chair to wait for the mail. I watch The Duke vanish under the running boards. Seven a.m. I could set my watch to him.

I look through the kitchen door into the only other room in my apartment. The place is a mess. Clothes and records are all over the floor, the sheets are unwashed and balled up in the middle of the futon and beer bottles clutter every surface. There was a time when I folded that futon up every morning and kept the place neat and organised. There was a time when I opened the windows, when my plants didn't look like desert island castaways.

The red light is flashing on the answering machine.

I put together bands, spent days on arrangements, set up studio time, handed out demo tapes, made phone calls, waited for hours to talk to bar managers, spent entire winter nights when it was twenty below postering for gigs (the glue solution in the bucket slowly freezing over my hands), phoning in substitutes at the last minute, teaching uninterested rich kids from Westmount... I was so busy I was just hanging on, catching quick naps here and there, home for just long enough to shit, shower and shave, pick-up my phone messages and check the mail, make a few calls then off to the next gig, lesson, meeting or rehearsal. I was careful about how much I drank, so I wouldn't be too hung-over for the next event, whatever it was. I was careful how stoned I got before gigs so I'd be in top form.

Then I got what I thought was a break. I was invited on a cross-country tour with a former teacher of mine. Jerry Barber, a well known trumpet and flugelhorn player, had put together a bop quartet to tour in support of a CD he had just released on a small Canadian label.

We left in a van, four of us, and headed west from Montreal in the middle of January. I was the youngest by about ten years. Watching Montreal disappear behind us, to the sound of Coleman Hawkins, was so exciting I could barely sit still. I was like the puppy in the back seat, hyperactive and much too talkative.

The tour was gruelling. We played nearly every night in some snow-swept factory town, in some half-empty club or restaurant all the way to the Pacific. We would arrive in time to stretch, eat a greasy meal and get a few drinks in before warming up. When we hit a city, say Toronto, Saskatoon, Edmonton, whatever, we played a longer engagement, maybe a week. There's nothing to do when you're on tour. Especially in the winter. You can't just wander around the city, see the sights. Besides, we were usually broke and exhausted.

At first I really had to work to keep up with the guys on stage. It was mostly original numbers and I didn't know them well. It was a lot of up tempos and tricky key signatures. After a couple of weeks I got a handle on them. I began to suggest changes, ways to keep them interesting for the band, to keep our solos edgy. Most of my ideas were ignored and I thought it was because they didn't like them. Then I realized, they didn't want anything challenging or difficult. They couldn't be bothered.

And all the while we drank and drank, and drove and drove. The prairies were the worst. Every morning we smoked huge joints just to numb us from the boredom. You can drive for two days and see nothing, just field upon field of snow. So flat and empty, it's like the surface of the moon. You drive and drive and then with a sudden violence, office towers shoot out of the horizon. Winnipeg. A city dropped from the sky.

The sun comes into my apartment for about twenty minutes in the morning at around 8 a.m. I move my chair and sit in the middle of the room to enjoy it.

We became uncomplicated types. The drummer, Dave, cracked the jokes and told the stories. Zach the bassist was quiet, but good at handling weird drunks, calming down rednecks and generally dealing with 'situations', as he called them. Jerry knew the bar managers and had all the contacts, he ran things. Me, I was the kid who everybody had a lesson for, I was the guy paying the dues, which means I was the butt of the jokes, the one who carried the heaviest gear. For a while I fell into this role, cleaning the van, running errands to music shops, writing out the set lists and fetching take-out food.

Moosejaw. Seventeen below. Jerry parked the van and he and Zach and Dave split in different directions. It had been a long day and we were all sick of each other.

Jerry tossed me the keys, "Get the gear inside. We'll see you in an hour."

The club was still locked so I headed for a drink myself, intending to come back in half an hour. I ended up drinking for two. I ran back to the club, slipping twice in the snow, in time to watch Jerry carry in the last of the kit. He stopped in the doorway and stared at me, then disappeared inside.

We set up in silence. The place, surprisingly, filled up. The band played like absolute crap. And all night we just got worse.

By the last number we were all plastered and it really started to fall apart during Jerry's solo. I stepped in, attempting to bring the tune around by playing some background licks that I'd shown Jerry earlier in the week, that he'd virtually crumpled and thrown away. I was in the wrong place and the number got even worse. Zach just stopped, Dave took an unaccompanied solo and we managed, just, to play the head out.

And then, during the hesitant clapping, Jerry bawled me out, right there on stage in front of everyone: "Charlie, what the fuck do you think you're doing? Have you got ears? Are you listening? Jesus you piss me off. Never, never jump in and cut me off like that. You think I don't know what I'm doing? Is that what you think? I'm embarrassed to be on stage with you. You're a fucking talentless amateur. Next time fucking pay attention."

The club was dead silent. All eyes were on me. Jerry walked off stage, stumbling a little, knocking a glass off a table. Nobody moved. I turned to Zach and then Dave, and neither would make eye contact with me. I packed up my horn and sat down at the bar while the place emptied out.

That's when I met that drummer. He'd heard the music and wandered in. He introduced himself and bought me a drink. I told him I was thinking about leaving the band, about trying to catch a ride back east. I told him about the tour and how I was sick of the music and the guys and being a doormat, that the guys in the band didn't even really care about the music at all. He listened to me complain for a while, shaking and nodding his head.

After I'd finished he said, "Man, you're way too uptight. Nobody in these clubs is even listening. They're not listening to you, and when I play a gig they're not listening to me. You're furniture, man. People want you around to make them feel sophisticated. This isn't Birdland and you're not Parker. So don't take yourself so seriously – you're never going to make it otherwise. Roll with it man. Things will change. Fighting against fate never helped anyone."

I press play on the answering machine: "Hey, man, it's Adrian. Uh, listen I'm just calling to say that I can't sub-in for the Carlos and Peppés thing next week. I've got a bunch of rehearsals with Barber, 'cause he wants me to go down to the New Orleans Jazz Fest with his quartet. Can you believe it? Anyway, I'll, uh, talk to you later. Bye."

After that night, things changed. I stopped being the lackey for the band. I looked after my horn, did my share of the driving, played the numbers and drank. By the time we got to BC spring had broken and the band got invited down to LA to play in front of some record guys. It was an invitation for a trio. They gave me a hundred bucks and left me on the corner of Commercial and 6th in Vancouver, a newly initiated alcoholic, 3000 km from Montreal, not knowing a soul. As I hitch-hiked back across the country I cursed Jerry in every city, town and crossroads.

It was only when I got back I learned the reason I'd been invited on the tour. The original sax player, an old buddy of Jerry's, Andrew Schnider, broke his hand two weeks before they were due to leave. They couldn't get anybody else to go on tour with such little notice, so I was hired.

Six months later they turned up in Montreal again. No record deal. And at that point Jerry's wife had left him. One tour too many, I guess. According to Jerry, she and his kids were just gone. He said he had spoken to her a week before he got back and everything seemed OK. Only his records, his stereo and some books were left.

It's been two months since they got back and last week I went over there to pick up some cash for a gig I played for him (you can't stay mad at one of the best-known players in a scene as small as it is here), and there he was, sitting in the middle of that big empty living room transcribing a solo from a Parker album. He hadn't done anything to the place.

This is pathetic.

I need to make some phone calls.

I need to get back on a practice regiment.

I need to clean this place up.

I walk into the kitchen and throw the half-full beer bottle into the garbage. I hear it smash on the bottom with satisfaction.

Diminished scales.

Chord extensions.

Rhythm changes.

Man, my rhythm changes are weak. I need to work on my intonation in the upper registers. Jerry gave me some exercises, I think. Where did I put those?

I'm in the bathroom. It's a disgusting mixture of mildew and pubic hair. I turn on the tap and run the shower.

I should call Gord and Steve, and see where those guys are working these days. Maybe we should record a new demo. Better call Lisa and see if we can't get some studio time in the next couple of weeks. I should check in at the University, I haven't talked to Dave in weeks, maybe he's got a few students for me. Tri-tones. I need to do those tri-tone exercises. I step into the shower.

I'm still wearing my clothes. Including my shoes.

Fuck. Fuck. Fuck. I bang my head against the tiles. Man, pay attention.

Still under the steaming water I remove my shoes and toss them through the curtains to the tiled floor. I take off my socks and hang them on the shower curtain-rod. I remove my water-logged pants. I flip them over the rod as well. Just as I pull my shirt off and fling it up, the whole rod and curtain crashes to the floor. Water is going everywhere in the bathroom. A sock floats in the toilet. I finish undressing, tossing the rest of my clothes to the bathroom floor and then pick up the curtain. I wedge it back up and finish my shower. The steam is filled with the warm smell of urine.

Dressed again, garbage bag in hand, I scurry around the flat picking up clothing to wash. Then with another garbage bag I pick up all the bottles, pizza boxes and bits of paper. I fill the sink up with sudsy water and stack the dishes to soak. I put all my tapes, CDs and records into their cases, books back onto the shelves and sheet music into folders. Then I push my furniture into the centre of the room and mop the whole place.

While the floor is drying I grab my laundry and head down the block to get a start on my washing. As I walk my mind is still spinning about the people I should call, the things I should practice, the gigs I need to get. I walk into the laundromat and open the bag in front of a machine.

It's my garbage.

Heading back to my apartment I dump it in an alley. I notice a paint sale in a hardware store. I buy a gallon of white paint, a brush and a roller. I return to the apartment, get my laundry, go back to the laundromat, start the cycle and return. I push my furniture back in place and finish tidying up.

It's one-thirty. The place is back to the way it used to be. I feel ready to pass out from exhaustion. The paint-can stares at me. Do it today, while you've got the momentum going.

On my hands and knees on the kitchen floor I use the brush to do the areas along each wall. I have no tray for the roller. Fuck it. I pour some paint onto the floor then roll it smooth, until the whole kitchen floor is gleaming white. I stare at it, feeling a little stoned from the fumes. How even and perfect it looks. My own reflection stares back at me.

I try to clean the brush and roller. Of course it's oil paint and I don't have any paint thinner. Never mind, I don't need to paint anything else. I go to the kitchen to throw them out and almost step in the paint.

Ha! Paying attention.

I'll throw them away later. I open the windows to let a little air in. I'll go and sit in a café and make up a list of the things I need to do. Yeah, I could use... I can't leave the apartment. I've painted myself in.

Never mind, I'll make the list here. I sit down on my futon and scribble down all that needs to happen. I divide the list into calls, things to practice, new gigs...

I wake up on my futon fully clothed. I sit up quickly. I look around at the neat and tidy room. Outside it's dark. I look at my watch. Six-thirty a.m. I remember my laundry and get up and check the paint in the kitchen.

And there, in the middle of the floor, is the spider. The Duke. His legs sealed into the paint's shiny finish, the way the Mafia might give an enemy cement shoes. I imagine him setting out like normal, and then stepping into the goupy paint. Then with all six legs coated, he might have stopped to try and clean them off, but that would only coat his legs heavier. And those delicate appendages would've become heavy, soaked with the toxic stuff and he would become tired. He would exhaust himself struggling and then would simply stand there as the paint hardened around his legs.

I walk over to one of the windows. I rest my chin on the sill; my eyes level with the sidewalk. I watch the feet of Montreal pass by in the dark, on their way to work.

For David Brown

DINA RABINOVITCH

Extract from **The Spice of Life**

Last night there were three cooking programmes, one after the other on the telly. Who's it for? When I was young, dinner was something you swallowed, or else you jolly well spent it thinking about the poor little Africans.

The Sunday papers are no better – look at this: six sections, and five of them about food. I'm not exaggerating. Grown-ups eating fashionably, children eating faddily, duchesses on cranberry juice. The food revolution they call it. And meanwhile, all the time, on our road, a mother was starving her daughter.

Famous mother, she was too. You've probably seen her on the box. She's part of it: one of the cooks who shows other people how to cook. We were expected to learn at school. You made a sponge, a scone and a tuna turnover, and you could eat for England. These days it's only properly cooked if it's done abroad, with a camera crew.

Well, except for Delia, that is. But I can tell you something; the other cooks, they don't rate Delia very highly. Oh no. Joanna, the one on our road, used to call her a jumped-up au pair. Apparently, they all get together at awards ceremonies, all these famous cooks, and none of them speak to Delia. She's not a real cook, according to them. Well, she's not, is she? She's just like one of those women who used to teach us at school.

Joanna's the same generation as me; in fact, she's probably the same age as me. I'm 57. She looks younger than me though – she does her hair. I would colour mine, it's not like I'm partial to boiled grey. Only the first boy I ever fell in love with, his mother had a brain tumour, and they said it was the hair dye she used that caused it.

Anyhow, Joanna. I won't give her surname. Joanna's husband left just after their third was born. That's when Joanna started seriously writing her cookery books. I have wondered if I would have been famous if my husband left. But of course, he hasn't. So I just cook for him.

Joanna, I will say, was never all that tempted by fame – in fact she could get quite impatient when people began to stare at her in Waitrose, trying to place her. 'I'm already friendly with all the people I shall ever want to know,' I remember her snapping to me once. But she did see the cook books as a way of making some serious money. The fact that Delia has, and Joanna hasn't, well, I think there may be just a touch of jealousy there.

You see, Joanna always cared about money. Counted her pennies I mean. Though she had no need to. We'd go round for dinner and take a couple of bottles of good wine; they'd come to us bearing nothing. Shows in her recipes actually; it's always a pinch of this, a pinch of that, never what I'd call a proper teaspoonful.

You want to know why she was like that, is that what you're asking? Oh, I couldn't say; there's far too much psycho-rubbish around these days as it is. It's like the food, isn't it – too much of a good thing's no good at all, and never will be. For me, it's not the why that counted, it was the how. As in, how to stop Joanna doing what she did.

Joanna's older two used to play with mine. Mine always sat down to a proper tea after school – pot of course, and biscuits, on a plate. Joanna's children ate theirs up fast, gobbled down almost before you'd offered them round in fact, but I didn't take particular note. Manners is as Mother does, I always say.

They'd go off without a thank-you, so I'd stand on the doorstep and call out, 'thanks for having me,' in a merry way, and that'd make them stop in their tracks and look back at me, puzzled. The older one was quickest to catch on, after a nudge, they'd both turn and say, thank you for having us. I did my bit.

The baby, Sandy, was too young to come round then. She was born eight years after the others. She always seemed like an add-on, Sandy. I felt sorry for her. At first, the children – my two, and Joanna's two – had quite liked playing with her. After a bit, though, they started saying her crying was annoying – 'Oh, she's always crying, Mum,' they told me.

Ben – Joanna's husband – left just three months after Sandy was born. Flew off to New York with an air hostess fifteen years younger than him. Short men do that sort of thing, have you noticed? But he did leave Joanna provided for. That house was worth a bit for a start, and there was never a question of her going without. I know, because my Jeremy's a solicitor of course, and he handled all Ben and Joanna's affairs. So we knew there were no financial worries. Maybe that's why I never could take my own suspicions seriously – any little niggles I felt about what was going on in Joanna's house, I mean.

BEN RICE
Jamaican Bananas

"Guys! Hey! Wait!"
It was 2 a.m. and I was walking home from the party I hadn't been invited to. There were no cars on the road and no lights on in the houses.
"Sebastian! Louise!"
I was approaching the woods. I really didn't want to be alone going past the twisted trees, and so I broke into jog and then into a run.
The party had been at Julio Kloof's house. Julio Kloof was a student at the Academy and the holder of the Hans Hectorfield Scholarship for Outstanding Potential. The rumour was that he was a Star-Grade Alpha-rating student from the Emanuella Zmatlova School of Excellence and that he had achieved an average of nine point nine nine (nine) in his Diploma of Cognizance Exams. It was also whispered everywhere that he was on the verge of producing a groundbreaking Quasi-Treatise, entitled *Redefining and Re*something-something-ing *the Apocrypha of J.S. Limeshield*.
Anyway, I had overheard someone saying that anyone-who-was-anyone was going to this party at Julio Kloof's house. And so finding myself at a loose end, and unable to concentrate on my work, and feeling a little anxious as to why I hadn't been invited in the first place, I waited until midnight and then left my flat with my baseball cap pulled down low over my eyes, and went and hung around outside Julio Kloof's house just to get a measure of what it was that I was missing.
And besides which, I wanted to see Sebastian and Louise.
I'd had a good feeling about Sebastian and Louise ever since I was introduced to them at the Academy Induction about a week before. We hadn't had much chance to speak, but over the next few days I made a point of sitting a few rows behind Louise in the lecture theatre so that I could see the patch of tender white skin at the back of her neck. She nodded and laughed at

the same things I nodded and laughed at. She put her hand up and asked questions when I wanted to ask questions.

I had been observing Sebastian too. He was barrel-chested and had dark hair, a small mouth, and large quiet eyes. He was the sort of person who was reticent and introspective, but understood things, and once he looked at me over someone's shoulder and nodded a definite acknowledging sort of a nod, as if to say: "We'll meet. We'll become friends soon enough. Don't worry."

"Louise! Sebastian! Slow down!"

I quickened my pace. I wanted to be walking with them stride for stride. Like I say, there was no way I wanted to be going past the dark wood on my own.

As I gained on them I tried guessing what Sebastian and Louise were talking about. I imagined they were discussing the lecture Dr Grierson had given that afternoon on E. Z. Hammerstein's *Labyrinthine Utterings and Parlances*. And I supposed that Sebastian and Louise were also assessing Julio Kloof's party as they walked. I guessed they were talking about the people who had been there. About who was who. About who was worth it and who wasn't. And who had the real brains and the ideas, and who didn't. About who was acute. And who wasn't acute.

When I had eventually arrived at Julio Kloof's house the door had been left ajar and so I put a foot gingerly inside the door on the carpet, as though I was testing ice to see if it could stand me walking on it. And then I took a deep breath and walked into the party.

Julio Kloof's house was smoky, and crowded. The hallway was dimly lit with blue bulbs. I squeezed through the crowd, keeping my head tilted down. There was the thud of music coming from down the hallway, and energetic conversation swarming from a black door straight ahead. I'd paused outside the door and grabbed a beer can from a table, half-thinking that if I kept sipping at it, it might serve as some sort of mask. And then I eased open the door and peeked in to the living room.

There were about 70 or so people inside. Some were clotted around a sofa in conversation. There were groups standing laughing with wine glasses in their hands and about twenty people dancing in the centre of the room, some with hands around each other's waists. I'd made sure no one saw me come in, and then I'd sat down in a dark corner in a big leather chair, pretending to sip from my beer can all the time. And then I scanned around the room, keeping an eye out for Julio Kloof.

At first there seemed to be no sign of the host, but then I noticed in the far corner of the room a huddle of people from which a single low mutter was emanating. I remember thinking two things: firstly that it was strange that a mutter could be heard over the loud music and party noise, and secondly that Julio Kloof himself must have been at the centre of the huddle and the source of that mutter.

Because I had not been able to hear what Julio Kloof was saying I'd grabbed a handful of pretzels from a bowl on the sideboard, and then I just retreated back into my dark corner and chewed on them, and smoked a cigarette, and observed the goings-on at Julio Kloof's party. I tried to look inconspicuous, as though I had been at the party a long time, and just wanted some time sitting on my own, staring into space. After a while I became fully reassured that no one had seen me come in and so I was able to relax a little and take in the detail of Julio Kloof's living room.

There was plenty to look at, but the most remarkable thing by far was the ceiling which boasted one of those huge and distinctly English intricate Victorian ceiling roses. The strange thing was that the rose was not positioned in the centre of the room around a light fitting, but directly over my head, as though it had sort of picked me out and followed me over into the corner. The ceiling rose was, of course, floral in its design, but it had obviously been painted over a few times with white paint, and after I had stared up at it for a while, the detail blurred and it appeared to take on a different shape, so that it began to look, I don't know, like a forest, or a sponge maybe, or the workings of some sort of brain or something.

Feeling suddenly dizzy I pulled my eyes off the peculiar ceiling rose and panned around the room, taking in everyone, and keeping an eye out for Sebastian and Louise. There was no sign of them, however and so I settled my gaze on a beautiful oriental woman in a silver dress who was holding a black cat to her breast and talking to it. I leant forward on my knees to try and catch what she was saying between the beats of the music. She had a high-pitched flutey voice which rose above the background noise, and what she was saying was: "There, there, Debussy. There, there! Lovely cat! There, there Debussy!"

I stood looking at the woman and the cat for at least ten minutes, unable to stop my eyes fixing on her arms and breasts and her neck. It was almost hypnotic the way she was stroking that cat, the way she buried her face in the cat Debussy. After that I felt hot at the back of my neck and my legs started to get restless.

It had clearly got to that stage of the party where people were getting up and starting to think about leaving. The room seemed to be thinning out, and so, worried that I might be recognized,

I stood up and left the room while the going was good, still concerned that someone was going to notice me and expose me as someone who had not been invited.

It was then that I saw Sebastian and Louise. They were standing talking in the hallway by a coat-rack. I moved closer and heard Louise say to Sebastian, "Listen, I've had enough of this." And then they headed off before I could ask them if I could join them.

I paused and considered whether or not to run after them, and eventually decided that I wouldn't, but then five minutes later I was alone in the street facing the prospect of the long walk back with only my own mind for company. And so I set off in pursuit.

"Guys! Wait! It's me! Mark! You know! Mark from the Programme."

I wanted to be walking along with them, wading the orange husks, kicking conkers, chatting about what a terrible party that was, and those ridiculous people, and that muttering Julio Kloof whose party it was. So cocksure sure about what he thought and what he said.

I finally caught up Louise and Sebastian by the skip with the old mattresses in.

"Hey there! I'm glad I caught you up, guys," I panted. "Remember me? I'm Mark."

Sebastian and Louise stopped suddenly and turned around.

"Mark!"

"Mark!"

"We're glad you caught us up, Mark," said Sebastian. "How the devil are you?"

"I couldn't be better," I said.

"That's good, Mark," said Louise. "Were you at that party too?"

"Was I ever!" I said.

We didn't say anything for some time, each of us thinking about the party, maybe. Louise kicked an old windfall along the pavement. Sebastian stuffed his hands in his pockets and gave me a firm smile.

"Louise and I, were just talking about the party, Mark. Didn't you just think that was the worst party in the entire universe?"

I felt a glow come up under my ribs and spread all over my body.

"Absolutely," I said. "I didn't want to say anything in case you guys were really into it. You see, I thought you might really like Julio Kloof."

"No, no," said Louise, "You're joking! Us like Julio? That arrogant bastard? And all those fakes? All those people thinking they've got something to say?"

She spat onto the floor.

"I can't stand that guy," Sebastian said.
"Me neither. I hate him," I said.
"Oh I don't *hate* him. That's a bit strong," said Louise. "No, no. I just *dislike him intensely*. That's all. But not hate."
"Yeah. That's what I meant," I said. "I *dislike him intensely* too," I said.
"I was talking to Carol Froude about Signor Kloof the other day, as it happens," said Louise.
"No? Really? Carol Froude. You hang out with Carol Froude? I thought Carol Froude was a friend of Julio's," I said.
"She was. She was chairperson of his society. She resigned though, as a matter of intellectual differences. She dislikes him intensely now, after what Julio said in his Manifesto."
"What did he say?"
"Ha! Get this. He said: 'there's only two people worth knowing in the world: yourself and yourself. The rest can burn.'"
I snorted and shook my head. Sebastian put a finger down his throat and pretended to gag.
"That's such a complete *Julioism!*" he said
"Exactly," said Louise. "That's just what I can't stand about him. The way he speaks through his nose, as if there's some biographer around who's waiting to put it all down into *The Life of Julio Kloof*."
The woods were coming up.
"You know what? I hate these woods," said Louise, "They give me the creeps. I'm glad I'm walking with you two."
I felt my arm brush against Louise's arm as we walked. I knew we were going to be friends for a long, long time.
"They're pretty spooky, those woods, I agree," said Sebastian. "It's irrational to be afraid, though. Just a bunch of trees."
"'You cannot rationalize fear,'" said Louise, quoting Lichendort, page 76, Chapter Three of *The Brave Cranium*. "'Fear is an intrinsically ineluctable and irrational force.'"
"Good point," said Sebastian.
"Hey?" Louise said suddenly. "Guess what. Speaking of ineluctable. I heard something the other day. Some vague rumour about Julio saving a woman from someone in the woods? Did you hear that rumour?"
"What rumour?" I said.
"It could just be nothing," Louise said, "but I'm pretty well sure I heard Julio saved someone from something in these woods. I think it was this summer, a while before the Programme started. Someone was hasselling someone, or something, and apparently The Great Kloof stepped in, scared off the assailant, just like that."

"That must be just a rumour," I said. "I was here all summer. There would have been something about it in the local papers. Anyway, it's impossible. Wasn't Julio Kloof in America this summer solving mathematical problems for the U.S government?"

"You're probably right," Louise said. "It does sound unlikely, doesn't it."

"I really hope it's just a rumour, anyway," said Sebastian, "I don't like the idea that Julio Kloof is some sort of action hero or something as well nine point nine nine (nine) Star-Grader from Zmatlova."

"I'll bet he made it all up," Louise said. "He's so totally self-mythologizing, it's incredible."

The first trees appeared on our right. No one said anything for some time. I pulled my baseball cap down lower so I could see only the pavement in front of me. I gritted my teeth and listened to our jeans rubbing, our shoes crackling the twigs, and I tried to think of something to take my mind off the sinister woods. But strangely, as we walked briskly and urgently past the woods, all I could think of was that girl at Julio Kloof's party, stroking the cat and calling it Debussy, and that strange impending, ceiling rose, which had seemed to follow me into the corner and then transformed from a sponge to a brain before my eyes.

A cat shrieked suddenly from the dark.

"The thing about Julio Kloof is that he's so *affected*," I blurted out in a quavering voice. "He doesn't know anything about real life. About getting your hands dirty. He doesn't know about fear."

"Yes, apparently he's from quite a privileged background," said Sebastian, breathily. "You know what? I heard he's the son of Pietro Kloof."

"Really, Pietro Kloof? As in *Pietro-Misconstruing-the-Vortex* Kloof?"

"Yup."

"Oh my God," I said, "I hadn't made the connection. That explains everything!"

The others nodded in agreement.

The wind flapped its wings somewhere up high in the branches.

As soon as we were past the woods I breathed a sigh of relief, and I could tell Louise and Sebastian were glad to be past them too. And then quite suddenly I felt the fear slip off my back altogether, and I was extremely positive about everything again. My unease about those woods gave birth to a surge of enthusiasm about being out in the night, walking home with two friends, two fellow thinkers, talking so intimately.

And then suddenly my excitement formed into an idea, and I couldn't stop myself from voicing it.

"Hey guys! I've just had a really excellent idea!"

"Oh yeah?"

"Yeah. You know what we three should do? We should never go to one of those pretentious parties at Julio Kloof's house ever again. Yup. You know what? We should have our own meetings. I've got a hut out the back of where I'm living, down by the canal. I've been working on it for a while. I've painted the inside, and I've got music. You know the new Silver Spoon CD? Well, I've got it. And we could have fires and sit outside. There's an old couch I could rig up and, yes – I know what we could do – we could have a kind of cook-out. How about that? We could eat Jamaican bananas. You know? I used to have them when I was a kid. Jamaican bananas. It's easy. You cut the bananas gently down the middle and then you arrange chocolate in them, and then you wrap them in tin foil. And when the heat gets to them the chocolate melts all over the banana, and snuggles into it, and the banana softens. And the banana and chocolate mingles together. You'll see what I mean when I make them, guys. Go on. Just the three of us! We could get a bottle of whisky. Some tobacco. Talk about what we think is really important. Unpretentious things. You know, we could even not bring any books with us. And it could be just the three of us in it together. And we could all bring an idea and tell each other why we thought it was good. See? It would be great to have each other's company. We could discuss the latest ideas while we're sitting by the fire, eating Jamaican bananas, and then we could just kind of sit there getting warm and absorb the autumn, and have a toast to sort of celebrate our…our likemindedness."

There was a long silence. I could almost hear my excellent idea fingering its way into the heads of Sebastian and Louise and taking a grip.

"That sounds good, Mark," said Louise said eventually.

"Yeah that sounds excellent Mark."

"But, hang on. These Jamaican bananas, they're not racist or anything are they, Mark?" said Louise.

"Racist? No. Why racist? God no, they're just bananas and chocolate, that's all."

"Oh good. That's fine then. I was just concerned they sounded a bit on the hegemonic side," she said.

We stopped walking at the wonky telegraph pole.

"Tomorrow then?"

"Yeah OK, tomorrow, why not," said Louise. "Down with Julio!"

And then we all shouted together: "Down with Julio Kloof!"
"Great," I said. "Tomorrow at eight then."

And then I wrote down my address for them on the back of a receipt, and I said goodbye and continued the walk alone down the avenue, feeling excited because I already had this picture of the three of us sitting outside together, our faces glowing in the firelight as we talked.

I spent the next day gutting the shed and getting things arranged. I aligned the couch. I got deckchairs. I ran an extension cable from the house for the music. I moved out a stack of books and a pile of tapes and CDs, and then I went to the local store and bought cigarettes, a hand of large bananas, silver foil, and a family-size bar of milk chocolate and a bottle of whisky. And, when everything was finally ready I sat there outside the hut waiting for Sebastian and Louise and wondering whether I ought to make some sort of introduction speech or just let things take their course.

And then, as it was getting a little cold, and realizing that my friends would almost certainly be a quarter of an hour late out of politeness, I lit the fire, relishing the idea that Louise and Sebastian might be able to see the smoke over the rooftops from the road as they approached.

And then when the fire was up and running I had the idea of getting a couple of Jamaican bananas on the go immediately so that they were sweet and done for when Sebastian and Louise arrived. I particularly liked the idea of Louise smelling it as soon as she walked through the gate, and her nose curling, and me being able to say: "Perfect timing, guys! Have a Jamaican banana!" So I started cutting slits in the bananas and placing chocolate in and wrapping the foil around them.

And then there was nothing to do but sit and prod the fire, and I'm not afraid to say I actually went through a little bit of a rehearsal, it being quite a while since I had played host to anyone. And then before long the bananas were ready and smelling sweet, and Sebastian and Louise still hadn't turned up, and it was 8.40 p.m. and so I began to just pick delicately at the foil around the end of one banana, and before I knew it I had made a little hole accidentally in the foil. And then I unwrapped it completely.

And then I ate one of the hot Jamaican bananas myself with a teaspoon, and felt the warmth of the banana spread from my tongue all over my body.

And then I ate another one. And I ate it extremely fast so that Sebastian and Louise wouldn't suddenly arrive and come in to catch me in the act, and tease me about it. And it was easy to imagine how it might become a kind of legendary joke throughout our friendship – that is: me being caught in the act of guzzling the Jamaican bananas.

But I shouldn't necessarily have worried because I easily finished the banana without my friends having arrived, and consequently I had more time to sit and dream about their arrival. But the next time I looked at my watch it was suddenly 9.30, and there were other things to worry about, such as the possibility that something had happened to Sebastian and Louise on the way to my house, or that they had got lost, or mislaid my address.

I couldn't wait anymore, and so I stood up and poured water over the fire so that it hissed. Then I locked up the house and went walking up the Avenue, keeping my eyes on the road ahead, expecting to see my friends coming towards me at any moment, shouting: "Mark! Sorry we're late Mark! We were just buying some wine for the meeting!" I walked up almost until the woods, with the taste of Jamaican banana in my mouth, and then I stopped and waited for a while, and listened to the wood breathing.

And then I held my own breath and ran helter-skelter past the woods.

I didn't stop running until I was a quarter of a mile away, and I don't remember quite how I got there, or why, but before I knew it I was walking down The Avenue all over again, past the park and down Julio Kloof's street.

And the next thing I knew I had stopped outside of Julio Kloof's house.

There were voices seeping from the windows. It occurred to me that it would be good if I could creep over to the window and spy on our rival through the curtains, and report back to Sebastian and Louise, and so I tiptoed over the flowerbeds and crouched down by the smaller of the two outfacing windows. And then I slowly raised my head and looked in through the gap in the curtains.

I was looking straight into Julio Kloof's kitchen, and strangely the first thing I saw was another ceiling rose identical to the one I had seen the night before. This time the ceiling rose not on the ceiling at all. It was high up on the wall above an extractor fan and a shelf of cookery books. It was as though the rose from last night had actually slid through the wall from the living room.

Before I had time to dwell any further on this peculiar fact, however, I heard Julio Kloof talking and someone laughing and whispering to somebody. I leaned in and put an ear to the gap in the window.

Julio Kloof seemed to be muttering to some friends. I caught the conversation in snatches. I heard words like 'preposterous' and 'torment' and 'infantile' and 'punish'. But at that point the conversation was muffled by the sounds of crockery chinking and rustling. Before long I heard the whispering of words like 'likemindedness' and 'hate' and 'dislike intensely' and more laughter and then suddenly I recognized the voices of Sebastian and Louise and then I heard Julio laugh and repeat the words 'Silver spoon' and 'Jamaican bananas' over and over again. Jamaican bananas. Jamaican bananas. Jamaican bananas.

And then quite suddenly I got a whiff of sweet banana coming through the window and I realized what I was hearing. Sebastian and Louise were making Jamaican bananas with Julio Kloof.

I felt suddenly dizzy and sick then, and the undigested banana rose up from my stomach and up my throat in a kind of urge and scalded the back of my throat. And then Julio laughed again, and I suddenly felt my heart give, and a sense of panic swell up inside me. I bit into my knee as I sat there crouched under the window and I started to feel myself shake. Eventually I slouched away and squatted behind the rear fender of a parked Volkswagen Beetle. And I remained there feeling dark and empty like the car I was behind.

I waited there in a crouch until Sebastian and Louise came out of Julio Kloof's house, and then I sprang up, and stood in the road with my hands on my hips, the anger welling up in my head. And I heard Julio Kloof say, "I'd love to see the look on his face!" and Louise said, "Goodbye darling," and Sebastian called out: "Ciao Julio!"

And then I stepped out into the road and blocked them off.

"Sebastian!" I shouted, "Louise! What's going on? I thought you were coming to the hut tonight. "

They jumped and stepped back. Louise looked at Sebastian. Sebastian had his hands behind his back. He stood with his feet wide apart on the road.

"We went to your place, Mark," he said. "You weren't around."

"Rubbish! You didn't go there. You never came. You can't have done. I waited for ages. I had just put out the first Jamaic..."

I stopped myself, before I finished saying it but it was too late. I saw a sneer appear on Sebastian's face.

"OK then," he said, "What if we never came? What if we met Julio on the way and went straight to Julio's house instead?"

"But you dislike Julio intensely! You said so last night!"

"Ha! We liked him all the time. We were just testing you. To see what you would say. And now we've told him everything you said. About how you hate him."

"I never said I hated him."

"Oh, yes you did. And we found out why. We found out things from Julio tonight, Mark. Things about you."

I went suddenly very uneasy.

"What things?"

"The woods, Mark. That's what things."

The word 'woods' made me shiver to the core. Coldness slunk up my arm.

"Julio told us about you and the woods. About you and what you did in the woods. And how he caught you. And the girl from the library. "

That was enough. I suddenly unleashed this huge blood-curdling scream "It's a lie!" I yelled. "It's a bloody lie, I'm telling you. He's lying!"

"What's a lie?" said Louise with a smirk.

"Yeah. What is it, Marky? What's a lie?"

"Nothing. The woods. Nothing. I haven't done anything in the woods. How many times do I have to say. I don't know a girl from the library. It was an accident. I didn't do it. I couldn't speak. They bound me up. The woods bound me up. There were thousands of them. Trees. I couldn't see properly. There was a girl. I didn't know her. She followed me. She wouldn't let go. The trees clung onto me. I threatened her. The trees were threatening her. I intervened. The trees intervened. The woods. Everything. She was smiling. She wasn't making any sense. She was accusing me. Honestly. She was. I'm not dangerous. Honestly. I'm not crazy. Louise! Sebastian! It was the woods. It was the crazy woods. It's all lies. It's a Julioism. There's nothing wrong with me. I never did anything. It was the girl. It was Julio. It was a trick. Louise, he's making it up. He's mythologizing. She didn't need saving. She was out to get me. I never touched her. I was confused. I was lonely. It was Julio!"

Sebastian took something from behind his back. He had been holding a plate. On the plate something silver was shining. It was tin foil.

"I bought you something, Marky," he said. "Mmmmm, Mark, Mmmm," Julio took a taste of the bananas. "Mmmmm. It's delicious. Mmmm. Jamaican bananas. Shall we go and eat them in the woods, Marky? Shall we? In the woods? Bananas in the woods? Shall we follow a black girl into the woods. Shall we try to touch her, Marky? Shall we offer her some Jamaican bananas? Shall we ask her to come to your hut?"

"No. Shut the fuck up. Shut the hell up, Sebastian!"

"Shall I go tell the police, Marky? Shall I? Shall I go tell the police about how you were – "

"No! Stop!" I shouted, "Stop!"

I spat on the road by his feet, and then I turned and ran. I ran all the way up the avenue hearing Sebastian's voice hissing in my ears. I ran until I came to the woods, and this time I ran off the road and went plunging into the undergrowth.

In the middle of the woods I lay down on my back, my heart hammering. My head began to spin. The twisted fingers of the trees moved in around me. Through them I could still see Julio Kloof's terrible ceiling rose hanging in the sky like a huge moon.

"Get lost!" I yelled. "Get lost, all of you!" I rolled over and buried my eyes in the grass and the leaves.

I'm not saying anything else.

RHIAN SAADAT
Leave of Absence

Leaving

belongings are the least of it;
we found that out early on –

useful perhaps, only
for muffling the cold.

no, it's the roses I shall miss,
there, and there in corners
tucked away like words
that never quite
unfolded.

he would bring them home
on Monday nights – a ritual
I christened 'Saved from Death
by Hanging' – I tied the stems
preserved their scents.

I'd always wanted a garden –
we had shelving without the sun
the kids and I foraged the market
for English speaking blooms
to plug the draughts.

there was nothing in the end
I wanted to take – just essential
sanity and winter clothes, with
a few powdered petals I hoped
would sometimes recall

the perfumed pauses that filled
rooms now emptied of their clutter
where shadows wave to shadows
nodding about the roses
gone missing before winter.

The Bird-Woman of the Boulevards

Monday. I am washing dishes.
The French have a word for it – plongeur – conjuring a diver of
the suds, a grease-smasher
The acrobat in the kitchen sink. Chic.

I've got one eye tightroping the distance between me and the
house next door, House Beautiful - creeper covered facade -
ecru tasselled hammock suspended between hot-house trees.
Strung lights for party nights. Dogs for decor. And constant
deposits of foie gras and objets d'art from Galeries Lafayette.
Dressing up clothes. Fresh flowers.
An encore of lights fantastic.

I am my Own Woman. Elle next door is a victim of rampant
lust, a prisoner in her maquillage and fully-staffed wardrobe. I
spin the plates on the end of a mop. own woman. Wash the
dishes. Oop-la. Watch me dive.

I lived life with feet on the ground, until we moved here,
amongst the trees. Discovered my prehensile roots. Painted
them, red, white, blue, and began to walk ropes to pay the bills.
Later came the balancing tricks. Along the branches reaching
out for us.

Come to the edge! Fly. The children have started to grow
feathers. On their feet. Like birds tightly packed in an eggbox
nest. Some days we might hear a bird. Or two. Singing. In cages.

They wanted to fill Paris with birds whistling the Marseilles. But we
hear only canaries, and they sing songs to break our hearts, of love
and red roses. The mannequin in my kitchen window rocks in her
hand-painted hammock. Her gardener whistles the latest Jonny
Halliday as he waters the roses. She's the only bird he knows.

LEAVE OF ABSENCE

Monday. I am washing dishes in a spangled leotard. Plonge. Plonge. The kids are practising chucks with diabolos instead of cats. Like me, they want to join the circus when they grow up. Like everyone. We have posters of Marceau pinned to our walls. Faded to match.

Da Daa. Husband enters holding a bunch of wilted roses. Red, or white. Never blue. The smile I wear is gash wide. I am clowning. Juggling with cups.
Five at a time.

I have taken to wearing a white all-in-one for special occasions. I pretend the flowers were picked right that moment, from Elle's Garden Perfect, for me. The Big Act. Of pity for these roses have been working hard all weekend, being beautiful, perfumed, in a breathless joint at the Marche Serpette.

Hanging from the pipes in the bathroom, remaining scents drip down. Petals crisp to brown and rust. They will crumble with deep sighs when the pipes begin to shake.
We will catch their tatters on clean dinner plates.

Monday. I hope to die like this one day. In my leotard.

RHIAN SAADAT

theory number five

that umbrellas offer inadequate protection
against the thousands of silvery creatures
                tumbling daily
out of the sky as
leakage from a suspended sea just beyond

the reach
        of gravity.

It is thought that many of these living raindrops
are indigenous to the super sargasso, becoming

                displaced by

intergalactic flotsam

resulting in flotilla of fish

large-mouth black bass
goggle eye
and hickory shard
                landing in our streets.

what we need are paludaria of
enormous dimensions
in which to pamper these downpours of

                bumblebee gobies
                        banded clowns
orange chromide
        or star-gazing dorads

LEAVE OF ABSENCE

not to mention those other sightings of snakes
spiders, sea sponges, lizard, and myriads of
small annelidae protected by casings of gel

        free-falling

onto our streets

causing chaos generally, where systems are,
at this present time geared only to downpours

        of a liquid kind.

le bain

Because he'd always wanted her
that image in the Puces, the one
he lied, reminded him of me, and
whilst I knew how hopelessly untrue
I bought it – one vacant afternoon
a let's make up and kiss gift
                presented it with tea.

I'd hoped we'd somehow celebrate
but he said he needed space to enjoy
her silver bromide body, skin – light
Glad you like her, sensitive emulsion.
Even the lichened stone she clutched
with phosphorescent hand was aerated
like mousse,
                filtered over passion.

He ignored my kiss, forgot his drink –
dark gree – mumbled about radiant energy,
smoothing the amber voile soaking her legs.
I left the room and she, in turn, ignored him
to focus on some distant point beyond
the edges of her frame   as if
grass must surely be greener off
                photographic paper.

But naturally it never is
a real green   more a verdigris
a   distant   shade   of   frequency
its tiny dots creating shapes then
gradually
            gradually

LEAVE OF ABSENCE

loosening their hold   until
one day
they wash away like tea leaves   or

like a misting woman in a

                                  cooling liquid
photodegradable

Metamorphosis

As a woman, once out of the city
she discovered she could fly easily
through the spaces between trees.
Her clothing burst across the shoulders –
She must have grown wings
in the night.

Her new skin satisfied;
a transparent velvet, through which
her internal workings glowed.
She spun her thoughts
into sonar beams.

Picking up speed, and humming,
she noted her ability to translate
vibrations from the earth –
and considered how language,
in her past, had always
left her mumbling.

Caviar Fast

This Spring we gave up chocolate for eggs, ate their tiny tear drops in clusters, on the rims of teaspoons, on corners of folded sheets of palest bread – reflecting the crepes we see sugared and rolled on street corners, the Caspian salt watering the maps of our tongues curled, wet nests for rows of sea-black eyes reflecting the grooves in the lids of our mouths, their pearl round dreams of swimming a life time of sea melting under liquid waves. Their tastes had us praising wordless, the nature of love, its brine, its acts of suspension like arabesques in opaque sighs, bodies gutted of secrets, each secret enveloped in a perfect sphere of black.

Missing Person

She arrived in the world
with some preconceived notion
about being human, warmth –
whatever it was,
it was never quite enough.

The absences between people
and their spoken lines
suggested more
than the words themselves –
few, and far between.

She grew, then shrivelled
in corners with the rolling dust
where the elimination of music
pulled at the corners of her mouth
so that, grimacing clownlike
she played the dying down.

Adam and Eve

These days, it's a matter of how we place our fig-leaves,
And where.

Forget genitalia,
The breasts.

My leaves are attached to the temples. I no longer see from side to side.

You wear yours like bank-notes.
Grafted.
To the palms of your hands.

Haunting

The new house was steeped in the smell of it –
stealing their breath in a way the city pollution
had never done. They put it down to change of scene,
laughing at the way their hair turned a sudden grey
and newspapers slumped into waves the weight
of sodden earth –

> the air grew thicker by late afternoon
> and their first night, unhinged by misgivings.

They found themselves waking in strangled sheets,
crying out for lost limbs, with waterless tears,
winding themselves tightly inside each other, feeling out
the tracks of familiar human maps, sharing
restless whispers of some hidden knowledge
welling up to close the surface openings,
decomposing nightly into musted odours of
webbed leaves, ancient plastered walls –

> each morning they swept out a dark crumbling
> soil, heaved up by the sighing rooms.

Later, the shock of finding the moths in the cellar,
hundreds of freeze-frame documents, unwritten, poised
invisible pins through each brief heart
bellus, hypolitus, zalmoxis, zephyritis –
secreted recipes for immortality, causing
their human dreams to shatter, reach for the light
against the shut tight window panes,
hecuba polydos, demophanes, euphorion,
interrupted – half-lived beings tightly held somewhere
between the illusion of life, and the humus beneath,
picked off, sealed without rites, a haunting in flight.

Sharon Sage
The Change
a short play for radio

[*An eerie wind blows and whistles... it slowly subsides...*]

OLD LADY   Tha's an ill wind

CLARICE   Said the old lady as she stood on the opposite pavement and watched the scene of dramatic devastation. This is the tale I really wanted to tell, the one that fires my belly. This is the tale of a brave and blameless woman, and a chicken-shit man. Anne-Marie and Butch, I'll call them. Of course those are not real names. His real name was Adrian; he used to use it occasionally, when it suited, or with his parents, who couldn't stomach Butch. It doesn't really matter any more now, not after what happened.

ANNE-MARIE   Aren't you being a bit melodramatic?

CLARICE   And why not? This tale has plenty of melodrama, all the right ingredients – man woman conflict – but with a specifically domestic, woman's slant. Only fly in the ointment being the enchantment, I'll admit that gums things up good and proper. It suits me to tell it, too. I'm your born exaggerator, everyone always says. Your original unreliable narrator, except of course that his tale happens to be true... I'm Clarice

ANNE-MARIE   [*half laughing/groaning*] Clarice?

CLARICE   What's wrong with Clarice? It comes with some connotations, bags of its own, ready made bona fide luggage, it has style, clarity; CLUH for clarity, slight exoticism from the possible Frenchy element. Sadly we can't all be double-barrelled beauties.

ANNE-MARIE   Whose story is this anyway?

CLARICE   You're absolutely right. Totally legitimate question to ask of any drama, even a melodrama. Let's be clear about this, from the outset: this is the story of my friend here, Anne-Marie –

ANNE-MARIE   Anne-Marie?

CLARICE   Yes – two names but neither of them guileful... a case of a good fit, name to nature, if we're in the business of naming names, no dramatic mismatch there. It's also the story of Butch, who wasn't Butch at all, never had been... his name never fit. In fact neither of them did, there was a definite schism, between who he was, and who his names gave-him-out-to-be. You might say there's nothing unusual about that, apparently a lot of people are walking around giving signs of other selves from behind names they feel don't fit. Somehow, in the naming of names, his two couldn't mesh tightly enough to hold the outside together. When he was young, it seemed that Butch had been papered on to him by mischievous mates, who saw him as a pretty boy, often misread by men in pubs.

ANNE-MARIE   Anyway, I feel fine about my name, thank you. Now, who's the main point here? I mean let's just keep asking the question until we get it straight; whose story is it?

CLARICE   It's Anne-Marie's story, the story of how she had decided to trust him again but was betrayed by Butch. But it's also the story of how, unbelievably, by the agency of a magical coin that was passed into her change, Anne-Marie's husband had a bit of a mishap, and she was released from her unhappiness.

ANNE-MARIE   A bit of a mishap...

CLARICE   OK, he and his mistress –

ANNE-MARIE   – Don't tell the story before you tell it, you'll spoil it, I want to enjoy it.

CLARICE   Mmm, telling it first would be a mistake. Although by now it's only the pay-off that's left to reveal. I've told the bare bones of the tale already. Why should the end be enough to keep you with it? Surely it's the middle where all the real meat and potatoes are?

THE CHANGE

ANNE-MARIE   Well, yes, that's true, although the way you've set it up, it does make you wonder...people do like a good twist, and they'll go a long way to get one. It seems like there's a lot of pleasure in riding along knowing your horse is going to throw you into a soft pile of hay, just as you reach the stables.

CLARICE   We're not in a fairy-tale, where every one knows how it ends, things are a little upside-down. The test is for the heroine to survive the middle – however predictable – and make no mistake, she is the heroine, there's no room in this tale for a Prince. She has to open her hand for the change. In this tale, when Sleeping Beauty awakes, she doesn't get the usual reward for sleeping virtuously all that time, I would say that this is altogether more savage...

ANNE-MARIE   So. On this particular day, Anne-Marie is driving Clarice out to the boot-sale.

[*Fade-in interior of car driving over bumpy ground*]

CLARICE [*reading*]   Between moments of time
catch the light that shines
Through the flickering leaves of a tree...
Jesus, where did you find it?

ANNE-MARIE   in his overalls – I was doing the washing. He said it was from before, but it gave me a bad feeling.

CLARICE   I suppose he was too embarrassed to say he'd written it himself.

[*Bouncing over uneven ground in the car, they come to a stop, park, the engine is switched off*]

ANNE-MARIE   It's vile, give it back...It goes on and on like that. I want it to disappear, to never have been, but I know it can't, none of it will, how can I be back in this terrible place, again?

CLARICE   What did he say, exactly, when you showed it to him?

[*Fade into interior of Anne-Marie's house, domestic appliances humming*]

BUTCH [*wheedling*]   Come on, that's all finished, all over, I told you, that must have been in my pocket for weeks.

ANNE-MARIE   When did she give it to you?

BUTCH   It must have been when she came to the site one time, it was before, I don't see why we have to go over and over the same ground –

ANNE-MARIE   – but it's horrifying, I don't want to find this stuff, I hate the way it makes me feel, on edge.

BUTCH   Well, how do you think I feel, I'm trying to get over it too you know, it makes me feel terrible that you can't trust me, it's like you're looking over my shoulder all the time. You've got to trust me, or we can't make any progress –

[*The phone starts ringing,* **Butch** *goes to answer it*]

BUTCH   OK...I'm on my way, [*uncomfortable*] Yes...I'll be there as soon as I can. Look [*to* **Anne-Marie**] I'm late, I was s'posed to be there hours ago. All you need to know is, I'm not gonna lie to you...we'll talk later, yeah?...OK?

ANNE-MARIE   OK.

BUTCH   I promise, there's nothing for you to worry about,

[*Domestic appliances fade into the interior of the car, we are back at the boot-sale*]

ANNE-MARIE   He said: I promise, there's nothing for you to worry about.

CLARICE   [*narrating over*] But Anne-Marie had a bad feeling, she felt on edge, on the edge, where there was nothing for her to worry about, but she was worried, worried that there was really nothing to worry about any more...everything that there had been to worry about was gone...[*back in the car*] Come on, I'll buy you a coffee, we'll have a wander round, get some air, look at bedding plants and souvenirs of Benidorm. It's a powerful recipe for clarity.

[*They get out of the car, and the wind takes their breath, the sounds of the boot-sale grow as they walk: buyers and sellers, generators for the hot dog and bacon roll stalls,* Tie A Yellow Ribbon *distorts over the tannoy. Children and babies are calling and crying*]

ANNE-MARIE   How can you be clear – it's like a whirl-wind dumped its eye in a field and left a maelstrom of junk.

CLARICE   That's the beauty of it, the magic, you can feel the randomness that brings it all together – it makes no sense, but the truth is, it makes as much sense as everything else –

ANNE-MARIE   This isn't like some horrible cosmic equation you can add me in to you know. Two negatives make a positive, is that the theory?

CLARICE   I just mean that there's something comforting in it...there's a wonderful sensation that hums off all that stuff.

ANNE-MARIE   It seems such a horrible trick, everyone working so hard to make a system of it. Sometimes what's in the skips between the aisles is the same as what's on the stalls.

CLARICE   That's the point – there's no logical rhyme nor reason, but somehow it gets sorted into valueful and valueless – it's a job of work –

ANNE-MARIE   – to make something out of nothing.

CLARICE   If you ask me, seems like the only dignified thing to do, given what a mess things have become.

ANNE-MARIE   [*narrating over*] But Anne-Marie was unable to get any clarity from the junk, she had been overtaken by a spooky sensation of foreboding. She remembered that morning, early...

[*The boot-sale fades, and we are in* **Anne-Marie's** *bedroom*]

BUTCH   Come on, stay a minute longer.

ANNE-MARIE   [*reluctant to go, forcing herself awake*] I said I'd go.

BUTCH   [*pulling her back, close*] You could say you'll stay – I want you to myself, Jamie'll be back from your mum's later, and then it'll be too late.

ANNE-MARIE   Stop trying to tempt me…

BUTCH   Ssssss….like the serpent in the garden.
ANNE-MARIE   [*laughing, struggling to get free*] Very true.

BUTCH   Misunderstood, just like me. [**Anne-Marie** *has got free and is moving around, getting clothes, shoes on*] That poor old snake was just offering a girl some good honest fun.

ANNE-MARIE   Just like you.

BUTCH   Just like me…as honest as the day is long. Look into my eyes [*he lunges across the bed, grabs her and there's a mock fight*] You just don't know what's good for you.

ANNE-MARIE   Strangely enough, I've never really had much doubt about that until recently, [*She gets free, they're both out of breath,* **Butch** *gives a sharp intake of breath in mock horror, the tone has changed, broken into earnestness*] I'd been thinking that was more your trouble.

BUTCH   You're good for me.

ANNE-MARIE   Yes, but are you good for me? I don't want to play these games.

BUTCH   If you could just stop, start again from now. I won't lie to you, whatever happens, I promise.

ANNE-MARIE   Which one are you, which one is the honest one? Adrian or Butch? Or is there someone else in there who can give me a straight answer?

BUTCH   Why are you being so unfair? – after everything that's happened, why would I lie?

CLARICE   [*narrating over*] This is the point in the tale where you need to hold on tight to those memories of swinging on granny's knee, when she told you how bad stuff can happen if you lie. What exactly happened defies rational explanation, but that doesn't mean it didn't happen. When Anne-Marie closed the front door, Butch disentangled his mobile from his jacket on the floor. [*A whirlwind building*] While he dialled the numbers a whirlwind far off somewhere started: its eye was on him, and full of deadly flotsam but he didn't know that yet.

THE CHANGE

[*Whirlwind, debris falling, garden gates slapping, digital phone dialling*]

BUTCH [*in an intimate new tone*] Hey, How's it going...I'm at the house, listen, I've got some free time, how'd you feel about coming over? [*The wind blows the bedroom window wide open with a sudden crash, the wind whistles round the room, and* **Butch** *has to raise his voice to be heard on the mobile*] Shit, no, it was the wind. [**Butch** *goes over to the window and struggles to close it while still talking, he locks it, the wind howls but from outside*] OK. Yeah, she's gone out, it's cool, at least for a couple of hours...a lot can happen in a couple of hours... [*laughing*] I remember, unlikely to forget. Look, lets stop wasting precious time, just get yourself here.

[*Fade-up boot-sale; outside noises, generator close by*]

ANNE-MARIE   Clarice, could we go?

[*Burgers and bacon frying on a huge hot plate nearby, chips being drained, their sieve banging against the side of the deep-fat frier*]

CLARICE   Naah, lets not go yet, here [*to the man at the bacon roll stall*] two coffees please.

BACON ROLL MAN   Two coffees, one twenty-five. Don't forget the change...

CLARICE   You get the change, I'll carry the coffees. Ow they're hot –

BACON ROLL MAN   One twenty five, one thirty, fifty, two pound, three, and a nice shiny new two pound coin –

ANNE-MARIE   Ow. Ow. The change is hot, never mind the coffee –

BACON ROLL MAN   – makes five. Sorry love, the coin box was parked next to the deep-fat frier.

ANNE-MARIE   [*dreamily*] The deep-fat frier.

CLARICE   Let me see your hand...it's burnt, 'scuse me – could I have a wet cloth or something, the change burnt her hand.

[*Background of boot-sale fades away*]

CLARICE   The change. When I looked under the cloth, the mark was gone, but I had seen it, it had left a perfect red imprint on the soft palm of her hand. Probably crossed her life-line. That was the change. The agent of change; Anne-Marie was blushing and flushed but this was no hot-flush-change, not the kind of change euphemistically known as The Change, the one that usually re-shapes a woman's life without her instigating it. This was just Hot Change. Her life was about to change, and things were about to get hot.

[*In the kitchen of Anne-Marie and Butch's house,* **Butch** *is making coffee, putting the kettle on the stove using the clicking ignition button. The* **Mistress** *muses to herself, and then turns from the kitchen mirror to* **Butch**]

MISTRESS   Mirror, mirror, on the wall…What did you tell her?

BUTCH   Nothing, sweet nothings, actually. Enough to keep things sweet while I figure out a few little nothings.

MISTRESS   Meaning?

BUTCH   Meaning, I need to set things up, move the money around. Come here [*he pulls her over to him, kisses her*] Mmm…yum yum I don't want anything to go wrong. For us, this is a whole new life.

MISTRESS   She must be sleepwalking.

BUTCH   She badly wants to believe I'm someone else, although I firmly believe he never existed. So it's no great challenge to keep her on hold. It won't be long –

MISTRESS   I do hope you're right. I'm not sure I can wait.

BUTCH   Just hang on till I've taken care of the last little details, I don't want any child support crap…

[*The phone rings, they are embracing. He is undressing her*]

MISTRESS   Why don't you let it ring?

JAMIE   [shouting from the garden] Dad, phone's ringing.

[**Butch** *lets the phone ring, goes to the door and shouts out into the garden*]

BUTCH   OK, I've got it. Just another half an hour out there, OK?

JAMIE   [f*ed up*] OK

[**Butch** *closes the door, but the wind blows it open and papers and flotsam blow around the kitchen. It whistles violently around the room. The last bang of the kitchen door on its hinges switches us back to the boot-sale*]

CLARICE   Does it hurt?

ANNE-MARIE   Does what hurt?

CLARICE   Your hand.

ANNE-MARIE   Oh. No, not really, it just feels hot. What time is it? Jamie... Jamie'll be home. I need to go.

[*Back at the house,* **Butch** *is struggling with the back door, trying to close it. He bolts it, top and bottom. The bolts are unused and hard to wriggle across. He uses all his strength, and just as the last bolt crunches into place, he pinches his hand*]

BUTCH   Ow...[*He sucks his hand*]

MISTRESS   [*laughing*] Here, let me look at that. I think you've been an all round very brave boy, and you deserve a big reward, I wouldn't manage to keep a straight face.

[**Butch** *pushes his* **Mistress** *up against the cooker. The automatic ignition clicks continuously*]

BUTCH   That's the easy part – [*change of tone, to earnest as before*] it makes me feel terrible that you don't trust me.

[*The ignition button is clicking furiously, and above the sounds of their undressing. Heavy breathing, frenzied, violent clinches. There is a loud woomf of gas igniting*]

BUTCH   [*back in seductive tone*] Now if I'm not much mistaken, we had about half an hour to transact some serious business – why don't we go upstairs? I don't believe I've shown you the master bedroom –

[*Up close the gas roars loudly through the tiny jets of the gas ring. Behind the roar,* **Butch** *and the* **Mistress** *run upstairs*]

BUTCH   If we're lucky the bed might even be still warm…

[*The fire ignites in the chip pan, and grows huge. It leaps around the room; furniture crashes, glass breaks, and roars, fuelled by the wind which has blown a window open. It becomes increasingly loud, and overpowering, when it suddenly stops*]

CLARICE   Most domestic fires start in the kitchen. This one was no exception, and chip-pan fires are amongst the most violent … having begun with such a super-heated source, a house fire that starts in a chip pan can rage through a house in no time flat. [*Fire engine sirens draw closer, several go past, drawing the Doppler effect as they go*] Now I'm sure some people will say that it was the betrayal that lit the fire, and it was the lie that soaked through the house like kerosene soaks through a rag; it was the deceit that locked the doors and windows preventing their escape. But I'm here to tell you that a magical coin found it's way into my friend's hand, and when it found her it did a job of work.

ANNE-MARIE   So that's Anne-Marie's story.

CLARICE   A brave and blameless woman, who was freed by enchanted means from a cowardly plot to betray her.

ANNE-MARIE   And I imagine she lives happily ever after?

CLARICE   Oh, I think so, don't you?

[*Fade-up news reader*]

ANNE-MARIE   Two bodies were revealed by fire investigators, although it may be some time before they can be named, such was the ferocity of the fire. One occupant of the house and her son are safe and well, having been out with friends and relatives at the time the blaze started.

J. SHAW

Extract from Pusher

Julia didn't sleep that night, but sat on the couch wrapped in a blanket with every light in the house blazing. Shadows couldn't move if they weren't there. She kept the TV on, as loud as she dared without risking a noise complaint and flicked between infomercials and the home shopping channel. Sometime after 3 a.m. she ordered two gold bracelets and a Supa-Mop. She smoked and drank coffee to keep herself awake and worked very hard at not thinking. HSC proved very helpful in that endeavour. When the cigarettes ran out, she ransacked the medicine cabinet and found some Vivarin that was only a year and a half out of date.

At 7 a.m. she found herself drinking cold coffee and staring at an Addams Family rerun. She remembered when she was seventeen and going through a Goth phase. She'd dyed her hair jet black like Morticia Addams. Her father had made her cut it all off, Pat Benatar short (which was years out of fashion by then), and dye it back.

"Fuck this," she said to the television and got up, spilling coffee on the rug. She grabbed some shorts and a T-shirt out of the hamper, dug her wallet out of her purse and stuck it in her back pocket. She had to get out of her apartment so she could think. And so she would be gone if they came back for her.

Outside, she avoided the parking lot and her car and walked instead. They might know her car, tag it, track it, something. She thought of the high-school kid in the parking lot. The doorman at Rodney's. The new cleaner. Invasion of the fucking body snatchers much? Or she could be going insane. That was always an option. Maybe more appealing too. They had medication for insane people didn't they? And didn't the body snatchers win at the end of that movie? Fucking mess.

From her apartment Julia walked west, towards the carefully maintained yuppie haven that was downtown, full of pricey hair salons, bridal boutiques, and antique stores. Early morning on a

Saturday and there weren't many people around which she was glad for. If Jacob was telling the truth, everyone was an enemy. Or maybe he was insane; a crazy stalker with twisted Anne Rice delusions. Stalkers always got arrested or killed in TV movies. That she could handle. And what about the others, she asked herself. Are there groups of crazy delusional stalkers now? She had no answer.

Downtown, she wandered past closed shops and dark cafes. She walked for an hour, circling the blocks four times and saw only a morning jogger and an old lady walking her dog. The jogger passed on a cross street a block ahead of her, but she crossed the street to avoid the old lady and only felt slightly stupid. Any form we wish, he had said.

But the world slowly woke up and the safe haven of desertion was spoiled. Julia sat on a bench and watched a smiling, middle-aged woman in a knee-length skirt flip the sign of her shop from closed to open. As the shops opened, people arrived, mostly women, cluttering the sidewalks with bodies and chatter. Young wives, still attractive in slim-fit jeans, dragged toddlers behind them as they shopped. Older wives adopted loose cotton shorts in pastel colours and leather Keds. Julia watched them all with suspicion and growing panic. She knew she couldn't sit here forever, suspicious of the world. She wanted to buy cigarettes but was afraid of talking to a clerk. She was afraid of everything. Afraid of the things in her apartment, of the people outside of it, afraid of what they would ask her to do. Jacob was right; payback's a bitch.

There was a payphone on the corner, an actual box of square glass and reflective metal. Julia stared at it and decided she would call Joey. She would go to Joey's. Joey would make sense, take charge, tell her what to do. Or at the very least Joey would have cigarettes. Julia got up from the bench, fishing in the change pocket of her wallet for 35 cents. She suddenly felt better, having a plan. She knew Joey, trusted her, and most of all, would know if Joey wasn't Joey.

She stepped into the phone booth, picked up the receiver.

"Please, please be home," she prayed to the phone god as she shoved her money in the slot. "Please be home even if I have to wake you up." She dialled, the numbers beeping in her ear. It rang on the other end.

But only once.

A forefinger depressed the hang-up lever, cutting off her call. Anger rose and then fell, trading places with fear. The phone booth was doorless and standing in the opening was a young girl, thirteen or fourteen, her hair bunched into a single ponytail. She smiled, and her teeth shimmered with the metallic correction of braces.

"Julia," she said, in a voice still high and sweet. "Jacob says Hi. And to look over there." The girl pointed through the glass of the telephone booth to a small stationery shop across the street. There was a man leaving the shop, a balding man with glasses and a briefcase, dressed up for a Saturday in a business suit. He looked like an insurance salesman.

She looked back at the girl, dread making her tongue thick. "What does he want?"

The sharp glitter of the braces smiled at her.

Push him. Such a simple thing. A single motion of the arm and hand, a short and efficient movement of muscles. Julia swallowed nausea. The intersection bled heavily with traffic fed by the tollway ramp half a mile down and the sprawling commercialism of the shopping mall cradled by restaurants and office buildings. The road was two lanes in each direction and cars flashed by in a smooth stream of shiny metallic skin, rushing past with the continuous roar of engines and exhausts. Across the street the orange Don't Walk sign pulsed at her, ticking off the seconds. But here the light catered to cars not pedestrians. People began to collect around her, behind her, waiting to cross the rushing divide between the decaying strip mall and its more affluent neighbour. Julia tried to fold into herself, avoid contact, touch with any of the gathering crowd. Any of *them*. The whispers invaded her head still, the low expectant hum of scavengers waiting to feast on the kill. They could be anywhere, in the crowd, or passing by, close enough to watch the show. Wait, watch, and feed.

It was ninety-degree heat but she shivered. She could feel sweat slide past her temple leaving a cold trail of melted ice. The air, clogged with the thickness of heat and fumes, choked her. The orange signal throbbed at her and the crowd shuffled and mumbled, pressing forward, the impatience of waiting brewed into shifting restlessness. To her right, a heavily set woman in a green tank top brushed against her, the doughy flesh of the woman's arm sticky and moist. Julia swallowed the acidic taste of bile and the scream that rose in her throat with it.

In front of her, the insurance salesman looked at his watch and shifted his feet. She'd followed him here, the distance from the serenity of downtown to the busier shopping district surprisingly small. He was sweating under the layers of his suit. Julia could see the small pools of moisture gathered in the patch of bare skin on his head. He looked common and ordinary. Harmless. She couldn't push him.

But they whispered at her still, cajoling, threatening, impatient, the words themselves lost in the tangled jumble of so many voices, tiny slithering snakes slowly poisoning her.

The traffic light changed from green to yellow.

Her time wound down, the seconds decelerating into the interminable void of indecision. *I can't do it*, she told them.

Babbling, screaming, screeching, voices that coalesced into the single command. *Push him.*

I can't do it. Her brain was frozen. *I can't do it.* Her body paralysed, stuck in the litany of refusal, caged within the human restraint against murder. *I cannot kill.*

Silence. The voices gone, leaving the echo of emptiness waiting to be filled, the climax of the play when the actors fall silent and the audience draws in that baited breath. *I can't kill him*, she said, pleading with the void.

Then fat woman in green touched her.

And Julia pushed.

It was a half step forward, the raising of one arm and one hand, a sharp shove. The insurance salesman tumbled into the street, clumsily with sprawling limbs, like a child's doll knocked off its shelf. It was a bread truck that hit him, speeding through the yellow light. It was painted a bright white and said 'Wonderbread' on the side. It hit him with the crackling thud of metal against flesh and the thin-edged scream of tortured brakes. Julia felt the diesel-fuelled wind of the truck as it flashed past her, the back end jumping the kerb as the heavy vehicle skidded under the brakes. More brakes screeched and tyres twisted. In front of her, the front end of a red Toyota folded neatly under the back of a Ford pick-up, the bed of the truck impaled the windscreen of the smaller car leaving a spider's web of cracks and schisms. Smoke rose from the engine block of a Cavalier that had jumped the divider and hit the traffic light. Everything screamed.

The pedestrian crowd scattered in chaos and terror like a herd of animals fleeing after the first blast of the hunting rifle. But there were predators among the prey, feeding on the horror, pain, and death she had created, like kids at an all-you-can-eat ice cream buffet.

At her feet was the insurance salesman's briefcase, lying there like a toy abandoned by a fickle child. There were initials engraved into the clasp. R. A. H.

Julia turned away, her earlier nausea returning with more force. The population of the former crowd mixed and milled with the confusion of people who need someone to tell them what to do and soon. A few feet away, Julia saw the heavy woman in the green tank top comforting a crying teenage girl.

The woman saw Julia looking at her, and smiled. Not the sorrowful, commiserating smile of someone who has just witnessed the same tragedy, but the pleased, prideful smile of a parent to a child, or teacher to student, the slight, toothless upturn of lip and cheek that says, Well done.

Julia turned around again, the muscles of her stomach clenching, and vomited, narrowly missing the briefcase of the late R. A. H.

CLARE SIMS

Extract from **Dusk**

ONE

Joel Pearce, formerly of the Pearce, Lehmann and Associates architectural practice, whose design for a museum dedicated to the paintings of Henrik Klinge had appeared on the cover of a tourist brochure for the town of Vyburg, and whose 'New Ideas in the Fenestration of Leisure Buildings' had been published in a 1984 edition of Architectural Digest along with a series of photos of a mall he'd designed in Weyburn, had lived his whole life within view of the solid geometries that carved light from dark, the dimensions of which could be laid out on graph paper, subject to ruler, T-square and triangle, only to find, in his sixty-fourth year, that the straight lines were trembling, softening, exhaling at last – as if after a long, intricate deception – and were returning to what he had always suspected their true nature to be: smoke.

What Joel occasionally wondered, as he felt his way through the town, north of Mexico City, where he intended to wait out the remaining years of his life, was when it had all started. When was the first moment the light shimmered, and the lines moved, and the centre began to void itself of its objects? The cigarette he raised to his lips he could see only as a pale shape against the paler air; the smoke he exhaled was invisible. With his other hand, he felt his way along the cathedral gate. He could dimly make out the iron bars as they flipped past. The alley narrowed ahead of him, the walls on either side mounting to uneven peaks. In the far distance, where Calle Hidalgo intersected with the next street, Joel saw only a cloud of debris, as if the stones of the houses were disintegrating, and offering themselves up to the air.

"It is not uncommon," the doctor had explained, "for a patient who has suffered an overexposure to light to experience, in later life, withering of the visual cells and blood vessels in the choroid, leading to a condition known as macular degeneration."

The examination had been brief and confusing, almost like an embrace. Dr Anderson sat close enough for their knees to meet.

"Look there," he murmured, pointing over his shoulder. A white ray shot into Joel's eye. The room behind it went dim. He could feel the other man's breath on his face: short, concentrating puffs that smelled of earth. Something cold fell against his hand – the button from a lab coat. Joel allowed the saliva to pool under his tongue so that he would not have to jar the silence with his swallowing. The ray moved into the centre of his left eye, and then clicked to the right. Abruptly the doctor wheeled his chair away and a waft of air chilled Joel's neck. White spots with black holes in them drifted slowly downward from the ceiling.

The doctor handed him a square of laminated paper and asked him what he saw on it.

"It's a grid."

"Anything else about it?"

"Some of the lines break off." He paused and looked up.

"Whereabouts?"

Joel traced his finger over the centre of the grid, where a few of the blue lines were shifting from foreground to background, obscured as if by the momentary intercession of a waft of white cloud. "These squares here, they're incomplete."

Joel looked up to confirm what he knew must be true – that the grid was intact – and noticed the frames of the doctor's glasses appeared to be undulating, as if they lay under a thin veil of water. On the far wall was a white poster with a handful of black letters scattered across it. A box on the desktop held a set of lenses. Close to his head, he sensed the grey form of the autorefractor, its eyeholes embedded in a thick casing of metal. These objects, strewn around the room, took on an insistent clarity. His palms went damp, and he flushed with a feeling of overwhelming and cosmic shame that usually only children suffer.

When the blood had stopped ringing in his ears the doctor was in mid-explanation. "Degeneration," "ageing," "irreversible," a few stray words pierced through. He held out a textbook, open to a glossy photo of an eye which had apparently been lit from the inside of the skull, showing the blue iris like a mottled pane of glass, scarred with a trail of white spots.

"This is where the tissue in the choroid has started to break down," the doctor was saying, "so you get deposits of dead cells, and they obstruct the light from going through to the retina. That's why it's your central vision that has the problem – that's where the build-up is. The degeneration is gradual, you'll hardly notice it from week to week, and if you're careful about not putting any strain on your eyes then you can count on having good sight for a long time yet. I've seen people with this condition keep their sight well into their seventies, even older."

The letters on the poster across the room pulsed, like dim stars.

"Have you got some prescription sunglasses?"

"No."

"I'll give you a prescription. You want to avoid strong sunlight."

"What about these?" Joel said, tapping the case for his reading glasses.

"Those should still be fine."

"But that's what I told you – they're not fine, not for reading, not anymore."

"Mr. Pearce, we're not talking about adjusting your eye's ability to focus. There's a breakdown in the lens tissue, and with this disease, I'm afraid there are no easy solutions. Your eye's going to keep breaking down and the more scar tissue you create – and that's one of the risks of surgery – the more obstruction you're going to have."

Joel was silent for a minute, staring at a point in the air about a foot ahead of him, letting his eyes drift in and out of focus. He knew there was some thought he had to formulate or overcome, beyond which the uncertainty of this moment would be dispelled and he would be able to rise from his chair, shake Dr Anderson's hand, and walk out with an air of polite indifference.

Whatever the thought was, it refused to materialise. He pressed down on the vinyl armrests and found himself standing. The doctor handed him the prescription, and also the grid.

"Try to take a look at this every day and keep a record of what you see."

"A record?"

"It's one way of monitoring the progress of the disease."

As Joel moved through the revolving doors of the office building, holding the square with its shifting pattern of grid and cloud, he had an uncanny sensation of being lifted up, shaken round, and tossed gently back on his feet. It was at that point that the thought he had been struggling for back in the office crystallised. He would go blind.

After the first, cold shock of it, the thought dwindled into something thin that pressed up against the walls of his mind. He found he could move his limbs normally again, and the strange, disorientating heat in his face and ears faded. He walked out of the shadow of the skyrise, past a Chinese grocer, where, in the window, a twist of brown herbs hung beside a red paper lantern. The news that light had damaged him came, oddly, as no surprise. What he wondered was when the assault had taken place. That it was an assault – a sudden, brutal gesture – Joel was convinced. He sensed it, lurking somewhere in his past: a moment of intense overexposure that had burnt away some protective covering inside his eyes. But no matter how hard he strained, he couldn't bring the event into clear focus. It flickered away, just out of reach of his memory. This idea, that he had been attacked by light and then had forgotten it, stayed with him in the years that followed. In his dreams he moved through a vast building without windows or light fixtures, that was nevertheless suffused with an unworldly glow that seemed to emanate from the walls themselves. Sometimes the walls would implode into shimmering portals through which he could see a flat landscape of snow stretching to the horizon in every direction. The light in these dreams intensified over time, until, in the last three years, since he moved to Mexico, it reached such a crescendo of brilliance that he seemed to be dreaming at the centre of a lightbulb, his head resting between the two burning filaments. But each morning he woke to looked more like dusk.

TWO

How Joel found himself standing in a lecture theatre, addressing an audience of fog, on the subject of the hyperbolic paraboloid roof in modernist architecture, through a Spanish interpreter whose voice emerged from the darkness somewhere to his left along with the jangle of heavy jewellery, was something he no longer thought about, or even remembered with any particular clarity. It was three years since he had come to Mexico, on a short-term lecturing contract in the department of architecture at the University of Guanajuato. When incidents from his former life occasionally did cross his mind, it was in the same way he might remember a drafting pencil he had once owned, or a building that had been visible from the window of a hotel bedroom where he had spent a few nights.

Once, his buildings had been launched with the traditional beer ceremony, foundation stones had been laid, conferences had been attended at universities in Berlin, Tel Aviv, London, and Stockholm. Articles had been written, prizes won, partners engaged, partners retired. There had been sketches, thousands of sketches: charcoal drawings on tracing paper, ink on water-colour paper, and long ago, the supple feel of a conté crayon – short, with a black wooden handle, and a softness somewhere around a 4B. There had been surveys of vacant lots, renovations, and demolitions. There had been a brief dalliance with set design that led to some interest, which for reasons of money he never pursued, from directors at Stratford, Ontario.

There had been an interview in an obscure Parisian periodical, where the influences of his team were traced (inaccurately, as it turned out) to Mondrian. There had been three wives and three divorce settlements. There had been two sons and one death of a son. There had been collaborations with international firms of no little distinction, and letters of application from graduates who wished to intern at the office he shared with his partners, which was furnished with a collection of chairs Joel had designed using leather and black ironwork. There had been numerous affairs. There had been Bloody Marys drunk in the business class lounges of airports, and a steady supply of hand-made shirts from a tailor in New York who kept his measurements on file. There had been a collection of Japanese wood block prints he donated to a gallery in Regina, and Christmas cards from former clients who owned valuable property in the Los Angeles area, some of whom were minor celebrities.

If it hadn't been for certain – as they struck him now – quite unnecessary mistakes, that list of things might still exist, defined as a unity by the fact that they all accrued to him. Consider the library of the Robert Sprung house, which might have been a strong building, possibly one of his finest. Joel had designed an octagonal space, with windows arranged on the ceiling in an abstract pattern of rectangles and squares. But the truly unique feature was the balcony he proposed to construct out of glass reinforced by sheet metal, and which would run all eight sides of the walls, suspended from the ceiling by iron chains attached to pulleys. During construction, however, the northeast pulley broke, and one end of the balcony came crashing down, damaging the fretwork and dislocating a workman's shoulder, not to mention Sprung's confidence in the whole design, which had been shaky to begin with. A simple question of engineering, evidently not a problem in design, since, the fact was, it had already been done by Frank Lloyd Wright 90 years earlier. Still, this resulted in endless arguments with Sprung, who took this opportunity to object to the use of glass as a building material, and to suggest the inclusion of marble columns to buttress up the balcony, and who knows how long this wrangling might have gone on, except that the construction was eventually held up due to reasons of finance. Apparently Sprung had his money tied up in a scheme for mass producing a tool used for centuries by the Inuit to strip skins off seals which he intended market as an all-purpose kitchen utensil. This fell through in the end, and a year later he was forced to sell the property, and the half-built library was demolished to make way for a swimming pool.

After that, people began to whisper about his eyesight. He was forever catching glimpses of half-concealed conversations, bodies pressing themselves behind doorways, glances half turned away. He took to pouncing on his employees, snatching their work out of their hands and barking corrections, then stalking off, tossing the pages back down on the table, to rustle in the aftermath of silence and vague shock. He sat behind the bubbled glass door of his office, brooding over the shifting squares on the ophthamologist's grid, and then, once he'd pencilled into a green-backed notebook the number of squares that had effaced themselves from the centre, he sat back in his chair, and shut his eyes. He would sit a long time like that, with his head tilted back, but even so, the glare from the ceiling lights would penetrate through his lids, and he saw particles of light moving across the darkness, like sparks drifting in the smoke above a fire. More and more, as the months passed, he turned the lights out and sat in the grey solitude of late afternoon, examining the myriad permutations of dark orange and black behind his closed eyelids that he had never noticed before.

He designed buildings in his imagination, more perfect than any he had previously conceived, and which, when he drew them on paper (to this day he could draw clearly), invariably offended the tastes of his clients. These buildings were spare, delicate, void. Some had window patterns descending in jagged strokes down the walls, that looked like lightening bolts when viewed from the outside. Often there were spaces carved out in the centre, like elevator shafts, that could serve no human purpose but which might be stumbled upon, at the ends of hallways, and gazed wonderingly into, before being left and forgotten. There were long, narrow corridors with no doors giving off them, slab-like rooms to be entered on hands and knees, and staircases ascending toward empty space. All the interiors would be lined with sheet metal, curved, and painted a luminous white, to create a sensation of transparency, like the thin, beaten glass of a frosted light bulb. Eventually he stopped sketching out the blueprints, there didn't seem to be any point. His clients today wanted architecture as collage; they wanted to combine rusticated brickwork with granite, bamboo with glazing, gabled roofs with ionic columns, marble staircases with half-timbered exteriors. It was this kind of intellectual and aesthetic chaos that Joel saw as portentous of some great global decay, and that he believed had been entirely absent in the days of his early career, which he remembered in terms of the tension headaches that gripped his temples whenever he wrangled with the fine points of the concept of *mu* in Japanese tea house architecture.

In the end he was forced to hand over most of the design work to his office. The fact was, he found it increasingly difficult to distinguish one commission from another. Casting an eye over the blueprints, he corrected and harangued, and then stalked away, bringing his office door to a resounding crash behind him, satisfied that he had given a display of interest. There, he would turn out the lights, rest back in his chair, and contemplate his own private designs. They shimmered and floated behind his closed lids, gaining ever more detail and definition, as if they were approaching a final climax of clarity at which point (he anticipated) they would burst, fully formed, into shape around him, just as his own vision gave way.

Of course, nothing like this had ever happened. The closest he ever came to it was in that meeting with the Grossmans. They were a wealthy Montreal family who had solicited proposals from various international firms for the design of a new theatre, and had selected Pearce, Lehmann and Associates on the basis of a set of drawings and a model constructed by a team in the office, under the supervision of Harry Bledworth, a man whose rise through the ranks of Joel's office staff Joel could not account for, especially since he couldn't remember ever having hired him. Harry simply appeared at Joel's elbow one afternoon, in a puff of smoke, wielding a calculator as if it were a remote detonation device. Whenever he punched it, which he did with a ruthlessly stiffened finger, Joel imagined one of his buildings, on a tree-lined street in Assinaboine, imploding to dust and ruin. All Harry's movements had this quality of reckless violence – he tripped over doorsteps, careened across rooms, even his hair struck out blindly whenever he swung his head round. Joel could not help feeling that he did these things deliberately: observing him out of the corner of his eye as he slung off his jacket and whipped it onto his chairback, releasing the whirlwind of his arms grabbing at pens, telephone receiver, coffee cup, Joel was forced to consider whether there was not some connection between Harry's disordering presence and the way the stripes of the venetian blinds snapped in and out of existence, how the edges of doorframes leapt at him without warning and threw him off balance. But whenever he came close to assaulting Harry with the same sort of abuse he lobbed readily at his secretaries, draughtsmen, engineers, Joel found himself holding back, partly out of a suspicion that the offence was too great to find adequate redress in yells and insults, and partly because he preferred to steer clear of the swift, brutal movements of Harry's hands and torso.

And so, on that day when Joel was presenting the new model to the Grossmans, when Harry interrupted, saying 'I think what Mr Pearce means here,' it was with a kind of relief that Joel was able to snap at him that he knew quite well what he was saying. It was a moment of truth, when the younger man had at last declared his antagonism, so that Joel might be seen, in the company of witnesses, to condemn him; he might reach out a paternal hand and set those flailing limbs still.

Mr Grossman shifted his bulk in his chair, while Howie, his son, let out a choked cough, a gold ring on his finger snagging the light. For a second the room went still, and Joel, feeling vindicated, went on describing the vaulted ceiling made entirely of glass, the thin sheets of metal that served for walls, the hallway that would funnel people, as if through a fluorescent tube, up to a balcony overlooking dead air, a sheer drop down a cliff with nothing visible at the bottom save a white circle of floor, until a chink of awareness opened up in his mind, the tiniest aperture, like a lancet window. Growing uncomfortably hot, he reached for his glass of Perrier, which thrust itself at him, cold and wet, before spilling all over Harry Bledworth's lap. There was a moment of confusion. Paper towels were sought. The model was moved to a safe distance, and someone brought Joel a new glass of perrier, which he slurped in an enraged silence, while Harry, after making a few swift stabs at his slacks with a kleenex, said, "If I may pick up from Mr Pearce here, I'd like to point out the low hanging ceiling in the main theatre space, panelled with struts of dark wood, which is specially designed for acoustic effect, and which you'll find echoed in the wood panelling of the lobby..."

And Joel saw, from the oblique angle that was all that was left him of visual clarity, the architectural model, which had, as if from pure spite, wrenched itself free of his own description, and withered into a bulbous, black shape, like a mausoleum.

After the meeting, Joel stormed off down the hall, refusing to speak to Harry, who was anyway still sharing a laugh with Howie Grossman, with whom he appeared to have struck up a suspicious intimacy. In his office again, he stared hard at the various objects that surrounded him: a *shoji* screen angled beside a jade plant, a leather chair, a black desk, as if his gaze were a series of hard, cruel punches, that could bully the shapes of the world back within their own outlines. Surely he was not so far gone as that, he thought, after all, he could still make out the shape of a woman's red kimono in a Japanese print that hung on the wall, he could dimly see the CN tower, with its blinking lights, against a pale indigo sky. He seized the ophthamologist's grid and concentrated on the centre, which now showed a cross-hatched enclosure of emptiness. Then his eye fell on a framed photograph with a slice of sunlight reflecting in the gloss. Sliding his glasses further down his nose, he bent down, and peered at it. It was a picture he had taken himself nine years ago, on a trip to the Rockies, when Casey was still alive. That was the summer he was living in a cabin just outside Golden, working for some unlicensed outfit called Alpine Adventures. His job was to guide tourists up and down Mount Yamnuska, twenty miles east of Banff National Park, and when Joel went out to visit, he did the climb too. The photo was taken from above, although now Joel didn't see how that was possible, since Casey had climbed up first on that day, hammering the pitons into the rockface, clamping the metal krabs over the rope, kicking the spikes of his boots into crevices. But here he was, seen from above, with the whole length of the mountain furled out in his wake, a sheer drop of burnt umber and grey ending with the flourish of waves on a river. Six months after that, Casey was climbing the north face of Huarascon Sur in Peru when, having just ascended past an overhang on a steep ice wall, a chunk of ice gave way under his axe and he fell twenty feet, twisting there, suspended by the safety rope for twenty minutes, while his partner sought enough purchase on the slope to haul him back above the overhang, until the friction with a shard of ice caused the rope to fray, and Casey fell away into the blind white. But when Joel imagined the fall, he did not picture the ice axe, the rope, the ten minutes of exertion and shouting. He saw it only in terms of a simple, pale gesture: a relaxing of vigilance and a plummeting away into light. As he stared closely at the photograph, he saw the grainy texture of dolomite rock, and further below, a trail of other climbers, all splaying their arms and legs against the mountain in postures that expressed a vague quality of distress, but the face of his son, at the centre of the picture, no matter how hard Joel strained to hold the features intact, dissolved into a dust-cloud of flesh-coloured tones, that spun and swerved so violently that he was forced to unfocus his eyes so he might catch a glimpse, at the corner of his vision, of the sharp rectangle of window, so far to his right it was nearly behind him, and to wait for the beats of his heart to retreat back down from his throat and into his chest.

It was around this time that he received a letter, with a stamp depicting a flowering cactus, that he read with the aid of a magnifying glass.

Señor Pearce, it began…

JESSICA SMERIN
Extract from **Killing God**

This is the opening of a novel about Joseph Mengele, former head doctor at Auschwitz concentration camp.

The red pile on the theatre seats was packed hard with flakes of dead skin. The arm rests were stained with spit and burns and vengeance. Lights at the ends of pens slashed words through the dark as critics turned to make sardonic comments about the play to the row behind. Leigh bent back her neck and shut her eyes against the invisible roof. The deep, narrow auditorium was windowless, like the hull of a cargo ship under water. Inside it, Leigh made plans to leave at the interval for a drinks party at the House of Commons. She calculated the time it would take her to reach Westminster, factoring in the comparative probabilities of finding a taxi on Whitehall or the Strand and the percentage uplift for traffic congestion. Briefly, she formulated an outline for her review, based on the failure of the script's new translation to match the rhythm of the original Greek.

As she did so, she felt the quality of the audience's watching change. The air around her grew thick with emotion, pulled her back into the theatre. Dropping her head to the black stage, she saw a dancer posed in a spotlight funnel, one leg trailing, one arm lifted. The line from the dancer's wrist to her jaw, to collarbone, shoulder and ankle was flawless. She spun on one leg and slunk across the stage, edge to edge and back. The light hit her costume sharply, reducing her body to three lines which swelled and flattened like the contours of a flame. From the wings, the cast chanted about a hunt. The dancer moved as if she had become the dogs, and the boar, and the steep mountain. She bent the words around her body with vivid, precise wrenches, making their sounds visible.

Leigh hunched forward, staring at the stage. Her hair was bleached out and cropped close to her skull, exposing its narrow bones, its socket temples. She looked starving. She was wishing that she could dance. That it was her standing in the heat of the spotlight, living like the theatre was empty, feeling her muscles twist her bones into pictures, controlled by a choreographer instead of her own relentless thoughts. Her thin fingers caressed the pen that hovered above the notebook in her lap. Without dropping her eyes from the dance, she brought it down in a staccato rush and wrote: 'Lands from split jump, crouches, curled. Brings up left hand, slow, looks at palm, wrist, forearm. Like for blood. Stands, stares at hand, turns, throws arm open, stretching arms out showing clean, jumps with three limbs wide, up, high, one toe at floor. Is called arabesque?' Leigh's notes trailed into a ragged line, like the record of a heartbeat. As she stopped writing, her brain slowed, her consciousness shrunk into her eyes. They sucked the methedrine beauty of the searing, psychotic dance.

The actor ruined it. He strolled on stage with his body loose and his head turned to wink at the crew in the lighting box. As the dancer skimmed towards him on the points of her toes, he swung an arm back and slammed the weight of his elbow into her stomach. She fell on her hip and shoulder with a crack that hit the back wall of the theatre. The audience giggled, embarrassed, nervous. The actor grinned and began to drawl his speech to the front row with confident intimacy, ignoring the dancer dumped on the stage behind him. She recovered, sliding up from the boards with the anguished arms of the rejected, miming a scene in which her master had chosen to punish her. It was done with such skill that the bulk of Leigh's mind believed the new story, even as her pen scrawled: 'Who the fuck does he think he is?'

He thought he was a god. He was playing Dionysus, and he was good at it. He looked like a Greek statue animated by dreams. Carved on a tragic slant, his face was the gold of mediterranean stone, his dark red hair a slash of time-proof paint. His body was divine. Leigh loathed him; he had ended the only calm moment which she had experienced in months spent fighting with words spoken and written and printed by her antagonists. Tension caged the back of her spine, and she let it out between tongue tip and top teeth with a hiss as she wrote: 'I'll get you. Be a chat show host when I'm through. Welcome to daytime satellite, tosser.'

As the last line before the interval was delivered, Leigh rose from her seat. The actor paused as he turned to leave the stage, looking towards the disturbance that Leigh was causing as she trampled the feet of people in her row. Their eyes seemed to meet, but Leigh knew that with the stage lights in his face he could not see her, and was only reacting to noise. She smiled at him, pleased with her anonymity; him the animal petrified in the head lamps, her driver choosing to gun the car or swerve. In her mind, she put down her foot and felt fuel ignite. Swinging away from the stage, she ran down the aisle as the house lights came up and the audience clapped. She recognised the tall, black man in the back row as the director, Alex Travers, and dropped her eyes as she passed with a short flicker of shame at what she was going to do to his production of *The Bacchae*.

In the empty theatre lobby, Leigh took a glass of wine from the cordoned press area, drained it, and carried a second glass with her into the street. The November night was so cold that tears seeped from her eyes and froze to her skin. A girl was asleep on the steps of the theatre, her face calm with junk and her cover of black plastic bags tucked neat around her feet. Leigh did not look down at the girl, she squinted, anxiously, towards the church clock at the end of St Martin's Lane. The drinks to which she was invited would begin after Parliament had voted on whether to keep benefits for the homeless. With a sudden gut clench, she thought that the clock said nine because its hands had frozen, that she was late and had missed the vote. Under shards of panic, she pulled a mobile phone from her pocket and called Mike, a reporter from her paper who was already at the House of Commons. He said that that the vote would not be taken before ten. Leigh deftly manipulated him into confirming that this was in an hour's time without revealing her fear of frozen clocks.

Elated by the victory, Leigh strode down the narrow, yellow street, under the crooked gilt of bars and theatres, feeling the pavement mould itself to her feet. She was a journalist, wielding the strength of a paper hydra which hung its legs into every hidden place in London. As she stepped out into Trafalgar Square, she saw the sky flare above her like a black fountain. Although it was Friday night, the square was empty because of the cold. Its flag stones shone with ice, sweeping wide across the opening space. She stood above it and spread her fingers across the lion sculptures, preparing to write her review in the spare hour before the vote.

Her wine glass rang at she set it on the stone edge of a plinth. Lighting a cigarette, she allowed herself one look – the length of a long drag – up Nelson's Column, length flung to a height where proportion vanished. The lights of an aeroplane, shifting blinks of white and red, disappeared for a moment behind the dark of the pillar. She watched for them, then twisted her mind into focus with a movement as practised as an athlete's press up.

With the cigarette jammed in her teeth, its end staining her white jaw orange, she flicked through the press pack for *The Bacchae*. The dancer's name, she discovered, was Roxanne. Only eighteen years old, she was a Royal Ballet School graduate making her West End debut. The actor, Sasha, was 25. He had appeared in several recently released and prestigious British films. Leigh opened her laptop computer and typed with gloveless fingers, set at rigid angles by the cold: 'Barely off the Edinburgh fringe, Sasha Kohn thinks that if he hangs an elegant profile in the air the body of a performance will follow. But like Carroll's cat, he leaves the audience with nothing but the image of his grin. The only tragedy for Kohn is that newcomer Roxanne Eliot acts him off the stage.' She went on to praise Roxanne's performance effusively, but damned the production in general, and Sasha in particular. 'This man puts the crap into "pile of",' she concluded. She had argued earlier that day with the sub-editors of her paper's arts pages about the use of the word 'crap' and, having won, wanted to stress her dominance.

At ten minutes to ten Leigh finished her review, found it was 63 words too long, cut 63 words, closed her computer and stubbed out her last cigarette on a lion's paw. Ash stuck to the front claws. She called Mike again, and he told her that Parliament had just voted in favour of keeping benefits for the homeless. This news was not going to cause any papers to rewrite their front pages, as they would have done if the vote had gone the other way. Purged by her revenge of Roxanne's injury, Leigh began to relax, deciding that she had time to walk to Parliament Square along the Victoria Embankment. As she crossed Northumberland Avenue she felt water pull under the road tar, currents that ran underground, down to the Thames.

Leigh was always drawn to the river, its tide mud, its flat smell, its pipes that plunged from concrete sides into filthy depths. She loved its breadth, its bridges, its surface that chopped endlessly across a grey spectrum. That night, as she leant on the Embankment, it was too dark to see the water, but when she closed her eyes she sensed it all the way to the river bed. There, layers of London's history rotted; pulped paper, machine parts, dead weeds with suckers that still clung to fragments of bones. She opened her eyes to a maze of lights which hid the water's surface; strings of lights from bulbs slung between lampposts covered with cast-iron fish, strobes from the dance floors of pub boats, warning lights on the London Eye wheel that was going up that week, and hung at 30 degrees from vertical. As she watched, the lights on top of the wheel were wiped out by shifting cloud.

The tide was out. Leigh drank the dregs of her wine and threw her glass into the river, believing for a moment, as it left her hand, that she was strong enough to make it reach the mudflats on the opposite bank, lying formless as liver in the dark. Instead, she heard it fall close to the Embankment, the sound of the plunge cut by a train crossing the Hungerford Bridge to Waterloo.

Big Ben began to strike ten, and Leigh realized that she had watched the water until she was late. She hailed a taxi and cut across the driver's reluctance to accept a passenger whose trip would take half a minute by slapping her press card on his dashboard. Before he had travelled 30 metres, she forced him to stop at a news stand. There, she bought an early edition of the following day's paper and scanned it, determined that no politician should ask her about a story with which she was not familiar. As she passed the security checks at the entrance to the Houses of Parliament, her eyes remained fixed on the newsprint. Only when she was inside and half-way up the stairs did she stop reading and start hunting.

Leigh's leather coat and shaved head clashed with the suits of the Members of Parliament who she passed, yet none of them looked at her twice to question her right to be there. They recognized her through signals so secret that she did not know she was sending them, nor the politicians that they received them. She bore the stamp of one who had grown up sharing the clubs and colleges of their England. Moving with the untroubled tread of an insider, she scanned their faces for those who were known to hold strong views on homelessness, and would be worth asking for a comment on the result of the vote. With the automatic eye of a critic, she also checked the faces in the portraits lining the high walls for those with artistic merit. Critiques of inferior brush strokes wrote themselves – distractingly and inappropriately – on the screen-saver of her mind. Switching it off, she ordered herself to concentrate on politics.

The Conservative backbencher who had invited her to the drinks stepped out of a meeting which he had been holding behind a statue, and pulled her through a door hidden in the shadow of a pillar, into the party. Leigh took a glass and inhaled the alcohol fumes for reassurance.

"Lovely of you to pop down for this little bash," said the backbencher.

"I'm sure a result like this means more than a little bash," she replied, adding, like a prompter: "You must be very disappointed."

He flashed the prompting look back at her and said nothing, forcing her to continue. "Are you determined to carry on trying to take cash away from the only ones who really need it?" she asked, charmingly.

"Pardon?" His face turned purple fast, as if blood were being poured into it, filling up from neck to forehead. His ingratiating expression was wiped out by mockery. "Haven't you bothered to check the result of the vote?" he spluttered. Shocked, Leigh did not reply. She knew that the news reporters on her paper were unhappy that she, an arts journalist, had begun to write for their pages. She had not realised that Mike would resort to lying to her. "Get your editor to send someone else next time," said the backbencher.

Leigh could see Mike standing on the other side of the room, eating his way through a tray of fish as he talked to a journalist from a rival paper. Leigh marched towards them, told the other journalist to go away, took the tray from Mike and handed it to a waiter.

"Why'd you tell me the vote had gone against?" she asked.

"You must have misheard me," he said, blandly. "It was a terrible line."

Leigh poured her glass of claret down the front of his shirt.

"Never mind," she said. "It was a terrible wine."

Mike winced as the wine began to seep into the front of his trousers.

"Why don't you fuck off back to the theatre and leave political coverage to people who can handle it?" he said.

Leigh's review of *The Bacchae* was published that weekend. On the following Monday, Sasha called her at work. She was used to dealing with actors whose judgement of their own importance vastly exceeded the media's.

"Sasha from?" she demanded.

"Don't pretend you don't know who I am." His anger distorted the line. "It's your job to know who I am."

"Oh, I know. You're a bloke who cocked up, complaining about the fact I noticed it. I'm putting you through to the arts editor."

"You're not."

"It's our policy to let the editor take all abuse. That's why he earns more than me."

"You just write the abuse?"

"Got it."

"And what gives you the right to write it?"

"Nothing but my genius. Sorry, forgot that was your field."

"Exactly. Your sort don't create anything, they destroy it."

Leigh switched to a voice developed for the benefit of teenaged theatre administrators who asked her to review pantomimes in Milton Keynes. "Listen, Mr Kohn, fascinating as this debate on the nature and role of criticism – with particular emphasis on the stage production as a vulnerable artefact in immediate pre-millennial western culture – is, I have a meeting to get to."

"And I have a question to get answered. I'll take you out to dinner to answer it. Tonight, as it's the only day this week I'm not on stage. Don't say it's not your editorial policy."

"You've a story for me?" Leigh asked, thinking of her half empty arts diary column.

"Story?"

"Gossip. Behind the scenes."

"I won't give you gossip," he replied, lowering and calming his voice. "I'll make you the subject of it."

"I think not," said Leigh.

"What time you finish work?"

"Later than you've ever finished a play."

"That's not good for you. I'm dragging you out of the office at eight," he said, and hung up. Leigh dialled her switchboard and instructed it not to put any more calls from Sasha through to her. She phoned the security desk at the base of Canary Wharf, and told the guards not to let him in.

But the ramifications of Friday night were not over. From his seat on the news desk, Mike was glaring at Leigh. She had not spoken to him since she had thrown the wine. Now, she opened her mouth slightly and flickered her tongue at him. The silver stud which pierced it rolled on the wet flesh like a trapped word. Snapping her teeth together, she turned her back and went to the water dispenser, where another reporter was drinking.

"You OK, Leigh?" asked the woman, her voice undulant with concern. "Mike told me how you got bawled out of the House last night. You know, sweetie, if you're trying to write news you need to check, check, check every fact. Never assume anything. I know it's different where you come from – "

"The only fact I need to check is the force needed to give Mike a black eye without actually breaking his jaw," said Leigh.

"You've been watching too many films, sweets. Still, that's your job, no?"

Instead of holding a cup under the stream of water, Leigh let it run over her wrists and fingers, numbing her hands until they set in elegant lines and no longer desired to make obscene gestures at Mike. Still, she did not feel cold enough. She crossed the office – whose furniture seemed angled to trap her in claws – and stood by the window, pressing her palms against the glass to feel the air outside freeze through it. On the far side of the docks, cranes rose above offices like ships' rigging. She wanted to see the buildings spread sails against the white sky, break from their foundations as the tide pulled, and swing down the Thames towards the Essex marshes, leaving nothing on the banks but the slewed mud and stunted trees which the Romans had found there.

Junior writers shifted nervously as Leigh stalked back to her seat on the arts desk. They worked in fear of her vicious perfectionism. She swept a pile of theatre publicity material from her desk and slammed down a copy of the parliamentary *Hansard*. A photograph of Roxanne, fallen from the press pack of The Bacchae, skimmed to the floor. Leigh picked it up. The dancer had been caught in the air, and the photograph cropped so the ground beneath her was gone. Leigh thought she looked like a hawk, her arms and legs powerful with expression, her dark face sharp and dedicated to freedom. Leigh propped the photograph on top of her computer and began to write.

By eight o'clock that evening Leigh's body was painful as she crouched over her shorthand, straining to decipher the interview with a film director which she was transcribing. Every time she looked up, she was aware of Mike's aggression on the far side of the open plan floor. Her telephone rang with the tone of an external call.

"I'm downstairs," announced Sasha. "Security won't let me in. They're immune to my charm. Where did you find the mutants, Chernobyl?"

"We train them specially to keep out terrorists and thespians. How d'you get my direct line?"

"You're a journalist. You know how people get people's direct lines. Are you coming down or am I coming up?"

Leigh realised that she was no longer able to see her article clearly. She needed a break, and to return to the office once Mike had left for the night. She wanted a drink to calm her down, cocaine to wake her up and sex to take her outside her head for a moment. She was not sure that sex with Sasha would be worth the effort of talking to him first. But she supposed that if she was rude enough about his play he would be capable of providing her with an argument. She loved arguments.

"Five minutes," she told him. Saving her file, she took a mirror from the drawer of her desk, shook a pile of powder out and chopped it into two lines with her paper knife. Suddenly, Mike appeared beside her.

"Go on, give me one," he said. "I'm totally shagged, I've an interview with Straw to file by three this morning." Leigh was furious that Mike was attempting reconciliation without apologising directly.

"You'll have to excuse me," she said, lightly. "I'm an addict. Addicts kill for coke, they don't share it."

"Are you now?"

"Are you not? What a shame. You can't achieve without addiction. All the hacks I admire are addicts; to words, to coke, to fame, to booze, to sex."

"Sex?"

Leigh sorted through her arts publicity and found Sasha's photograph. She presented it to Mike, who was gay.

"What do you reckon?" she asked. His pupils flared to take in the strength of the image.

"Nice."

"Who're you doing tonight?" she taunted.

"The Home Secretary," said Mike, and returned to his computer. Jealous, Leigh dipped her head like a lizard, snorting both lines of cocaine. She sat back and stared at her screen, running her finger around the edge of her mirror and licking off the sharp powder. As it froze her sinuses and dripped bitter snow down the back of her throat, her interview on the screen retreated into perspective. It had been a mess of quotations that had to be skewed and facts that had to be checked. Suddenly, it became an integrated expression of Leigh's authoritative opinion; letters etched out perfectly in black electricity on white. She laughed, imagining Mike's envy when he read it in print.

"You've got a brain the size of a planet," she told her reflection in the computer screen. "Love you madly, really do."

Leigh left her computer on so that people passing her desk might think she was still working, and slipped into a lift.

When she stepped out among the silver pillars at the base of the Canary Wharf tower, the street was deserted. She crossed it and leant on a rail by the water of the West India Docks, watching lines of trains pass on its far side, brighter and further away than they seemed when she was not high. At first the water was invisible, ironed smooth and black by the night. But as she swung her body further over the rail – looking down to where the pool seeped beneath the props that held up road and offices – the dark split for her, and she saw a faint stream of water pouring from a hole in the side of the wharf. It was solid as rope, and it fell in an ugly churn of froth deep into the dock, sending simple charcoal rings spreading so cleanly that they seemed disconnected from their source. Leigh thought that she was becoming as cold and clear as the rings; a woman made of ice and rock and black wood. High on solitude and hypnotised by water, she did not hear a car stop behind her.

"Get in, hypothermia's not painless," called Sasha, through his open window. She turned, recognised him, and climbed into his car.

"Would you like me to expand on my criticisms now?" she asked, turning down the volume of his radio. "Or shall we deal with your dubious taste in music first?"

"Tell me how to get out of this desert first." Sasha accelerated past flights of marble steps that led to squares filled with floodlit fountains, chrome sculptures, and journalists drinking hard at carefully designed tables. "Unless you want to eat here," he added.

"Nothing worth eating here."

"What's worth eating?"

Leigh named a very expensive restaurant by Tower Bridge, on the cusp of Docklands and the City. She watched the confident lines of his face for signs of panic, but none appeared. "It's on my expenses," she added. "You're a contact." Seductively, she added: "It's just round the corner from my flat."

With apparent indifference, Sasha watched the road. Metres on from the tower, the sleek development was replaced by the massive excavation well of a building site. Security lights on the sides of mobile cabins showed trenches and tunnels carved in frozen mud, from which concrete lumps sprouting bunches of iron rods emerged; the flimsy foundations of foundations.

"Why do you live in Docklands as well as working here?" asked Sasha. "Doesn't it get to you? It's a load of American coffee bars slapped on top of where ordinary people used to live. It's not a real place."

"I find reality excessively tedious," said Leigh, with an irony that she intended to appreciate alone. She thought about how the creek which her flat overlooked would drain away at low tide to its mud bottom. She loved to stand on the bridge which crossed the empty channel and look into the spaces which the water had kept private. The contrast between the new bridge – a sophisticated construct of silver springs and wires – and the old wood struts of the wharf – plunging their slimed, worn bulk down at crooked angles into the mud – always delighted her. That weekend, she had seen a traffic cone three-quarters buried, stripped of its fluorescent colours and faded to the green brown of the river, and a plastic bag shaped like the fossil of a greyhound, breaking the ripples of mud dragged out by the Thames.

Drugged into manic acuteness, Leigh became uncertain whether she had spoken her opinions on the reality of mud out loud. In case she had, she launched a tediously detailed description of a news story which she was working on, using Sasha's attentiveness to rehearse the pitch which she intended to make in a news conference later that week. She had familiarized herself with the subject to the extent that she could recite misleading press releases verbatim and, as she talked, three-quarters of her attention passed out of the car into the dark street. As they crossed the Isle of Dogs she watched a fox trot across a wide, bare roundabout. Fleetingly, she became the fox, displayed the glory of its tail above her head, felt its sharp teeth against her lip, stared from behind its famished eyes at the barred, broken windows of derelict warehouses. She did not point out the fox to Sasha.

They parked in a deserted street near the back of Leigh's flat, behind Butler's Wharf, and began to walk towards the water front, beside a patch of wasteland marked for development. As they passed bollards swathed in bubble wrap and packing tape, newly cemented into the new pavement, Leigh was saying: "So on the one hand the private sec's telling me it'd been placed in the library weeks ago but the response in *Hansard* clearly showed no such thing was intended now why would the PS lie? Well I don't think he did much more likely the minister meant to say it and jibbed in the Commons and the little jerk thought he'd done what he'd said and didn't think to check the records well that's one more tosser for the chop isn't it?"

Sasha touched her shoulder, stopping her with an actor's focused, economical gesture. He looked across the twilit patch of wasteland with a precise gesture of his head, so that she saw what he saw. It was an iron anchor forged on an inhuman scale, rusting among piles of broken concrete from demolished buildings. When she had passed the site before, Leigh had admired the crane or wave or god which had chosen to dump the anchor there.

"Well there's your answer," she told him. "That's why I live in Docklands. It's easier to see the surreal here."

"It's not surreal at all, no more than the old East End's more real than the offices they've built on top of it. Everything's equally real – "

"No it's not," Leigh interrupted, pleased when she saw he responded to argument with increased attention, not defensiveness. "I'm going to tell you about mud."

CHERRY SMYTH
Playing Celine

It was in the summer of 1958, when I had the chance to sojourn in Paris at the Hotel de Serifos at the south-west corner of Rue Saint Jacques, that something curious happened. It was one of those small hotels, where people would only stay a night or two and seldom unpack. It was run by a Greek family, which I welcomed, having often found Parisians aloof and self-regarding. The hotel is occupied by an accountancy firm now and all that remains are the elegant, diamond-shaped deco tiles around the front entrance and the wrought-iron balconies.

I was touring with a theatre company from Dublin, doing a week in the intimate Theatre des Beaux Illusions after a successful but subdued run in Ireland. The response to the revival of a little-known, bilingual play called *Trois Coins* by Maud Gonne was destined to be select and I was already beginning to find the demands of the leading role draining, despite my enthusiasm for the part. It was not easy to play a woman who had killed her young lover, the wife of her son. Within the play, the logic of the words and the shape of the scenes protected me and charged me, but it was afterwards that I feared the character began to unhinge from the role and roam in parts of me, unrehearsed.

My hotel room was one of those French rooms with beautifully proportioned tall, slender windows, a bed with starched linen sheets and a bolster that was as hard as bone. Although relatively bare, it brought me a sense of immediate peace. It possessed the faded grandeur at which the French so excel and the late afternoon sun cast extended shadows on the walls and floor. There was a fine reproduction of a Corot print on the wall, a plain wardrobe and a simple gilded mirror above a walnut dresser. In another corner stood a writing desk covered in brown leather, dotted in black and blue ink and peeling up at the edges. The adjoining bathroom showed years of use and as much cleaning, so that the enamel from the tiles, sink and bath was worn thin, rendering the surfaces porous and matt, like the icing on a wedding cake.

I washed my hands, removed my make-up, splashed my face and without looking at the critic in the mirror, returned to the bedroom and lay on the bed.

My thoughts went to Celine, the character I was playing. I idly wondered what she would have been doing in such a hotel, alone. Would she be waiting for a lover, a spy, a meeting with a rival? She would smoke. I longed to. She would go to 'Le Monocle' dressed as a man. I doubted if the club still existed, but the idea that women like Maud Gonne and Celine de Bacourt had lived in Paris seemed to be captured in the flavour of the room, as though all the excitement and unknown desires pressed themselves against the windows and imbued the very air. Old cities have that quality about them, a whisper of ether that belongs to other people in other times, but only cities one doesn't inhabit long. Dublin's ghosts are so present they are no longer greeted with surprise.

I must admit, at that time, I found myself off-stage making gestures which belonged to Celine. Only a wave of my hand at first, to emphasise a point, but then I would catch myself walking her walk, arguing flirtatiously with dinner guests for the rum pleasure of it, and then laughing a laugh not unlike Celine's. I remember one night my husband got up from the table and pushed his dining chair smoothly up to the edge in a tacit reminder of good manners. I was giddy and held my breath until he had left the room and then snorted, "I thought he was going to bow!" I'd been staring at Amelia Reidy all evening and I leant in to kiss her on the lips. I was clearly not myself, not that I didn't enjoy her mouth. She was a little too shocked to respond. Her husband did though. He laughed and clapped and winked and puffed on his cigar until Amelia snatched it from him and drew extravagantly on it. I had no idea what would happen next. I can only say that it was similar to the sense one can get after too much Moroccan coffee, when your actions and words seem to happen through someone else's body, which is no longer in perfect synchrony with your own. It is only a fraction out, but through that minuscule and imperceptible opening, a whole new personality takes shape and is born.

And nothing really did happen. Amelia and Victor, and Ginny and Seamus all went home and I cleaned up the dishes and climbed into bed with my make-up on. No one believed that I had been completely sober.

Back in the hotel, I must have fallen into one of those unbidden, dreamless afternoon naps, that can leave you completely refreshed, but I woke feeling weary and a little disorientated. I got up quickly to unpack.

I always open every cupboard, wardrobe and dresser in any room in which I sleep. I am never sure if I am searching for something I have lost or looking for a future hiding place, but the action allows the comfort of a good night's sleep. Perhaps it's a way of fully occupying the room even if I do not fill the space available. That's what I adore about acting – being everywhere in a large, crowded room at once.

I hung my dresses and suits in the wardrobe and began to fill the dresser with smaller items – stockings, underwear and gloves. The top two drawers were empty and released a smell of cedarwood. In the middle drawer on the left was a bunch of seven assorted keys attached to a wooden Pinocchio keyring. I set the keys on top of the dresser and filled the drawer with cardigans and an evening shawl. I opened the drawer on the right to reveal a black and gold fountain pen. I set it beside the keys.

Although I had fully unpacked, I tried without success to open the bottom double drawer. I automatically tried the keys on the keyring. One fitted and turned the lock. There lay a scattering of papers – a shopping list, several bus tickets, theatre programmes dated from the thirties and a folded letter. The moment I touched the letter, I experienced a strange relief, as though I'd made contact with a lost loved one at a railway station. I felt no sense of impropriety as I sat down at the desk and began to read. The first page was missing, so I had no idea of the time or place from which it was sent. It was written in French, in black ink, and read as follows:

... about you that made me feel part of the world in a way no one has ever done before. I don't mean simply happy and connected, I mean alive in every cell and atom of my body, as one who has been a ghost becomes embodied and can breathe once more. I know you'll scoff for you've never lived what could be called a shadow life; you've always pounced on experience, laughed off troubles with an indomitable laugh that is recognized and imitated throughout Paris.

At first my lust invigorated me, it's true. Everything seemed to coalesce that year – my career, my new apartment, the life of my heart. I accelerated and you loved my energy, relied on it, shone through it. You said I brought you back to the world. I was younger than you, more naive and desperate to know another reality. All that happened to you happened to me. We were indivisible. Those who came before tried to warn me to step back but they couldn't love you like I did. I would succeed where others had failed. When I looked in the mirror, I saw your face, Celine, that broad smile, those frank eyes and I loved what I saw, like love grafted on to me. I wore you well. I loved that you existed in the universe even when we weren't together. That knowledge drove my days.

You were my nights! I yearned for darkness, welcomed the first star over Sacré Coeur like my first spotlight. I played for the indigo sky. You showed me Venus, that dense, hurtling planet that outshines all others, its edges trembling like a drop of mercury about to spill and run. How could every night with you be the same and yet entirely different?

Everyone began to want more of you. I'd shown them what you could do, how glorious you were. The great Celine Ernoult eclipsed me. Miss Julie! Miss Julie! they called after I missed my first cue. They battered on my door. I wept among the fan letters addressed to you in a dressing room scented with your bouquets.

I let you down and, from that moment, ceased to abandon myself.

I've heard that a young woman from Nantes has taken you on, but that her laugh is shrill and her eyes dead. She has not got what it takes. But I cannot stay in a city where your name is whispered with mine. I'm leaving for South America tonight, to a place where I can understand my own face. I know you shall never read this and I wish there was a way I could tell you how I have loved you. And do still.

Your,
Julie.

At first I thought it was a joke. I looked over my shoulder in a moment of guilty panic and some terror. The placid room gave up nothing. My thin red scarf still lay across the bed. I turned the letter over to search for signs of forgery. I leafed through all the other pieces of paper in the drawer and there, as though it had been waiting to be discovered in a previously established sequence, was an old programme for *Trois Coins*, dated April,1938. My fingers trembled as I opened it and found her name – Julie Bachelier as Celine de Bacourt.

I happened to glance up at the window. I had neither closed the shutters nor pulled the drapes and could see my reflection clearly in the glass. As I stared, my body stiffened. My face bore a look I had never seen before. It registered for a long moment, then vanished and my features settled into familiarity. I could see the resemblance to my grandmother, who had been dead for over twenty-five years. My name for her, 'Nainee', turned over in my head.

The lights in the street beyond came back into focus. I took a deep breath as though I had not inhaled for some minutes. My hands were icy.

Somehow I knew that the look I hadn't recognised was the face of Celine de Bacourt, or rather Julie Bachelier as Celine, which had flitted across my eyes. In that moment of recognition, both Julie Bachelier and I had perished. It had been Celine in the glass, Celine who existed in the room. By banishing her image, I had won something for which I did not even know I had been in battle.

When I looked at my watch, I discovered that it was nearly eight o'clock. I had almost missed my opening night! Such a thing had never happened before. I must have detached myself from being the actor, from all the roles I had ever played, from time itself and wandered into a zone where nothing had any claim on me. And yet the core of me, which I can only call my soul, was burning, vital with assertion, as though it had been fully seen and wholly loved.

I stood up a little shakily and closed the shutters. My pale hand against the frame made me think of Julie Bachelier's hand once making the same movement. I avoided looking at the bed.

I wondered why no-one had called from the theatre. I checked the phone and found that it was disconnected. I put on my cape to go downstairs to complain and to make a call to the stage manager. As I moved towards the door, I experienced a lightness and clarity that were almost blissful. Mental fatigue and numbness had fallen away. That night I knew I would bring something intangible yet powerful to the part of Celine, for I had matched her blithe capacity for destruction with my own.

Trieste, December 1999

For Jacqueline Duckworth

ANNE F. STAIRS
Comfort Food

Peter removed a white envelope from his jacket pocket. Diana nudged him. "Wait 'til she's cleared the plates." Diana watched the young waitress remove Sam's plate. *He's not eaten much.* The remains of a rib-eye steak, chips, peas and a salad garnish were pushed to the rim of the oval plate, leaving a space in the centre. She couldn't see if Toby had eaten all his meal, his plate was underneath Sam's, in the waitress' hand. Peter's plate was empty. He'd had prawn cocktail to start, well-done rump steak for main. He'd decided against dessert, because everyone else had, but Diana knew he would have liked Death by Chocolate. The waitress removed Diana's plate, empty apart from the bones of her salmon steak.

"Happy Birthday, son." Peter handed Sam an envelope. He wanted to give him a hug, but he knew Sam would be embarrassed, as the restaurant was full and his mate Toby sat next to him.

"I know it's just money, but we weren't sure what you'd want." Diana kissed her son on the cheek. "I can't believe you're twenty, it only seems five minutes since…"

"Mum," Sam knew she was about to divulge some awful story about potty training or first steps. "No. Money's fine." He winked at Toby, "Just great, honest, thanks."

In the car park they did hug, all very macho and backslapping. "Thanks for coming down and the money, Dad, I'll put it to good use, don't worry." Peter didn't see the quick exchange between mates. Toby was standing behind him.

"I'm sure you will, darling," Diana said as Sam kissed her on the cheek. "Shame you'd already made arrangements for to-night, I always think dinner is better than lunch for a celebration."

"Lunch was fine Mum and any way it's not the real big one is it? We can have a real posh nosh for my twenty-first, yeah."

They said their good-byes.

"See you at Christmas," they all called as Peter edged the car into the traffic flow.

Diana snoozed the three-hour journey home. Peter smiled at his dozing wife. *Wine at lunchtime always sends her to sleep.*

Sam headed straight to the bank and paid the cheque in at the cash point.

"Shame it wasn't cash," Toby said.

"Cake looks good. Chocolate?"

"Chocolate mocha. Don't even think about it," Diana tapped Peter's hand as it hovered above the frosted top. "And what's in here?" He lifted the lid of the slow cooker, inhaling the aroma deeply.

"Ah, Peter please don't do that, it affects the temperature."

"Sorry." He nuzzled her neck. "What is it?"

"Brisket and root veggies."

"What time's the train due? I know you said, but I can't remember."

"Half-five and you're picking him up so I can get dinner organized."

"Traffic might be bad, better leave at five."

"You'll be too early."

She'd been right. He was too early. The train wasn't due for another twenty minutes. He wanted to tell Sam about the tickets for Boxing Day. Peter walked up and down the platform, squinting into the distance. He checked the arrivals board. It was on time. He checked his quartz watch. He tapped the dial, no point in listening to make sure it was working. Pigeons fluttered in the station's Victorian steel rafters. Peter looked up at the blistered paint. *The sooner they complete the refurbishment the better*, he thought. He missed the engine creeping round the bend. The hiss of air brakes alerted him. Automatic doors swished open spilling out their contents. He was lost in the surge. Standing on tiptoe, he scanned the disgorged passengers. Within moments he was alone on the platform. He ran to the gate. Had he missed him? Was he standing waiting in the foyer? Peter looked back at the stationary train. Sam was strolling along the platform, a bag in each hand, headphones round his neck, grinning.

"Gosh, thought I'd missed you," said Peter, taking one of the bags.

"Sorry, Dad. Had to go for a whiz." Sam sniffed deeply.

As they negotiated the ring road, Peter asked his son about University, his course and his health. Sam replied to each enquiry, "OK." Peter couldn't contain himself any longer, he had to tell Sam.

"I promised your mother I wouldn't say anything till we got

home, but what the heck. I've got tickets for the match on Boxing Day."

Sam gazed at his reflection in the window screen. "What?"

"I've got tickets for the Canaries. You do still support them?"

"Suppose. Yeah."

"One of my new clients gave me tickets for the Director's box. So we'll watch them in style." Peter flicked the indicator lever, they blinked into Thunder Lane. "It's great isn't it."

"Oh, yeah." Sam was out of the car, before Peter had turned off the engine.

"Not eaten much love." Diana stroked his head as she cleared the table. "Not feeling too good? You've been sniffing quite a bit."

"I'm fine. Don't fuss." Sam smiled widely. "Just tired that's all, long journey and all." Diana looked him in they eyes, *they're bright enough I suppose.* "Are you sure?"

"Nothing that an early night won't cure." Diana and Peter laughed. It was always their answer when he tried to feign a sicky from school.

"Do you think he's all right?"

"Of course he is, don't fuss too much love."

"It's just that he spends all his time in his room. Says he's got projects to finish or he's on the phone to Toby. He hardly eats anything." Diana rearranged the cards on the mantlepiece. "And he seems so," she picked up Sam's sixth form photo. "Oh, I don't know. He just doesn't seem like his old self."

Peter held out his hand, "Come here." Diana placed here hand in his, "Don't worry, I remember when I used to come home from University, I used to feel as if I didn't belong."

"Peter this is his home."

"His life's in Oxford. He has a flat and mates there. He'll probably end up working there or London." He pulled her down onto the sofa.

"Just going to the pub." Sam's head appeared round the door. "Meeting up with a few of the lads from school. Don't wait up." He slammed the front door.

"See he's all right, remember how we used to tell him don't slam the door. He'll probably wake us at midnight when he comes in."

Peter and Diana settled into a night of Quality Street and television.

"Phone, for you Sam." He took the cordless phone from his mother and left the room.

"It's a girl."

"What?" Peter averted his eyes from the early evening news.

"On the phone for Sam. A girl. Very well spoken."

"Diana, don't give him the third degree."

"As if I would, but I'm only showing an interest."

"Any chance of a lift to the station, Dad?" Sam swung his leather jacket over his shoulder.

Diana noticed he'd gelled his hair and changed his sweatshirt and jeans for black chinos and shirt.

"Going out?"

"Yeah, need to catch the seven o'clock to Cambridge. There's a party. Annabel, just phoned."

"Annabel?"

"Toby's sister."

"You could take the car, couldn't he, Peter? We don't need it do we?"

"Better not. Probably staying over. You'll need it for the supermarket tomorrow."

"I'll take you then." Diana began to get up from the sofa.

Sam shot a glance at Peter.

"No love, I'll go. You'll miss Emmerdale."

"Thanks Dad," he said as they pulled out of the drive, Diana waving on the doorstep.

"It's OK. She's only interested."

"I know."

"I don't think there'll be a white Christmas somehow." Peter flicked on the wipers.

"Doesn't look like it," Sam glanced at his watch and sniffed.

As Sam got out of the car Peter fumbled with his wallet. "You could probably use this." He handed him twenty pounds.

"Great, thanks."

"Don't be too late back tomorrow, Christmas Eve and all. Give me a ring, I'll pick you up."

Peter watched him disappear through the misted glass doors.

They'd only been gone half an hour. Diana had vacuumed up the fallen pine needles, plumped up the cushions, made potato salad and coleslaw to go with the cold turkey and ham. She decided to iron the shirts, then watch the video Sam had given her yesterday, *Titanic*. Peter had taken her to see it at the cinema for her birthday. She'd wanted to go again, he'd refused. She took the shirts upstairs. Hanging up Peter's she noticed the slippers she'd given him in the wardrobe. Sam's shirts were neatly folded. He was going back to finish his projects. The holdall was all ready on the floor by his bed, *may as well put them in*, she thought. Placing the shirts on the bed, she lifted the bag, something fell out of the bottom compartment where Sam put his shoes and trainers.

She bent down to pick up a tin. The lid was dented and the snow scene was scratched. She turned it over and over in her hands. She prised off the lid and slowly sank on to the bed. She removed the items one by one onto the green and yellow duvet. She could hardly see them. A rectangular Stanley blade, a handbag mirror, two pieces of tinfoil folded into tiny squares, a drinking straw, like the ones for McDonalds' milkshakes and a small plastic bag with a self-seal top, half-filled with white powder.

From downstairs came the opening bars of the Bond soundtrack. She'd always watched it on her own, while Sam and Peter went to the Boxing Day game, every year. She looked down at the items on the bed, how long had he had them? She didn't notice the splashes on the freshly ironed shirts. She picked up Roland Rat, she always put it on his bed. Sam had begged and wished for it one Christmas. She hugged it to her and rocked back and forth.

"No. No. No," she said to Oasis above the bed, but they didn't answer.

She refilled the tin. She would have to hurry. The Bond film was over she could hear the closing music. They'd be back soon. She put the tin in his bag and went to the bathroom. Trembling as she washed her face in cold water. She didn't look in the mirror. She went back into Sam's room and put the tin in her apron pocket. Tactful confrontation the Drugs Officer had said at the school drugs awareness talk. That's what she'd do. No accusations or recriminations.

She heard the car pull into the drive as she came downstairs. She slipped into the kitchen, before they opened the door.

"We won," called Peter as he put his sheepskin coat in the hall cupboard.

"Need a whiz," Sam charged upstairs two steps at a time.

"Too many lagers," Peter laughed.

"Did you enjoy the Bond film?"

"No."

In his room Sam emptied out the holdall, he looked in his other bag. Shit. Then under the bed. He striped off the duvet. Shit. Roland Rat fell to the floor.

Diana and Peter stood at Sam's bedroom door. The room was reminiscent of his early teens, clothes, books, trainers and a toy, strewn across the floor. His mother's face was red and blotchy, his father's grey.

"Is this what you're looking for?" Peter held out the tin.

Peter held Diana's hand as they mounted the clinic steps. It was in an old country house. They'd chosen it on the advice of Dr Walton, their family doctor. On New Year's Eve they'd dropped Sam off. They weren't allowed to stay. For two weeks they'd telephoned daily to see how Sam was, to be told, *he's making satisfactory progress in detox.* Sam made contact after three weeks. He invited them to visit.

In the oak-panelled hall Diana sat on a cracked leather chesterfield and touched-up her chocolate pink lipstick. Peter slowly strolled the length of the hall, glancing at the pictures on the wall. He didn't notice they were painted by past residents. He was trying to push the cashed-in endowment policy to the back of his mind. It had been meant for Sam's education, but he won the scholarship. So Peter had earmarked the fund for an improved retirement. He joined Diana on the edge of the sofa.

A man in his middle thirties, dressed in jeans and a blue jumper appeared from a room opposite where they were sitting.

"Sorry to keep you waiting, Bill Davenport." He held out his hand. Peter appreciated the firm handshake.

"Peter." Bill took Diana's hand and squeezed it gently between both his, "Diana. You are both most welcome to Maybury Manor. We like to keep everything informal, come in."

The room was large, three long windows reached to the floor. "Have a seat." Bill gestured to a circle of armchairs. "I'm Sam's counsellor. I thought I'd update you on his progress before you see him. Also, fill you in on a few things regarding his discharge."

"He's coming home?" Diana clutched her handbag tightly.

"Oh, not for a few months yet, but we find it's better to let parents know what the options are."

Bill spoke to them for twenty minutes. "Any questions?" he asked. Diana and Peter shook their heads. "You'll probably find when you get home you think of something. You can always telephone. I'll take you to Sam. He'll be in the conservatory, having tea."

They followed Bill through the corridors to the rear of the house. At the door of the conservatory he stopped. They could see Sam sitting at a wicker table talking to a girl, with long chestnut hair. She had rings on each finger of her right hand.

"Remember," said Bill. "It's all about trust."

They negotiated their way round tables and chairs, occupied by residents and visitors, many still wearing their coats. *Ready*

COMFORT FOOD

for a quick get away, thought Peter. As they neared the table Sam glanced up, then said something to the girl. She got up and left.

"Hi." Sam pushed his chair back. It screeched on the tiled floor. Diana shuddered.

"Hello Sam. How are you?" Peter asked.

"Would you like some tea? The cakes aren't too bad either. Not as good as yours though, Mum." Without waiting for a response he headed to a serving hatch on the far side of the room.

"He won't be here 'til five."

"I know, but I want to get things done and I've the hairdresser at eleven. There was no need for you to get up."

"I was awake," he lied. He wanted to say; *your pot walloping woke me forty minutes ago and I've given up trying to get back to sleep.* He watched his wife put a baking tin in the oven. "Chocolate mocha cake by any chance?"

"Of course, it's his favourite."

"You could have made it yesterday."

"It tastes best on the day it's baked. Any way there wasn't time with the cleaning." Diana wiped the butcher's block and began chopping carrots, parsnips, onions and swede. With each cut the skin at the top of her arm wobbled. He wondered how long it had been like that. "As you're here can you get down the slow cooker." Peter shuffled across the tiled floor, tightening the cord on his robe. The chair screeched as he pulled it into position.

"Lift it, you know I can't stand that noise."

"Sorry. Forgot." Peter heaved himself up; he could feel his pyjama bottoms beginning to slip. "Diana, take this will you."

"What are you like?" Diana took the slow cooker, thumping it onto the worktop. Peter wriggled up his pyjamas, climbed down and sat on the chair. There was a time when she would have laughed and pulled them off. Each impact of blade on board rang through his body. He looked at his shabby slippers, the left, Dennis the Menace and the right Gnasher. Sam had bought them as a joke two Christmases ago. When Sam was about six or seven, Peter had dubbed him Dennis. Not that Sam was very naughty. He just liked boyish things, mud pies, catapults and super-soaking any cat that dared to venture into the back garden. Sam's mischief was aided and abetted by Sooty, his black mongrel. Peter placed his feet side by side, a boy and his dog. Diana had given him thermal lined tartan slippers this Christmas, they were still in the box in the bottom of the wardrobe.

"You may as well get dressed now." Diana put the brisket of beef, another favourite of Sam's into the slow cooker and surrounded it with the chopped vegetables. Peter lifted the pine chair and placed it carefully next to the matching table. Diana stood at the sink. Pink rubber gloved hands moved rapidly through the suds. Her green and orange Dash tracksuit hung in folds round her hips. How she'd agonized in the shop when they bought it. "Does it make me look fat? Am I too old for this?" He'd reassured her, "You look fine and for goodness sake you're only forty-five." She'd be forty-seven in a month. He placed his arms round her waist, her hands stilled. They looked out onto the garden. The sun was creeping over next-door's leylandii hedge. The first rays caught the greenhouse gable, fractured, sending beams across the lawn.

"I'll be able to given the lawn its first cut soon," he said, nuzzling into her neck. "It'll be OK."

"Will it?"

"Would you like a cuppa before I have my shower?"

"No, you go on," Diana stirred up the suds.

In the hall he paused to pick up the newspaper. Diana turned on the radio.

"I suppose they know what they are doing, letting him come home on his own."

"I would hope so it is their job after all. They deal with it all the time." Peter placed his hand on her knee as they waited for a green light. "Don't you remember the counsellor said, he has to feel he's trusted."

"I know what they said, but..." the lights changed. Peter pulled on to Riverside.

As they parked in front of the station Peter said, "We're in plenty of time."

She looked at her gold watch with the champagne face, "You gave me this when Sam was born."

"I remember."

"We're too early."

"I'll buy you a coffee in the new buffet."

"The tables and chairs might be new and they've painted the walls, but the coffee's the same." Diana took a peppermint from her bag and gazed at the posters offering Family Fun Days, Cheap Day Returns to London. "We always said we'd go on that." She pointed to a poster, the Bittern Line to the North Norfolk Coast.

"We did didn't we," Peter drained his paper cup. "It's about due now."

They walked hand in hand to the platform.

LORNA THORPE

Extract from **The Ashram**

ONE

The train journey from Bangalore to Dharwad takes fourteen hours. Alice Chase tries to sleep but she is too nervous, too excited about reaching her destination; after all, she's been waiting almost a year – no, almost a lifetime – for this. After a noisy meal, the family sharing her carriage wished her a good night and retired to their sleeping berths. Now she sits alone by the window, looking out through the smoked glass at great expanses of dark land, broken now and then by the silhouette of a tree or the dim lights of a small town. She is heading for an ashram in the heart of Karnataka, for a meeting with Swamiji, for what he calls a cleansing of the doors of perception, that she might at last clear away the static she's accumulated over the years and get in touch with her true self.

She has reached the stage in life when the only option is to go to India.

NEW YEAR'S EVE, 1999

She wakes at five-thirty, an ungodly hour, surely meant not for waking but for returning home barefoot, shoes swinging from carmine-tipped fingers, sweet, aimless thoughts accompanied by the lingering music of parties or the taste of stolen kisses. And yet, while the rest of the world slumbers in downy comfort, she must wake. She shakes her head to free her mind of the crumbs of the night, bristling with a virtuosity that will, she hopes, overcome her inclination to slip back into the crusty embrace of sleep, if only her body – or her mind or heart, whatever it is, wherever is located the dark impulse to fight every step of her unsteady progress towards enlightenment – if only that part of her which clings like a blood clot to the past would give up its feeble but irresistible protest and link arms in the struggle to ascend to where the air is thin and clear. Immovable mass. Her limbs dead-weight heavy. Even yawning overtaxes her facial muscles and yet the tiredness she feels is so immense, so engulfing she is unable to stop yawning, her mouth stretching wider and wider until she imagines she might swallow herself whole. She wakes to a roar of silence and the smell of India. She wakes to the inevitability of finding her skin swollen with a fresh rash of ugly bites because the mosquito net, like every net before it, is riddled with holes big enough for a flight of bees to swim through and because, if she's to meditate before the sun comes up at six, if she's to get herself to the hall in time for yoga practice, she has to leave the relative safety of her shroud while the wretched bugs are still active. Every muscle in her back aches from sleeping on a mattress that does nothing to cushion the hardness of the wooden slats beneath it. Her ear throbs from pressing against a solid pillow all night. Her mouth tastes of asafoetida. Well – let her body complain. The point is that she is endures these hardships, no welcomes them. She gets up at five-thirty, meditates, plunges into a cold shower before taking her thin blanket to the yoga hall for six-thirty. She does these things! She, Alice Chase, embraces the austerity of the ashram because that's the whole point, to live simply, to sharpen herself until there is nothing left but what is pure, essential.

And so she must move. She leans over the edge of the bed, long hair falling like a veil around her head, the net settling in soft folds around her shoulders as she scrabbles in the pitch black for her torch. She closes her fingers around it gladly. There is some solace in its cool, metallic body but she hesitates before switching it on, her heart fluttering with the panic of a captured bird at the prospect of what may yet lie hidden under the cover of night. Better not to know, sometimes, better to lie in peace in your bed, oblivious to the bugs and insects as they make silvery trails across the floor and walls, blind to the many-legged creature that surely hovers just inches above your face, waiting to drop into your open mouth. Better to not comprehend what propels the shadows that slide beneath the door at dawn. And the ashram is supposed to be a sanctuary, she thinks. Oh but it is. My god, she has only to cast her mind back to the hotel in Bombay – slime green walls and blood-specked pillows – she has only to remember the hustle of the streets, people stepping over the woman and child who lay sprawled across a filthy pavement (who could have been dead for all anyone cared), she has only to remind herself of these scenes to be grateful but the room is too dark and, yes it's ridiculous to be afraid of the dark when you're forty-two but Swamiji is dead – dead, can you believe it? – and there is always the possibility that he will appear to her in these twilight hours.

And whilst his appearance is something she longs for, whilst she wants nothing more than to see him – white beard shining in the dark, eyes as bright as they appear in his photographs, lips mouthing words so sweet they would act as a balm on the yearning that tears at her heart – whilst this divine materialisation would fulfil her most ardent dream, at the same time her body stiffens at the prospect of coming face to face with his shimmering image. Why? Because she will recoil from his ghostly likeness? Or because she is convinced that, rather than her seeing right through him, he will see right through her? Oh, but why worry. It won't happen because she tries too hard, that's always been the way. If only he were here, alive. After all, she has waited almost a year for this and no matter what they try to tell her, that his presence will be with her still, it's not the same as meeting him – an adept, a truly enlightened being! – face to face. Why couldn't he have waited, when she gave up everything to be here?

With the torch blazing the dark mystery of the room retreats to its farthest corners, shadows shrink away from its fierce beam. Alice first guides the circle of light across the concrete floor, pausing briefly as her stomach leaps at a suspicious shape at the foot of the bed which, on closer inspection, turns out to be a pair of blood-stained knickers. (And that's another thing, the temple is only opened one day a week and she will not be allowed to enter this divine domain because she is having *masik dharma*; she is menstruating.) She slides the beam over the walls and ceiling. As usual they are speckled with black-shelled creatures which may be crawling or simply shimmering in the unsteady light (but surely they must be moving, surely that sound is the scritch-scratch of their crunchy bodies against the rough plaster) and a Pollock-like spattering of blood. Ought she to be killing the mosquitoes given Swamiji's stand on non-violence? Probably not but if it's a choice about who dies, rather them than her. It was only once she got to India, only once the place leapt out from behind its ethereal name and her curious sepia-tinted image of it, only once the sub-continent burst to life in a blaze of colour, spices, fumes and horns that she began to question the wisdom of relying solely on homeopathic remedies to protect her western system against malaria and dysentery. What had she been thinking? That some half-hearted belief in a form of medicine no-one could actually prove worked would keep her safe from the entire gamut of strange bacteria and disease that could invade her body? That her body would find a means of filtering out the unwanted, a method that her mind, bombarded with an overload of sensual detail every day, had yet to uncover?

She peels the sheet from her legs. Is Patrick up yet; is Patrick also meditating? No doubt he is in a deep trance by now, his spirit caressed by Swamiji's long fingers; no doubt he meditates for at least three hours every day, without fail. No doubt he is no more than a whisker away from enlightenment. She hadn't been expecting another westerner. In the sixties and seventies there would have been swarms of visitors, of course, in those days you had to book your place well in advance but few had kept the faith. Over the years the numbers visiting the ashram dwindled. Swamiji was not fashionable; he did not encourage liberated sexual practices; he did not market himself to a western audience; he did not have a computer or collect cars. On the contrary, his books were published only in India; a motley collection of local men took care of his affairs. Alice only discovered him through Michael who had taught her to meditate, who had stayed here for months at a time because of his special bond with Swamiji. Michael had painted a pretty accurate picture of the ashram so that, when she arrived at here three days after Christmas, she had not been surprised to find herself the only visitor. At that time, standing lost and confused in her bare little room, wondering what she should wear to prayers, she would certainly have appreciated finding another foreigner. Yes, it would have been good then to have someone to teach her the ropes but once she'd begun to feel her way through the long, shapeless days she became used to her solitary status, became fond of it, even. And then, yesterday morning, then there was Patrick, stirring up a billow of dust as he dumped his battered rucksack in front of the office, striding right on in and engaging, without a moment's hesitation, in thick conversation with Mr Basham when all her efforts to talk to the ashram manager had been so awkward, the poor man's discomfort so plainly manifest in the continual adjustment of the small, wire-rimmed glasses that perch half way down his beak-like nose, that she had begun to feel, and then behave, as if she were standing in front of him naked, until eventually her own discomfort became so acute she was forced to break off each discussion abruptly. Patrick, on the other hand, was in the office a good half an hour. Alice happened to notice him as she passed the building on her way to visit Swamiji's shrine and then again, thirty minutes later, on her return. He raised an arm in greeting but she looked away and then he ran after her – a slap of sandals against soles – as she approached the concrete block that houses the guest rooms, stopping her to introduce himself and explain – oh, very tactfully, naturally – that she should go to the dining hall at six o'clock in the evenings, not six-thirty, OK? because she had been holding everyone up. She nodded and thanked him. His skin was the dirty tan of someone who has been in the sun for many months, his hair bleached blond. He looks the part, she thought.

"Guess we'll catch one another later," he said. She replied that she thought so, and turned to make her way to her room, resisting the temptation to look back at the man whose presence she felt still standing in the dust, watching her until she climbed the steps and closed the door behind her.

She steps onto the floor. Her feet recoil at the first contact with the ground, toes curling and arches lifting like the back of a cat. Dust everywhere. No amount of cleaning will shift it. Her sandals, nut-brown when she arrived, have taken on an orange hue, the dust deeply ingrained in every pore of her shoes. When she stayed in the Hotel Metropole in Mysore – the lap of luxury, with a claw-footed bath and her own rattan sofa on the verandah where septuagenarian 'boys' bought her drinks of iced lemonade – she would hesitate to touch her freshly laundered and rigidly ironed clothes, knowing that the briefest contact with supposedly pristine hands would leave a trace of sandy powder over their spotless surfaces. Here, even the sheet on her bed is dusty and so she wears knickers at night because she doesn't want the gritty ash... she shivers the thought away but not before she sees dank caves with glistening walls, bald scars on the ground where fires once burned. She switches on the light and the room takes on the sickly glare characteristic of all lights turned on in the hours between sleeping and waking, the dim hope of lights that burn all night in the rooms of the ill and dying. That's enough of that, she thinks, as she gathers together the paraphernalia for meditation – the candle, the incense, the crystal – after all, she's left all of that behind her.

Om mani padme hum, om mani... back home tonight their minds will be on nothing but parties. They will spread their black dresses and best underwear across their beds; they will run their hands through new stockings; they will chill champagne and ice vodka for pre-party drinks. They will line up the coke, warding off the moment for reflection and the making of resolutions. No doubt about it, this will be a New Year to remember but she should have come earlier, she thinks. She should have come five years ago, when she first became sick of her life. She should have come before Swamiji died.

How can it be that, once again, she's left with nothing but herself?

Patrick is already sitting at the long table when Alice reaches the steps leading down to the dining room. He is sitting in her chair!

Well, of course, he won't know that's the chair she's chosen for every meal but even so she finds it hard to return a smile that seems to say welcome as though she were the new arrival and he the one who had already established himself. She descends the stairs slowly, her heart sinking more with every step. She has never found this a comfortable room. Set halfway below ground level, the only light coming from frosted glass windows at the upper reaches of the walls, it is always dingy but she hates the glare of overhead lights, especially during the day and she is pleased to see that Patrick has not switched them on. She nods in acknowledgement as she passes the table and makes for the small washbasin at the far end of the room where she turns on the stiff tap and lets the cold water run over her hands. This is another area of the dining room she dislikes. It is even darker at this end of the room, so dark she has to squint to see into the deep, square basin and even then she can't see clearly enough to make out the dark shapes offset against the white enamel. Every time she leans across the basin to wash her hands she holds her breath against whatever it is that might make some sudden movement and scuttle along the surface towards her. Until this morning she never noticed how the sound of the water splashing into the basin echoes throughout the dining room but now she is acutely aware of everything: the musty smell of the room, the rise and fall of her own breath, Patrick's presence behind her.

"Don't you have, you know, washing facilities in your room?" Patrick calls out.

"Yes. Why?"

"The hand washing. Seems kind of excessive."

Alice feels the flush rise from her neck to her forehead. Why should she justify herself to the little jerk? But she has no choice. She'll have to explain because what's the alternative? To appear as some finicky western woman obsessed with cleanliness; the kind who can't handle a bit of dirt; the kind who should never have come to India? She turns off the tap, shakes the water from her hands and pats them against her trousers. "Rusi, the man who serves us food, made a point of showing the wash-basin to me the first day. I assumed it was some kind of ritual."

"Oh, OK. I don't think it is though."

He leans back in his chair, raising the front legs and stretching his arm across the adjacent chair back. He's only been here five minutes and he looks like he owns the place, she thinks, checking herself with a minute shake of her head. How come she's still reacting with the kind of comment her mother would make?

"Maybe not but I do it, all the same."

"Even when they're not watching? I'm impressed."

"Why, do you think it's only worth doing things for show?"

She pulls out a chair opposite him and sits down. She is facing the wall, him and the wall, and even in a room with no view, even in a room such as this with nothing to look out on except bare floor and ceiling, she never likes to face the wall.

"Hey, I didn't mean anything by it." He looks at his watch. "I thought Basham said breakfast at eight o'clock. It's nearly ten past."

Alice sits a little taller in her seat. So, he is hung up on time. She swings her hair over her shoulders. "Well, it tends to arrive at roughly eight o'clock but I've waited twenty minutes before."

Patrick sets his chair square on the ground, stretches his arms across the table and begins drumming with his fingers. Is there no end to his irritating habits? "Could be they've forgotten us. Maybe I should go and check. What do you think?"

"You can if you like but I've always sat it out. They turn up in the end." How cool this sounds, how nonchalant and yet she has sat rigid in here on two or three occasions, her breath becoming more and more shallow, beads of sweat trickling down her back, wondering the very same thing, *had they forgotten her*? And always, as she was on the point, finally, of leaving the table to brave the sunlight and ask someone, Rusi would appear, as he does now, bearing a wooden plate of grapes and a pan of sweetly spiced grain, laying the food down on the table and smiling, as he always does.

Until Patrick arrived, Rusi, because he is the only other person apart from Mr Basham who speaks English, has been her sole source of conversation. They never speak for long but she has learned that he gave up a good job as an engineer and left his family in order to serve Swamiji; that serving guests is an act of devotion; that he has been at the ashram for four years and that, while he is deeply saddened by Swamiji's death, he feels his master's presence still as he goes about his business every day. She can tell Rusi is a spiritual man because of his peaceful manner. He walks and speaks quietly, saying and doing no more than he needs to fulfil his tasks. There is nothing superfluous about Rusi, nothing inessential. His serene features are framed by a thatch of white hair that offsets the white shirt and dhoti he's worn every day since she arrived. Alice aspires to his calm. This is what she is aiming for; that she will achieve serenity, peace, that all her unnecessary traits and emotions, all her frills, will be trimmed away.

Across the table from her Patrick eats hungrily, scooping up the grains with flat bread and lowering his head to shovel the food into his mouth. Alice approaches her food more slowly although she, too, is always hungry in the morning. The food at the ashram is simple and lightly spiced, exactly as it should be, but she has difficulty in eating here; the spiced food for breakfast, the reappearance of food from one meal to the next. She'd like to eat the grapes, Rusi told her they grow the grapes on the ashram, but the tiny fruits are dripping with water and crawling with ants. On previous mornings she has detached a small bunch and wrapped them in tissue, throwing them beneath a bush when she goes for a walk. It's all so pathetic. From the start Rusi has said, 'please tell us if there is anything you don't like and we'll change it if we can,' but she can't say anything. They're all so good to her, she doesn't want to appear ungrateful and so she eats what she can and, if that doesn't appear to be enough, she finds a means of disposing of the rest. At least with Patrick here it looks as though food disposal is one thing she won't need to worry about.

For most of the meal they eat in silence, Alice taking the opportunity to glance up at her new companion from time to time. How old is he? Early thirties probably although it's hard to tell, as it always is these days. His hair, thick and blond, hangs to his shoulders, his frame is thin, his flesh barely covers his bones. His clothes hang off him, the way they do on skinny people. His lips are too large and the lower half of his face is poised on the verge of a smile which implies the owner knows something about you that you don't know yourself.

"Where are you from?" he asks, between taking in more food. Although he has the voice, the transatlantic drawl, and the attitude, he's not old enough, doesn't have the facial lines and bags for an old hippy. A faker, she thinks. He doesn't belong here.

"Brighton."

"Ah, Brighton," he says, and while he doesn't actually say it, his words are laced with the sentiment, far-out. "Last time I was in Brighton I spent some time by the West Pier, you know? ... the drummers?"

Oh yes, the drummers and now they'll have to have the conversation about what a cool place Brighton is, nowhere like it, when the truth is she'd been glad to leave. But that was a favourite spot of hers, the stretch of seafront by the West Pier. She had done a lot of walking over the past few years. It wasn't something she'd ever gone in for before and at first she didn't even know why she was doing it but there was that moment... one morning, several years ago, thick with a hangover; she was escaping one of those typical little scenarios at home and she went down to the beach because at least by the sea there was space. There was air to breathe and she inhaled gobfuls of it, gulping down the salty smack of the sea, trying to ignore the tempting wafts of bacon carried by the wind. Why did she get herself into these situations? She paused to look at the pier and listen to the squawk of the seagulls and the crash of soupy grey waves, the drag of tide against pebbles, the anxious tapping of rigging against masts. For some reason the West Pier, neglected for decades, always made her think of Miss Haversham's room; bridal weeds of seaweed and slime dripping from a fretwork of girders which had long ceased to connect the body of the pier to the shore, the old concert hall the bride cake, gnawed away not by mice but by swarms of seagulls, pigeons and starlings, the latter of which swooped through the broken windows to dance, she imagined, to ghostly music-hall tunes, to soar and dive over shattered glass and broken seats of dusty velvet. She used to come to this pier as a child, had always preferred it somehow to the Palace Pier even though the West Pier had fewer amusements. She remembered them making *Oh, What A Lovely War* there, wanted to be on there herself, watching the sea move beneath her through the gaps in the slatted walkway. That morning she had woken with that awful sick feeling, like her life had settled at the base of her guts. She had not been alone. Nothing unusual in that, but for the first time she seriously thought that something had to change, the old philosophy wasn't working any longer. But what was the alternative? As if she might find the answer on the streets or in the swell of the sea, she continued eastwards, head bowed against the fierce wind, not knowing where she was going, unable to clear a space in her mind to think, just walking towards the Palace Pier, the pier that couldn't help but be much too much as it stretched out from the shore, neon-bright, wheels spinning, shrieks carrying across the Channel.

KATE WEINBERG
Reflex

Elma peers through the window which is opaque with frost, gives it a brisk rub so that the glass squeaks.

A tramp and his dog, Petrovic, have found themselves on the wrong street. It's just like any other in the quarter, skinny grey buildings covered in drains, but as they pass one of the houses, the tramp stiffens. His eyes follow the ghostly finger of a creeper plant, which, blackened by winter, trails slowly along the wall, up the steps and points darkly at the half-open door. Petrovic has now bent to sniff the steps, and gathering him by the scruff of the neck, the tramp jerks him away and drags him forcibly down the street. The dog whines in complaint, his claws scraping thin tracks in the snow.

Elma lets her bloody knife clatter to the surface, sighs, wipes her forehead and lumbers down the corridor to slam the door shut. Hair-thin rivers of red have sunk between the mounds of her fat palms. She blames this on the professor, whose hands are lily-white. Most days, that is. Sometimes they drip with blood, thick as paint, but the water washes it away and then they bear no traces.

Grasping the ham again, Elma begins to saw through a thick vein of gristle. As the slice leans, leans and folds suddenly in a deep bow, a bell sounds from the professor's study. Twenty-to-twelve. Elma catches sight of her soupy features in the glass of the clock and bares her teeth so that they glint. *Lets see what we can do today, my dear.*

Most days there is a draught in the professor's house. It rattles the floorboards and whistles up mouse-holes. Strange then, that it never seems to cleanse the air, which hangs dankest in the professor's study. Elma stands in the doorway, under a crust of recycled night-breath and fart-mingled sleep, and smiles brightly.

"Yes, Professor, you wanted something?"

The professor heaves his face out from his papers; ponderously, as if it is held down by a thick layer of cobwebs. His eyes dart to his bell, which stands, motionless, on the edge of the desk, and then back to Elma. He blinks and his face changes.

"Playing *sil*-ly games again, are we Elma?" The professor likes to separate syllables occasionally, to push words on their side and pull at their individual toes to show he is in control.

"No, sir. But I thought you might want 'to issue me with my weekly reminder.' Lets see, today's Thursday. I'd say its just about time for you to remind me to go to the butcher's."

They both look up at the clock, which reads eight minutes to twelve.

"I'm aware of that, Elma. But its not quite time is it?"

"Nor have I yet 'astounded' you, Professor, or 'managed by my very existence to disprove your theories on animal' – "

"Yes, yes, you've proved your point." The professor's head drops back to his papers. Elma eyes flicker round the room a little wildly.

"I mean, all over St Petersburg, scientists are flocking to…"

"*You've made your point, Elma*." The professor's voice glints like steel. He sits looking at the clock for a couple of minutes, and begins to smile. Reaching over, he gives the bell a short, definitive ring. Then he looks down at his papers again.

Elma's face begins to quiver. The blush rises slowly, mottling her neck and then sweeping over her features like an expanding flower. She opens her mouth minusculey.

"Yes, Professor?"

The professor looks up. His eyes squirm behind his glasses like maggots in a jar. "Ah, Elma. So prompt today. You *astound* me. I was just going to issue you with your weekly reminder. Let's see, Thursday. I think a little trip to the butchers is called for. Perhaps you can do me the honour of purchasing five steaks?"

Elma's nostrils widen slightly as she tries to regain control. "Why, yes Professor. I think I can manage that…"

His voice follows her down the corridor like a clammy hand on the neck. It constantly amazes her that out of all the people crawling over this earth, he has been given such a gift. The way he uses a knife, she'd swear it's the devil's touch. It irritates him when she breathes over his neck, but sometimes she can't resist; she can just get lost watching him slit open skin, his eyebrows bunched in concentration.

Next to the sink, a plate is stacked with fat from the ham. Flies squat on its white surface, vomiting microscopically. Elma grasps a hoop of fat and shoves it defiantly into the pocket of her coat. Swinging open the door, she watches her breath freeze.

Elma totters in her booted feet as she walks through the back door and into the garden. It is a sharp spring day, and she is wearing a tight coat that makes her arms stick far out on either side. Her face is soft and buttery, uncooked by age, and it is already apparent that she is a chubby child. She stops a few feet away from Ivan.

"What's that behind your back?" she asks him. Ivan keeps silent. His hair is jellied over to one side of his scrubbed face and he is squashed into new, tight trousers.

"You have to play with me today, Ivan. Mother told me that if I came out back and asked to help, that you would play with me."

"Your mother's fat." Ivan kicks a clod of soil viciously. "Besides, you can't help me today, I'm weeding."

He bends down and begins pulling at stems, hurling them over his shoulder so that their roots flail for a moment before disappearing behind him.

"Oh no," puffs Elma, horrified. "Those aren't weeds, they're flowers. Look, let me show you…"

She bends down in the soil and carefully picks out a small scrap from amongst the patch of flowers. Ivan scowls. "I hate flowers," he says. His glance flickers back to Elma. "Well, when's she coming then?"

"Your aunt? Oh, I don't know. Soon," replies Elma, sensing power. "Your mother told me but I've forgotten."

But Ivan has already lost interest. His eyes fasten on something in the soil.

"How many worms do you see, Elma?"

She follows, with instinctive anxiety, an earthworm slinking across the ground. "How many, Elma, how many?"

What can he do if she answers?

"One."

"Wrong!"

Song of triumph and metal as the spade whizzes through the air and hits the ground, guillotining the worm into two. Ivan leans on the shovel and watches the two wriggling parts with satisfaction.

"Who asked you to come over, anyway? My aunt doesn't like girls, especially poor ones. She only likes little boys like me."

Elma unglues her eyes from the murdered earthworm and looks back up at Ivan.

"What's she like then, do you know?"

"Who cares?" replies Ivan. "She's rich anyway, and if she likes me she's going to take me away with her."

"Where to?" asks Elma, suddenly scared.

"St Petersburg. Better than this dump. I'm going to become a famous scientist. You might be able to come too. I could probably arrange it," he adds carelessly, "even though she wouldn't like you."

"Would we get married then, Ivan?" asks Elma, still in a whisper.

What a silly thing to say. Ivan has always said she is a silly girl, and besides, she's going to run to fat, his mother said so last week as she watched her scrape the gravy off the bottom of her plate.

Ivan's aunt arrives just before lunch. She swoops in the door that Elma holds open, head-to-toe in a silver fur coat. A blue-eyed husky steps importantly by her side. Elma has a whiff of something sweet and intoxicating, and like a bee drunk on honey she floats back upstairs to Ivan, who is sitting in his usual position with his legs dangling between the banisters.

"She looks ugly," he says as his aunt lifts a hand to slip off a fur hat. Her wrists are clamped with silver.

"She does not, Ivan," breathes Elma. They both fall silent as his aunt looks up and sees the two of them sitting on the landing. Sweeping up the staircase she bypasses Elma and crouches down in front of Ivan.

"What a beautiful baby," she cries as she opens her almond eyes wide. "And so exactly like my dear Pietr, God rest his soul." She grasps his face and brings it closer to hers. "I think we shall enjoy getting to know each other, Ivan."

Just as they begin lunch, Elma feels something stab at her thigh. Looking down she sees Ivan is digging a fork into her plump flesh.

"Pass it here," he hisses with a jerk of his chin.

Elma's eyes are hot with tears as she passes the small lump of fat under the table. Her hunger has been bubbling all morning as she helped her mother cook the stew and dust the best plates that usually hang on the wall. She watched greedily as Ivan's mother served her, fishing around between the best pieces of meat and ladling gravy with a thin smile.

Blue eyes glow from the shadows under the table. Ivan suspends the dripping lump of fat a few inches away from the husky's head.

"Watch him, Elma."

Elma watches, sickened. Within a few seconds saliva coats black gums and teeth, and stretches in thin strings to the carpet. Ivan waits until the head lunges before snatching the meat away. He pops it into his own mouth.

"People like you go to hell," Elma whispers out of the corner of her mouth, between chomps of potato. But Ivan just looks at her with his jellied hair and dark, sly eyes, and his mouth curves into a perfect bow.

The queue for the butcher's trails out like an intestine into the snow. Elma recognizes a knot of women, their coats converging in a shaggy clump, breath steaming in the air.

"Getting worse isn't it?"

She looks at the scraps of faces for a response – here a red nose, there a watery eye, but the air blinks back, fogged and expressionless. Their coats bunch closer, squeezing Elma, a fat wordless question mark, off the edge of the pavement and onto the road. Someone titters and she shuffles back further. Her eyes dim with resentment as she makes her way to the end of the queue, hairy boots crunching with indignation.

When Elma finally makes it inside the shop, the slight warmth brings tears to her eyes. The sawdust-covered floor feels soft beneath her boots.

"Bang on time, Ma'am. How many mouths to feed this week?"

"Five steaks, please, Viktor."

"Got some newcomers, have you?" enquires the butcher. He wipes his hand on his apron, and begins picking the steaks off the ice. "That's what I thought. I've heard…well, let's say, news travels fast, especially when you're in this business."

"What news?"

"Let's not be shy, ma'am. My boy has friends who do some of your groundwork."

"And?" says Elma icily.

The butcher winks conspiratorially and leans over the counter to give her the parcel. His bulky hands are as blood-stained as Elma's. She feels the warmth of his breath against her cheek.

"Well, I'm not one to judge. Others might, but not me. I'm just the butcher. Let's just say that some of your newcomers aren't just lying about in the gutter waiting to be picked up, are they?"

Elma scowls, slams the rubles on the counter. The butcher's voice follows her out onto the street.

"See you next Thursday, Mrs Professor."

It isn't snowing now but the wind whips stiffly through her clothes, and blasts black branches of trees. Most figures on the road are solitary, bundled into old fur and lumbering awkwardly along the road like bears. Every so often Elma lifts a hand, finding her mouth amidst the unfeeling slab of her face, and wrenches at the strip of fat. She chews slowly as she approaches the milk shop.

It squats at the far end of a small street and smells of rot. Elma waits as an old crone, bent almost double by a diet of cold and potatoes, feeds the milk through a funnel.

"Three quarts again? You're squeezing me dry, you know. Don't think my other customers don't notice."

Words fizz at Elma's lips, but she keeps them pressed together. In the corner something is scrabbling in a hemp sack. The old woman ignores it, even as it grows more persistent.

"Is that a rat?" asks Elma finally. "We've run out. Maybe I should take it for the professor. Do you know what colour it is?"

"Rat-coloured, I'd expect," says the woman sourly. Her hooded eyes flicker up. "Getting well-known round here, isn't he? Not for the right reasons, though." The flow of milk wobbles as she savours Elma's expression. "I hear certain dogs have gone missing. Rich peoples' dogs. I've seen posters up in the square, there's a reward, you know. Fourteen rubles," she adds, holding out a claw. "That wouldn't be anything you'd know about would it?"

"No," says Elma fiercely, as their hands touch. "There's just no point in talking to any of you. Someone's making history below your noses, and you're all gossipmongers, with nothing to do except talk about this and…that. But your children will know better, and your children's children. The whole world will know who he is, and," she adds on a hiccough, "…and me."

She strides back out onto the street, the bucket of milk clanging against the makeshift doorframe so that it shudders. For an instant, she thinks – wishes – that the whole edifice, St Petersburg, perhaps even Russia herself would collapse into a pile of rotten sticks. She takes an icy breath and begins shuffling down the street, clumsy with parcels, age and fat that grows steadily on her like guilt.

"Sir sir, do you have the time?"

She squints at an unshaven face, too late recognizing him for a drunk.

"Well, let me see, I don't. Though the bell-tower over there says its half-past the hour," says the tramp. Both he and Petrovic turn to watch the frozen bundle of snot, steak and milk as it hurries quickly down the street, skating over patches of ice. Elma's eyes water. *I'm on my way you old bastard, I'm on my way.*

The husky bounds up the stairs, two even three at a time, loosing saliva with every shudder of its pink tongue. Elma, who is sitting on the curve of the landing quietly digesting lunch, sees it first. She grips the railings.

"Ivan!"

The husky ducks nimbly round her and skids to a halt in front of Ivan. Its legs lock and its belly tenses in a low growl. Ivan twists, still sitting, to meet bared teeth and slavering jaws a few inches away from his face. His eyes bulge. The dog lets out a murderous snarl and the two creatures stare at each other, crimson-eyed.

"Elma! Get mother!"

Elma may be a podgy child, but it would be wrong to call her slow. She scrabbles to her feet and races down the stairs, two at a time, her mouth dry. As she skids round the bend towards the final few steps there is a splintering sound. Glancing up behind her she sees Ivan sailing past in mid-air, starfish hands swimming for grip.

Up on the landing the husky's face peers through the broken banisters. Ivan bounces on his skull, once, twice, and there is a loud crack before he comes to rest on the tiled floor.

Elma opens the door to the laboratory, lets out a breath of frozen air and dumps the parcel of steaks on the side. The room is even smaller than the kitchen and the smell of entrails fugs the atmosphere.

She mutters to herself, straining as she bends over the cages and peers in through the gridded windows. Most of the dogs are sleeping, a couple are slit-eyed, still recovering from the anaesthetic. She glances in at one, an ugly black mongrel, the hair around its belly matted with blood. A tube dangles from its stomach, and there is a large hole in its throat. Elma sniffs the air, revolted. This one was such a pig before the operation, she is secretly hoping it won't revive. Out of all of the experiments, the sham-feeding is Elma's personal worst. She has to sit around half the day as it chews the steak, pick up the morsels as they drop onto the floor through the hole in its throat, and then re-feed it. By then, the gastric juices have started pumping through the funnel from its stomach, and often as not they miss the rim of the bucket and spill onto the newly-washed floor.

The professor's chart hangs on the cage, with a number circled at the top. It's the twenty-seventh dog he's tried to make the stomach pouch for. Most of them were huskies, hulking great things that are virtually impossible to sedate, but the professor is at his jolliest when the boys haul one off the streets. Out of the lot, only two have come round, but most of the other scientists say that with all the blood vessels in their stomachs, even that's a miracle. As far as they're concerned the whole set up is a con, a butcher's shop. The professor laughs when they troop into his lab, bending over cages and shaking their grey heads.

"Wait and see, Elma. They'll crawl back, tail between their legs. People have won the Nobel Prize for less. They'll be talking about it for generations, me and my dogs," and he pats one of the comatose creatures absently on the head, with his bloody glove.

The bell severs the still air. A few of the dogs lift sore necks, a couple show the white film of a half-opened eye. Elma heaves herself to her feet and walks back into the kitchen, leaving the door ajar. She pours the tea, stacks the ham, and busies with the tray for a few minutes. *On my way, husband dearest.*

Wedging her backside against the door, she boots it open.

The professor's head snaps up. His lips stretch into a smile, so that she can see the drool gathering about his teeth. "Ah, lunch," he barks.

DAVID WHATLEY

Extract from **The Eye of a Little God**

Occasionally I am aware of Kate turning over in the small bed above me, or in the early hours padding to the kitchen to get a glass of water. Hearing her footsteps, I slip from the edge of a food dream – a repetitious Christmas lunch – back to the tangible shapes of window-light on a black wardrobe.

I twist about inside my sleeping bag. I concentrate on my breathing whilst listening to Kate's. The rhythms are syncopated, a kind of wheezy dialogue. Then Kate stops breathing altogether, or sustains a longer than usual out-breath, the whole tune falling apart and having to be put together again. It makes me think of round robins in the classroom, 'London Bridge is falling down, falling down, falling...'

I think of toast before smelling it. I look up at Kate's bed but it is empty. I can hear Mel in the hallway singing *Yellow Submarine*.

"Hey, Kate, there's a postcard from Tom. Says he might be home for Christmas."

I hear Kate emerging from the bathroom.

"That's brilliant news."

"Not so sure, he sounds really pissed with Beverley Hills, says the sitcom sucks and everyone's really anti-smoking."

I sit up and the room spins. The pain in my lower back crawls around my spine and digs in. My bowels shudder. I lie on my back in preparation for my morning work-out. I run my finger along the space between the elastic of my boxer-shorts and the dip of my belly. The gap allows me to insert an index finger without moving the waistband. Good. I place both hands flat against my hips. I run my fingers from navel to neck, feeling the bumps and crevices as if reading the small-print of my body in Braille. I smooth the backs of my hands over my jawbone. I press my hands against my chest, measuring the ribs, feeling for the strange bone which pokes from the middle of my chest and wondering if it has any use. I place the tip of a finger against it.

I move it back and forth. It responds like a well-oiled ball-bearing. Only it is soft, too soft. I check my stomach. I knead the flesh. I squeeze inches of excess skin. I turn on to my stomach. I arch my head into the pillow and count the bones on the back of my neck, one, two, three, four, five, six, just to be sure. I put my finger on the bone at the base of my spine and repeat the same exercise, this time counting the small curve of bones to my rectum, one, two, three, four, five. Good.

I turn over and sit up again. I place the thumb and forefinger of my left hand around the top of my right arm, just where the muscle swells out. The flesh gives slightly until my thumb and forefinger meet. I do it again, this time concentrating on the flesh, how much there is, how much it has to give in order to accommodate the touching of thumb and finger. Because some days I really have to squeeze, some days the flesh has ballooned overnight. So I press ever so gently and feel it – the muscle – hardly move. The tips of my fingers touch effortlessly. It is good.

I pull the purple sleeping bag tight around my waist and stand up. The room spins again and a noise like tinnitus being released through a small valve rushes around the inside of my skull. I grip the edge of Kate's dressing table and take some quick, rhythmic breaths, deliberately keeping them short to avoid fuelling the oxygen fire in my head. My heart is beating fast, the demon in my back is scratching at inner layers of skin . I scan the surface of Kate's dressing table trying to locate her tube of Deep Heat. Hairspray, moisturiser, a nail file, a stray condom. I manoeuvre myself in the direction of the door, hiking the sleeping bag to my chin, pulling the door a crack, an inch, listening to Mel and Kate. I prepare for a casual entrance. Not easy, especially when trussed up in a purple maggot-skin.

I make my entrance. Mel looks up, her lips parted and pushed forward, whatever she was about to say locked in her throat. I inch my way across the room, hoisting my purple hobble skirt tighter. I feel their eyes follow me before their mouths, too, respond.

"Hi."

In unison.

"Bathroom," I say, disappearing down the hall and locking myself into the white room. Someone has already showered, there is steam on the mirrors and the air is thick and humid. It smells of warm soap and excreta.

I remove the sleeping bag and reach under the basin for the scales. The glass eye has steamed over. I clear it with my finger and the red marker shivers slightly. My stomach feels like it has been glued to the interior walls of my back.

When I step onto the scales I notice that the glass eye has steamed over again so I balance on one foot whilst I bend down and wipe it with my finger. I ignore the red marker, the rotating disc, with an impunity which is strange and oddly satisfying. I straighten myself and place my other foot onto the plastic foot-pad. The disc rotates. The black numbers spin. I hold my breath. And wait. The disc shudders. I concentrate on the eight, breathing out. I watch the eight spinning back and forth.

Eight.
Eight.
ten, ten, eleven, ten, nine, nine
ten.
I am seven:ten.
I am a pound from my goal.
I look again,
ten; seven:ten.
I repeat the process.
Seven:ten.
I shift the scales into a different part of the room.
I repeat the process.
Seven:ten.
Fat cunt fat cow fat chance.

Putting the scales back under the basin I run a quick check-list. The vodka, but that was two, nearly three days ago. Since then I have had nothing, a coffee on Sunday – or was it Monday? – which, with milk, may have made the difference. But I had it black. Is it the scales? Is the steam ruining their accuracy? Or am I destined to fail? Maybe my destiny is in the hands of an invidious God who will turn me into a walking effigy of the men I see all around me and who wear track suit bottoms because their belts no longer fit.

I take a deep breath. I'm reminded of the two men force-feeding the Creme de Menthe to the young girl at Covent Garden, their paisley waistcoats stretched over paunches, the expensive suits a waste of effort and money. Wide-boys. I can still see the stream of green bile spraying from the girl's timid mouth. I have a sudden impulse to shove my fingers down the back of my throat. I stare into the lavatory bowl and see my disembodied head looking up at me. What would be the point? In search of a two-day-old cup of coffee? I remember seeing the same girl in the Lamb and Flag, how her hip-bones poked through the worsted fabric of her skirt. I wonder where she lives. Or who with. I wonder what she does when she is not with people from work. Perhaps her hip-bones are her secret full-time job. Because that is what it is. I think of the hours and hours stretching ahead of me. Or my mouth swallowing up the days.

Days and weeks of nothingness. I look into the toilet bowl at my face. It is smooth and round. Failure days. Hours and hours of hard labour. I spit into the toilet and watch my face shimmer. I pull the flush and my skull disappears.

There are six days left.

There is still time.

Hours and hours.

I find Kate's tube of Deep Heat and anoint myself.

Kate's bedroom is cold; the morning light silver and alert.

I decide to do the mirror fully dressed.

It is hard to define my upper body due to the immensity of my jumper but I am pleased with my neck. It is long and smooth. There is the shadow of a bone on my right cheek.

I turn sideways and lift my jumper. I tug at the waistband of my jeans, pulling it forward with my fingers in order to examine the gap between my belt and my stomach. I relax, letting my breath out in a steady stream. My stomach is connected somehow to my diaphragm. No, that is not what I mean. The entire front section of my body, from chest to penis, is made up of one muscle. This is especially so on the out-breath. Except, now I examine it in more detail, the muscle quivers. There is no definition, just a solid mass of flesh. It is ruining the sharp relief work made by my ribs. So I breathe in, just a little. The gap between the front of my jeans and the ugly promontory of flesh is three or four inches. I let the breath out slowly. Next, I hook both thumbs either side of the waistband and hoist the jeans above my hips. I peer down, looking through the wide gap. I pull the waistband as far it will go, outwards of my hips, and, looking down, try to see the carpet through the bottoms of my jeans. For this my feet are wide apart, my legs pushing inwards at the knees. I stare down at the floor, my chin resting against the thick collar of my jumper. The carpet winks at me from the gaps at my ankles. There is minimum effort which, again, is good. I let the jeans fall to around my hips. I look into the mirror. I press the seat of my jeans around my buttocks looking for some kind of shape, some tell-tale deceit. The jeans hang loose and flat. Next, I place my thumb and forefinger around my upper arm, as before, but this time I am squeezing through the thick material of my jumper. I apply more pressure and again the fingers touch. It is good. Still looking in the mirror sideways on, I tilt my head forward and place my right hand on the back of my neck. I brush a finger over the protruding bones, counting as I go, one, two, three, four, five, six. I take my hand away and glance sideways. I look at the individual bones, the ones at the top, just below my hairline. Each bone stands out. Again, it is good. Only the extra pound nags at me and as my jeans settle around my hip bones I feel my stomach press into the taut material. I turn to face the mirror, my thoughts knotted. My face looks back at me. It is blank. Despite the growing panic I can't help noticing that my face is a dead face. It is pale, that is all that can be said for it. It is pale and there are dark rings under my eyes. I open my mouth and yell. The noise bounces off the astonished glass. Then there is silence, the yell swallowed up by the mirror-mouth. There is an embarrassed echo. In the mirror I can see Kate's holiday snaps. She is arm in arm with Jules. They are sniggering at me.

I lift my jumper. I breath out to ensure I am not cheating. I stand closer to the mirror and it offers me ME in close-up. I stare at the smooth belly. I twist my pelvis over to the right. The skin remains taut. There is nothing spilling. I stare at the strange bone in the middle of my solar plexus which has no use; at the mysterious shadows in my upper chest; at the sheer scoop of my collar bone; at the hollow sand pit in my throat. But it is no good. My belt has a strangle-hold on my midriff. I consider loosening it but that would be sacrilege, I could not live with myself. There is failure and there is failure and *that* is the worst sort imaginable. No. There is nothing I can do. Except wait. There is too much time ahead of me. But that is good, because that is what I have, I have time. Time sustains me. So I stay where I am. I lie down. Waiting for time to waste me. Wasting time. Here, on the floor beside Kate's bed. I will lie here all day. My body will measure the seconds, the hours. It will count and be patient. I will barely move a muscle. I will watch the light shift colour, from lunchtime through to evening supper, aware of my breathing, of the steady pulse keeping time in my chest, or my neck, slender inside my jumper, it is my neck and not my heart that is beating time, it is my neck that is keeping me alive.

In the end I thought fuck it.

The next day Kate super-glued the tuner to her handbag and said she was sorry. We looked at the scratches on the side of my face in the bathroom mirror. Kate found some antiseptic cream which she applied to the livid stripes, dabbing with the tip of a nail, the side of a finger. Afterwards I packed some things into a rucksack and headed west on the underground. I'd arranged to stay with Ben who, through an acquaintance of his father's, had landed a flat off Neal Street near Covent Garden. It was above a Greek restaurant which had a clientele of minor celebrities, business men and American tourists staying in the hotels off Russell Square.

I didn't have a plan. All I knew was that Kate and I needed some time apart. I thought about Nancy a lot.

I next saw her over a liquid lunch at the Marlborough Arms. We met by chance. My time at drama school was nearly finished and with nothing much to do I wandered in off the street. Nancy was sitting alone drinking lager, chain smoking and reading an austere-looking novel. She had tied her hair into bunches with ragged pieces of white lace. She was wearing a short black T-shirt, ripped Levis and a pair of motorbike boots from Shelly's. The T-shirt had a logo. It said, 'Robert De Niro's Talking'. The hair and the cigarettes made her look like a truant schoolgirl. The clothes, though, gave the impression that she was the singer in a pop band bored with waiting for the sound-check. She dragged on her cigarette, the novel raised in front of her face. She blew smoke from the side of her mouth in a continuous stream.

I sat nearby. I asked her what she was reading.

"Hi Stevie."

And she closed the book and stubbed her cigarette as if she'd been expecting the interruption all along. She held the book up and I read the title: *The Master And Margarita*. I'd never heard of it. She told me it was set in Moscow at the turn of the century, that it was a satirical fable – amongst other things – about so called modern values, that it was a love story too, but not like you'd imagine. She lit another cigarette and for the next few hours we flirted with Formalism, Nancy taking the lead. She blew smoke rings and made the words intention and performance sound sexy. Over several lagers we arranged to meet at the Nags Head Covent Garden Saturday night.

The following day Kate and I spoke on the phone. I told her I wasn't really sure what was happening. I hinted that I thought it was over but without saying anything definite, deliberately keeping phrases like *let's just be friends* or *I need time to myself* out of the conversation. Vague. Having my cake and eating it. And that was another thing. Kate suggested we meet up Sunday around midday and maybe go for a picnic in Regent's Park. I agreed to without really thinking, afterwards staring at the receiver and realising that Sunday would be my sixth day without food, the longest I'd ever gone.

The Nags Head was full: weekenders, day-trippers and tourists. Having lived in Covent Garden for a full week I'd developed an acute snobbery about the place, clinging to its unfamiliar corners, ousting my way through the crowded bars as if my very own party had been invaded by gatecrashers.

I sat in a corner sipping lager, aware of how quickly the alcohol was reaching my brain through lack of food. I chain-smoked. It took the edge off my hunger. To my left a group of adolescents were drinking bottles of Pils and talking about Body Popping. They were wearing identical black and yellow tracksuits with gaudy trainers. I fingered my palm-tree haircut and wondered what the next craze would be and what it would turn into.

When Nancy arrived she apologized, saying she'd taken the wrong exit from the tube and had ended up halfway down the Haymarket. Her blonde demi-perm had been back-combed into velvet skewers. It was held together by an invisible halo of hairspray. Everything else was deliberately low-key; no make-up; a plain T-shirt with an off the shoulder neck-line; faded Levis. She asked me if I wanted a top-up and I nodded and she went to the bar. Watching her manoeuvre through the roving eyes of lads and middle-aged men with paunches I felt a thrill of sexual anticipation. There were four skinheads standing near the bar. Their heads were periscopes, turning at exactly the same speed as Nancy walked past. My stomach groaned and I lit another cigarette.

I told Nancy I was living just down the road with Ben. I didn't mention Kate or what had happened. She asked me about the scratches on the side of my face. I said Ben and I had been messing about in the flat doing some drunken stage-fighting moves and he'd accidentally slapped my head against the wall. I asked her why she had decided on acting as a career and she said she hadn't really, she'd always wanted to paint but somehow the acting opportunity had come along and she thought she'd take it and see what happened. She looked at the group of lads sitting to our left, but not really at them, through them. One of them made a joke, his hand over his mouth, the word tits spilling through his fingers. His mates laughed and Nancy pretended not to hear. She looked at me and her smile was weary. She said she didn't think she was a very good actress but that she had a certain look which she figured would sell. She stubbed her cigarette and the subject was closed.

She talked about literature intimately. I was aroused and intimidated by the amount she had read. She leaned into me, her face inches from mine, her tangled hair smelling of smoke and pine needles. She placed a hand on the hollow of my arm and said words like fantastic and brilliant. Dostoyevski was definitely brilliant, but Bulgakov, with his handle on the surreal, was absolutely fantastic. I was aware of two middle-aged men sitting to our right, one of them wearing a straw boater with a black feather. He leaned towards his friend.

"Tolstoy, amazing fucking costumes, 'nuff said."

They laughed. When last orders were called Nancy stood up. She fished into her purse and, standing over the man in the straw boater said, "It is not a matter of wishing to extend the licensing hours to a state of contemporary capitalism. On the contrary, spirituality and the techniques of aesthetic theory would suggest that Marxist criticism of the conglomerate breweries looks for an extension anyway simply because we all like getting pissed." She dropped her cigarette into his drink (tss) and headed for the bar. The straw boater stood up and grabbed at her only he stumbled into the skinheads. They called him a dirty old sod. One of them took his hat and tossed it across the room.

I joined Nancy at the bar. She was laughing and swaying. It felt like someone had pressed cushions against my ears and I realised I was already drunk. She ordered two beers with tequila chasers. She sprinkled salt onto the rim of her hand, dabbed at it with her tongue and swallowed the tequila straight down. Her eyes lit up and she asked me where my flat was.

"Just down the road."

"And Ben?"

"He's visiting some mates for the night."

In the bedroom it became apparent Nancy wasn't fussed about foreplay. Which was a relief because the walls had started spinning. We undressed separately, bumping into things. I lay back on the bed. The ceiling turned into a merry-go-round and Nancy climbed on board. She sucked me until I was hard and then got on top. She told me it was all right, she was on the pill. Her corkscrew hair had wilted and was all over her face. She pressed her hands either side of me and began rocking up and down, getting faster, her head pointed at the ceiling. It was solemn and mechanical and all I could think of was pornography, Nancy's breasts accentuated by the narrow waist and sloping rib-cage, her body going through the motions. My prick felt as numb as a dead trout so I tried thinking of other stuff but all I could hear was Kate's voice saying, 'So what about The Body, do you want to fuck it like Tom?' Nancy's hips were moving in circles, faster and faster, but it was no good, I couldn't feel anything. I remembered Tom's words, 'Yeah, but what a body.' I imagined him watching with salacious envy, his hand reaching inside the front of his jeans. I tried to think of other scenarios. I closed my eyes and saw Tom fucking Nancy from behind, his beer-gut slapping against her and making a bat-wing noise, Nancy begging for it like in a porn film. But nothing. Nancy leaned forward and I felt her hair brushing against my chest. I opened my eyes. Nancy's face was inches from mine, her solemn stare fixed on the wall. The smooth coupling of cunt and prick became a dry friction and Nancy toppled from me in a heap of sweat and sinew. The walls had started spinning again. Nancy climbed under the duvet. My head found the pillow and when I closed my eyes there were yellow and red lights, Nancy's cigarette dropping with a 'tss' into someone's drink.

At first I thought Ben had forgotten his key. But then I remembered that Kate and I had arranged to go for a picnic in Regent's Park.
"What is it?" said Nancy, turning to face me, the intercom buzzing in the hallway like a trapped fly. Her breath smelt of booze and stale bayleaves. I told her.
"Shit, Stevie, why didn't you warn me?"
"I forgot," I said, and suddenly she was stuffing stockings into a Tesco bag and pulling on her jeans. The sides of her hair were sticking out at right angles. The buzzer kept on going and I grabbed my dressing gown and ran into the hall. I picked the receiver off the wall and heard Kate's voice saying, "Stevie? Coming out to play?" I stared at the wall, trying to think of a reply. Nancy emerged from the bedroom. Kate's voice spat at us through the intercom, "Stevie? Stevie?" Nancy looked at me and shrugged.
"If you sort things out give me a call."
And then she was gone, heading down the short flight of stairs to the front door. When she opened it I heard her say sorry. I could hear her heels through the intercom clicking down Neal Street, at the same time Kate's feet on the stairs. Then Kate and I were face to face in the doorway. Her red mouth was a big O. She said "Stevie?" as if trying to prise into the silence. My dressing gown had fallen open. I pulled it round my midriff, still holding onto the receiver. Kate was carrying a small hamper. She was wearing a new summer dress. She'd had her hair cut into a short bob which suited her. I wanted to tell her only I couldn't. She shoved the hamper against my chest and I wrapped my arms around it, the receiver falling from my hand and banging against the wall. Kate ran down the stairs and onto the street, leaving the door gaping. I considered running after her but my head was heavy and I realised it was six days since

I'd last eaten. I took the hamper into the sitting room and sat on the sofa and gathered my dressing gown around my middle. I examined the contents of the hamper: a packet of mini pork pies, some celery and dips, an avocado, a potato salad. I started on the pork pies, popping them into my mouth whole. I then devoured the dips and celery, shoving the stalks into my mouth faster than I could chew. The food felt good but I was ashamed with myself for eating it. I went into the bathroom and pressed my fingers against the back of my throat. At first it was just a dry retching but eventually the mixture of foods jettisoned from my mouth in a brown stream of mashed pastry and liquid. I looked at my face in the mirror. It was puffy with booze and bad sleep. I pulled the flush. I went into the bedroom and slid beneath the duvet. The pillow smelt of Nancy. Every now and again a breeze made the front door bang against the wall. I could hear footsteps on the street coming and going.

I awoke with a dry mouth and a headache. I went into the kitchen for water. In the sitting room I flicked on the TV and fingered the remains of Kate's hamper. There was a newsflash on the screen, something about two bombs in central London. A lot of people had been killed. My head hurt and I didn't feel like watching. I buried my face in the sofa, my hands pressed against my temples. The voice on the TV was saying something about Regent's Park, that the bomb had been deliberately planted beneath the bandstand in order to cause a maximum number of fatalities. I looked at the screen and thought of Kate.

I got dressed in fits and starts. I swallowed two aspirin and ran down the stairs.

The entire area had been cordoned off and I wondered what I was doing. Streets surrounding the park were a mess: snarled traffic, orange and white tape and a migraine of blue lights. 'Why would Kate have bothered coming here?' I kept thinking. At the same time I needed to find out, I wanted to see for myself. I pushed past some people who had gathered outside a pub on Gloucester Place. My head hurt, it was hot. The sky was clear and blue. On the streets there was a jam-packed silence. It was ruptured every now and again by the shriek of an ambulance. I got to the end of Gloucester Place and couldn't go any further. A policeman asked me what I was doing and I said I didn't know, I thought maybe a friend... He looked at me and I felt guilty.

On Tottenham Court Road I rang Kate.

"It's Stevie."
Silence.
"When I heard about the bomb – I thought –"
"Fuck off."
It was the second time in a week I'd heard her swear.

I walked back along Tottenham Court Road towards Neal Street. The roads were crawling with rush-hour traffic. The whole of London, the city and the suburbs, felt as if it had been compressed into a giant bottleneck. The air was heavy. The back of my throat tasted of stale pastry and celery. For the first time that day I remembered the night Kate and I had slept in Regent's Park with the others. I stepped into the road and a car-horn screamed at me.

Later I went to Nancy's. She'd heard the news. We sat in silence for most of the evening, drinking wine and lying on her bed. She asked me if I wanted food and I shook my head. She asked me if I'd spoken to Kate and I shook my head. We slept without sleeping. We kissed without touching.

In the morning we read the papers.
At exactly 2 p.m. the bandstand erupted into splinters of scorched wood, twisted bits of brass and human limbs. Office workers in high buildings said they saw the cloud of smoke first, were aware of something quite devastating before the noise reached them. Others heard the echo somewhere above them in the blue sky and looking down tried to connect the dull thud with the glittering carnage.
The second bomb went off minutes later at Hyde Park. A horseback regiment were parading in full regalia. The streets were lined with Londoners and tourists. The bomb issued a hailstorm of nine-inch nails which tore into horses and bystanders alike.
Nancy and I read the papers sitting up in bed and drinking coffee. Looking at a picture of the desiccated bandstand I thought again of the night Kate and I had slept there, Tom standing on the frail platform performing his audition speech from Henry V.
A many of our bodies shall no doubt find native graves, upon the which, I trust, shall witness live in brass of this day's work.
Or in the morning Ben shouting 'catch that you fat bastard' and lobbing Tom's Mickey Mouse alarm clock into the air, Tom sliding on his belly with outstretched arms, the clock all in pieces by the bandstand.

Nancy said it made her feel sick when she thought of all those horses.

I looked at the photo of a ripped up horse, its insides all over the pavement. I was hungry but the sight of it made me nauseous. Nancy said she couldn't look, that they shouldn't have printed it. I stared at the photo, at the black flesh and poking ribs, trying to bottle the sensation of feeling sick.

KATHARINE WHITFIELD

Extract from **Unreturning Track**

ONE

His face looks like a college kid's, though I know he's a few years older. A City boy, which means he's paid well, better than I am. He'll be paying me himself on this one, and then I can pay my bills. I study him with some hope, and notice how differently he sits from the *pro bono* cases I usually get. He's crouched forward, watching me. Maybe he'll have better manners than usual. I light a cigarette, offer him one to be polite. To my surprise, he takes it. Lycos don't usually smoke.

"So." I say. "You realize the charges are serious. Your best hope is in proving that you tried to get to a lock-up but couldn't."

"I did." He says this as if it were obvious. My hopes of a courteous client slip a notch.

I sigh. "I don't suppose you remember the actual crime?"

He gives me a look: I've asked a foolish question and called what he did a crime. "Of course not. I can't even identify the man."

I flip a picture across the desk. "His name is Johnny Marcos. He's got a wife and three kids, and since you took his hand off he's on restricted pay and worried sick about their education. He's a very decent man."

"You know him?" My client looks surprised. "I thought legal advisers weren't meant to take cases where they're personally involved."

Bright boy. "This is the DORLA, Mr Ellaway. We all know each other. It's a small world, we're less than one per cent of the population. And since we all do – " I stop myself from saying dogcatching " – full moon duties sometimes, that could have been any of us. And since you'll get a non-lyco judge, you're going to have to work hard at convincing us it wasn't your fault." I don't mention how well I know Johnny; he doesn't need to know that.

"Why can't I have a normal court? Any bareback judge is going to be prejudiced against me."

Bareback, well, there we are. He's no better mannered than any of the tramps I usually get. I give my illusion about the gentlemanliness of the monied classes a little kiss and send it on its way.

"Like I said, Mr Ellaway, this is the Department for the Ongoing Regulation of Lycanthropic Activity, and we handle our own affairs. Now suppose you explain to me what you were doing running around on a moon night."

The story is a simple one. His car broke down; he was lost, and was trying to find a shelter when he started furring up. There are enough government lock-ups; you can always reach at least one by walking between dusk and moonrise. At least, that's the theory. Like most of our theories, it's prettier than the real world. Winos are the biggest problem since they're too drunk to make their way, but this guy's story might be true for all his manicured nails. It happens every month. Then again, it might not. It's not much of a story. And the fact remains that when Johnny tried to round him up, Ellaway bit his hand off at the wrist and shredded the remains. Most lunes don't do that. They go for you; of course they do. We've all got scars. There's a deep slash running up the inside of my left forearm from my first dogcatch; a heavy dent in one of my hips from when I was 22; a map of lacerations around my calves – and I'm a good catcher, I get mauled less than most. But breaking bone is something more. Lunes aren't usually savage enough to hurt you that badly before you get them tranked. Some of them don't even go for you that much: they consider the point made if they've drawn blood. Or they even give up once they realize they're caught; I once collared a wolf who licked my hand and rolled over to have his belly rubbed. It all depends what kind of person they are. This City boy has to have something in him to make him capable of mauling my friend.

I get out a map of the area. "Now, you say you were round here when your car broke down, yes? And you started walking east. There's two lock-ups within walking distance."

He sucks on the cigarette I gave him. "I told you, I don't know the area."

"You should know enough to stick to the main roads. You would have come to a shelter if you had."

He shrugs, and lounges back, his legs a-splay. I take out another file. "I've got your record here. Dangerous driving, twice, driving over the legal limit, and possession of narcotic substances. I have to tell you, Mr Ellaway, it doesn't look good."

"They dropped the narcotics charge." He drops ash on my floor.

"Were you using anything that night?"

"Drugs are illegal." He looks amused at himself.

"How about a little nicotine withdrawal? Cross because you couldn't fit a cigarette in your jaws?"

"Hey, hey." He sits up, waving his hand. "I didn't come here to be accused. I'm your client, you know?"

I run my hands into my hair. "Mr Ellaway, I'm just trying to tell you the kind of things they'll ask you in court. You've crippled a man for life. If you can prove it wasn't your fault you were out, then it's just wolf-state and you'll get off. And if you can't, then it's negligence, grievous bodily harm, the works, and you are looking at years. Years, Mr Ellaway. Judges don't take kindly to this sort of thing."

He shrugs again.

The telephone rings. "Excuse me." I say, and pick it up. "Hello?"

"Lola?" It's Josie. She's been working on reception ever since she let two lunes get away in one night. "Lo, I got a call from your sister. She says she's gone into labour and could you go to the hospital. She's at St Veronica's."

My throat jumps a little. "I'll get on it. Thanks, Josie." I turn to Ellaway, who is still dropping ash on my floor. "Mr Ellaway, I have to go. I'll see you again tomorrow, and I want you to think about what I've said. I need as many details as possible, so remember everything you can. Now, good morning."

"Good morning." His handshake breaks several bones in my knuckles, and he's still sitting in the chair.

"Mr Ellaway, you can go now."

"Oh. Right. I'll see you tomorrow." He gets up and swings out of the room.

"And could you close the – " He disappears, leaving the door wide open. I express a few opinions under my breath, and go to close it myself.

I call my boss and explain. "Is it all right if I take the day off? I'll work overtime next week."

"A baby." His voice sounds reflective, not that it ever sounds any different. "Well, off you go. You can see if it turns out to be one of ours."

I can't tell if this is a joke, so I laugh just in case. I get my coat and squeeze out of my little office. On the way past reception, there's a hand that comes down on my shoulder.

"Miss Lola May, you save my life." It's Jerry, one of my winos. He smells like a dustbin, which means he's fallen off the wagon again. "Wanna thank you frall your good legal advice, Lola May, you're good legal vice lady."

"Hey, Jerry." I say. "What are you doing here?"

"Got stuck out last mooning. Wasn't my fault, tried to shelter, you know always try. Don't mind shelters, quite like them ashually. Can't always find my way, not my fault if I try, Lola May. This guy says I pissed on him when he tried collar me but would I do that? Wouldn't. You know I'm nice guy, Lola May." He rocks back and forth, his eyes wide like a kid's. "Think they'll sue me for cleaning bill, you gotta help me Lola May. Don't wanna pay cleaning bill. Not mon – not mada – mada money. Tel 'em I wouldn't ever piss on a guy juss doing his job."

I've seen him worse than this: he's pretty bad, but his sense of humour hasn't drowned out yet. "What's he in for?" I ask Bob, who's standing a little back from his charge.

"Moon loitering. This is the twelfth time. He's not doing well."

"No cleaning bill?" says Jerry, swivelling his head.

"Jerry," I say, "what happened to your AA program?"

"M'wife left me." he says.

"Yeah? Was that before or after you fell off the wagon?"

"Ohh Lola May you gon break my heart. You're hard woman, Lola May."

My feet are starting to itch. "Look, Bob, I'll take this case if you can hold it over till tomorrow, he's one of my regulars."

"Lucky you."

"He's harmless."

"I," Jerry declares, "am a gentleman. Do my best."

"Can you just put it on hold for a day?"

"I think I'll put him in the lock-ups to dry out." Bob says, grinning.

"Don't wanna sleep on straw. Not no lune now. Lola May tell him I don wanta sleep on straw!" Jerry wails as Bob hustles him down the corridor.

I turn to head out, and that's when I see there's a man on the chairs who's been watching the whole exchange. His hair sticks up in tufts; his eyebrows are trained into fierce peaks. He sits with his lips a little apart, baring his teeth. The effect is meant to be vulpine, but it looks more like a bad photograph.

"Excuse me." I say.

The man doesn't take his eyes off me.

"Are you being seen?"

He turns his head aside, slowly, and spits through his teeth onto the floor. Then he looks back at me.

"Fucking skins," he says.

I take the bus to the hospital. My sister Becca and I are not really close. I'd hoped we might get along better since the baby, but I've got some doubts.

The baby could be one of two men's. There's her husband, but there's also a DORLA screw-up that's just another wedge between us. Caught between home and work one moon night, Becca presented herself at the nearest lock-up like a good citizen. It happened to be Friday, and there were a lot of people there; Fridays and Saturdays are always the worst. So some genius put her in a cell with some man she didn't know. Which would probably not have had serious consequences, except that Becca is one of those unlucky women whose menstrual cycle tends to be at mid-point around the full moon. When she furs up she goes on heat. If I'd known that at the time, I could have told her to take the Pill and knock her cycle out of sync, but I didn't hear about it till later.

It's a government screw-up, not hers, so legally neither she nor this anonymous man are responsible. But unfortunately for Becca, her husband didn't see it that way.

I never liked him, to be honest, and I think if he hadn't left her for that he would have left her for something else. This is not something she would thank me for saying.

Like a good sister, I went with her to the ante-natal classes. I helped her with breathing exercises. I held her hand. I put her onto a good agent in DORLA to fix her flights; flying across time zones three hours ahead of moonrise so she wouldn't change shape and miscarry. I even promised to stay with her when she went into labour. Throughout the pregnancy, though, there was a barrier between us, and I could guess what it was. It isn't just that I work for the department that's responsible for her being a single mother, my conservative sister's worst nightmare. It's that she couldn't tell me how much she hoped her baby would be normal, because that would be telling me how much she hoped the baby wouldn't be born the way I was.

More than most people, she has a horror of having a non-lyco baby, and that is because of me. It was only when we were very little that she didn't notice the difference at moontime. She'd lock up at home with my parents, and spend the night grooming or whatever, while I would be opted out of it and taken to a DORLA creche. She gave me looks like I was refusing to share something. And later, I couldn't join in the excitement of choosing a career, because we all know what happens to barebacks: they get conscripted into DORLA. There's a choice of what you can do within it, but no question, ever, of not working for them. It's too big a job, and being non-lyco is too rare a birth defect: we all double up and do several jobs at once as it is. That is decided for you at an early age. Becca never says that I wouldn't get into the spirit of things at home, but I know that's how she thinks. As far as she's concerned, DORLA stole her little sister. If it steals her baby, I don't know what she's going to do.

It takes me a while to convince the receptionist to tell me where Becca is, as she has doubts what a woman so obviously not pregnant as I am wants in a labour ward. Finally I get directions, and head off down the beige and green corridors which look like every other hospital corridor I've seen. When I finally get to the labour wing, a young man with flapping hands stops me.

"Excuse me, this is as far as you can go."

"I'm here to see my sister. I'm her labour partner."

"I've heard nothing from reception." His hands do a twirl of officialdom.

"Look." I tell him. "My sister has been relying on me for months to be her labour partner. I'm no doctor. I'm not that desperate to be here, but my sister, Becca Keir, is expecting me, and you are intruding on my family duties."

"I'm not meaning to intrude, but this section isn't open to the public."

I have just about had it with this hospital, so I decide on a short cut that I would, in a good mood, disapprove of. "Look, my name is Lola May Galley, you can ask if she knows me. You want to see some identification? Here." And I pull my DORLA ID card out of my pocket.

His hands stop flapping me away – they keep flapping, but more as if they're bowing to me. "She's in Ward Three."

"Thank you," I sing, and go past him. I can see him giving me a resentful look as I pass. We both know what I've done.

Becca is in the middle of a white bed, her dark hair in a mess that in other circumstances she would be ashamed of. She gives me a polite smile as I come in, that just about covers the disappointment that I'm not her husband.

"How's it going, sis?" I say.

Her voice has a different accent to mine, because of the lyco schooling: even when she's this tired and stressed, she sounds classier.

"The doctor says everything is going fine, it should only be a few more hours."

A few more hours sounds like quite a while to me, but then Becca always said I have no patience. I settle myself down in the chair by the bed, which, like the rest of the stuff in this place, is not going to make me any more concessions than it has to. Becca appears to go into a contraction, and I let her have my hand. Her grip is harder than Ellaway's.

"Breathe," I remind her.

I want a cigarette, but if I lit one in this place they'd have me arrested, DORLA card or not. Becca pants on the bed, and I inhale the sterile air, trying to imagine it is ash-grey. It tastes of disinfectant.

A man with a green paper hat comes in with a purposeful stride and examines my sister without making any comment. After a couple of minutes, Becca releases my hand and I flex it, trying to get the flesh back to where it was before. The green-capped gentleman nods to himself and says something about dilations to the nurse. He begins to aim for the door.

"Hello," I say to him before he can reach it.

"Hello. I'm Dr Parkinson, the consultant – I assume you're a friend of hers?"

"I'm her sister." Becca flops her head back on the bed, and doesn't say anything.

"Well, she's doing just fine," he says in a soothing voice. "I'll make a few more calls, but there should be no problem."

Becca's face creases for a moment with anxiety, then she turns it away from me. Evidently she hasn't asked him what's uppermost in her mind. If no one's told her different, then probably the babe will be a lyco; the odds against it are less than 1 per cent. Becca, though, is not one to let this calm her; I don't suppose she's spent a day in the past nine months without remembering that the kid might not be normal. She would have done better to ask behind my back before I got here. Since she hasn't, though, she's not going to say it to my face. She isn't fooling me, but I appreciate the gesture. Though I'd appreciate it more if she didn't need to ask him so badly.

"Is it laid right?" I say.

"Pardon?"

"Is it going to come out feet first like it should?"

He makes the beginnings of a deprecating sound, and I cut across him. "Only I was born head-on, you see, and my sister and I agree that one non-lyco in the family is enough."

"Ah. You're from DORLA?"

"Yep." Becca is silent, not looking at me.

"Well, there's nothing to worry about. I'll see that everything turns out just fine." And out he swans.

"There you go." I pat Becca's hand. "No need to worry."

She speaks without looking at me. "That isn't fair, May. You know I never said anything about not wanting it to be… to…"

This is true. She didn't.

I have a choice here. I can lie, and say it was just me who was worried, and I only brought you into it to give my worries weight; or I can tell the truth and say, yes, but I know that's what you were thinking. I'm quite relieved when another contraction starts up and gives me some time to think about it.

My sister toils on the bed. I sit and watch. No doubt she is in great pain, but she was probably right. I can't get into the spirit of things.

By the time the contraction is over, I've made up my mind to go for the lie.

The consultant returns at intervals. I wonder how she's affording him: money drips off him instead of sweat. A few hours down the line he delivers her of a fine baby boy. I'm not mad keen to see it, but it's best to check, so I tilt my head round and find that the desired end is coming to pass. His tiny feet appear, then his tiny knees, by which time it's perfectly clear that he's going to be a lyco.

"Perfectly sound in every way," Parkinson pronounces, as he hands the little mite over for the nurses to excoriate.

Becca's face is running with sweat; she's almost sobbing. "Oh thank God. Oh thank God, oh thank –"

Then she remembers that her bareback sister is listening.

"Don't worry about it." I say, and shrug. "At least you get to keep him."

Another contraction comes along, this one for the afterbirth. I give her my hand and squeeze back as hard as I can. This is to stop her from crushing it altogether. Perhaps it feels like solidarity from the outside.

By the time I get home, I have three separate back aches. I swipe card my way through the door, get in the lift and go all the way up to the seventh floor. The building is a little scuzzy. There are dust mice under the radiators and peeling paint on the windows; when I take a bath, I've been known to get bits of plaster in my hair. All of this means that it's cheap, which means I can afford it. And also, lycos don't live here, not adult ones anyway. It started out with nons moving in because of the low rent. The rooms are small anyway, and lycos prefer to have at least one biggish room for a lock-up. After a while, the lycos moved out because there were too many damn skins around, and now it's pretty much lyco-free. We tend to have lyco children, as the condition's not inherited, and some of us marry lycos, but there's a non in every flat. This has its advantages, the biggest being that no one acts like I'm about to arrest them.

I get to my apartment. I've painted the rooms red and blue, trying for cosy, but really they're just small. The bedroom is a double bed where I sleep alone, and about an inch of space each side. The kitchen is narrow, but it has my food in it. I haven't thought about food for a few hours, so I'm not yet hungry, but I will be in a while; I need to work myself up to it. What I've been looking forward to is a hot bath, the first major consolation of the evening.

My feet hurt. I kick off my scary-lady shoes, and hobble towards this goal. When I open the door, I find that there's a big wet patch on the ceiling, pouring a narrow stream of grey water down into a minor flood on my bathroom floor.

This is a disappointment I do not want to have to deal with, but I cannot have a bath with the room in this state. I make my way upstairs, shoeless, and knock on the door of the Cherry family, the people responsible for this misfortune. The kids, I discover – lycos both – are babysitting themselves tonight and have forgotten to turn off the tap.

"Could you turn it off now?" I say. "My bathroom is full of water."

The boy giggles; the girl says, "We're sorry, Miss Galley, really we are." She looks so worried I'm half-inclined to apologise, but she has a giggling brother who flooded my ceiling, so I don't. They take off to repair the damage, and I head back downstairs, wondering if life will be good enough to let my ceiling dry by itself.

I'm at my door when I'm caught by my neighbour opposite, Mrs Kitney. Mrs Kitney is an old biddy from Personnel who somehow manages to make everything she says sound like she's sympathizing about some intimate medical complaint.

"You're back late, Lola." she says.

"No, I'm fine." I say. This is not the most apt of answers, but the way she talks, I can't help myself.

"You don't have any shoes on," she confides.

"I was just going upstairs for a minute. The Cherry kids forgot to turn a tap off."

"Ohh, but it's terrible news about poor Johnny Marcos, isn't it?" she says, shaking her head at me.

I don't think she knew him well, but she's bound to have heard. "Bad lune. I'm advising him, but he doesn't have much of a case. The judge isn't going to go easy on him."

She frowns. It's possible she's surprised that I'm betraying client confidentiality like this, but only in the same way it's possible I'd win the lottery and be a millionaire.

"You're advising him?"

"Yeah, the man who took his hand off. Someone's got to do it. I always get the no-hopers."

"Oh, you haven't heard!" She claps her hands to her mouth, then leans towards me. "It's not his hand, Lola. It's him.

Someone shot him this afternoon."

Back in my apartment, I lock and bolt the door. I don't know whether I'm frightened or whether I want to be alone. I don't know anything. Closing my eyes, I try to bring up Johnny Marcos's face, but all I can think of now is his brown eyes. Somewhere in the afternoon when I was sitting in hospital, Johnny Marcos has gone in an instant from a person to a memory. I've lost a friend.

The sound of a slap makes me jump. I must be nervous. I go to see what's wrong, and see, through my bathroom window, a body of water fall through the air. It lands with a smack seven stories down, and another one follows it. It takes me a minute to put together that the Cherry children are throwing water out of their flooded bathroom window.

I can't stand this. Johnny Marcos is gone beyond hope of retrieval and I can't listen to any sharp sounds. I go through to my sitting room. The walls cramp in on me, and I switch on the television to block them out with noise.

The news headlines fill my flat. There's a war in Africa. There are earthquakes warnings in San Francisco. There's a move to lower inflation rates. There's an enquiry into the health service. There's a new toy invented that sold out within an hour of shops opening.

Some of this is local, but there's nothing about us. Johnny didn't make the news.

CLARA WIGFALL
Slow Billows the Smoke

Across the lawn, Nathaniel is dancing. Alone in the morning half-light. Dressed entirely in white apart from his shoes, the leather darkening slowly as the dew seeps upwards. A veil hangs across his face so that his features are fogged, indistinct as if seen through steamed glass. He side-steps across the grass and pauses. His gestures are utterly precise, lingering. He circles ninety degrees, then takes a careful pace towards the sun bleached pale in the distance. Like a displacement of time caught on slow-moving camera film, his movements seem in retrospect. It is as if the very air resists him. Gravity tarries his steps.

And all the while they crowd the sky about him like a dense scattering of neatly-sewn stitches. Poised. Watching. The silence of the morning muffles the hum of their wings.

Standing in the doorway, I dare not move a muscle for fear the sound might carry across the green and alert him to my presence. My insides echo the line of Nathaniel's movements. I can feel the data diffusing itself within my mind, lodging within the quietly compact curls of my brain. A fine hand reaches from behind and closes across my eyes.

It is over. I know it is over for I hear at least a hundred, if not more, disperse into the very vaults of heaven. His step is straight as he walks across the grass towards us. With that distant prickle of irritation he will by now have seen us through the fine mesh of his veil; a girl standing straight in a red dress, her eyes covered by another's hand. As he passes us unspeaking and disappears within the house, the white cotton of his jacket brushes against my bare arm.

My eyes are crushed closed beneath his fingers still as Thomas leans over my shoulder and presses his mouth to mine.

His passion is apiculture.

"Apiculture? What is that word?" I kick off my shoes and stretch my legs up onto the dash. We are driving under an arch of trees and the sunlight dapples the tan of my stockings. How the bright shapes move. Fast. Like trying to watch raindrops on paving slabs. He holds the wheel with one hand, smoothes it from side to side as the road dictates, while the other hand reaches to twist the dial on the radio. "I said, what was that word?"

He settles the needle at an early Schubert sonata. "Apiculture. The cultivation of the Honey Bee, *Apidae*, my Céline. Say it."

And I mouth his words carefully, watching him all the while, not trying too hard for the clipped accent because I know he likes my disregard. "Apiculture. Cultivation of the Honey Bee, *Apidae*." I smile with my eyes not my lips and Thomas gives a quick glance back over his shoulder, then pulls the car into a siding. Leans across the leather seat and slides his hand along my thigh. The motor is still running and the Schubert plays on.

When we draw up at the house we see Nathaniel distanced by the lawn. He's dressed for the bees, but as he walks towards the car he lifts the nets covering his face and slips off his gloves. I'm leaning forward to replace my shoes as Thomas skirts the boot of the car to open my door for me. We emerge just moments before Nathaniel reaches us. His face surprises me because it appears so passive beneath the wide netted brim of his hat. He is marginally less pale than his outfit, with skin that reminds me of dry paper once heavily crumpled and later run through a press. He only smiles when he comes to a point on the grass just a pace or two away from us, and even then it is a slim smile, wintry.

"Old chap." Thomas has his arm about my waist but holds out his free hand to Nathaniel. I can sense his excitement.

Nathaniel nods and holds his smile. "So good to see you."

Tilting his head towards me, "Céline, my pretty French wife." Thomas' laugh hangs a moment above our heads before diluting in the sky.

Lifting my hand to his kiss, Nathaniel fixes my eye. "*Enchanté, Madame.*"

"*Enchantée,*" I repeat, lowering my gaze.

We take the cello to the music room. This house has a hundred rooms, or so it feels. A room in which to read, to dine, to dance, to take tea, to breakfast. Rooms with closed doors that he doesn't take us into. When Thomas was a child, he used to spend his holidays here. And yet there is an awkwardness with which he follows Nathaniel's step.

Across the parquet floor, the sunlight slants its dusty path through the high windows of the music room. The walls are lined with blue brocade, the green-tinged off-white blue that surprises when you peel a quail's egg. I have to stop myself from running my hands across their silken surface. Above the mantelpiece hangs Apollo with his lyre, corpulent cherubs reclining in the foliage at his feet, their expressions beatific. Another painting is leant shyly against the wall. It is a tiny Cubist work with a guitar and a wine bottle sliced across the canvas. In the afternoon light a piano basks, its lid lifted, innards flashed; somehow indecorous as a young girl with skirts raised to sun winter-white thighs. Crouching opposite, a spindle-legged harpsichord balks in the grand presence of its colleague. Above its keyboard stands a manuscript, left open at a middle page as if someone had walked away mid-piece. A quartet of other instruments is positioned about the room; a viol, its wood burnished dark, a shining bugle, a filigreed harp, and an oboe resting languorous upon a wooden cabinet. They surround like an expectant audience.

Thomas takes a seat in the centre of the room and opens his cello case. He folds back the felt wrappings, careful as a mother with her babe, lets down the stand, and cradles the instrument between his legs. Is it jealousy I feel low in my chest each time I watch him take up his cello? He tightens the bow, slides it in long slow strokes across the rosin.

"I had the room aired for you," announces Nathaniel. He's standing against the piano, toying with a tuning fork, his right side ashen in the sunlight. He's just about to say something else as Thomas begins to sound the strings. Satisfied with the pitch, he begins with Bach. The clear notes exhale the fresh air into the room that Nathaniel's opened windows couldn't hope for. Thomas loves the precision of Bach, the understatement, and suddenly I realise that these are the qualities I recognise in Nathaniel. The thought makes me lift my eyes in his direction and I am surprised to find him staring directly towards me.

The Principle of Bee Space
Until the middle of the last century, a harvest of honey could only be obtained by killing the colony inhabiting a hive. That was until, in 1851, the apiarist Lorenzo Lorraine Langstroth discovered the principle of 'bee space', enabling him to revolutionize world practice. The distance left by bees between each wax comb is, precisely, nought point two-three of an inch. He takes a sip of tea. In light of this discovery, artificial hives could be manufactured which, allowing for this space between adjacent combs and the end frames of the hive, prevented neighbouring combs from attaching

themselves to one another. The combs could, therefore, be removed to harvest the honey and wax without the killing of the colony.

Nathaniel likes to lecture.

He places his words carefully, as though they are well-preserved specimens laid upon a display dish. These dishes he presents to Thomas. When I ask a question, it is Thomas who receives the answer.

The way in which he relates to his bees consequently surprises me. I ask if I might see them after tea, and he nods his head slightly and tells me of course I might. He disappears upstairs to find some of his old equipment.

"Am I right in thinking bees cannot detect the colour red?"

"Correct. But we don't want to take unnecessary risks, do we, Céline?" And he hands me an outfit of his to fit clumsily over my dress. Thomas and I laugh to see one another.

He slow-billows the smoke amongst the combs, and I can't help myself standing back as the bees begin to appear. Rising lazily within the smoke. With stiff-gloved fingers he lifts one of the combs and gestures us to look closer. It's thick with a dark mass of the insects, crawling rapid amongst the yellow of the comb. Their combined hum is insistent on the ear, rising in intensity. I reach for Thomas' hand and, feeling my touch through the cloth of his gloves, he catches my eye momentarily and smiles.

"Can you see her?" asks Nathaniel. We both lean forward to scan the densely moving creatures. My sudden in-breath tells him I have located her. Lying magnificent, not as large as I had expected, but somehow regal none the less. Regal and yet very vaguely wanton, like an exquisite thing resting prone in a fur coat, long legs sprawled, her wide eyes expressionless and shining. Other bees bow round her, their wings and antennae moving fast. "She's beautiful, yes? Over three years old – I've never had one last that long before." He gestures his finger to a worker bee, her abdomen waggling while the crowds circle eagerly. "Look, we surprised this one dancing. She's mapping the path. And you see the drones? Quite powerless – can't sting, can't even feed themselves. Alive solely for procreation. And the larvae in the cells. See that? Nursed by the workers. Just one or two will be privileged – fed exclusively with royal jelly – they'll grow up to be queens."

I turn to watch his dialogue betray the distance I've come to expect. His voice low so as not to disturb his colony, and yet he almost stumbles once or twice in his haste to release the words from his mouth. Looking at him, I know how he longs to stroke his cheek against their velvet backs. Through the mesh of his veil I see a few beads of perspiration glint on his forehead, the hairs on his brow are terribly fine and blond, his cheeks are flushed slightly. I turn my eyes back to the bees and feel my own cheeks redden.

"You don't like him. I can tell."

I'm sitting in front of the mirror, my fringe pulled back from my forehead, wiping cold cream under my eyes. Beyond my face, I see Thomas pacing in the candlelight. His collar is loose, hair ruffled into dark points about his head. I look away and say nothing.

"God, Céline, speak to me. Admit it. You think him arrogant, oblique, patronising, that's it, isn't it?" He sits heavily on the edge of the bed. His back to me, head in his hands. "He's been like a brother to me. You could at least pretend to like him. Why don't you say something?"

"I think he might hear you through the walls."

The words slip toneless from my mouth, devoid of emotion.

"Good God, Céline." He takes a long breath.

I say nothing more. This runs deeper than me or Nathaniel. As I stand before him, Thomas looks up at me and we both understand that. So often with Thomas, it's the notes he leaves out which hold the real passion. In their absence lies their eloquence.

I watch us in the mirror. The satin sheen of my robe glowing dully, the line of his shoulder blades, my face lost in the shadows. Slowly, Thomas runs his thin cellist's fingers down my side and, with my eyes still fixed on our image in the mirror, I am pulled to the bed. I hope he hears us through the walls.

We wake early to walk in the grounds. How lush the English countryside looks in June. Curvaceous, the hills and valleys seem about to breathe; like a parachute silk held aloft, air billowing underneath. A fine mist clings to the horizon and the soil treads damp underfoot. Cattle graze quietly in the fields behind the house. Beyond them a thick line of trees.

By the time we head back for the house the mist has risen and the day is growing warm. "This is where you spent your summer days?" I ask as we walk.

"This is the place." Thomas rolls his head back to take in the sky. "It's vast, isn't it? We'd be let out in the mornings, our hair combed in place, our knees clean. We were so god-damn tired by the time we returned. The days seemed so long. We knew each other better than anyone else during that time. Speak of the devil, heh?" I look ahead, across the bowed heads of the cattle in the field, to see Nathaniel vertical before the house. A tiny figure in the distance. Staring out towards us. Standing quite still.

Thomas is playing his cello in the music room. We've left the doors open so that the sound can travel through the hallways. In the library, I'm looking amongst the shelves. Many of the books relate to apiculture. Often, when I slip a spine towards me, dust falls from the pages. The leather bindings powder my fingertips. I'm picking at titles that attract me. Turning slowly the rippled pages. Reading a line here or there. Sounding the phrases that surprise me. I take down a copy of Don Quixote written in an archaic French. I like how the words sound against my tongue. I lift the yellowed leaves to my nose; I love the smell of old books. They smell of history.

A noise from behind startles me and I turn around a little too fast.

"Nathaniel, I thought you were tending your bees."

"*Not yet.*" He's speaking with my language. His accent perfect as only a foreigner can make it. He turns to the shelves on the far wall, reaches for a book with obvious indifference. He's looking down into its pages as he speaks, "*Thomas tells me you are French. Is that right?*" The question is ridiculous, made more so having been executed in my own tongue. I don't know whether to answer.

"*I'm from Normandy.*"

"*Ah, I know it well. Fought there.*" He continues to peruse the book before him. Shuffles the pages with delicate movements. All the while, the sound of the cello filters from the music room.

"*Thomas told me.*" I haven't moved since Nathaniel made his presence known. I sense that he can feel my awkwardness. That he's testing me. Waiting for me to break. I remember something else Thomas once said, about a game they used to play. How they'd take a match and hold it under the other's hand, wait to see who'd give way first. Nathaniel could always hold out longer, whether he were holding the match or not.

He replaces the book on the shelf and continues along the wall in my direction. He's running his hand along the spines, following the titles with his eyes.

"*Do you like my bees, Céline?*" His questions come offhand, or at least, they sound that way. I nod in reply and although he doesn't look up I know he's acknowledged the movement.

"*Thomas really isn't bad on his cello these days, is he?*" He's quiet, his right hand moving slightly in time to the distant music. "*He'll never be a...*" He breaks off to look at me. "*But we both know that, don't we?*" This time I don't nod. I don't move at all.

"*What a pretty dress you are wearing, Céline.*" And as he says it he reaches forward to finger one of the buttons at my collar. I move backwards very slightly but he holds tight to the shining sphere. "*So, shall we fuck?*"

Precise, polished, the words fall like cold marbles, leaping sharply before rolling away across the wooden floor. And then I'm gone. Walking fast through the doorway, across the hall, and out over the back lawn. I head briskly towards the line of trees until I'm out of breath and only then do I look down and see the torn strand of red thread hanging where once was sewn a tiny round button.

It's growing dark by the time I walk back to the house. The inside lights have been lit and from a distance the windows are tiny squares of glowing orange cut into the blue horizon. I let myself in and go straight upstairs to our room. Thomas is sitting on the bed, dressed for dinner. He rises as I walk through the door.

"God, Céline, where have you been?" He takes my hands.

"I was just walking." There is something else hanging in the air, I can tell it. But Thomas couldn't possibly know. He was playing his cello.

"Nathaniel's bees are dead."

"There's no explanation, Céline. They're just dead. A disease or something, he doesn't know." Just before we enter the dining room Thomas leans to whisper against my ear. "Don't mention a thing, all right?" Nathaniel is seated at the far end of the table. Straight in a high-backed chair, a glass of whisky in his hand. He barely acknowledges us as we walk in.

I see it before I sit down. There, lying centrally on the white china of my soup bowl, the button from my dress.

As I sit, I pick up the button with finger and thumb and place it next to my napkin. Nathaniel swigs back his whisky and refills his glass from a decanter on the table.

"A good walk, Céline?" As he says it, he leans across the table to fill our glasses with wine.

The evening is excruciating. The air in the room hangs pregnant above our heads, laced with the candlesmoke; like a sullen animal it slopes about the room, smearing against the walls, easing against the window panes only to discover them closed fast against the night. It is uncomfortably warm. I can feel my brow damp, my cheeks flushed. Nathaniel keeps having our glasses filled and the alcohol presses tight below my skin. Clearly, he himself is quite drunk. Shapeless like mercury, the conversation idles awkwardly between the serving dishes and silver cutlery, pausing abruptly whenever someone enters to serve the next course.

We're sitting in silence, waiting for the port and cigars, when Nathaniel, all of a sudden, rakes back his chair and strides from the room.

I'm wondering if we should go after him when Thomas, sharing my thoughts, says he thinks it better if we leave him alone. "Those bees were everything to him." And so we don't move, remain silent at the table, like polite children waiting for permission to leave. How long might we have waited so? We're jolted by a swoop of light behind the curtains and the sound of wheels turning fast against gravel.

"He's taken the car," and Thomas has run out through the door. I follow him without thinking, into the dark of the night. We can see the lights of the car in the distance, careening across the fields.

"The bloody fool will kill himself," shouts Thomas. His words are almost lost, for he's running across the grass in the direction of the car. I wonder how it would look from above – the car swerving wildly as it traces its drunken path across the fields, and behind it two small figures, one several paces ahead of the other, each racing across the fields in the direction of the car.

It works in counterbalance; when the car finally comes to a stop we move somehow even faster than we have been, as if its sudden stillness grants our legs new speed. Because it doesn't come to a halt with any practised ease – when we started to run somehow we knew it couldn't possibly be stopped that way. All happened so quickly, so monumentally, with a hideous, jolting crash that seems to reverberate through the very earth. And yet it is not the sound of the crash which remains in our ears as we run, instead our ears echo with an inhuman sound that rang out at the same moment, a primal, guttural bellow of pain. The scene appears frozen now. Thomas reaches it first. Dimly, I see him yank at the driver's door and then another silhouette rising from the seat to be enveloped in Thomas' arms. As I draw near them, Thomas lifts his eyes to me and mouths over Nathaniel's shoulder, "He's alright. He's safe." My breath is rasping with the force of the run, as is Thomas's. He clasps me tightly round my waist, pulling me towards them. Three figures huddled together in the middle of a dark field. The sound of the night roaring about our heads.

Lying in the rough grass before the car, lit up by the beams of the headlights, is a cow. Its neck is twisted backwards at an unnatural angle. The eyeballs are rolled within the sockets leaving pale globes threaded with red. Distended towards the light curves the huge belly of the beast, the flesh gaping due to a sharp slice which cuts across the white fur. Already that fur is matting, turning dark as the blood flows fast. The sight is both horrifying and mesmeric. Now that we've looked, we can't turn our eyes away. And that's when we see the first of them. Crawling intoxicated from the flesh, their legs unstable, their wings sticky with blood. How slowly they emerge at this stage. Glistening against the night. And then they start to appear more rapidly, surfacing *en masse* from the gashed stomach of the cow. Hundreds, thousands of them. It's the noise, that rising monotone, the heady hum that assures us we're not hallucinating. They've begun to lift into the air, swarming darkly in the headlights, disappearing as they ascend into the black of the night.

I couldn't sleep. That's why I came downstairs. Followed the dawn to the open doorway. Stood there quiet in my bare feet.

Across the lawn, Nathaniel is dancing.

JOANNA WOOD
The Fire Mountains

The road was in fact worse than it appeared on the map; an intestine snaking across the mountains. He said nothing, but concentrated on skimming the flimsy hire car around the hairpin bends, catching his breath in between each turn. She sat in the passenger seat, plaiting her hair and delighting in the colours outside. The dramatic contrasts pleased her; the orange mountains glowing against the blue sky, the white foam, the endless grey stretches where nothing grew but bright green cacti.

"They're weird aren't they?" she said. "They look like something out of a sci-fi film." She backcombed the end of the plait so it would stay in place and moved on to the next one.

"Maybe they actually are aliens," he said, his sunglassed eyes fixed on the road. "You don't know that they're not."

"Now you're just being silly," she replied and then cursed as she dropped one of the strands of hair and the plait unravelled itself.

On either side of them the volcanoes bubbled. The last eruption occurred over two hundred years ago. Without warning, the earth had opened up and what had for centuries been a solid mountain, suddenly became a lawless torrent of molten lava, torching the island to ash. Even now, the temperature was four times that of boiling point just six metres below the surface of the ground.

The road straightened out again. He relaxed and yawned. She had woken him up early that morning, enticing him with soft boiled eggs that she had placed on the table on the terrace. Perfectly cooked eggs with runny yolks that would congeal if he left them too long. It was the last day of their holiday and they wanted to make the most of it. He did not know it then, but she had planned for them to do the coastal walk at La Hoya and by mid-afternoon it would be too hot. He did not like walking. He thought it was pointless. Why bother to exert yourself on holiday, when you could be sitting about reading or eating or just doing nothing. She found it almost scandalous to do nothing when there was still so much that needed to be done. So much to be seen, to experience, to learn. And she prided herself on telling the most adventurous holiday stories amongst her group of friends.

She had known that the road would be an obstacle. But despite the fact that she did not drive, she had insisted that it would not be anything like as difficult as it seemed from the map. Things never were when you actually came to them, and he was such a good driver. Whilst he was scooping out the last sliver of egg white and rolling this thought around in his head, she had told him about the rock pools. "Just think darling, emerald green pools. We'll plunge in and then," she had moved her hand just slightly further up his thigh, "Well, then who knows..." She had giggled naively, as if she had only just met him and was still a little shy.

It was as she was clearing away their plates, balancing them carefully on her arm so that she did not have to make two journeys, that she had dropped in the bit about the cave. She knew that this would put him off. He steered clear of anything that might be dangerous. But she also knew that if she did not tell him about it now, he would be angry later for not having been warned. It was really the cave that interested her. The guidebook said it was enormous, with a cloistered entrance opening back into the face of the cliff. The thought of the cave filled her with dread. It also reminded her of failure. When she was thirteen, she had been on a school trip to Brittany. One night a few of them had sneaked out of the hotel with a group of French boys they had met. The boys had given them whisky and driven them out into the countryside where they had tramped across fields to get to some caves. They had dared each of them to go alone into the biggest cave. She was the only one who had refused to do it, terrified of what might lurk inside.

They turned into the car park, got out and looked around. It was completely deserted. Behind them the tiny squares of the salt pans gleamed, like mosaic tiles glued on to the basin floor. Beyond these they could just about make out two white dots that might have been houses. They headed up to the top of the plateau, sliding over loose fragments of lava which cluttered the path like broken crockery.

"I bet this is what it's like to walk on the moon," she said, pleased with her comparison. Without stopping, she unknotted the turquoise sarong from around her waist and stuffed it into the rucksack on his back.

She strode ahead of him in her bikini so he could admire her body. She had a rich tan now, which they were both very proud of, and her skin shone under its permanent coating of oily sweat. Sweat was as much a part of the landscape here as the volcanoes. Even showering didn't disperse it, the heat was always so intense. She liked it. It was very erotic, she had told him one night, before he took her out to dinner at the fancy restaurant cut into the cliffs. Looking out on to the natural lagoon that shimmered in the candlelight, he had agreed that it was a spectacular setting and that they could certainly open another bottle, as she was right, it would be a shame to drink anything other than champagne in such a romantic place. She had popped a delicate fizzy laugh and congratulated him on his taste whilst prising open another shell and dropping a fleshy mussel into her mouth.

They got to the top of the cliffs and paused. She spontaneously assumed the look of someone who was in awe of nature, but was quickly bothered by another thought and examined under her bikini to check she was not getting any strap lines. Below them, the sea was pounding against the cliff. In a few years time, the rock they were standing on now would be gone. A huge wave rammed into the cliff face, splitting on impact and shooting froth high into the air. They looked out, and in the distance they could see the bump of the next one. They watched it build steadily, waiting in fear for that exhilarating moment when it would smash against the rock. She made a well-structured comment about how powerful the sea was, not expecting him to reply. But he did, informing her that it wasn't just that the sea was powerful, but that it was unpredictable.

"And what about the volcano?" he continued, speaking with a passion that surprised her. "Imagine what that must have been like." His eyes flashed at her. He seemed almost angry. "Boiling hot lava, surging across the island and hitting the ocean. Fire and water, the two great superpowers colliding with each other. Fighting it out for supremacy. Which do you reckon won?"

"The water, of course."

"I'm not so sure. The lava could have boiled away the water – "

"Ha! Nice idea. But let's face it, the fire didn't stand a chance."

She turned to him and smiled, expecting him to smile back, but instead he was staring at her with a peculiar look on his face that she had never seen before. It made her feel invisible. Trying to ignore it, she hooked one arm around his shoulder and pointed with her other to a mirror in the rocks below.

"Come on, I'm dying for a swim." She led him towards the rock pool, unfastening her bikini top on the way.

The rocks were reflected in the surface of the water making it appear scaly, as if the pool itself was a silvery fish. Satisfied that there was no one else around, she wriggled out of her bikini bottoms and posed for a moment.

"Isn't it wonderful," she enthused. "I feel so free and natural," and she arched her back and sucked in her belly to make her breasts seem fuller. She dropped to her knees, disappearing slowly into the shallow water and thought that she must look like Botticelli's Venus, only in reverse. Lying flat on her back, the warm water lapped around her gently. Clearly uncomfortable about the fact that he was naked, he followed and lay down beside her. She remembered what she had promised and knew better than to go back on her word, so she pulled him on top of her and encouraged him to enter her, all the time feeling satisfied that this was by far the most exotic place that he had ever made love. His body was heavy and her back hurt as he pressed her against the rocks. She twisted her head to the side to look into the clear water. Next to her big toe was a white crab and she panicked, experiencing the irrational fear of seeing a living thing without a face. Sensing that he was about to climax, she kicked it with her foot, expecting it to scuttle away. When it didn't, she realised that it was not a crab at all but the dead shell of a crab.

They finished, separated and emerged from the pool, congratulating each other on the fact that they had finally had sex outdoors. She shook the black dust out of her bikini bottoms and pulled them back on. He put his shorts on and picked up the rucksack. All that was required of them now was to find the cave and the day would be perfect.

They continued walking along the coast. In the distance they could see the pointed Ajache hills, strewn across the plain like witches' hats. The landscape was bare and lifeless and when they saw a village strung out along the edge of an elevated plateau, they said to each other how strange it would be to live there. They passed the blue and white desalination plant, the wooden cross and finally the white concrete trig marker which indicated they were standing above the cave. They peered down, careful not to overbalance. It was steep and dangerous. They dropped to all fours and proceeded like goats.

At the entrance to the cave, he sat down and got out his book. The breakers were still crashing up against the cliffs and every time one came over the top it sprayed his book with foam. She looked at him in astonishment.

"You go in, I'm quite happy here," he said.

"But you're getting wet," she said, as if this was what

concerned her. And then, when he still did not move, "but we came all this way to see the cave and now you're just going to sit outside?"

"You came all this way to see the cave. I came all this way to be with you," he said, without taking his eyes off the page. She hesitated. She didn't want to go into the cave without him. But she had to go through with it now.

"OK, I won't be long," she said and ducked through the entrance into the darkness. Fear bubbled inside her, but as she forced herself on and listened to the silence, the terror gave way to an unusual, but by no means unpleasant feeling of solitude. She crawled to the back of the cave and sat cross-legged, imagining she was a pearl inside a giant oyster.

When she came out he had gone. The book was still there, sodden wet now, and next to it the rucksack, but he had disappeared. He must have wandered off for a minute, she thought, still reflecting on her achievement. She walked about, waiting for him to appear. She sat down and waited, the waves spraying up against her flip-flopped feet. She got up, clambered back over the cliff the way they had come, looked around again and waited. She sat down again and waited. Gazing out at the sea she waited. And then the panic began to build. It rolled through her body, steadily at first, but gradually picking up speed and power until it smashed against her insides what had happened. It was the worst possible explanation. He had been swept into the ocean.

She had no idea what to do. She had seen no one during the walk, they were so far off the tourist track. She picked up the rucksack and started running back towards the car, tripping over the shards of lava, uncertain whether she was going in the right direction. But eventually the shiny salt pans caught her eye and she knew that the car park was just in front of them. She trembled toward it, wondering what she would do once she got there.

And then she saw him, standing next to the car, one hand on the roof, staring up at the fire mountains. She hurled herself at him waving.

"Oh, thank God. It's you," she cried. "I thought you'd – "

"Me?" He turned and looked at her. It was that same peculiar look as before.

"You," she repeated. "My –"

"Your what? You must be mistaking me for somebody else."

"But you're my – " she began and then stopped as the word fell away. She realised how ridiculous it would sound. You should not have to tell someone who they are.

He got into the car and turned the key in the ignition, shaking his head as if she were crazy.

"What are you doing?" she shouted and tried to open the door. It was locked. She started banging on the window. He stared back at her from behind the glass. It was only when their eyes connected that she suddenly thought perhaps she didn't recognise him after all.

She stepped away shaking. He reversed the car out of the car park and she watched as it sped between the volcanoes and vanished.

Biographies

Clare Allan was born in 1968 and lives in North London. She would like to thank the Eric Evans Memorial Trust, Goldsmiths' Charity, the Metropolitan Hospital Sunday Fund, the Reeves Foundation, Richard Cloudesley's Charity and the St Vincent de Paul Society for generously supporting her studies at UEA.

Alison Boulton was born in London and grew up in Oxfordshire. She has lived in London, India and Amsterdam, and has worked in publishing and teaching. She now lives in Suffolk with her three children and is working on a novel.

Helen Cleary was born in 1971. She has been published in *The May Anthology of Oxford and Cambridge Short Stories 1994* (introduced by Stephen Fry), and the *Asham Anthology of Women's Writing 2000* (including work from Helen Dunmore, Barbara Trapido and Kate Mosse). She is a freelance editor and writer.

Martin Corrick is a journalist and lecturer. Sunshine House is an extract from *The Navigation Log*, a novel in progress.

Douglas Cowie was born in Elmhurst, Illinois, USA.

Fflur Dafydd was born in Wales in 1978 and educated at the University of Wales, Aberystwyth. She writes in both Welsh and English and has recently been commissioned by the Welsh Arts Council to write her first novel.

Deborah Davis started working for the screen in 1997 after working as a freelance journalist and TV researcher. In 1998 *Balance of Power*, her first full length film script was selected for development by Euroscript. She was selected for the Bridge Film Company bursary this year.

Rebecca Deans was educated in Ripley, Derbyshire and at UEA where she completed a BA in English Literature and Creative Writing and, after a year of Wordsworth and telephone banking, took the MA in Creative Writing. Her first novella, *Exposé* was published in 1998.

Sarah Fairhurst grew up in the South Island of New Zealand. She has spent the last eight years living and working in London.

Lara Fisher was born in New York and resides in North London. She has taught writing for the past seven years, and is currently an instructor for the first CD ROM based writing course for The John Hopkins University.

Adam Foulds was born in London in 1974. He also writes short stories and is currently in the early stages of work on a novel.

Sophie Frank's first story, 'Birth', was published in Heinemann's *Best Short Story Collection*, 1988. Subsequent work appeared in British journals *Ambit* and *The Fred*, in the *Australian Meanjin* and *Overland Extra*. Faber published her in *First Fictions:* Introduction 11 1992. A novel, *The Mattress Actress* was published by Faber in 1993.

Clare George was born in 1969 and grew up in Dorset, Essex, Kent and Cheshire. She lives in London, having worked in marketing for seven years.

Leonie Gombrich was General Manager of a touring dance company for five years before coming to UEA. Previously she worked in the US in the music industry, in publishing, and as the office manager for a four-doctor psychiatric practice. *The Assumptionists* (working title) is her first novel.

Nicola Johnson is currently studying the MA in Creative Writing at the University of East Anglia and will graduate this year.

Panos Karnezis was born in Greece in 1967 and came to England in 1992. Before joining the creative writing course at UEA he studied engineering and worked in the manufacturing industry. 'Deus ex Machina' is from a collection of short stories.

Simone Knightley lectures in art and design and visual culture. She has worked as a graphic designer for *The Sunday Times*. She started writing poems after an art history degree research trip to India.

Michelle Lawrence, the *Magpie* illustrator and cover designer, is currently in the second year of a BA (Hons) Graphic Design at the Norwich School of Art and Design. She is now specialising in illustration to further her knowledge and skills. She likes to travel to experience different cultures and ways of life. Her influences are culture, mixed media and computer generated images.

Julia Lee was born in 1978. She took a degree in English and American Literature at Warwick University. She lives in Twickenham, south-west London. *For Bumpa*.

D.W. Lewis was born in Lisburn, Northern Ireland, in 1974. He attended the Royal Belfast Academical Institution and the University of Nottingham. Since graduating with a first in biochemistry and genetics he has worked in a number of occupations, most recently as a journalist.

Kenneth Macleod was born in Glasgow in 1972 and has worked as a newspaper journalist in the UK and Germany. Last year his story *Something Burns* was shortlisted for the inaugural Canongate Prize for Scottish Writing. He is currently completing a novel and a collection of short stories.

Paula Main was born in Scotland in 1968. She moved to London when she was 19 and did a BA in Writing at Middlesex University. She now lives with her boyfriend, Haggis, in Norwich and is completing her Creative Writing MA at the University of East Anglia.

James Mckenzie served five years in the British Army. He has lived in Berlin for the last four years where he works as an English language teacher. He has written for *The Guardian*, *The Independent* and the *Berliner Zeitung*, and is currently working on a collection of short stories entitled *slow learners*.

Jane Monson, born in Slough in 1974, grew up in and around Bristol. She has a degree in American and English literature from UEA, the third year of which was spent in Portland, Oregon, where she started writing poetry seriously. She is currently working on a collection of poems and photographs.

Sandra Newman was born in the US but has been living in the UK since 1984. She has worked as a typist, a freelance copywriter, and a professional blackjack player.

Kate North is from Cardiff. She studied English at the

University of Wales, Aberystwyth. She is currently working on her first collection of poems as well as several prose projects.

Jeff Nosbaum was born in the US in 1971. Since 1993 he has lived in Ireland and the UK.

Andrew Proctor was born in 1973 in Toronto and has lived and worked in Canada, the USA, Australia and England. Whilst studying in Montreal he mounted two of his own productions and published poetry and prose. He is also a professional saxophonist. He is currently writing a novel.

Dina Rabinovitch is a journalist living in London, with three daughters. She started this MA intending to write about Israel, but ended up with stories set in a nightmare mix of Hackney and Detroit.

Ben Rice was born in Devon in 1972. His novella *Pobby and Dingan* will be published in hardback by Jonathan Cape in October 2000.

Rhian Saadat lives in Paris, where she teaches English and Drama at The International School of Paris. She has had one children's story published by Ginn. She is working on her first collection of poetry.

Sharon Sage

Jamie Shaw is from midwestern America and considering expatriatism. Agewise, she is younger than most and older than some. UEA's Creative Writing course is her fifth year in. To the chagrin of her writing peers, Jamie is often distracted from her work by the cute contrivances of the cat.

Clare Sims was born in Montreal, Canada, in 1971. She studied Philosophy and English literature at McGill University, and then worked for six years as an actress. She now lives in England.

Jessica Smerin was educated in Paris and Cambridge and has worked as a journalist in London for five years. She is 27 years old and also writes for the theatre.

Cherry Smyth is an Irish writer living in London. She is the author of *Queer Notions*, Scarlet Press, 1992 and *Damn Fine Art* by *New Lesbian Artists*, Cassell, 1996. Her work is included in *The Anchor Book of New Irish Writing*, 2000. She wrote the screenplay for the short film, *Salvage*.

Anne F. Stairs is Anglo-Irish. She has been a closet writer for years. Her outing process began in 1993, culminating in a place on the Creative Writing MA. She lives in Norwich with two of her three children.

Lorna Thorpe has been published in *Cheatin' Hearts*, a short story collection from Serpent's Tail, and shortlisted for the Ian St James Awards twice. The extract published here is from her third novel. She is a freelance copywriter.

Kate Weinberg graduated from university in 1997. Prior to the MA, she spent most of her time travelling and teaching abroad.

David Whatley trained as an actor at RADA and has worked in the theatre as a writer and performer. He studied English Literature at the University of Sussex. *The Eye of a Little God* is his first novel.

Katharine Whitfield read English at Cambridge, where she won the T.R. Henn Prize for Original Composition, and was thrice published in the May anthologies. She is currently working on two novels; published here is an extract from one, *Unreturning Track*, based on an idea suggested by Joel Jessup.

Clara Wigfall was born in Greenwich in the summer of 1976 and now lives in the Czech Republic. Her first book will be published by Faber and Faber in June 2001.

Joanna Wood was born in Stretford in 1976. She studied English at Wadham College, Oxford and is currently working on a collection of short stories.